Coastal Treasure

Coastal Treasure

Mark Alan Griffis

Bent Tree Creek Press™

ISBN 13: 9780998942100
ISBN : 0998942103

Edited By - Sara W. Brown
Cover Design - Joe Merkley merkleymarketinggroup.com
Cover Art - Michael Lewis

For My Unbelievable Wife,
Tasha
Who Never, Ever Allowed Me To Doubt!

To the wonderful people of the Fernandina Beach and Amelia Island - Thank you for your gracious tolerance regarding the literary liberties I have taken with the geography of the towns and waterways. Please understand it is my love for the natural beauty of the area and the charming historical district that compelled me to set the story in Fernandina Beach.

Thank you to my early readers (who endured a ginormous first draft) Cynthia White & Sam Mathias.

Betty Nall, thank you for your amazing feedback and encouragement.

A special thank you to Jennie Blue and the ***U.S.G.I.R.L.S. Reading Club*** for their insightful commentary and willingness to review this work .usgirls04.wixsite.com/usgirls

When a great man dies for years beyond our ken, the light he leaves behind him lies upon the paths of men.

-- *Henry Wadsworth Longfellow*

CHAPTER 1

"It was the best of times, it was the worst of times." When Charles Dickens opened a *Tale of Two Cities* in 1859, he never could have imagined that a century and a half later those words prophetically depicted flying on Christmas day. My day began at the nearly deserted Harrisburg, Pennsylvania airport. There I said goodbye to my wife Karen and our two teenage daughters, Carrie, and Rae Ann. As we hugged the girls were quiet and seemed almost burdened. It was rather surreal because on the most important day of the year to be with family, I was heading south and they would board a plane for Nebraska.

By the afternoon, I was thrown amongst the holiday hoards in the madhouse known as Atlanta Hartsfield. I finally landed in Jacksonville, Florida well after dark. This placed me within thirty miles of my destination, Fernandina Beach. A wonderful little hamlet sequestered at the very edge of Florida. Any farther north and you're in Georgia, any further east and you're in the Atlantic Ocean.

I exited the well-lit interstate onto Heckscher Drive. The two-lane road wove for fifteen miles around and over the marshes and tributaries that funnel off the Intracoastal Waterway. Unlike traditional holiday travel where the warm embrace of loved ones beckons the weary journeyer, this trip held no expectation for a joyous reunion. The return to my childhood home was not so much a trip as it was a duty, and by default the week between Christmas and New Year's was the best time to address it.

Passing the port where giant loading cranes hulked, menacingly silhouetted against the yellowish hue of commercial grade lights, civilization yielded to the expanse of the estuary. The landmarks I now anticipated were of God's rather than of man's design. Little and Big Talbot Islands hugged the coastline where the Intracoastal merged with the Atlantic Ocean, signaling the Fort George Inlet was just around the bend. Despite the long day, my heart's cadence quickened as I approached the bridge spanning the inlet.

Crossing the new bridge, I pressed my face to the window. Peering across the dark water I could just discern the outline of the old bridge. The activities occurring on and around that bridge were some of the most cherished recollections of my youth. The moonless night cast a hint of malevolence on the inlet and it brought to mind a similar blackness that descended all too quickly on a sweltering afternoon. A darkness that brought with it near lethal consequences.

It was the summer of 1973 and my best friend Rory Perkins and I were on the inlet just west of the bridge. Our fishing platform that afternoon was a raft of our own making. However, it was more than mere lumber and barrels. It was a magic carpet that ushered us to adventures that profoundly shaped our lives. Yet on that summer day our raft glided us to the very edge of mortal existence. From that fragile craft, Rory and I peered helplessly into death's cold abyss.

It began innocently enough, while facing west with the bridge to our backs, an almost chilly breeze enveloped us. Rory being otherwise occupied with a hooked fish took no notice, but I ventured a glance towards the bridge to investigate the origins of the welcomed breeze. Whereupon my blood turned cold.

Beyond the bridge, a veil of inky blackness concealed the sky. I had never seen nor could have fathomed a more menacing cloud. Its color was completely uniform, a deep blackish gray that covered the eastern horizon. Its ever-widening grasp was rapidly encircling either end of the bridge. Westerly it was a pleasant sunny day, easterly however, a demonic darkness was pressing in and would soon engulf us.

"Rory, we gotta move!" I said with what I believed was adequate urgency.

"Oh yeah! Got another one," Rory said as his rod bent. He sprung to his feet and began reeling in his catch.

"RORY, WE GOTTA MOVE! NOW!"

"Man, what is the prob….." That's as much as he said before turning and seeing the apocalyptic storm descending.

"Holy Crap!" he said.

As if the storm desired to reiterate Rory's pronouncement, a jagged lance of lightning split the darkness and thunder cracked instantly.

"That was close!" said Rory.

Shouting to be heard over the rushing wind I said, "We gotta get to the bridge!"

Rory popped open his knife, cut his line and joined me at the front of the raft. Feverishly we pulled hand over hand against the mooring rope. Despite our efforts, the raft was moving far too slow for our situation. We were hindered by not only the incoming tide but also the storm's effects. The fierce wind churned the inlet into three foot swells topped with white caps. Several waves crested the front of the raft, the surge of water rising above our ankles. More lightning strikes flashed across the sky and echoed like cannon fire under the bridge while giant raindrops punctuated the surface of the inlet.

"Owww, my eye!" Rory screamed and released the mooring line. His hand covered his left eye and when he pulled it away a stream of blood ran down his face.

"Something cut me, felt like a rock," he stammered.

There was a nasty gash just outside of his eye. Before I could rationalize what happened, a dice size piece of hail pelted my arm.

"It's hail! We've gotta get to cover!" I yelled.

Rory joined me on the rope and we frantically pulled as hail pelted us and bounced off the deck of the raft. Finally, the raft edged beneath the protection of the bridge. Safe for the moment, we paused to watch the barrage of hail and lightning assault the inlet.

In between heavy breaths Rory said, "Wow, that was close. How's my eye?"

Using the hem of his shirt he dabbed the wound and I took a closer look, "It's OK, just a nasty cut. You'll have a cool scar to remember this."

"I won't need anything to remember today," Rory said.

"I'm just glad we're out of the worst of it," I added.

We were definitely not out of the worst of it. The big storm of '73 was just getting warmed up, and soon Rory and I would experience a degree of fear reserved for old world mariners caught in the clutches of a deadly blow.

Wump, wump, wump, wump, loud thumping noises rose from under the car as the left side tires rumbled over the road reflectors next to the bridge rail. The jaw rattling vibrations shook me from the memory of the big storm bringing me back to 2003.

Nearing the end of the bridge, I glanced northwest across the darkened marsh. "The old place would have been about there," I said recalling the old man's house perched precariously over the creek. It was barely more than a shack, but it had been the home of a remarkable man who had forever touched my life. A man I had the profound privilege to call my friend.

Entering Fernandina Beach, I made several turns through pleasant suburbia before embarking right on Loggerhead Lane. I slowly turned into the drive and the headlights shown across the darkened house. Turning off the engine I sat in the stillness of the moment, overcome by the awkwardness of the empty house.

Once on the porch a biting cold wind whipped at my face as I fumbled with the keys in the glow of a much too small light. Flinching in the chill I smiled thinking of my coworkers who envision all of Florida as palm trees and South Beach discos. This was North Florida, the land of century old oaks, Americans whose primary language is English with a Southern dialect, seasonal cold snaps, and really sweet tea.

Nudging the front door open with my shoulder I was met by the smell of my parent's home. The interior aroma of the 1960's ranch style structure included elements of Cheer laundry detergent, Pine Sol, fried chicken, and just a hint of cedar paneling. Add in the furniture and carpet that screamed 1980 and it was as if I had stepped back in time.

Standing in the foyer, stamping the cold from my feet I realized I could see my breath. Dropping my bags, I proceeded through the formal living room to the main hall in search of the thermostat. The power engaged and the smell of burning dust soon permeated the house. I took a quick detour into the dining room. There *it* was. Safe in the china cabinet—second shelf, on the right hand side. The most prized possession of my childhood. A wave of relief and quiet joy rolled through me. Though it was an irrational fear, I had worried for the last seven months about the security of this heirloom.

Hefting my bags, I was struck by the oddness of being in my parent's home completely alone. This was my first time back since my father passed away seven months earlier. In May Dad had a massive stroke and languished for a month before quietly slipping into the Lord's presence at 4:39 am on the third of June. While in ICU he was mostly incoherent, but we shared a few precious moments in which Dad returned to me. He had been alone since Mom died of cancer five years previously. As he passed, his final audible utterance had been my mother's name

After the funeral there was no time to settle Dad's affairs. The summer months are my busiest time of the year and I had already been away from my post for a month. I authorized Dad's attorney to do what was immediately required, but any significant decisions had to wait until I returned at year end.

Before returning to Pennsylvania I gathered the most important and valuable items—my mom's jewelry, Dad's collection of uncirculated silver dollars, his papers and medals from the war, the .32 pistol that belonged to his father, and a 20-gauge shotgun affectionately referred to as "the quail killer." As careful as I was to pack my parent's precious items, the moment I fastened my seat belt on the plane, I realized I had forgotten it. The one item in the house that was most important to me, an irreplaceable relic of the greatest summer of all time was left behind.

Deciding for unknown reasons to sleep in my childhood room rather than the guest room, I traversed the long hallway. As soon as I dropped my bags my eyes were quickly drawn to three shelves laden with trophies, Boy Scout awards and a row of plastic sixteen ounce cups. Picking up a cup bearing the likeness of Brooks Robinson, Hall of Fame third baseman for the Baltimore Orioles, I chuckled recalling the mockery I endured from my wife and girls about my Slurpee baseball trading cups. My standard response was, "Make fun you scoffers, but one day Cooperstown will need these cups to complete their collection, and I'll be able to name my price."

I missed being with my girls on this most special of days. Dad's illness and subsequent death was tough on all of us. But for Carrie and Rae Ann the loss of "Pop" was more profound than I expected. I surmised that even at this late hour, Karen, her parents and her three brothers' families would still be celebrating Christmas. There would be a fire in the hearth, a table of decadent desserts and the great room filled with extended family. I wondered if they were thinking of me?

Suddenly feeling famished I walked to the kitchen pausing again to peer into the china cabinet. I rooted through the freezer and was rewarded with a Stouffer's turkey dinner. Minutes later the microwave dinged and I settled down at my parent's red dinette table, opened the *SkyMall* magazine I liberated from the plane, and in quiet solitude devoured my Christmas night feast.

After dinner, I returned to the china cabinet and ever so carefully lifted the purple glass vessel. I slowly navigated it around a tea cup from the Cotswolds, and a paper mache' bowl I made in the fourth grade. The bottle was heavier than I remembered and I made sure to have a firm grip before I carried it back into the kitchen.

Examining its radiance in the bright kitchen, my appreciation of its beauty was as pronounced as it had been in 1973 when Rory and

I discovered it. Was it valuable? Absolutely, but far above its intrinsic value was the wealth of memories it conjured. For this was no mere glass bottle—this was coastal treasure.

CHAPTER 2

Spring 1972

The origins of our treasure hunt can be traced to Louisa May Alcott's literary classic, *Little Women*. After suffering through the laborious saga of Jo, Amy, and the other March girls, the seventh-grade boys were rewarded with Mark Twain's *Huckleberry Finn*. Our follow up assignment was to depict our favorite scene on a poster board.

Planning to work on it together, Rory spent Friday night with me. Since his parents divorced two years previously, it seemed he spent as much time at my house as he did at his.

I didn't really understand why his parents split but one evening I overheard Mom talking with Dad. "Stan Perkins felt he needed to go all the way to the Pacific Northwest to figure out the meaning of life." Dad referred to Stan as Peter Pan and said, "He had a wife and a son and it was time to be a man, but he couldn't or wouldn't do it. Instead he went to Oregon, to be with a bunch of other twenty-seven-year-old Peter Pans."

While working on our assignment that rainy Saturday, Rory offered what was to be a life altering suggestion, "You know Jake, we should build a raft just like Huck did."

I smiled at him with complete admiration, "Best idea ever!"

Rory beamed a satisfied grin. My sometimes too competitive friend always had to win. Perhaps the competitive drive was due to his stature.

He was smaller than most guys our age and a good half foot shorter than me. His dark thin hair absolutely refused to do anything but lie perfectly straight, as if he had just emerged from a steam room. His face sported a somewhat pronounced nose that was narrow like a blade. Rory's trademark clothing was his black high-top tennis shoes. It didn't matter the season or the event, if Rory was wearing shoes they were Converse black Chuck Taylors.

Having a navigable raft would not only serve our adventurous yearnings but would also provide a preferred fishing platform. Fishing from the bank or a bridge was too limiting for anglers of our ilk. If the fish happened to be where you were, that was fine, otherwise you were just feeding the crabs. However, a raft would enable us to leave the confines of the bank and pursue our quarry. And just like for Huck, a raft would mean independence.

The areas we wanted to fish were the tributaries that veered off the main creeks, and of course the Fort George Inlet. The inlet was situated just east of the Intracoastal water way, and this particular section of the Intracoastal was less than a mile from the Atlantic Ocean. Meaning it was a super highway that ushered game fish to the inlet.

Fishing, like any other pursuit, mandates the right equipment. A good salt water rig was expensive, but it meant the difference between hooking a fish and landing a fish. A couple of hard working boys with a lawn mower could easily pick up five or six yards and clear $75 a month. If we saved our mowing earnings for the rest of the spring, we could buy new reels and still finance the raft.

Part of the plan hinged on our ability to commandeer rather than purchase the raft materials. There were several viable places to procure these raw materials. However, our Moms unilaterally declined to take us to the city landfill or to cruise the county's rural dirt roads seeking a communal dumping zone. We knew of one other possible source. Along Timuquan Road there was a vacant lot where we sometimes fished. The lot was cleared and several loads of lumber were stacked near the water. But for unknown reasons the project was abandoned.

The following afternoon Rory and I mounted our bikes and sped towards the lot. The lot was almost invisible from the road due to thick palmettos and a cluster of oak trees. As we followed a path between the trees I heard voices. We stopped abruptly and quietly moved behind a large oak.

"Who is it?" Rory whispered.

"Can't tell by the voices," I answered.

"Let's take a look."

Sliding our heads around the tree, we saw a group of boys sitting on the pile of lumber. They were laughing and smoking, but they only had one cigarette and were sharing it.

"Are they smoking what I think they're smoking?" Rory asked.

"Yeah, I think so," I replied.

"Smoking pot in broad daylight, who would be that stupid?"

Before I could offer a guess, the boy sitting with his back to us stood up. We both recognized the profile, Wade Brown.

"Well look who it is, I'm so surprised," I said in a whisper.

"Wade Brown," Rory answered. "Man, I hate that guy!"

This was Rory's Pavlovian response. If his dark inset eyes saw Wade Brown his mouth involuntarily proclaimed, "I hate that guy!" He was not alone. Every kid in Fernandina Beach echoed Rory's resentment.

Wade was almost seventeen but still in the ninth grade. He had barely graduated junior high school, needing two tries to pass seventh grade. He was on the same path in high school, this being his second year of ninth grade. Being separated from Wade over the last two years was a relief for most boys at Roger Chaffee Junior High School. However, with his performance thus far in the ninth grade, we would all too soon catch up with him. Again, the lambs would be in the same cage with the tiger. Actually, a tiger was far too noble a beast to be associated with Wade Brown. A hyena was a much better comparison.

Wade was tall and lanky, but not skinny. His hair was long like some of the rock stars of the day and it was always greasy. On this particular day, it was loosely corralled in a ponytail. His face was pock marked by teenage acne and he sported a very poor example of a mustache. Wade got his jollies from terrorizing kids smaller than him, which was just about everybody in our school. After nearly suffocating a kid in a headlock or bending his arm behind his back, he forced him to the ground and rubbed his face in the dirt. During the beat down he said horrible things about his mom. It was pointless to fight back, he was too big. For most of us the best defense was not to cross paths with Wade, and if you did, to break hard and run fast. He was truly a deplorable human being.

Suddenly Wade looked in our direction. Quick as a whip we pulled our heads behind the tree.

"Do you think he saw us?" Rory asked.

"No, cause if he did he would already be pounding on us," I replied.

Ever so quietly we pushed our bikes across the road and hid in the woods.

Fifteen minutes later Wade and his friends emerged from the lot and went their separate ways. Rory and I waited a while longer before venturing back to the lot. As we walked around inspecting the discarded boards we also noticed the numerous burned butts on the ground.

"Those guys must be smoking here all the time," I remarked.

"Well that's that!" Rory proclaimed. "We can forget building the raft here."

"Maybe not," I said.

"Are you kidding?" Rory asked. "Not only do we run the risk of running into Wade and his pot head buddies, but if he got wind we were building so much as a bird house he would make it his personal quest to destroy it. "

I continued, "Rory, this place is too perfect to just let Wade have it. Look around you, there's plenty of wood, a lagoon to launch from, and we're fairly close to the inlet. This spot is primo. All we have to do is figure out a way to make Wade disappear."

"Jake if you can figure out a way to make Wade leave town you could run for mayor," Rory answered.

"We don't have to make him leave town, we just need him to leave this lot."

CHAPTER 3

Over the next two months Rory and I hypothesized and dismissed several schemes to evict Wade from what we began referring to as Twain's lot. The plans were discarded due to their silliness, such as posting signs proclaiming the site as a nuclear waste dump. To the absurd, digging large camouflaged pits complete with sharp punji sticks. By late May we were out of ideas and it seemed once again Wade Brown had bested us. However, sometimes fate gives you a perfect pitch with the bases loaded.

On most Saturdays, Rory and I made our way downtown. It was close enough for us to ride our bikes, and it gave us an opportunity to make the rounds, so to speak. We generally stopped at Western Auto as our bikes were always in need of a screw or a piece of wire. If we had a little money, we may stop in at the DeLuca's Italian restaurant. Mr. DeLuca's daughter, Mary Grace was a friend of ours, which guaranteed a sizable discount on a slice of pizza and a soda. After lunch, it was on to Big Mike's Bait and Tackle shop. Big Mike's had the area's best selection of salt water reels. Crafted with Swiss watch precision, and priced similarly, the reels glistened under the glass display case. They called to us like the Sirens of Greek Mythology.

Our last stop was Tyson's Dime Store. Tyson's was an antiquated emporium that owed its longevity more to its location than its business model. It was similar to thousands of generic dime stores that dotted the landscape of America's small towns. Except for a few items, the décor and much of the inventory could have been from 1972 or 1959. Things just hadn't changed that much.

Our primary interest in Tyson's was its selection of models. Rory liked ships, mostly warships, while I liked muscle cars. Entering the store, we passed the "L" shaped glass counter containing pocket knives, Zippo lighters, and Kodak instamatic cameras. On most days retired Chief Petty Officer, Francis Wolshisky manned the helm behind the counter. After thirty years in the U.S. Navy, the last dozen attached to the Mayport based *USS Saratoga*, the chief decided North Florida would be home.

At first sight, Chief Wolshisky was an imposing figure. His hair, still cut in a traditional flat top, was underlined by bushy eyebrows which rested over his piercing eagle eyes. He furrowed his brow much of the time which over the years had created craggy canyons in his forehead. His attire was always crisp. A starched white shirt, a blue tie with a US NAVY tie clip, and shined shoes, whose brilliance rivaled that of polished steel.

The Chief was accommodating to customers, with one exception. He had neither love nor patience for long hair hippie types. He classified all of them as dope heads and draft dodgers, and neither they nor their money were welcome at Tyson's.

Entering the store, the chief barked, "Morning swabbies!"

"Everything ship shape in town today?" I inquired nodding towards the police scanner on the shelf behind the Chief.

"Yes sir, all is well," the Chief answered.

Though Fernandina was largely void of lawlessness or mayhem, the Chief still liked to be in the know. Periodically he touched base with his favorite law enforcement officer, Deputy Reuben Bowers. If there happened to be a stranger in town that in the Chief's opinion was acting odd, he'd call Deputy Bowers to check 'em out.

We headed off towards the model section but were frozen in our tracks by a harsh directive.

"Forget something sailors?" the Chief said.

We both turned and very sharply brought our right hands up to our forehead and waited for the Chief's reciprocal salute.

Reaching the models, I searched for new arrivals. Rory picked up a box and showed it to me.

"Here's an A-10 Thunderbolt. It's the new tank killer, have you ever thought about building a plane?"

"Naw, airplanes were Will's thing."

Rory paused before slapping his forehead "I'm such an idiot, sorry man."

"Forget it buddy, it's OK," I answered.

I settled on a Ford Galaxy 500, and headed back to the counter. There was an older lady ahead of us trying to decide on #6 or #8 embroidery needles and while waiting I scanned the racks behind the counter. There, in the cigarette section, I was hit with an epiphany. I leaned over and whispered for Rory to follow my lead. I placed the model and two dollars on the counter.

"Ford Galaxy, nice. Had one in '64," the Chief said. As he opened the register I pointed towards the cigarette section and said to Rory:

"Hey, those are the papers we saw at our fishing spot."

The Chief stopped in mid change, "What papers are you talking about Jake?"

"Those, next to the Camels," I answered.

The Chief picked up the package. "These are rolling papers boys. People use these to make those funny cigarettes. Where again did you see these?"

"The vacant lot off Timuquan Road. There were burned nubs all over the place."

"Really?" the Chief replied. "All right then, you boys have a great day, and stay away from dopers."

Once outside I stopped under the store awning pretending to examine the model. Watching the Chief through the window he picked up the CB transmitter and began speaking into it.

I said to Rory, “Right now, he is talking to Deputy Reuben Bowers about a bunch of kids smoking dope on a vacant lot.”

CHAPTER 4

THE FOLLOWING MONDAY AFTERNOON, JUST as quick as Rory and I stepped off the bus, we headed for Timuquan Road. If our plan worked, Wade and his crew would be there smoking and Deputy Bowers would show up and take them all to a juvey farm.

As we waited in the woods across the road, Rory again congratulated me on the plan.

"Jake, I just gotta say it again, you are brilliant. I still can't believe you came up with this, I mean it's so perfect, yet so simple."

"But this has to stay just between us. If Wade ever finds out we're responsible for him getting busted—we're dead!"

In the cover of palmetto bushes we nervously waited. Nearly a half hour later, a Nassau County police cruiser slowly drove by and pulled off the road in front of the lot. Stepping out of the car, Deputy Reuben Bowers adjusted his gun, slid his police baton into his belt and donned his cowboy style hat. Fully equipped for his one-man raid, he quietly closed his door. Resembling Ichabod Crane with his tall gangly physique, his efforts at a stealthy approach appeared awkward and comical.

The excitement of the moment and the high humidity caused sweat streams to run down my face. Tiny beads dropped from my nose and upon hitting the dry leaves made a small "pop" sound.

After what seemed like an eternity, Deputy Bowers escorted five boys out of the woods. To our great dismay none of them were handcuffed.

Rory whispered through his teeth, "Why is he not in cuffs?"

I made no verbal response but simply mouthed, "Shut up!"

Deputy Bowers directed the boys to line up against the cruiser. Speaking to Wade he said, "I know you, Vernon Brown's boy, right?"

Wade nodded. Displaying his lack of surprise Deputy Bowers chuckled and shook his head side to side. "Keeping up the family's good name I see." He stepped backwards to address the entire group, "Now I got a tell you, based on the number of butts out there, you boys have a cannabis problem." Bowers paused and examined the group, "You seem confused. Allow me to explain in terms you dip wads can understand. Cannabis is the scientific name for what you morons call reefer, wacky weed, Mary Jane, pot, or loco weed. Now I could run your sorry asses downtown and let you spend the night in jail. Know what you'd have then? Anybody?"

Deputy Bowers paused before saying, "You're all dumber than ditch water. You'd have a record. And if the judge was in a particularly foul mood you might get six months on the county farm. Is that what you want?"

He received a few grunts and head shakes in response.

"Boys, I don't think I heard you," he remarked.

Each boy gave a weak "no sir" except the tall kid on the end. The nonconformist appeared older than the others, he was tall and because of a ridiculous Prince Valiant haircut, very odd looking. Deputy Bowers walked over stopping in front of the boy. After peering down the road in both directions, he whipped out his nightstick and slammed him in the stomach. The boy doubled over and hit the ground in a crumpled heap. Bowers tapped the nightstick into his open palm and said to the others, "Any other tough guys?" Pulling the boy to his feet he asked his name.

Through coughs the boy said, "Skyler, Tommy Skyler."

"Tommy Skyler, you ain't no minor, are you?"

"No sir, I'm eighteen."

"Know what that means? It means your candy-ass will go to adult jail. Those animals would have a lottery for you the first night. Now, I asked you a question, sport. Do you want a criminal record?"

"No sir."

Bowers continued, "Now I'm gonna let you go this time. But I got your names, especially you two," pointing to Wade Brown and the Skyler boy. "And if I catch any of you with pot, alcohol, or just loitering on somebody's private property, I promise you'll experience the full impact of the penal code for the state of Florida. Now move before I change my mind."

With a fair sense of urgency, the boys headed south on Timuquan Road.

Bowers cranked the cruiser then fished a cigarette out of his chest pocket. He pulled out onto the road and blew a plume of smoke out the window as he passed.

Rory and I brushed off the leaves and made our way out of the thicket. We were both disappointed with Deputy Bowers' apparent lax attitude toward the country's drug laws.

"I can't believe he let them go," Rory said.

"Yeah, so much for my brilliant plan," I said.

"You know," Rory started as though he was slowly putting his thoughts together, "Maybe it did work? Even though Wade's not going up the river, our real goal was to keep him away from the lot, right?"

"Yeah, I guess."

"So, after that encounter with Deputy Bowers, would you come back here to smoke with your friends?"

"No," I said finally getting what Rory was saying, "I'd find another place. Ha! I knew it was a brilliant plan."

Two days later we returned to the lot, to our joy there was no sign of Wade or anyone else. As a precaution, we collected the discarded butts. That way we would know if Wade returned and resumed his illicit activities.

The cleanup complete, Rory ran to the stack of pressure treated poles and deftly clambered to the top.

"These logs are perfect," he said.

And perfect they were. Eight feet long and at least nine inches in diameter, these logs would be excellent raft timbers. Rory squatted down and reached his hand under the top log, attempting to get a feel for its weight.

"I wouldn't do that if I were you," I said.

"Why? Rory asked.

"Number one if you dislodge those logs while you're on the top, our great summer adventure may be over, at least where you're concerned. And number two, if I were a snake, that's exactly where I'd be hiding," I answered. Rory withdrew his hand as if it were on fire. He stood and without pause jumped the six feet to the ground. Landing somewhat awkwardly, he tumbled to his knees. Rory was a tough guy for his size, he didn't back off from much, but when it came to animals without shoulders he recoiled in terror like a little girl. His fear was so debilitating that on our school trip to the zoo he refused to walk through the reptile house.

I assured him we would devise a plan to unstack the logs without having to reach our hands into dark recesses. Our summer adventure was back on track.

CHAPTER 5

It always began the same way, gentle and nurturing. "Jake, Jakey its time to get up," followed by a chorus of, "Wake up, wake up the sun is up."

I mumbled the universal kid response, "Five more minutes."

This would be followed by two more relatively gentle urges leading up to the inevitable threat that if I was late for school I could forget baseball practice.

Realizing she had all the leverage, I pulled my cow licked head out from under the covers. Sitting in bed shaking the sleep from my brain, Mom issued a new directive, "Jake, before you put on your school clothes you need to take the garbage to the road."

Oh, how I loathed this chore. Stepping out the back door I stopped short at the edge of the concrete landing. It had been a heavy dew the night before, and like a cat avoiding wet snow, I tip toed through the grass. Granted, calling it grass was a bit generous. Yes, it was green and it covered the yard. But from a horticultural perspective it was not technically grass. Let the record show that this assessment should in no way reflect negatively on my Dad. He fertilized and watered religiously, but the odds were stacked against him. Our home was less than two miles from the Atlantic Ocean, and thus, our yard was simply an extension of the beach. Dad could have made things much easier by just planting sea oats.

The dented, rust accented can was embossed with a giant "F" in blue spray paint. "F" was for Forrest, my last name. According to my Father this was necessary to prevent someone from stealing the family's garbage receptacles. Straining to haul the over weighted can to the curb, I seriously doubted garbage can larceny was a serious crime issue in Fernandina Beach.

Upon reentering the house, Mom notified me that I needed to hurry up as she was taking me to school, ensuring the geography diorama arrived in one piece.

After a quick breakfast, I dressed and the last item I donned every morning was an MIA bracelet. The bracelets honored U.S service men who were either being held in Vietnam prison camps or reported missing in action. Engraved on my black bracelet was "Lieutenant Commander Michael Hoff, U.S.N.," a Naval aviator who resided in nearby Orange Park. He was shot down in January 1970. For most kids my age it would be impossible to understand the anguish experienced by Captain Hoff's family. However, for the families of the 58,000 men who never came home, of which we were one, the brutal reality of the war's cost was all too real.

I dreaded the times Mom drove me to school, as it was always an ordeal. All morning she would be urging me to hurry up, and each time I would be the one in the car cooling his heels. The problem was that Mom would not leave the house unless she was "dressed." That meant makeup, a nice outfit, hair just so, and perfume, way too much perfume. Born in the late nineteen-twenties she was raised in a time when women took great pride in their appearance. This was a far cry from some of the younger, sloppily dressed peacenik mommies of the current era. There was however a real upside to my mom's fastidious attention to her appearance. I would never suffer the indignation that befell many kids at school. The moment when you heard some poor sap's Mom yelling "Wait, you forgot your lunch!" Turning you would see a woman wearing bedroom slippers and sporting a head full of giant pink curlers running up the sidewalk, lunchbox in hand. Given the choice between that level of embarrassment or going hungry, most kids would choose starvation.

Given my Mom's focus on appearance, it's not surprising that one of her most cherished memories was the first time she laid eyes on Dad. He was in his Army uniform and she described him as "a sharp dressed handsome cut of a man."

This handsome man, Eric Forrest, grew up in the middle of the Great Depression in the backwoods of southeast Georgia. His family made their living to a large degree off the land, and most of their provisions were grown, caught, or hunted. By the time my father was eighteen, he was an experienced trapper, farmer, rail road section hand, and turpentine harvester.

Dad might have been required to carve out a career from one of the aforementioned jobs, but an unexpected letter was his gateway to places and experiences far from his backwoods home. The letter began, "Greetings, from the President of the United States," and it was his draft notice. Dad's travel itinerary, compliments of the Army, included the plains of Kansas and the streets of San Francisco. He endured a seventeen-day crossing of the Pacific on a troop ship for which his reward was a freezing winter on Hill 418, less than a mile from the 38th Parallel. But of all the places the Army sent Dad, the most impactful was Fort Benning, Georgia. While in basic training there, he met the love of his life, Connie Cahill. An education major at nearby Auburn University, she and several dorm mates attended a USO dance. Little did she know she would meet her husband that night.

My mother was raised off a rural route in Alabama, in between the thriving metropolis of Opelika and Auburn. She was the fifth and final child born to John and Mabel Cahill. They were a hard scrabble family who eked out a living on cotton and tobacco.

At the height of the Great Depression, her father's credit ran dry and most of the family farm was lost to foreclosure. All that remained was the house, barn, and several outbuildings. Like many of their neighbors, the Cahill's considered turning their backs on Alabama and heading west.

During this period of soul searching, John retreated to the woods with his shotgun and best birddog. He came upon a man surveying land for the CCC, or Civilian Conservation Corps. The CCC was part of President Roosevelt's New Deal Program aimed at putting America back to work.

A God-fearing man, John believed this was no accidental encounter, this was providence. A CCC survey meant there was a project planned for the area. A project required a camp filled with workers needing provisions and supplies. In addition to farming, John knew how to turn trees into lumber. He rehabilitated an abandoned band saw and established the Cahill Family sawmill. The majority of the boards used to develop the Chewacle State Park were stamped, "Cahill Lumber".

In her own good time, Mom exited the front door and quickly stepped to the car. Becoming bored at the long wait I had found an ant bed in the front yard. Like most boys, I was compelled to kick it just to see if anyone was home.

"Jake honey what are you doing? We're running late and you're playing in an ant bed," she said.

I smiled, as by in large these were good times. In fact, as a family we had experienced quite a run of calm periods in the last few months. There had been no occurrences of what dad referred to as the "shadows."

The tires crunched along our coquina shell driveway as mom backed the 1968 Chevrolet Impala into the street. The air conditioner blew cold and chilled the sweat streams that ran from my sideburns. Granted, on the edge of thirteen, I really didn't have sideburns. But with hairstyles being what they were in the early seventies, a skilled barber could create the illusion of sideburns. Although it was only the first week of June, the effects of summer had enveloped this little corner of Florida. Temperatures had climbed well into the miserable range but there was no need to complain or try wishing it away. You just had to endure the oppressive heat until early October when fall would finally push its way into the Sunshine State.

When mom drove me to school it was always a push to avoid being tardy. At each stop light, she intuitively sensed when it would turn green. At that moment, her sandaled foot jammed the gas pedal to the floor. The car made a noticeable *vroom vroommm*, a distinctive sound all too familiar to mom. She pointed her index finger at me and asserted, "Darn your Father, he's been messing with my car again."

In this case Eric Forrest was guilty as charged. Like most men, he had a thing about cars. He loved to drive them, he loved to talk about them, and he could tell you a model and make of a car from the 1930's forward. But for all the passion he felt for Detroit's finest export, it was a particular class of cars that could render him mute and cause him to stare like a love-struck adolescent, the muscle car.

Beginning in the late 1960's, the three wise men of Detroit— Ford, Chevrolet, and Dodge — began turning out unruly beasts with giant V8 engines, many exceeding 400 horsepower. Their christened names were Charger, Mustang, Chevell, Road Runner, Barracuda, and GTO. While black vinyl seats were the primary interior options, the exterior colors were as vivid as the times. Old standards like cherry red and canary yellow were joined by lime green, purple, and bright pink.

Despite his auto fantasies, my dad was a family man and he embraced all that the phrase entailed. He worked at a bank, attended church on Sunday, honored his wedding vows, and didn't leverage himself to buy toys he couldn't afford. His lot in this life was cast and there would never be a lime green Road Runner in our garage. But some dreams die harder than others, and Dad rationalized that even if his car was not a muscle car, there was no harm in it sounding like one. He routinely flipped the air handler lid upside down which created more intake, and hence the throaty roar my mom so detested. After tightening the wing nut he winked and said, "There, now it will sound just like Steve McQueen's Mustang in the movie *Bullitt*.

CHAPTER 6

Balancing my rain forest diorama, I navigated through the hordes of students scurrying to homeroom. Approaching my locker, I spotted Rory.

"Mornin' man," I said.

"Hey guy," Rory responded. "Got your project finished I see."

"Barely," I said. "I was up until eleven last night." Noticing his project I said, "Great use of a garbage can lid, I really like…" but was interrupted by another class mate.

"Good morning Gomer, Goober," was directed at Rory and me.

The voice belonged to Sean Jacob Horrowitz, a real piece of work. He was the product of a second-generation Irish mom and a Jewish father. This cultural combination was never more apparent than in the month of December, when Sean reminded us that celebrating Hanukkah and Christmas meant twice the gifts. His mom looked like she could have just gotten off a boat from Belfast. She and Sean shared red hair, fair skin, and emerald green eyes. But Sean had an extra layer of freckles. He also had a wretched sneaky streak. Mom often warned me that one day he would get me into real trouble. I knew she was right, but Sean made things happen. His mischievous ways were just too attractive.

"Hey Sean," Rory and I replied in unison.

"Looks like you clowns wasted a whole weekend on those projects. Nice beach Rory," Sean said.

"It's not a beach," Rory said. "It's the Sahara."

Rory had indeed been clever with his diorama. To produce the Sahara Desert, he placed sand in an upside turned garbage can lid, then added tiny palm trees.

"Besides, fart breath, where's your project?" Rory asked.

Sean reached into his book bag and produced a large potato. Tossing it in the air he proclaimed, "Right here losers."

"A potato!" I exclaimed. "You're kidding, right?"

"Allow me to explain. While you two goof balls were wasting the weekend on those lame projects, I was with my girl at the beach and the movies," Sean said.

"That's bull Sean, you don't have a girlfriend," I said.

"I do, but that's not the point," he remarked. "The point is that you knuckleheads lost a weekend and I had fun."

"But you're gonna get an 'F', it's just a potato," Rory said.

"OK jokers, listen and learn. My grandpa lived in Ireland, right? Many Irish people came to America because of the Irish potato famine. So, I can paint my diorama with my words and this spud. I don't need a fancy jungle, or beach"

"Desert!" Rory said and rolled his eyes.

"OK Sean, you're creative with your laziness. But you're going to get a bad grade."

"So?" Sean proclaimed with his arms outstretched. "I am sitting on a 96 in geography. I can make a 50 on this project and still nail a 'B' for the 9 weeks."

Tossing the potato in the air, Sean turned to walk away but offered a parting "Chumps," for good measure.

"Rory, Jake, my compadres, what is up?" Came the positive vibes from Freddy Sadler.

"We're good Freddy," we said.

'Righteous," he replied.

"Righteous" was Freddy's favorite phrase and he used it as an adjective, verb, adverb, and interjection. Freddy was one happy dude. His ever present smile was accompanied by a very infectious laugh. And if Freddy was laughing, we were all laughing. His big grin complimented his big head and a big body. He weighed at least 200 pounds and was easily the largest kid in school.

Freddy's sandy blond hair stretched well below his collar and was accented in the front by huge fly back bangs requiring him to constantly push it out of his eyes. Despite his girth, nobody ever called him "fat Freddy." Everyone seemed to understand he was too big of a bear to poke.

"You guys pumped this is the last week of school?" Freddy asked.

"Just four more days," Rory said. "It's going to be a rad summer, Jake and I are building a raft and..."

Rory was cut off in mid-sentence by Freddy, "Wow, here she comes."

As I turned the earth's rotation slowed. My field of vision blurred except for the very center of the hall, and I would swear I heard the Monkees singing "*Then I saw her face...Now I'm a believer.*" Walking towards us was Lacy McAlister, the most enchanting creature in the universe. She was not only proof of God's existence, but that He was partial to Fernandina Beach.

In every middle school, there was one who stood out, a woman among girls, a young lady who had matured ahead of the pack. For Chaffee Middle School that was Lacy. She was tall and gracious with shiny golden hair that rippled as it cascaded over her shoulders. Her perky nose was covered by an ever so slight dusting of freckles, much like the delicate spots on a fawn. These features paled however in comparison to her eyes, which were perfectly shaped pools of blue. No sapphire mined from the Isle of Madagascar could match the beauty of her eyes.

Yes, I was smitten, as was every boy in school that had clued in there was something mighty intriguing about the opposite sex.

"Good morning Jake, nice jungle," she remarked as she walked past.

"Oh, hey Lacy, uhh thanks," I somehow managed to mutter.

Rory interjected, "Lacy, how 'bout mine?"

"She gave a quick glance back and said, "Oh hey Rory, nice beach."

Rory growled in disgust. The world's confusion about his diorama was annoying, but for Lacy not to notice him at all was downright painful. He knew Lacy did not like me in a boy–girl way, it was just our friendship had deeper roots. Since fourth grade there had been several fate driven occurrences that placed Lacy and me in close proximity, such as playing George and Martha Washington in a school play, or being assigned to the same group on a school field trip. Perfect opportunities that allowed my charming sense of humor to be revealed.

My discussion with Rory about Lacy was cut short by a shrill voice, "Only in your dreams boys, only in your dreams."

We knew immediately it was Mary Grace DeLuca. Mary Grace was without question the smartest student in school and perhaps the entire county. In seven years, she had never achieved less than an 'A'. In sixth grade, she was the state spelling bee champ and in most years, was honored for perfect attendance. But from an appearance perspective, she had not yet hit her stride. She was gangly and saddled with brown rimmed glasses, an overbite that would only be corrected with years of braces, and thick black hair that was not to be tamed. But despite her awkward appearance Mary Grace projected absolute confidence. She seemed completely at ease being the best friend of the prettiest girl in school. In addition to her confidence, she also had a sense about what she wanted and was not afraid to pursue it. And the thing she wanted most was Rory Perkins. She had a bead on him like a Marine sniper, and had no reservations about making sure Rory knew her feelings. Rory likewise had no reservations in making sure Mary Grace knew he was not interested.

Mary Grace, her six siblings, her mom, dad, and maternal grandmother accounted for the total Italian population in our town. They had relocated to Fernandina in the late 1950s and brought with them sufficient family recipes to open the first authentic Italian restaurant in the county.

After Mary Grace's declaration that Lacy was out of our league, Rory and I followed her into our homeroom class. Settling in our seats we said good morning to Callie Vinson. Callie was a relatively new member of our ensemble of friends, having transferred to our school the previous year. An assertive person, she was ahead of the curve, environmentally speaking. Through her doe brown eyes, she saw the planet as something that needed saving, and she was the girl to do it.

Callie's diorama of the Arctic Circle included poachers killing baby harp seals. For added impact she splattered bright red fingernail polish across the white ice flows. As I quizzed Callie about her project, Clay Dawson clasped my shoulder with a firm grip.

"Morning Jake," he said.

Clay Dawson was by far the most unique individual in our friend circle. He lived just west of Fernandina Beach in the little town of Yulee. But for unknown reasons Clay's mom decided he should attend the city school and listed her sister's Fernandina address as Clay's home address. Clay was real country, his manner of speech, his appearance, and his values were all classic country. He had light brown hair, although it was hard to tell as he kept it cut high and tight. Clay only wore western style shirts complete with snap buttons, short sleeves in the summer, long in the winter, and I never saw him in anything but Wrangler jeans.

Although Clay was not what you might call athletic, he was as strong as an ox. He also confounded us with strange country sayings. Like when something surprised him he'd say, "Well I'll be a spotted squirrel."

One weekend the previous January, Clay invited the city boys to his farm for a campout. After building a fire and roasting hot dogs Clay led us up to the hay loft where we spread our sleeping bags. With the loft door open we fell asleep with an unobstructed view of the heavens.

The following morning, after slopping the pigs and brushing the horses, Mr. Dawson introduced us to Jewel the dairy cow. He suggested we try our hand at milking.

He pointed to Rory, "You, young feller, park yourself on this stool and show your friends how to milk ole Jewel." With a great degree of reluctance Rory sat on the stool. He slowly moved his hands towards the cow's udder, but stopped and looked up at Mr. Dawson. With no concept of what he was about to do, Mr. Dawson made a statement that would be replayed by us thousands of times and never wear thin.

In a plain deadpan tone he said, "Now boys, the first thing you do is gently grab her teat."

There was a brief silence before Freddy allowed a snort to escape his nose. The rest of us in turn lost it. Freddy was so tickled he couldn't stand. He draped himself over Jewel's back burying his face into her hide. Shaking his head Mr. Dawson walked away muttering something about "Damn city boys," as we stood around Jewel repeating the line over and over.

After that weekend, I had a better understanding of why Clay was so strong, and not just from a physical perspective. The farm was a difficult way of life and even at thirteen Clay's efforts were required to make it all work. He seemed like more of a man than the rest of us because, well, he was.

CHAPTER 7

Awards day was Thursday morning during the last week of school. The cafetorium would be full of parents anxious to see their little geniuses recognized. In addition to awarding the scholastic achievers, there were also certificates for students with perfect attendance (Mary Grace DeLuca), most outstanding student (Mary Grace DeLuca), and Science Fair Winners (again, Mary Grace DeLuca). Had there been an award for the most beautiful girl in the entire solar system, that award would be permanently bestowed upon Lacy McAllister.

In a strategy designed to avoid being drafted into chorus, most of my male friends and I joined the Patriots Club, a civic minded organization that embraced the spirit of the founding fathers. Generally, a member of the VFW in full dress uniform presented certificates to the junior Patriots, but as we proceeded towards the stage we were surprised to see the presenter was none other than Sheriff Earl Buddie Jr.

Earl Buddie Jr. obtained the position of sheriff the old-fashioned way. His daddy gave it to him. However as can happen in small towns, the circumstances were a little more involved than that. His father Earl Buddie Sr. had held the position for nearly thirty years, originally taking the oath in 1939. Earl Jr. followed in his father's lawman footsteps and by 1967 had climbed to the rank of assistant chief. In November of that year, Earl Sr. died with his boots on, so to speak. Although his death did not occur in the line of duty, he was technically on duty at the time.

For years Earl Sr. had maintained his keen crime fighting instincts by taking a little siesta every afternoon. The rest of the force became accustomed to seeing him leaning back in his big leather chair, eyes closed. On an otherwise uneventful fall day, Sheriff Earl Buddie Sr. took his final nap. The autopsy indicated the cause of death was a massive heart attack. The awkward but somewhat humorous part of the story is that no one noticed. Everyone in the station merely assumed he was taking an extra-long nap. It was nearly six in the evening before one of the dispatchers became curious and attempted to awaken Earl Sr.

After the funeral, the County Commission met and unanimously voted to allow his son, Assistant Chief Earl Buddie Jr., to complete his term. As the county was not overrun by outlaws or gypsies during the remainder of his dad's term, Jr. was rewarded with a landslide victory in the 1970 election.

It's a good thing his family had a solid reputation in law enforcement, because otherwise the options would have been limited for the young Earl. When your father decides to give you his name, he should carefully consider the lifelong ramifications. Sheriff Earl Buddie is a respectable sounding name, but when it becomes Sheriff Earl Buddie Jr. it can greatly limit your vocational aspirations. So are you Buddie Jr. or Junior Buddie? Either way there are only two options, a Southern law man or a stock car driver.

Buddie Jr. approached the stage in a deliberate, almost military like fashion. Though still in his thirties, he appeared considerably older due to his baldness. He had a distinctive face, so much so that he never could have been an undercover cop. Besides his premature balding he had a wide boxer's nose, a cleft chin, and side burns that followed his jaw line to the middle part of his cheeks. But it was his eyes that most distinguished him, flat gray eyes that seemed to peer into your very soul.

The sheriff carried a huge .357 Magnum service revolver, while the rest of the force was issued the smaller .38s. The position of top lawman was one of strength and influence in Nassau County, and Sheriff Buddie Jr. relished that power.

We were herded backstage per our grades and assembled in two parallel lines. There, behind thick blue curtains, I stood in front of Rory and next to Sean Horriwitz. While we waited for the sheriff to finish his comments, a measure of jostling and light horseplay ensued, prompting Miss Isenberg to walk between the lines snapping her fingers and shushing us. As the sheriff droned on about the importance of respecting the law, I glanced over at Sean. He was staring straight ahead, seemingly bored and oblivious. I thought it odd he had not offered a snide observation about the sheriff's remarks. It was if he was in some sort of trance. Then, ever so slowly, like a creepy ventriloquist doll his head turned and he stared at me. Still he said nothing.

"What?" I whispered.

The left side of his mouth curled up ever so lightly into a half smile, then slowly he turned his head back and faced forward. The one-sided smile was Sean's tell. I knew what he had done, and soon so would everyone else. Sean could produce a colorless, soundless, anti-personnel flatulent cloud anytime he deemed appropriate. And truly it was the level of toxicity that separated him from the rest of the herd. Like napalm, once Sean's poison gas stuck to you, it seemed the smell permeated not only your clothes but your very skin. There was no escaping the kill zone.

I quickly buried my face into the blue stage curtains. Seconds later a kid three people back groaned, "Jiminy Crickets, what is that smell?"

Simultaneously Freddie Sadler caught the drift and I heard him gag and then start laughing. By now there were coughs and gags echoing from a dozen boys and the curtains were being jerked and pushed as we attempted to move away from the odiferous cloud. My Mom later commented it was like a pack of wolverines trying to claw their way out from under a blue blanket.

The commotion prompted Miss Isenberg to charge in and quell the pending stampede. Making her way through the crowd she grabbed boys by their shirt collars and pulled them back in line, all the while saying in loud whispers, "Quiet!" Suddenly she ran into the Sean's death mist and stopped cold. "God in heaven," was all she could muster before mounting a quick retreat.

At the front of the line boys were spilling out onto the stage to find breathable air. This caught Buddie Jr.'s attention and he made a joke about how he had never seen young men so excited about meeting the sheriff.

CHAPTER 8

THURSDAY AFTERNOON THE BELL RANG at 3:10 signaling the last full day of seventh grade. Friday was all that remained before summer vacation and it was a half day filled with signing yearbooks, emptying lockers, and pizza parties. That Thursday afternoon Rory and I picked up our dioramas and headed to the stairs. As we plodded down two flights, Rory dropped little piles of sand with each step.

"Rory," I said. "You're spilling your beach all over the place."

Rory by this time had given up arguing beach versus desert, but nonetheless gave me a quick glare and responded, "Well it's heavy, what should I do with it?"

"That's an excellent question Rory, what exactly are you going to do with it? Is your mom going to proudly display a garbage can lid filled with sand on her coffee table?"

"No," he answered.

"Then as soon as we get outside dump it," I said.

Once outside Rory heaved the sand over the short side wall scattering it among the bushes. We were walking down the steps and he said, "There she is."

"Who?" I asked. But no answer was necessary, all I needed to see was her summer wheat hair and I immediately knew it was Lacy McAllister. She was sitting at the bottom of the steps in the shade of a sycamore tree that framed the front of the school.

"I think we should..." I started but at that moment Rory interrupted me. "Great, why did it have to be him?"

Based on Rory's tone I knew it had to be Wade Brown.

"I hate that guy!" Rory said with a snarl.

Wade rode up on his ten speed, which he had modified by placing a smaller wheel in the front, giving the bike a "jacked up" look. By repositioning the curved handle bars backward, he had the leverage to pop a wheelie and then catwalk effortlessly on the back tire. Rory and I could do it with our regular bikes but Wade was the only kid I knew that could do it with a ten-speed. He cat walked in front of Lacy much like a lizard would inflate the sack under his mouth to impress a potential mate.

"I think we should rescue Lacy," I said. The courage to engage Wade was more feigned than real, but this was about Lacy.

"No thanks. You're on your own, besides you're the one that wants to marry her," Rory snapped.

"We're in front of the school and there are adults all around, what's he gonna do? And I don't want to marry her, I just like her as a friend."

"That is such baloney Jake. OK, there are two of us, come on."

Yes, I would walk through fire for Lacy. But choosing to engage Wade ran counter to the basic laws of survival. We set our shoulders and walked down the steps just as Wade stopped in front of Lacy.

"Hey Lacy," I said, "What's up?"

I expected her gaze to be that of a princess who had just heard her knight's voice as the evil dragon approached, but there was no relief in her eye. In fact, there was no worry on her face at all.

"Well if it isn't Turd #1 and Turd #2," Wade said with a forced laugh. "I've seen better looking things than you under a Band-Aid."

"Shove it!" Rory said.

"You better watch your mouth Perkins, or I'll have to embarrass you in front of your friend," Wade said pointing towards Lacy.

"I'm still here," Rory said and was brandishing the garbage can like he was serious. I'll give Rory credit, he had a lot of fight for a guy his size, but even with the garbage can lid we were no match for Wade.

"What's with the garbage lid? Was that the best you could come up with for show and tell? That's pretty sad," Wade said and simultaneously glanced over to Lacy for her approval.

I had been on the sidelines thus far and it was time for me to show Lacy I was no slouch. "You know what is sad Wade, the fact that you don't have any friends, that's really pathetic."

"I got plenty of friends, runt."

"Is that so? Then why would you possibly need to be hanging around a middle school? What a loser."

I felt good right then, it was a respectable shot and it clearly annoyed Wade. He threw down his bike and started to come at me.

"I'll show you who's a loser Forrest," he said brandishing a snarl. My first instinct was to take two steps back and find an escape route. But Lacy was there, I had to stand my ground.

Suddenly Rory yelled, "Hey Mrs. Wells!" Mrs. Wells, the school nurse was walking down the steps. She had been oblivious to our situation but was now looking in our direction.

"Oh, hi Rory, Jake. Just one more day," she said with a smile.

Rory said to Wade, "Really Wade, you're gonna start trouble right here in front of school, that's not very smart."

Wade grimaced, "If you two have any brains you better grow eyes in the back of your head, 'cause when you least expect it I'll get you."

The statement itself should have stood alone, "If we had brains we should grow more eyes." It really did not need a rebuttal, but Rory was not one to let such an opportunity pass.

"Well, Wade if you had brains, wait never mind, if you had brains you wouldn't still be in the ninth grade."

Wade brandished a smarmy grin. He climbed on his bike and rode away. Rory and I plopped down on either side of Lacy, half expecting a 'thank you'. But instead she rolled her eyes and said, "Well that was pleasant, thank you both so much."

"Hey, he started it!" Rory barked.

I added, "He always starts it."

Lacy chimed in, "Do you guys ever wonder why Wade acts the way he does?"

"Don't know, don't care," Rory said.

I added, "He's evil, does it really matter why?"

"Sure it does," Lacy said. "There's something that makes Wade act so hateful. People just aren't that mean from birth. You guys know he has a bad home life, his Mom left and his Dad's a drunk. And his brother is even worse, he's already in jail."

Lacy was right, Wade's brother, Ray was certainly no choir boy. Several years previous he was kicked out of high school three days before graduation. Ray had foolishly taken a bag of pot and pills to school and showed it to a couple of friends. Those kinds of secrets never stay secrets and due to the quantity of his stash, Ray was convicted for dealing.

The conversation was not heading in a positive direction, and we were thankfully distracted by the sounds of a finely tuned manual transmission going through its gears. A racing green British MG was zooming towards us. A sports car of this caliber was rare in Fernandina, and we all knew it was Mr. McAllister's.

Rory and I excitedly accompanied Lacy to the curb. We pestered Mr. McAlister to tell us how fast it went and he whispered, "One hundred & eighteen."

"Whoa that's fast," Rory said.

"See you tomorrow Lacy," I said and she waved as they sped away.

If the MG was on the cool end of the car spectrum, we'll call it the Sun. The opposite end would be the planet Pluto, and in 1972, Pluto's standing as a legitimate planet had not been questioned. Bearing the comparison in mind, my dad was driving down the street in the planet Pluto, a 1964 Ford Country Squire station wagon. It was once dark burgundy with crisp wood paneling down each side, but time had faded both. It was as long as a delivery truck and could carry an entire baseball team.

Pulling up to the curb he said, "Afternoon boys."

"Hi Dad," I said.

"Hop in, we have just enough time to get you to practice."

"What'd you bring us?" I asked.

"Well there were some leftover doughnuts in the break room, one glazed and one cinnamon."

Rory quickly reached for the cinnamon doughnut. Dad continued, "And the Coke machine was low on everything, so it's a Tab today."

Despite the bitter tasting diet soft drink, we were in fine spirits. We both loved baseball. It did not matter if it was practice or a game, we were always ready to play. Of the two of us, Rory was by far the superior player. He was built for speed and had a gun for an arm. And once he got on base, there was no reason to question if he was going to steal because he went on the first pitch. Most of the opposing catchers learned to ignore him and not even attempt to throw to second.

Raw natural talent did not describe my baseball ability. If forced to comment the coach might say, "Forrest is a hustler, he tries hard." I truly played for the love of the game. Oh, and just for clarification, the steal sign was never flashed to me from the third base coach. I was definitely not built for speed.

CHAPTER 9

THE GAME DIDN'T MATTER. FOR a couple baseball purists like Rory and me that may sound blasphemous. But that's how we felt that first Saturday morning of June 1972. We just wanted to get through the six innings, grab some lunch, and spend the rest of the day building our raft.

Arriving at Twain's lot shortly after noon, our first task was to select and arrange the logs. Although very cumbersome, we discovered if we shifted one end off the stack and swung it around, gravity would handle the rest. Having moved the first six logs, we took refuge from the stifling sun on the shaded side of the stack. As we rested something at the bottom of the stack caught my eye. It was moving and it had no shoulders. A three-foot corn snake was slithering out from under the stack.

I stood motionless as the non-venomous snake moved past my feet. Rory was also leaning against the stack, his head buried in the crook of his arm. I waited, oh how patiently I waited for the snake to slink into the perfect position. Finally, with the snake practically rubbing the heel of Rory's shoe I said, "Hey is that a silver dollar?"

Rory's head jerked up and he shifted his feet. His foot brushed over the snake's back with sufficient pressure to agitate him. The snake owes its name not to the fact that it eats corn, but because it likes to hang around barns and that's where rats live and rats like to eat corn. Apparently, this snake perceived Rory's black Chuck Taylor's as a large rat. In less time than it takes to snap your finger, the snake wrapped itself around Rory's foot and began to squeeze. Rory, sensing the pressure peered down and was mortified to see his left foot completely enveloped in the intricate orange and brown patterns of the corn snake.

Rory's initial reaction was a blood chilling scream in an octave typically associated with the Vienna Boys' choir. That action had no effect on his attacker, so he began stamping his foot as if the concussions of his shoe striking the ground would prompt the snake to cry "uncle." Mustering his last vestige of courage, he stretched a trembling hand towards his foot. Unfortunately, his courage ran dry as his hand reached his knee. Ultimately, I decided to be the friend that Rory once thought I was and rescue him.

"Hold still, stop twitching or he'll never let go," I said.

"Get it off, get it off!" Rory shouted.

Grabbing his leg, I lifted Rory's foot off the ground to locate the head for this curse of Eden. Although non-venomous, corn snakes do have a row of small sharp teeth with which they latch on to their prey. I located the head which had an unyielding grip on Rory's shoelaces. Pulling and twisting it finally released its grip. Seeing he was free, Rory jumped to his feet and stepped back five paces.

Holding it aloft I stated, "Wanna pet him?"

"No jerk face!" Rory snapped.

"Jerk face? After I saved your life, that's the thanks I get?" I said through escaping snickers. "Rory, for the record bud I had no idea the thing would attack you. I thought you'd see it and jump out of your skin."

"Save it butthead!" Rory replied.

It was a good half hour before Rory decided to speak to me again. Yes, there would certainly be a payback in my future. But I was confident that he could never conjure up anything that would rival "The attack of the killer corn snake."

We worked steadily for most of the afternoon with little progress. The scope of the raft seemed feasible enough, on paper that is. We would connect seven logs which would provide a platform of eight feet by six feet. But we had not factored in the sheer weight of the logs, and the torque required to bind them together. Despite my Boy Scout experience with knots and lashings, the results were terrible. We pulled and wrapped until our tongues hung out, but the raft still had gaps between the logs.

To be sure, our expectation of launching the raft by day's end was not only unrealistic, we now doubted the viability of our plans for the entire summer. Completely drained from the work, the heat, and raw disappointment, we threw down the ropes in disgust and collapsed into the dirt.

Breathlessly Rory said, "So much for the best summer ever. We plan for months and we can't even get the darn raft together."

Wiping the sweat from my forehead I responded, "I know man, its way harder than I thought. I'm not sure if it's the design or if it's us. But I know one thing, I'm done. Let's rethink this and try again tomorrow."

"OK," Rory echoed then he added, "Do you think your dad might help us?"

"Maybe, I'll ask him tonight. After *Hee Haw* is over. He's always in a better mood after *Hee Haw.*

Every Saturday night my parents watched *The Lawrence Welk Show* followed by *Hee Haw*, and they seemed to enjoy both shows equally. Ballroom dancing and hillbilly humor, an absurd dichotomy.

With burned necks and discouraged hearts, we slowly peddled home. That night even my favorite dinner of turkey pot pie and crinkle French fries could not sway my defeated feeling. This was more than just a raft. It was the conveyance to adventures never imagined by Jack London or Edger Rice Burroughs.

Mom thinking perhaps I was ill, placed the palms of her hands on my cheeks and pressed her lips to my forehead. No thermometer in the world was as accurate as Dr. Mom's lips on your forehead.

"You are warm Jake, maybe you have a fever."

Fearing this matriarchal pampering was a guaranteed path to Sissyville, Dad said, "For Pete's sake Connie the boy's fine. He's cooked from the sun and he's pooped. That's all."

In a pitiful almost four-year-old like tone I relayed the frustrations of the day and how our summer was ruined. Leaving the table, I headed to the couch to watch TV. As I walked from the kitchen, I heard Mom begin working on him.

"Eric," she said.

"Yes, dear." He always responded in that manner when he knew Mom was about to suggest "we" do something. Problem was, Mom's "we" was in reality a single person activity, strategically camouflaged in a plural pronoun. She stood from the table, began clearing the dishes and continued, "We need to help the boys. Can't you just take an hour tomorrow and help them finish their boat?"

"An hour?" he said with a chuckle. "Are you kidding, I'll be there all afternoon. And who is this 'we' that you speak of?"

"Oh Eric, don't you want to help your son realize his dream?"

Dad ignored her maneuvering. Stooping and wrapping her arms around him she kissed his cheek and said, "If you help the boys I'll reward you with strawberry shortcake."

And there was Dad's kryptonite. Once Mom threw down the prospect of strawberry shortcake, resistance was futile. The man would have crossed the 38th parallel and taken on the entire North Korean and Chinese armies if he were promised a generous serving of layered cake toppled with strawberries in heavy glaze.

"Well, I guess I could give them some pointers. But that shortcake better not be skimpy on the whipped cream."

CHAPTER 10

"BLESS HIS HEART." MOM UTTERED these words in such a sweet tone I thought perhaps there was a lost kitten on our front porch. There was no kitten, just Rory. Rory and his mom attended the Lutheran church, and the service ended at twelve o'clock, no exceptions. I was never sure if this was a bylaw of all Lutheran churches or just particular to Fernandina Beach Lutherans. As Methodists, however, we were a broader minded bunch. On a limited basis, our pastors had the liberty to spill over into the noon hour. However, despite this gracious flexibility, even we drew the line at a quarter after.

After lunch and Dad's mandatory thirty minute Sunday nap, the three of us loaded the car with tools and drove to the lot. Once there Dad assessed our work. He examined the loosely constructed raft and tugged on the ropes. He then said, "Now boys you do realize this lumber belongs to somebody?"

"No dad this stuff has been here for years," I said.

"I understand Jake, but it still belongs to someone. Don't worry, I know the contractor who started this job and I called him to make sure you could use this lumber. But it's important for you two to understand just because it is abandoned does not make it yours. OK?"

We nodded.

Returning his attention to the raft he said "humph" a couple times, and then attempted to lift one end. Dropping the end, he groaned, "Holy cow this thing's heavy!" After which he stood up straight and stretched his back. "Jake, are there any lighter logs in that stack?"

"No sir, but there's a big corn snake," I said smiling broadly at Rory. He had no response, no facial gesture, nothing. He just focused his dark eyes at me in a cold stare. Clearly sufficient time had not elapsed for Rory's deadly battle with the corn snake to become a humorous recollection.

"The good news is your knots and lashings are good," Dad said. "But these logs are so heavy it would take a team of Clydesdales to pull them tight." He saw the bewilderment on our faces. "Clydesdales, you know the big horses on the beer commercial."

"Yeah, we get it dad, but I don't think I've seen any Clydesdales around here." At this dad smiled a confident smile that assured us he would figure out something.

As I matured I came to understand that Dad's absolute confidence was not something he was born with, but was a product of his upbringing. Where he grew up, the closest neighbor was three miles away. There were no grocery or hardware stores within twenty miles. These isolated homesteads required a strong sense of self-sufficiency and making do with what you had. Being raised in this culture, my Dad had the confidence he could fix or at least effectively Band-Aid any problem.

"Boys," Dad said. "I know where we can find a Clydesdale."

"Where, Mr. Forrest?" Rory asked.

He walked over to his car, slapped the roof and proudly said, "Right here, the ole Country Squire has 300 horses under the hood."

Rory and I were still confused. "Trust me boys, you'll see," he said. "But first we need to completely unwrap your handiwork from yesterday."

"Are you kidding?" I asked.

"Hey, no whining or I'm headed home," he said.

The three of us untied and unwrapped for the next twenty minutes. It was the hottest part of the day and our shirts were quickly drenched. Dad then instructed us to soak the rope in the creek, round up three straight pieces of steel rebar and as many cinder blocks as we could find. Again, we presented a clueless guise. And as before Dad assured us it would all make sense.

Once all the materials were in place Dad said, "So here's the plan. While the rope is still wet, we retie the lashings. A wet rope stretches, so as it dries there will be some natural constriction."

I couldn't resist, "Yeah constriction, like a corn snake." Perhaps I should have felt a tinge of guilt but absolved myself that emotional scarring at the hands of your friends is the essence of male adolescence bonding. As before, Rory found no humor in my comment.

Dad continued, "As I said, we'll lash it while it's wet, but we won't knot the rope at each individual log, we'll wait until we have them all joined and place a slip knot on the end. "

"But how is that going to be any tighter than what we did?" Rory asked.

"That's where the Clydesdale comes in," Dad answered.

Rory and I gathered the rebar and cinder blocks as directed. Dad drove the rebar deep into the ground at intervals which lined up with the lashings. He then told Rory and me to place the cinder blocks on the opposite side of the raft while he connected the lashing rope to the trailer hitch on the back of the car.

As the car eased forward, the rope tightened and the individual strands groaned. At the point that the raft appeared to want to lift on one side we signaled Dad to stop. We repeated the process several more times and then Dad encouraged us to climb aboard. We anxiously stepped onto the raft. It was as tight as a drum.

"Wow, we could sail this all the way to England," I said.

"Maybe not England, but possibly Bermuda," he responded. The final step was nailing 2'x 4' pieces for cross beams.

Rory said, "Done! Time to launch."

The three of us gathered around one end of the raft with the intention of pulling it to the water. Perhaps if the fourth member of our raft building party had been Andre' the Giant we would have been able to muscle up the logs. But the combined strength of two adolescents and a middle-aged man was woefully inadequate.

Gasping and holding his knees Dad said, "Stop, there's got to be a smarter way. Man, it's like an oven out here."

A few minutes later Dad clapped his hands and offered a hearty "Yes!" Signaling he had a plan.

"Boys, have you studied Archimedes?" he asked.

"Who?" Rory asked.

"Well that answers that," Dad said. "Archimedes was a Greek mathematician and one of his principals was that if you have a long enough lever and a solid fulcrum you could move the world." At which point he lifted his hands in the universal sign of "Ta Da!"

"What's a fulcrum?" I asked.

Dad's jubilant face turned to a disappointed scowl and he mumbled something about "Schools these days…"

"OK, guys," he said. "You'll get to Archimedes in high school perhaps. My point is that it's all about leverage. It's how the Israelites built the pyramids. And it's how we're going to launch this barge."

"It's a raft Mr. Forrest," Rory said. His matter of fact tone brought a smile to Dad's face.

"Well Rory, based on its gross tonnage it could be a barge," Dad answered.

Dad instructed us to wade across the creek and loop the rope around a small oak tree on the opposite side. He also lectured us about the danger of oyster beds and how even a small cut exposed you to a potentially nasty infection. He required us to take an oath that we would never leave the bank without shoes.

Rory and I waded into the cool brackish water and were immediately refreshed. With the tide being on the higher side, the water crested at my waist making it difficult to cross the creek.

The rope firmly attached to the car, Dad slowly applied pressure to the accelerator. The car was moving, the raft was moving, and suddenly the tree began moving. The strain of the rope was pulling the tree's root system from the ground causing a pronounced lean to the right.

Rory and I were on the precipice of our dream coming true. It was time to stop talking about our adventure and start living it. As long as the raft floated that is.

The raft plowed through the thick mud separating creek from shore. Slowly, the leading edge entered the green water. The lagging end of the raft slid along the trough and was punctuated by slurping noises as it moved through the muck. One log was longer than the others and it hung momentarily to the bank. A firm kick from Rory freed the raft from the primordial sludge. It bobbed up and down several times before settling in the tidal stream.

Rory and I gave each other "five" and shook hands as if we had just launched a Nimitz Class aircraft carrier. In jubilant pride, we stood on the bank admiring our little piece of nautical independence.

Dad soon joined us. Surveying the same glorious scene, he stated simply, "Well, it floats."

Immediately Rory responded, "No Mr. Forrest, *she* floats."

Dad chuckled and remarked, "Well of course *she* floats. Question is boys, will she float with the two of you on board?"

This was a query Rory and I had not considered. Given the size of the logs, we assumed flotation was a foregone conclusion. Dad pulled the raft next to the bank with the logs running parallel to the shore.

"Rory, you're the lightest, let's have you step on first," Dad suggested.

Rory, with a tad too much exuberance, launched himself from the higher section of the bank, thereby avoiding the slippery muddy slope. He landed not in the middle of the raft but closer to the left end. Upon impact the left portion of the raft submerged and the right end breached completely out of the water. Rory lost his balance and tumbled headlong into the creek, disappearing momentarily beneath the surface.

"Let's try this again Rory," Dad said through a laugh. "And this time try stepping, not jumping."

Rory carefully hauled himself up on the raft and slowly stood. It supported his weight.

Dad instructed me to step on the right, just off the middle. While at the same time, Rory was instructed to move to the left. I carefully stepped onto the raft. It lurched one way, and instinctively Rory and I leaned the opposite direction, which reversed and compounded the gyrations. It was part see saw, part mechanical bull. Gradually, Rory and I found equilibrium, but remained perfectly motionless for fear of capsizing.

"OK boys, you can breathe," Dad said.

"This is going to be more challenging than I thought," Rory remarked.

"It's like riding a bike, after a few days you won't' even have to think about the balance part," Dad responded. "If it were me boys I'd leave my good fishing gear at home for the first few days, you know just until you get the hang of it. It would be sad indeed for a twenty-dollar reel to end up at the bottom of the creek."

"Yeah," I muttered waving my arms to balance. With every move Rory or I made water sloshed over and between the raft's timbers saturating our feet.

Using two 1x4's, we pushed the raft back and forth across the creek. However, with each crossing we were further upstream. We quickly deduced the tide was going to be a force we had to work with, rather than against.

"Ouch!" Rory said.

"What happened?" I asked.

"I got a wicked splinter in my hand," he answered as he pushed his palm to his mouth and with his teeth attempted to remove the painful invader.

"We need to get some cane poles." I said. "They'll be smooth and plenty long enough. There's a big stand behind the Catholic church."

Dad cupped his hands and shouted, "I'm done, let's go before we get heat stroke!"

After fighting the current for five minutes, Rory and I were even further upstream. We pushed to the near bank, and like horse teams on the Erie Canal, pulled the raft back to the original launch site.

Through heavy breaths, Rory said, "We're going to have to know these tides inside and out. Otherwise, we may end up in the Bahamas."

We were filthy and drained to our core, but we walked to the car with a satisfaction that is only merited when you accomplish something the hard way. Driving home, much too tired to converse, the silence was only interrupted once.

Dad said, "You boys did good."

Dinner was late that Sunday evening, and by the time it was finished so was I.

"It appears someone got too much sun today," Mom said. "Jake honey, why don't you go lay on the couch."

I nodded and headed for the coldest spot in the house, the den. The large window air conditioning unit cooled the entire house, which meant the den was an artic zone.

Once I left the kitchen Mom presented Dad his reward, an extra-large bowl of strawberry shortcake and a big kiss on his sunburned cheek. As Dad plowed a spoon into the mounds of cool whip, Mom sat down at the table. She waited quietly, but expectantly. Momentarily Dad noticed her hovering and with a mouthful of angel food cake mumbled, "What?"

"Eric, I'm worried about my baby. This whole raft thing makes me nervous. What if they float too far? What if they get out to the Intracoastal and get run down by a ship? What if they float too close to Mayport and the Navy mistakes them for spies?"

Even though she was not trying to be funny, my dad could not muffle a spontaneous laugh.

"Connie, honey, what are you talking about? You're the one that made me help them build it and now you're worried?"

Realizing the contradiction of her stance she brandished an awkward grin.

"Sweetheart, you have to understand," Dad started, "this thing is a log raft, it barely floats. It's only slightly more seaworthy than a pile of bricks. With the maze of tributaries in the marsh and the difficulty in dealing with the tide there is no way they'll ever make it to the inlet. No way."

CHAPTER 11

December 27th, 2003

Rising early, I drove to town and slid into a booth at June's Diner. June's had been a fixture in Fernandina since the late 1950's. However, the original June was now slinging hash in that great eatery in the sky. But little had changed with the new ownership, two eggs, grits and toast remained reasonably priced and the red vinyl stools at the counter still spun 360 degrees.

One regretful exception from the original June's was the juke box. I recalled a large Rockola Juke box in the back corner and each table had selection pages and a coin box. June's catered to working class folk and as such Jimmy Hendrix, Lynyrd Skynyrd or Janis Joplin would not be found on the playlist. Selections were primarily country with a smattering of Elvis, and it's why to this day I know all the words to "Okie from Muskogee."

Breakfast concluded, I walked three blocks to the office of Jeremiah Kent, my father's attorney and friend.

Jeremiah was an attorney from a different era. His appearance and countenance easily distinguished him as a Southern lawyer from the early 1960s. Despite approaching his eighth decade, he remained sharp and maintained regular office hours.

Large gold stenciled letters reading "Jeremiah H. Kent, Attorney at Law" were eye high on the single glass door to his office. Entering the small sitting room, there were two large leather chairs, a small table with very dated magazines, a thread bare tapestry rug, and Rusty, a golden retriever who was ninety-one in dog years.

Rusty turned his head and appeared to consider rising to greet me. However, he had learned over the years that his master's clients would be drawn to him so why bother with hopping up every time the door opened.

Rusty had indeed surmised correctly. I sat in the leather chair closest to where he reclined and gave his head a rub. Jeremiah appeared and enthusiastically ushered me into his office.

Jeremiah was tall, with lustrous white hair that retained its youthful thickness. His hair was always long over the collar and it waved back and forth in rhythm to his quick cadence.

His shirts were heavy starched white and he wore the tandem of both a belt and leather suspenders. A bright purple bow tie with small yellow flowers decorated his neck, and a pair of spectacles rode halfway down on his nose, held firmly in place by a sizable hump.

Many years ago, Dad shared with me that the bump in Jeremiah's nose was not part of his original anatomy. Rather, it was his reward for trying to quell a cat fight over a completely worthless man. After catching her husband cheating, a scorned wife attempted to cave in his skull with a cast iron pan. Assault charges were filed and a young Jeremiah served as the prosecuting attorney. During the proceedings, the wife caught sight of the "Jezebel" sitting in the gallery and all hell broke loose. Jeremiah stepped between the women but was shoved aside by a bailiff attempting to restore order. He lost his balance and tumbled face first into the court room's broad rail.

Prominently placed behind his desk was a picture of his wife Ellie, who had passed away five months prior to my mom's death. Jeremiah sat down behind his big oak desk, which appeared to be as long as a couch. I sat in one of the chairs opposite nursing my fourth coffee of the morning.

"I like your tie," I said referring to his crisply knotted bow tie.

In a soft North Carolina accent he said, "Oh this ole thing, I bet I had this before you were born. You know it was Ellie that suggested I switch to bow ties. I kept coming home with soup stains on my regular ties and she said, 'Jeremiah if you'd switch to a bow tie that wouldn't happen, and you know you'd be the only gentleman in town wearing one.' She was right, hell, she was always right," he said as he glanced over his shoulder towards her picture.

"You know Jake, I sure miss your Daddy, he was a good friend."

"I miss him too," I said.

"Did you take his scatter gun home back in June?" Jeremiah asked.

"You mean the 'Quail Killer,' yes sir, it's above my fireplace in Pennsylvania," I said.

Jeremiah laughed. "Now your daddy did love that gun. You know we went hunting together several times last winter, four maybe five months before he passed. Mostly we were out for the exercise because we couldn't hit a damn thing. In fact, the quail that flew were the ones that survived. The only ones we bagged were the ones that hid and we stepped on them."

"I know better than that," I answered.

"Naw you're right Jake," Jeremiah said with a chuckle. "Right up until the last your dad was a helluva fine shot. In fact, he had a knack for staying on a bird that most folks would have let go thinking it was out of range. I'd say, 'Too late Eric its gone,' He'd wait another half a second just to make it interesting and bang he'd knock it down. Then he'd say, 'You don't mind waiting while I walk way over there to get my bird?'"

We both smiled, and I had no doubt he was doing my dad justice with this story.

Before tackling the remaining estate issues, Jeremiah inquired about my job. He noted my face brightened when I spoke about being a park ranger at Gettysburg National Battlefield, and was curious why it was so special.

"Well, it's exciting in the summer with the reenactments and thousands of tourists every day. However, you couldn't find a quiet moment in the park during the high season if your life depended on it. No, the park is special come fall," I continued, "Things change dramatically. Other than the weekends, there are hardly any visitors and even those leave well before sundown. Now I'll tell you this Jeremiah, in early November, just after all the leaves have fallen and you start getting some of those gray cold days, Gettysburg can be, well let's just say unsettling."

"What do you mean unsettling?" The old attorney asked as he leaned forward.

"Don't get me wrong, I'm not saying I believe in ghosts or anything. But there have been times I've been walking among Devil's Den or Little Round Top and I could almost feel the presence of the men who died there. And it's not something that would spook you, but rather it's more of an aura that permeates that hallowed ground."

"Huh," Jeremiah said.

"You know you should come up and visit sometime," I responded.

"Yes, just not in the late fall," Jeremiah said arching one eyebrow.

CHAPTER 12

CONCLUDING THE BUSINESS WITH MY father's barrister, I drove to the cemetery. I wanted to check on things and visit, for lack of a better term, my family. Pleased to find the grounds were well maintained, I replaced the faded artificial arrangement on my Mom's grave with a bright spray of mums. I removed the tattered remains of the American flags for Dad and Will intending to replace them before I left town. In addition to his name, birth and date of death, Will's marker noted he was a beloved son and brother, an airman in the U.S. Air Force and an Eagle Scout. An all too short life summarized on a block of marble two-foot square. Even after three decades I not only missed him but was also regretful, almost bitter, that we shared so little of our lives together. I was in my mid-forties, with a dash of gray in my hair and the beginnings of a paunch in my midsection. But Will was forever nineteen.

The heaviness of the morning's activities required a detour before returning to my parent's house to begin the purge. I grabbed a sub sandwich and drove to the one place that always soothed my soul—the marsh. Rory and I had spent large chunks of our lives in and around these waters. The marsh had also been a retreat when life had gotten the better of me. Whether it was a failed chemistry test, a poor outing in a baseball game, or a broken heart at the hands of a shortsighted young lady, the scenes, sounds, and fragrances of the marsh were always a comfort.

Within the town limits you can always discern the salty whiff of the ocean. But the aroma of the tidal tributaries is distinctly different. The vegetation, the mud, and the confluence of the fresh and salt water combine to create a much stronger scent. In fact, on a really hot day at low tide, this aroma borders on stench.

I pulled Dad's truck off A1A at a little bridge where a creek crossed under the highway. Within seconds of rolling down the window I was reacquainted with the salty musk of an old friend. A man could not have asked for a more perfect day to be in God's creation. The endless stretch of marsh and the cloudless cobalt blue sky would have made a perfect setting for a LL Bean catalog.

The tide, having recently reached its peak, now began the unhurried retreat eastward back to the Intracoastal Waterway. It was as if the marsh was fully dressed at high tide. The water covered the muddy banks and oyster beds leaving nothing but endless stretches of marsh interrupted only by the blue ribbons of its waterways. The seemingly single pattern of green and brown is actually millions of individual thick green strands which sway in unison as the breeze dictates.

My hunger, further enhanced by the sea air, compelled me to open the turkey sub. Taking a huge bite I felt the lower contents of lettuce, tomato, and pickles plop onto my lap. Opening the center console, I found a stack of napkins compliments of the "Golden Arches." Under the napkins, I glimpsed Dad's Bible. Putting my sandwich aside, I examined the exterior. Black leather with Dad's initials and *King James Edition* in gold lettering. Dad was traditional and always preferred the *thees* and *thous* in the King James version.

Allowing it to fall open, it settled in the book of Psalms. There was a wallet size black and white photo of my Mom wedged into the binding. She appeared to be in her early twenties and was sitting on a rock, her bare feet dangling into a lake. The sun was over her left shoulder which fully illuminated that side of her face and created a radiant luster on her hair. I felt a tinge of embarrassment as I looked at the image, clearly the smile she bore was intended only for her lover. The photo was traversed with creases and on the reverse, was Mom's unmistakable calligraphy, *Darling, know that I am missing you and praying for your safe return. All My Love, Forever and Always, Connie 1950.*

The date clearly explained the weathered appearance. This picture had accompanied Dad during his time in Korea. Over the years, Dad had shared many verses with me from his Bible, but this was the first time I had ever seen this picture. There was one other photo in his Bible, it was of Will and I dated 1968. We were standing on an airfield at a base somewhere in Texas. In the background was the huge unmistakable wing of a B-52 bomber.

Having finished the portion of the sandwich that hadn't fallen in my lap, I drove further south to where the bridge spans the Fort George Inlet. The inlet was center stage for much of the excitement and danger that resulted from our Huck Finn adventures during those two magical summers. It was also where Rory and I were caught in the storm of '73, an event that permanently impacted both of our families.

The Fort George Inlet is a wide expanse when compared to most of the waterways that intersect the marsh. Total distance shore to shore was more than a hundred yards. It was also unique from the surrounding waterways because of its high concentration of white sand, which rendered an almost tropical Caribbean appearance at lower tides.

Just past the bridge on the eastern side was a short beach that stretched for an eighth of a mile ending at the mouth of the Intracoastal Waterway. Moving to the western side of the bridge I walked along the sandy bluff until it spilled over onto damp mud. I paused under the thick power line stretched across the inlet. It was adorned every four to five feet with a set of sinkers and hooks that had become offerings to the gods of the bridge anglers. It struck me that with modern art being what it is, a length of this power line strung across the ceiling of a chic New York museum could conceivably command an appreciative audience.

Following the shore for another seventy-five yards brought me to an otherwise unremarkable creek leading off the main channel. Though it had no official name, Rory and I christened it "Bent Tree Creek." This simple little tributary, not more than fifty feet wide in any spot, was a byway to exploits that were far beyond our adolescent imaginations. What occurred on this creek not only hastened my journey towards manhood, but also revealed that treasure can sometimes be found in the most unlikely places.

A splashing sound drew my attention to the far side of the creek. Seconds later the fish again breached the surface, flew for two feet then disappeared beneath the briny water.

"Mullet," I said. And as the word left my lips countless memories overwhelmed me, "Amos, I sure miss you old friend."

CHAPTER 13

June 1972

It was *the* morning, perhaps the most anticipated dawn of my young life. This day, Thursday, June 14, 1972, Rory, and I would cast off the ties that bound us to the shore and realize our nautical destiny.

We procured smooth bamboo poles and salvaged a half cinder block to use as an anchor. Rory purchased a short canoe paddle at a garage sale to use as a rudder. The sea trials complete, we planned to arrive early enough the next morning to catch the tail end of the outbound tide. Our bikes were loaded like pack mules as we rolled down my driveway. The sun was already baking the landscape but we scarcely noticed. We were on the cusp of an incredible adventure. This excitement, this unbridled anticipation, must have been what was felt by the men who pushed off from the St Louis docks in 1804, with Captains Lewis and Clark.

Once at the lot we hid our bikes among a scrub of palmettos. This was most likely an overly cautionary move as Wade Brown and his future Folsom prison buddies had not returned to the lot since their encounter with Deputy Bowers. Arriving at the creek's edge we paused, relishing our handiwork.

Rory shot me a big stupid grin, "Jake old buddy, this is gonna be good."

Preparing to dislodge the raft from the bank, we poured our gear into the raft's final modification, a five-gallon plastic bucket. The bucket was wedged tightly in a cradle fashioned from lumber scraps.

Rory hoisted the cinder block anchor and gingerly climbed aboard. I gave the end a shove and as lightly as possible stepped on. Despite my nimble boarding, the end I was on dipped into the green water creating the inevitable seesaw effect.

The raft settled in the water. With the current's approval, we shoved off to boldly go where no Fernandina boys had gone before.

"Wow, look at that tree," Rory said as we passed the oak used as a pulley to move the raft. "That thing is way messed up." Messed up it was. It was leaning at an angle almost parallel to the creek, and like a sapling bent in a hurricane it would continue to grow in that direction.

Being inspired by the tree's sacrifice I announced with overtones of extreme importance, "I do herby proclaim this creek be called *Bent Tree Creek*."

Rory responded, "I second the motion."

"All those in favor say 'aye'?"

We simultaneously shouted "aye" and the motion was carried.

Ten minutes later the creek began a slow bend to the right. During our sea trials this was as far as we had ventured. We knew that somewhere downstream the creek poured into the Fort George Inlet. The inlet led to the Intracoastal Waterway, and eventually to the Atlantic Ocean. But what lay between here and there was ours to discover.

CHAPTER 14

DECEMBER 27TH, 2003

THOUGHTFULLY DISPOSING OF A HOUSE full of your parent's possessions is a daunting task. Walking from room to room I suddenly felt over matched for the job. I was confident that once I had developed an efficient strategy, I could cash in on the latest self-help book series. My entry would be entitled *Liquidating your Parent's Stuff for Dummies.*

As I opened each drawer I was faced with another question of "what do I do with this?"

Given I needed to be back home by New Year's, decisiveness was mandated. Clothes went to the local thrift store, the pantry items were picked up by the food bank, and other than a few of Dad's tools, most of the garage's contents would also be donated. I began setting aside a few items in the living room that were keepers. I located several of Dad's favorite hats, my Slurpee baseball trading cups, and countless stacks of pictures and photo albums. There were also at least two Rubbermaid bins of family VHS tapes.

The most difficult room for me was not my parents', but Will's. His possessions still filled the walls and closet. The bedspread and floor rugs were the same as the day he shipped out, stirring proof that there were aspects of dealing with Will's death that Mom could never face.

Glancing upwards I counted nine airplane models hanging from the ceiling. I carefully clipped the wires, wrapped them in towels and placed them in the keeper pile. Much of the rest, including a set of 1966 World Book Encyclopedias and a suitcase phonograph player, I placed in the donate stack.

I concluded the day by meeting with the realtor, a handyman, my parent's minister, and the president of the local VFW. Once home, I went straight to the den and plopped in Dad's favorite chair. These quiet moments were strange. The world, or at least the world that I knew, was out of kilter. The house surrounding me was filled with my parent's choices, accomplishments, and those things they held so dear. Like a dog that waits on the front porch for his master, it seemed the house was waiting for my parents to return.

While in the den, my eyes could not help but be drawn to the river rock fireplace. It was part of a sizable remodeling project my parents completed when I was nine. During the summer of 1968, an impromptu family reunion was organized in Alabama to coincide with Will's final leave before deployment. Late in the day after most everyone else had departed, Mom's and Aunt Shellie's families drove to the Wacoochee Creek, which straddles on the Alabama-Georgia border. The men fished, the women walked along the shallows, and the younger ones splashed about. Will and I had no interest in those pursuits, rather we preferred hearing Uncle Peresh's (Resh for short) war stories. He had been a waist gunner on a B-17 bomber and regaled us with heroic accounts of exchanging fire with German ME109 fighter planes. Uncle Resh represented a fascinating chapter in the Cahill's lineage. The limbs of the family tree took an odd bend when he, a Jew from Yonkers, New York married my Aunt Shellie, a belle from Alabama.

Finishing off a drumstick he somehow managed to sequester earlier in the day, Dad casually commented on the color of the creek rocks and what a terrific fireplace they would make. Mom overheard him and immediately latched onto the idea. Dad briefly protested, but quickly relented. The man was always a sap when it came to making her happy. We spent the next two days wading the shallows seeking the right rocks and it required a U-Haul trailer to transport the stones home.

While it was true that no other home in Fernandina Beach possessed a fireplace constructed of Alabama river rock, this was only one reason the hearth commanded one's attention. The other was Cousin Zeke, a twelve-point buck Dad killed when I was just a baby. While Mom enjoyed the resulting freezer full of venison, she loathed the thought of that deer staring at her from across the room. So, for years Cousin Zeke was consigned to the garage. With the construction of the den and perhaps in appreciation for his efforts with the stone fireplace, Dad's trophy was finally welcomed inside the house. According to Dad, Zeke was a real person and a distant-distant (he said it twice for emphasis) cousin of his. The lore of Zeke was due to his resolve to permanently retreat to the swamp rather than be arrested by revenuers. In addition to making illegal whiskey he was also making time with a number of local married women. As a moonshiner, Zeke did his work at night which freed him for more amorous pursuits during the day. The important point is that Cousin Zeke, the stuffed deer that is, became a valued part of the family and was occasionally asked to weigh in on important family decisions like what to have for dinner or where to spend summer vacation.

As much as my Mom wished Cousin Zeke was still making baby deer in the Osceola National Forrest, I can recall on several occasions hearing her privately speak to the glass eyed creature. The most haunting instance was late one winter night when I was about eleven. I awakened and wandered into the kitchen for a glass of water. Reaching the fridge, I noticed a soft light coming from the den. Approaching the entry way, I observed Mom sitting in Dad's lounger with her back to where I stood. She was silently reading her Bible but then quoted a verse aloud. The verse said something about "all things working together for good for them that love God." She paused and lifted her head in the direction of the mounted deer, "What do you think about that Cousin Zeke? Should that make me feel better about losing my boy?"

Sensing this was a terribly private moment, I slipped undetected back to bed.

My childhood was divided into two very different chapters, before and after Will's death. The memories and recalled emotions after his death were distinctly more detailed than the time before. One might surmise this was because I was older and therefore better able to retain memories. But I know the foremost reason was that after Will's death a measure of grief always shadowed our lives. Life would be flowing along at an almost normal rhythm when unexpectedly a jagged reminder would gouge a fresh wound in our hearts. It could be as simple as coming across a long-lost toy in a dark corner of his closet, or at Christmas when Mom would gently clasp one of Will's homemade ornaments before she placed it on the tree. Sometimes it could be as random as collecting the mail. There were times I opened the mailbox with an unshakeable fear that I'd find a letter addressed to Will.

We all loved Will equally, however, the impact of his death was not equally dispensed. Considering it from any angle, Mom's mourning was by far the most debilitating. After the initial shock and the ensuing detached numb period, each of us embarked on our own individual path through the haze of grief. Perhaps because she was a Mom and a woman, neither Dad nor I could really appreciate her pain or her path. It seemed she would take two steps forward and then fall three paces back. Despite her faith, which teetered at times but never crumbled, and encouragement from her surrounding friends and family, she would periodically retreat into a deep almost catatonic sorrow. Dad began referring to these episodes as the "shadows". Despite my youth, I too learned to see the signs of a pending descent. These shadow periods could last for three days to a week, sometimes longer during which Mom would completely withdraw from life. When they hit, Dad and I made sure Mom had what she needed, but mostly we made sure she was undisturbed.

It was rough on all of us, but there was a surreal positive aspect. Dad and I formed a special bond during those times. We shared many dinners and weekends just the two of us. As I couldn't help Mom, it provided me a sense that I was doing something important by being there for Dad. Like many men from his generation Dad sought to grieve privately. Even with his tough façade the pain showed on his face, especially in his eyes. He was like a bloodied brawler, who despite being way behind in the count, dutifully answered the bell every day and fought another round.

Given the times, and the stigma associated with emotional issues, Mom's issues were a Forrest family problem and therefore remained a family secret.

Sitting in the den watching the afternoon shadows creep across the backyard, I looked to the glass eyed trophy, "So Cousin Zeke, what in the world am I going to do with you?"

By five o'clock I was mentally and physically spent. Earlier in the day I called Freddie Sadler, who lived in nearby Brunswick, Georgia, to meet for dinner at DeLuca's restaurant. I needed a distraction and seeing Freddie's infectious smile and DeLuca's football sized calzones seemed like a perfect plan.

For two hours Freddie and I reminisced and consumed vast quantities of high caloric Italian cuisine. Try as I may, I could not keep pace with Freddie's voracious ability to eat. Always a large guy, a necessity for a college level offensive lineman, Freddie had not tamed his appetite even though his playing days were over by the age of 23. After four years at Florida State, Freddie was drafted in the late rounds by the Kansas City Chiefs. He hung around for half the season before being cut. After trying out unsuccessfully for several other teams he turned his football passions towards coaching. And at nearly 350 pounds Freddie was an imposing high school coach.

Glancing at a picture of Mary Grace DeLuca's flight crew gracing the wall of the restaurant, I smiled thinking about how hard she chased Rory. She certainly did the Class of 1977 proud. Homecoming Queen, Yale graduate, chemical engineer, and astronaut. We all knew she was a genius, even in elementary school. But if Rory had known the beauty she would become in high school he might have let her catch him.

"You still stay in touch with Rory?" Freddie asked.

"No," I said. "We stayed in touch until college but after that, nothing." I paused to take a sip of tea, "but I know he's still out in Oregon, and like you he's coaching." In my mind, I occasionally thought I should just ring him up, but never did. Perhaps I was waiting for him to call me.

We concluded the evening by hoisting our glasses in a toast to Clay Dawson. Even after all these years it was hard to comprehend his death, where he was that fateful day versus where he should have been. Of course, all recollections of Clay are unquestionably required to include his well intending father's attempt to show a bunch of city boys how to milk a cow. There in the rear section of DeLuca's restaurant, seated around the remains of three calzones and a burned down candle, Freddie and I quoted the perfectly innocent yet forever treasured line, "The first thing you do is gently grab her teat."

CHAPTER 15

June 1972

Over the ensuing days, Rory and I ventured further into the salt marsh. With each outing we learned more about navigating the labyrinth within the marsh and the need to pay critical attention to the tidal swings. Several times we found ourselves marooned on an oyster mound because of underestimating the retreating tide. On the first instance a passing boater towed us clear. However, on the second occurrence, we paid dearly for our oversight. Run aground on an oyster bed that gradually expanded in all directions, an impenetrable gauntlet of razor sharp shells surrounded us. Recalling Dad's warning that a mere scrape from these aquatic daggers would result in a certain and excruciating death, we were forced to wait it out. With no clouds shielding us, the sun was unmerciful and the scents that lofted from the mud became overwhelming. Late that afternoon two sunburned, nearly dehydrated explorers returned to the lot. As with previous days on the marsh, we had learned another valuable lesson, you can never take too much water.

Rory and I peddled off with as much gusto as we could summon. If we could just make a mile, an oasis with the promise of life giving refreshment awaited. Finally, we eyed the beacon that welcomed all weary travelers, the 7-Eleven. Entering the parking lot, the discarded bottle tops embedded in the asphalt lot shimmered like precious stones.

There were hundreds of Coke, Pepsi, and various beer brands, but we had to look close to find the rare ones. The scarce gems included anything Nehi and Frosty Root Beer.

Parking our bikes on the sidewalk near the bagged ice freezer, we pushed through the door and the attached cowbell announced our arrival. The first sensation to envelop us was the revitalizing cool air and the tantalizing smell of Southern boiled peanuts. We walked directly to the counter where on most days we found Doris. She appeared to be in her late fifties, and her frame carried a bit more weight than her slacks seemed to be able to manage. Her long fingernails clacked like Morse code when she rung up our order, and her hair color was flexible, some days it was a sandy brown and other times it could be Elvis black. Regardless of the color, it was always done. By done, I mean it was styled and then cryogenically frozen in place by highly flammable hair spray. Without knowing it, Doris lived squarely at the door step of Dante's inferno. Her hair was a bee hive of pyrotechnic potential, merely waiting for the catalyst of a hot ember.

In addition to her hair, Doris' other constant was something she held between her index and middle finger, a Virginia Slims 100. Once it was time for a purchase, she would let it dangle out of her mouth until she had bagged your goods and then it went right back between her fingers. A continual stream of smoke rose from the ash laden tip encircling her head in a nicotine halo.

The reason for proceeding directly to Doris was simple. She was the gate keeper, or more accurately, the key keeper. In addition to hydration and nourishment, the 7-Eleven was also the only available bathroom when Rory and I were mowing or fishing. Both the men's and women's restroom were on the outside of the building and therefore remained locked. Why? I have no clue. It's just another of life's great mysteries along with Bigfoot, the Bermuda Triangle, and what really happened to the famed hijacker DB Cooper.

"Hi Doris," I said. "Can we borrow the key?"

"I don't know boys, can you?" she responded.

"Doris, may we borrow the key?"

"Yes, you may," she said. "Just don't lose it."

We had borrowed the key dozens of times, but with each occurrence she reminded us not to lose it. The key was connected to the wooden handle that was once attached to a toilet plunger. It was two feet long and as big around as a broom stick. How we could possibly lose it between the store and the bathroom was a question that was always present, but we dared never ask.

Upon opening the restroom door, it was mandatory to stand back for ten seconds and let a modicum of oxygen replace the stale, urine laden air that resided in the men's room. The restrooms were situated on the western side of the store which meant on summer afternoons, the inside was as cozy as a prison farm hot box. I can only speculate on the cleanliness of the women's restroom, but I would bet a higher percentage of pee found its way into the toilet on the women's side. I am also confident the women's room was not covered in male anatomical drawings and clever poems about wenches, maidens, and girls from Nantucket. Most humorous was a note scrawled just above the sink, "For a good time call Doris!"

After washing our hands with the powdery residue that fell from the plastic bulbous container, we then faced a true life or death decision. As exquisitely appointed as the 7-Eleven's facilities were, it lacked paper towels. Instead, a large apparatus hung on the wall with a looped cloth towel. Each new guest would pull the towel to rotate it to a dry spot. Mind you, not a clean spot, just a dry spot. On any given day, my shirt would be covered in either dust and gas, or fish blood and shrimp entrails. In either case, I concluded it was more hygienic to wipe my washed hands on my shirt than the bubonic plague infested hanging towel.

After returning the key, Rory and I sought a nutritional snack. I was a Baby Ruth man, and Rory preferred Zero candy bars. During fall and winter, we would wash down the candy bars with our favorite soda, but April through August we opted for Slurpees. During the summer months, our Slurpee was served in an official plastic baseball trading cup. The 16 ounce cups sported a full color bust of a player with his career statistics on the opposite side.

Over time we had developed a degree of rapport with Doris and this came in handy during baseball cup season. As we approached the counter she would have two cups waiting for our approval. She allowed us to pass on a cup that we already had and if she was in a charitable mood she would also let us pass on a rookie cup. A rookie could be in the big leagues today and on a bus back to Pawtucket next week.

"What you think boys…are these keepers?" Doris asked.

We examined the cups.

"Lou Brock, Cardinals," I said.

"Hey, he's a base stealer, I'll trade you," Rory offered.

"Who you got?" I asked.

"Rod Carew, Twins," Rory answered and pushed the cup towards me.

"I'll make that trade all day," I said.

We put the cups back on the counter, and Doris asked. "You want the usual?"

"Yes ma'am, two suicides."

This would be the first and only time a beverage was consumed from these cups. They were now cherished collectables for display purposes only.

CHAPTER 16

THE FOLLOWING MONDAY, MARINERS JAKE and Rory headed out again. Heavy summer haze had settled over North Florida lending the sky and the water a monochrome gray hue. It was as if the colors of the marsh had been bleached away.

The outgoing tide was unusually strong, and Rory attempted to impress me with his knowledge that this tide's heavy pull was due to the current lunar cycle. I reminded him that school was out for eight more weeks and I did not care to hear his moon theories.

I further added, "Now if your smart girlfriend Mary Grace DeLuca was explaining the lunar cycle and its tidal effects, I'd find it more believable."

Rory glared at me, "You know I don't like her, why do you say crap like that?"

"I hear you say she's not your girlfriend, but she has other ideas. Maybe you're just confused," I added.

Rory paused for a moment, beamed a confident smiled and laid the wood to me, "Mary Grace is no more my girlfriend than Lacy McAlister is yours!"

The issue momentarily settled we returned our focus to the marsh.

Saltwater marshes are one of nature's great puzzles. At ground level it seems like a sea of grass with a river transecting its center, but it is quite different when surveyed from an elevated position. Numerous tributaries break from the main channel and most these are dead ends.

As Rory and I did not have a helicopter at our disposal, the only method we had of determining which channels transected the marsh and which were dead ends was trial and error. This game of nautical corn maze grew tiresome in a hurry.

Flowing along with the tide was not as relaxing and carefree as Mark Twain had described. Granted, we did not have to concern ourselves with being run over by a paddle boat, but the river we traversed was not nearly as wide as the Mississippi and Bent Tree Creek curved like a mountain road. This combination required us to continually adjust the raft's position in the center of the channel. Drifting too close to the edge could ground us on an oyster mound, or if we plowed too hard into the soft bank, especially at low tide, the raft would stick like a woolly mammoth in a tar pit.

Upon reaching a stretch of straight river, it was time to take a break and enjoy the freedom. We'd break out our rods and fish. Unfortunately, in these early excursions, our fishing success was anything but spectacular.

Following the main channel, we expected to see the Fort George Inlet around every bend. But alas, it was always more marsh. Around one of these unremarkable turns, the river widened and the pace of the current slowed. We interpreted this as a firm sign the inlet was near. Ahead on the right side of the creek a cabin perched precariously over the channel. The closer we got, the term "cabin" seemed an exaggeration. It could be more appropriately described as a shack of rusting tin and dilapidated boards resting on frail skeletal pilings.

"Let's pull up under that old place and grab some shade," Rory said.

"Good plan," I said. "It's gotta be a hundred today."

We angled towards the shack only to discover it was not deserted. Sitting motionless on the covered deck area was an old black man. Realizing we were now near the point of unwelcomed trespassing, Rory and I frantically pushed the raft away from the shack. This fevered activity caused it to sway both side to side as well as seesaw front to back and we nearly capsized.

I glanced up at the man on the deck who was now well within speaking distance. He had close cropped snow white hair and was wearing a faded blue long sleeve shirt with the cuffs rolled midway up his forearms. As we floated directly in front of his place, he bent forward in his rocker and leaned on the railing. Removing a pipe from his mouth, he tapped it several times on the rail. With each tap, small amounts of burned tobacco were expelled, only to be swept into the water with his other hand.

Feeling awkward about being so close to his house, I raised my hand in a friendly wave. And despite my mother's efforts to instill in me Southern graciousness, the only word I could muster was, "Hey." With only a slight hesitation the man returned the wave.

Despite being well out of earshot Rory said in a hushed whisper, "That was close."

"I'm sure he was thinking the same thing," I replied.

We floated downstream another fifteen minutes at which point the entrance to Fort George Inlet was finally in sight. Along this part of the channel the bank was lined by sandy beaches. On the left bank, there was a stand of oak trees casting lifesaving shade that stretched all the way to the water line.

Several feet from the shore we synchronized stepping off the raft. I sighed with relief as I stood in the cool knee deep water. The cinder block anchor thudded as it hit the bank and we retreated to the shade of the oaks. A huge fallen tree stretched across the clean soft sand creating a perfect back rest. As I plopped down, the water in my shoes trickled out and created small streams that advanced towards the channel but were soon absorbed by the sand.

Rory, who by this time was tearing into a box of Cheese Nips, commented that this would be a perfect spot for a camp out.

"All we'd need are sleeping bags and some cans of Beanee Weenees and we're set. We could even get the other guys to join us."

"Yeah, you're right," I said as I took a big swig from a half gallon jug of Kool-Aid. "This would be an awesome place for a campout except for one thing."

"Our Moms would never say yes," he said.

Nodding I said, "Pass me the Cheese Nips."

While licking the faux cheese dust from his fingers, Rory noticed the light reflections dancing on the underside of the tree's leaves.

"Wow that's cool how the sun bounces off the water like that. It kind of reminds me of that mirrored ball that hangs in the middle of the skating rink. You know the one they turn on when it's time to couple skate?"

"Yeah," I said.

"So Jakester, you ever asked Lacy to couple skate?"

Looking at him as if he had lost his mind, "No!"

"Why not? You know you want too."

"Cause."

"Cause why?"

"Don't be a dipstick, you know why. She'd turn me down. Then I'd be standing there like an idiot and come Monday I'd have to face her at school. No way man, too risky."

"Jake, you know the difference between you and me?"

"I'm tall," I said and then chuckled at my clever response.

"Jake, Jake, my big stupid friend. The difference between you and me is you don't mind taking a walk."

"A walk? You mean like in baseball?" I asked.

"That's exactly what I mean. You're OK with getting to first base with a walk, right?"

"Well, yeah. What's wrong with it? You get on base and it doesn't hurt your batting average."

"Me, I hate walks. In fact, I would rather strike out than take a walk."

"That's crazy! You're the lead-off batter. It's your job to get on base anyway you can."

"I know, and if I have to I'll take a walk. But I hate it. When the count is 3-0, I hope the pitcher throws a strike. Cause once its 3-1, I can swing away."

"So, what does that have to do with Lacy?"

"Everything," Rory said. "Jake by taking a walk you lose the chance to swing the bat and lace a line drive deep in the gap. How do you feel when you round first base and you see your ball has rolled to the fence?"

"Great!"

"Right. Do you feel great when you take a walk?"

"Well, no."

"Unless you swing the bat, the best you will ever do is take a walk. It's the same way with Lacy. Unless you make some kind of move you'll never know if she likes you or not."

Rory's analogy stunned me. It was so simple, yet so right.

He grumbled, "You're hopeless, why do I bother?"

"Because I'm your best friend, that's why."

Rory leaned back and chugged three large swallows of red Kool-Aid. Seconds later he produced a burp from the dark reaches of his gut. He began reciting his ABCs and the burp was of sufficient duration to allow him to get all the way to the letter "P."

"Very nice," I said.

"You know, that was kind of weird."

"What?" I asked.

"That old man living in that shack."

"What's weird about that, it's just an old man."

"Yes, but that shack's a dump, how does he live there?"

"I don't know?"

"It looked more like a place to hide out than a place to live."

"Maybe that's all he can afford?" I said.

"Well," Rory went on. "I still don't like it. He wasn't...right. Maybe he's one of those people that kills strangers, like on TV. You know like when a family's car breaks down and they ask some local farmer for help and they're never seen again."

"You mean like all the scary campfire stories?"

"Yeah, exactly," Rory said. "Besides, my mom warned me about colored people."

"What do you mean she warned you?"

"She told me to stay away from them. They're not like us. We shouldn't trust them."

"Why would she say that?"

"I don't know. Maybe it's an Ohio thing. Did you know she was from there?"

"No, but I'm ninety-nine percent sure he's harmless," I said.

"How can you be so sure?" Rory asked.

"Because he didn't have a hook for a hand you bonehead!" I said laughing as I contorted my index finger into a hook and shook it at Rory.

As in most cases Rory had to have the last word, "I'm just saying, something ain't right about that old man."

CHAPTER 17

THE EXCITEMENT OF EXPLORING THE marsh notwithstanding, the primary reason for building our raft was to enhance our fishing success. I had anticipated that within mere weeks my parent's freezer would be fully stocked with redfish, flounder, and speckled trout. Once we caught a winter's supply, Rory and I could then sell our daily catch from the 7-Eleven parking lot. We had not bothered to consider the legality of such a sidewalk fish market, but we felt confident that Doris would be agreeable if we gave her first choice.

However, after a week on the marsh we had yet to reel in our first fish. It was time for a different tack, and for that we needed bait fish.

Early the following morning, we pushed off from Twain's lot. The air was already heavy and humid but the searing sun was not yet high enough to initiate the daily roast. The tide was coming up on the high side but it would be another couple of hours before it turned. Rory and I flowed without effort further upstream from the lot, realizing that in a few hours we would just as effortlessly return.

I positioned us in the middle of the creek, as Rory unwound the white nylon cast net. Stretching his arms as far apart as possible he held the net aloft. With his teeth, he clinched the net and further opened the web. Twisting at the waist and bending his knees, Rory coiled like a spring. In one fluid motion, he spun and cast the net into the morning sky. It was poetry in motion. Like a deploying parachute, it opened a split second before the sinkers broke the surface of the water. Rory gave me a toothy smile, proof he had remembered to unclench his jaw thereby preserving his teeth. With great anticipation, Rory hauled the net aboard. However, it only yielded mud and a few oyster shells. Undaunted, Rory made five more casts before scoring three black tailed mullet.

Breathing hard and pouring sweat he said, "OK, your turn. Man, is it sticky this morning."

Being bigger than Rory, I knew my casts went higher and farther, and I also knew that bugged the heck out of him. On my first cast the net opened and falling water droplets created a ringlet of tiny splashes an instant before the sinkers violently plunged into the water. I caught several mullet on the next three casts which provided sufficient bait for the day. We spent the better part of the next three hours hooking up mullet and patiently waiting, but it was to no avail. The sun was high and our luck was poor so we called it a day.

Once on shore I pulled up the stringer with the remaining mullet.

"Well, there are seven left, want to split 'em?" I asked.

"You caught most of those so why don't you keep them," Rory answered.

"You sure?"

"Yeah," he remarked. "I'll take the next batch home."

Rolling into my driveway I couldn't wait to see Mom's face when I presented her with dinner. She prepared something from the ocean at least once a week, however I could not recall eating mullet. I walked to the back door, which was the only entry into the house I could access when I returned home dirtier than a coal miner. Opening it I announced, "Mom I'm home. Come see what I caught."

Holding the string of mullet behind my back to enhance the moment, I anxiously waited. Seeing me she said, "Jake Forrest you are as filthy as a pig. Go outside and hose off."

"Wait Mom, don't you want to see dinner?" I asked.

Softening her tone, she said, "Yes, Jake. I would love to see what you caught for dinner."

Pulling the string from behind my back I said, "ta –da!"

She stared at the fish, and then glanced at me. Then she looked at the fish again. "Why Jake that's a nice string of fish. What are they honey?"

"Mullet!" I announced.

With a measured response, she said, "Mullet, hmmm I see."

Without hesitation, I launched in again, "So how are you going to cook them?"

After a long pause, Mom said, "Jake sweetie, we don't eat mullet."

"Why not? Aren't they eatable?" I questioned.

"You mean edible? Well, yes, they are edible but mullet is somewhat of an acquired taste, like frog legs. They just aren't for everybody."

Raising my arm so the full string of fish could be seen, I said, "So you don't want to even try my fish?"

There I stood as if I were four years old, presenting her with a handful of buttercups. What could she do?

Mom approached me, and with a confident smile only a mom could muster, "OK, you clean them and I'll whip up some batter. We're having fried mullet tonight."

Dad arrived home, bid me hello and headed for the kitchen. His destination was always the same. After a hard day at the bank he needed a stiff drink. For Dad that meant three fingers of Coke on the rocks in his favorite high ball glass. The glass featured an image of John Wayne, and a quote, "*Life is Hard, it's Harder when you're Stupid*!"

Entering the kitchen, he spied my mom. "Hey babe, how was your day?"

"Oh, Eric you startled me," she said. "My day was fine, just fine. And yours?"

"It was, well it was," Dad paused, "Say what's that smell?"

"That's your dinner," Mom answered.

"I don't think so," Dad mused, "Perhaps my dinner is at June's Diner."

"Shooosh!" she said. Then in a whisper continued, "Your son caught these fish today and is going to be heartbroken if I didn't cook them."

"Are those mullet?" he asked.

"Yes," Mom answered.

"Did you tell Jake that we don't like mullet?"

"Yes I did, but that didn't matter. I had no choice. These boys have spent months dreaming of building a raft so they can fish. So how would he feel if the first thing he brings home is rejected by his mom?"

"Better than he's going to feel after digesting those foul tasting fish," Dad said with a chuckle.

Mom squared her shoulders and put her hands on her hips like a cheerleader, "Listen here Eric Forrest, you are going to eat it and you are going to like it!"

"Or what?" Dad said through a wry smile.

"Or no strawberry shortcake," Mom answered.

"Yes!" Dad said beaming. "You made strawberry shortcake? Well that's different then. Bring on the mullet, but don't be stingy with the ketchup."

As we settled around the table, we collectively eyed the heaping pile of fish cloaked in golden crumbles. "Well, who wants to go first?" I asked.

Dad said, "Champ, you caught them so you get first dibs."

I grabbed the biggest one near the top and Mom and Dad followed suit. "Well here goes," and I took a big bite.

"How is it?" Dad asked.

"A little chewy, could use some ketchup," I said.

Recalling that evening I marveled at my parent's zeal. We all managed to choke down one fish. No seconds were necessary.

CHAPTER 18

SEVERAL DAYS AFTER MY FAMILY'S mullet feast Rory and I were back on the water with a fervent determination to land tastier fish. Flowing with the outbound tide intent on making it to the inlet, Rory and I enjoyed the freedom of Bent Tree Creek.

Due to our mapping efforts, we were gaining confidence. We had mentally cataloged the natural markers such as the sweeping left hand bend we named "Darlington" after the NASCAR track in South Carolina. But with more time on the marsh, we began noticing the subtleties. This made it possible for us to know exactly where we were simply by "reading" the grass. Nearing the old man's cabin, I decided to have some fun with Rory.

"Rory, what 'cha say we stop by and have breakfast with the hook handed maniac?"

Rory responded, "No problem. But since I am the fastest runner and swimmer, you'll be the one he catches, not me."

"You're not a faster swimmer," I said.

"We'll see," Rory remarked

With the assistance of the current and our combined poling efforts, we were cruising along nicely as we approached the rusted shack. Rory was purposely steering us down the center of the channel well away from the clutches of the dangerous old man. He was sitting in his rocker as we passed. Rory wouldn't even glance in his direction, but I was too curious to pass up a quick peek. I saw him and he saw me. I gave a quick wave and he returned the gesture.

After several more bends and curves we could see the broad opening of Fort George Inlet. The mud of the marsh gradually conceded to the white sand of the inlet, the water changing from a grayish green to an inviting jade. Even on their best day, Crayola's color experts could not duplicate the hue of the inlet's water that morning. Above us, pushed along by a light westerly breeze, an expanse of puffy clouds moved towards the Atlantic. Their pace was leisurely yet unvarying, as if they were a migratory herd of white buffalo. A quick swim in the inviting water seemed an appropriate reward for our navigational accomplishment, and we simultaneously cannon balled into the inlet.

The current carried us to the bridge and once beneath the viaduct we were amazed by the temperature variance. Between the shade and the wind funneling through the straight it was an appealing place to escape the summer onslaught. Cars passing overhead produced *wump wump* sounds as the tires crossed the spacers in the concrete roadway.

The raft eased out of the cover of the bridge back into brilliant mid-day light. Rory tied us off at the last wooden piling of the channel marker. By my reasoning, if we were connected to the bridge then technically we weren't past the bridge. My Mom had been crystal clear when she stated, "Should you ever make it to the Inlet you stop right there. If I ever catch you past the bridge, that raft will make the biggest bon fire you have ever seen."

Preparing his gear Rory said, "This is the best man. Nothing can mess up a day this good."

I was about to concur but was distracted by the sound of an approaching boat. The tone of the growling motor indicated it was a small craft, which meant we did not have to worry about being run over. Due to the lattice work of the channel guard, we were unable to see the approaching mariner as he entered the shadows under the bridge. The boat broke into the sun and with it the captain of the small dingy was revealed, Wade Brown. Wade sat in the rear of the twelve-foot boat, his hand on the throttle of an Evinrude outboard.

He wore his ball cap backwards and his shaggy greasy mane was flapping in the breeze.

"Are you kidding me?" I said.

"I hate that guy," Rory said.

"Maybe he'll just pass us by."

Reaching for the short paddle Rory said, "You know better. But let him get close enough."

"He's not that stupid," I said. "But we can always hope."

The motor's RPMs slowed confirming Rory' prediction. No way he would cruise by like a normal person. He was a hyena, always looking for an easy opportunity. He cut the motor completely and the little boat drifted towards us.

"Well, if it isn't Turd #1 and Turd #2. What are you maggots doing way out here without your mommies?" he said.

"Move on Wade!" Rory said.

"You gonna hit me with that big ole paddle?" he said with a snide laugh. "What are you standing on? Did you girls steal a pallet from the IGA grocery store?"

I said, "It's not a pallet you ignoramus, it's a raft!"

By now the current was taking Wade past us and I had a glimmer of hope he would just keep going. But that was not to be. He re-fired the motor and came back alongside of us.

"Oh, I see now," he started in again, "It's tied together with ropes so it must be a raft. Please tell me you morons found it floating in the marsh. You didn't actually build that worthless piece of crap?"

"Yeah Wade, we built this!" Rory fired back. "In fact, it was a kit. It came in a box with all the materials. The instructions said anyone could build it, well anyone that can pass the ninth grade."

Rory's tongue was like a surgeon's scalpel. However, while lobbing the insult at Wade, Rory waived the paddle for extra effect. His gyrations caused the raft's equilibrium to shift and a wave crested over our feet.

Wade noticed the inherent vulnerability of the raft. "Huh, that pallet of yours ain't very sea worthy," Wade muttered. "You twerps best watch out for waves. Here let me show you."

Wade gunned the throttle and began making half circles around us. Back and forth he churned the water creating waves that hit us from all sides. With each pass, he came closer but still out of reach of our bamboo poles. Rory and I balanced as best we could and by some miracle did not fall overboard. Repeatedly, the swells washed over the raft and churning water surged upward between the raft timbers. Satisfied that he had sufficiently tormented us, Wade peeled off and headed down the inlet.

Reaching into my pocket I pulled out two eight-ounce tear drop sinkers. Because of the sinker's shape, if it were thrown heavy end first, it would fly as true as a lawn dart. Tossing one to Rory I said, "I've had enough!" Watching the boat move away I gauged the distance and speed and with all I had, launched the sinker on a high arching trajectory.

"Be right, be right," I said to myself. Watching the flight of the sinker I glanced down several times at the retreating boat, it was going to be close…real close.

The throw was a shade long. The sinker landed with a noticeable splash several feet ahead and just to the right of Wade's boat. But it was close enough to get his attention. He snapped his head around to look at us. At that precise moment, the sinker Rory had thrown whizzed past his head.

While my approach was a mortar round designed to rain down on Wade, Rory's was a bullet with practically no arc at all. Rory's sinker passed so closely to Wade's head that he lurched backward falling into the bottom of the boat. Once he had situated himself back on the seat, he gave us the one finger wave and sped away.

If one of the sinkers had hit Wade in the head, it might have killed him. On that day, at that moment, neither one of us would have harbored a trace of regret. Reflecting on it later, that moment represented a shift in the dynamics of our relationship with Wade. As long as we could remember Wade Brown had been a predatory menace. Staying clear of his clutches mandated cowardly tactics of running or seeking adult intervention. Until that moment, Rory and I had simply been his victims. In hindsight, it was unclear what brought about the change. Was it the surge of testosterone in our adolescent bodies? Or, had the experience of building and sailing the raft emboldened us with new confidence? Regardless of the motivating factors, that simple defiant act declared we would be victims no more.

CHAPTER 19

OUR ENCOUNTER WITH THE PRINCE of darkness concluded, Rory and I settled down to do some fishing. And *fishing* is all we did, because we certainly didn't do any *catching*. As the tide turned towards home we turned with it. After untying the raft from the bridge Rory asked, "What do you want me to do with these mullet?"

"Are they dead?" I asked.

Rory pulled the string out of the water, "Yep."

"Keep 'em."

"But you said they were terrible, why keep them?"

"Just leave them on the stringer. We'll deal with them later," I answered. I had a plan for the mullet but Rory didn't need to know it just yet.

We entered the mouth of Bent Tree Creek just as the tide was at its absolute lowest point. The unrelenting sun had robbed the mud banks of all discernible moisture. The ebbing of the water level created an illusion that the marsh grass towered above us much like if we were in a small canyon.

Making our way around the final bend before the old black man's shack, I allowed the raft to drift towards his side of the creek. Rory noticed us moving towards what he viewed as imminent danger and pushed hard towards the middle of the creek.

"Rory," I said. He did not respond.

"Rory!"

"What man, help me push already," he answered.

"Listen, let's do something nice," I said.

"What are you talking about?" he asked with a fair level of distress.

"Those mullet, there's no sense wasting them. Let's see if the old man wants them," I answered.

"What? You're crazy, no way I'm going over there!"

"Going over where?" I said.

He turned to point to the shack but realized that while he was so emphatically protesting the notion of approaching it, we were practically there. True to Rory's character, he expressed his disapproval with his patented dark eyed glare.

Up close the overall integrity of the shack appeared more abysmal than it did from across the creek. There was a deck that protruded out the back of the structure and hung over the creek. It was covered by a tin roof, rusted, and curled at the corners. There was a ramp on the left end of the porch which led down to a small floating dock. The ramp had boards nailed at regular intervals which served as steps. A cypress railing dipped like a rope in between the vertical supports. Attesting it was green and flexible when it had been nailed in place.

The tide was beginning to rise but we were still too low to see above the flooring of the deck. Rapping against the railing with my bamboo pole I said loudly, "Anybody home?"

In an angry whisper, Rory said, "This is stupid!"

I smiled and winked at him. Then we heard the squeak of a screen door opening followed by the thud of heavy boots.

"Who there?" came a deep baritone voice.

We both peered up to see the gangly black man staring down at us. His eyes seemed tired but his pupils focused intently. A nasty scar encircled the right side of his face running from the bridge of his nose around his eye and disappearing into his eyebrow. He wore a faded red, long sleeve buttoned shirt with the sleeves rolled up to his forearms. His blue jeans and leather brogans were equally aged.

"Oh hi .... I'm Jake and this is Rory," I said and then paused.

"OK," the man said. "What's you need?"

Clearing my throat and gaining my courage I said, "We caught some mullet today that we can't use and wondered if maybe you wanted them?"

The man paused a moment then abruptly asked, "What's wrong with 'em?"

"Nothing," I responded.

"Why can'ts you use 'em?"

"Well," I began, "We don't like them."

"Then whys you catch 'em?"

"Well, we were trying to use them as bait and we had too many," I said.

"Hmm," the man grunted. "Let's see 'em."

Rory, who until this point, seemed to be considering jumping from the raft and swimming for home pulled up the stringer of fish and handed them to me. I reached up as far as I could and the old man slowly bent towards me. His hand brushed across mine as he grasped the stringer. It was bone thin with heavily calloused palms, and his fingers seemed disproportionately long. The rocker groaned as he sat to inspect the fish.

To my right something caught, no something demanded my attention. It was an animal walking along the porch railing. The glare of the afternoon sun rendered only a silhouette of what was approaching me. It was huge and by the way it walked along the rail, my first thought was a bobcat, but I quickly dismissed that as ridiculous. The only other logical deduction was a big boar raccoon. This old man had a pet raccoon, *how cool is that?* I thought. As I smiled thinking about the prospects of a pet raccoon, a cloud shielded the sun and with the glare removed I could positively identify the creature. It was a cat!

The beast perched above me like a leopard, patiently gauging its prey. By now Rory too had noticed the Goliath feline. He muttered, "Whoa."

"These a nice mess of fish," the man commented, "You sure you don't wants 'em?"

"No sir," I answered, "We don't like how they taste."

"Well the taste is all 'bout how theys cooked," he said.

"My Mom fried them," I said.

"That's your problem," he said with a laugh. "You don't fries mullet. You smokes 'em."

Without speaking he carefully but proficiently walked down the ramp to the floating dock. Clearly unnerved by this, Rory's eyes darted around like a rabbit in a room full of coyotes. The man paused on the floating dock and stretched out his hand, "Name's Amos George."

Relieved, but still a bit intimidated, I slowly extended my hand, "I'm Jake."

"I know, you done said so. And you're Rory. Nice to meets you."

Rory paused a long uncomfortable moment before he stepped forward and extended his hand. This placed too much weight on my end of the raft and water cascaded over our feet. Amos said, "Looks like you gots a buoyancy problem."

Amos George retreated up the ramp and retrieved the string of mullet. He was mumbling about the fish then remarked, "This uns too small. Here cat!"

The beast jumped to the deck landing with a thud and pounced on the six-inch long fish. The sounds of bones crunching required a further inspection. Taking hold of the deck boards we pulled ourselves up to see the monster cat. At eye level his size was even more impressive. In addition to his dimension, his markings also differentiated this cat from any I had ever seen. He was almost all black except for a patch of white fur under his chin that gradually narrowed as it disappeared between his two front legs. He also had one white paw, the left forepaw. My initial inkling that he was a bobcat was further supported by the condition of his tail. Somewhere in his travels the better part of it had been left behind. The cat devoured the fish, head, bones, guts, and all.

"Almost forgots my manners," Amos said and stepped back inside the house. Upon returning he leaned underneath and handed each of us a bottle of soda. Ten ounces of Coca-Cola in the iconic green glass bottle. So cold that once it was exposed to the afternoon humidity the bottle was instantly coated in droplets of condensation. We anxiously downed a huge swallow. The cold burn from the caramel colored carbonated elixir immediately refreshed us. Rory and I alternated between long sips and rubbing the cool bottle on our faces.

During our rehydration, I noticed the remains of a row boat under Amos George's deck. Through the years, the outgoing tide had leached the wood of its cohesiveness causing the side walls to collapse. The only section of the craft that resembled its former state was the bow that remained above the high tide water line. It was royal blue and there was a hand scripted name painted at the peak. Holding to one of the deck's support timbers I leaned as far as I could and there in yellow letters it said "Lilly."

My focus on the rotten rowboat was broken when Amos asked Rory, "You plays for the White Sox?"

The remark caught Rory by surprise and he stuttered, "Huh? I mean, wait you're asking about my hat? Yes, I play for the White Sox."

"What position?" Amos inquired.

"Shortstop," Rory answered.

Amos smiled, "Thens you must be fast?"

With a level of modesty I rarely saw in Rory he answered, "Yeah, I guess."

I chimed in, "Oh, he's fast all right. There's not a catcher in the league that can keep him from stealing."

"You don't say," Amos continued, "So how's you with the stick?"

"You mean the bat?" Rory asked for clarification. Amos nodded. "I hit lead off."

I chimed in again, "And he's a lefty."

"Ah ha, so you already two steps towards first base befores you even swing," Amos said.

He turned to me, "How bouts you Jake, you play ball?"

"Yes sir," I answered, "Rory and I are on the same team."

"Where you play?" Amos asked.

"Mostly outfield, but a little at first base too," I said.

"So's you gots a pretty strong arm I 'spect?"

"Yeah, I guess."

"Where you hit?" he asked.

I paused for a second then said, "I bat sixth."

"Hey nothing wrong with sixth, that's the meat of the order. I 'spect there's usually somebody on base when you gets up," Amos said.

Rory answered for me, "Jake leads the team in RBIs, and he almost never strikes out."

Another big smile crossed Amos' face, "So you's the man the team can counts on what puts the ball in play."

There was a slight break in the conversation as Rory liberated the carbonation from his stomach with a thunderous burp. Realizing he was in the company of someone other than me, he quickly said, "Excuse me."

"That's OK Rory, you amongst the fellas," Amos said. "You know I's a fair ball player when I's young."

Without thinking Rory said, "Wow, they had baseball when you were young?"

Amos George cocked his head at Rory, "Yes Rory, we's played baseball when I's young, in fact Abner Doubleday was on my team."

Rory's face appeared as though he was about to say, "Really?" When Amos began laughing. "Rory, I knows I look old, but do's I look a hundred and twenty-five year-old?"

For the next little while the three of us conversed about a topic that is not hindered by age, race, nationality, or political persuasion–– baseball. Rory willingly joined in the discussion and seemed to let go of his concerns about Amos being a colored man. All too soon the gathering of dark clouds on the western horizon compelled us to head home. As we pushed away from the shack Amos spoke.

"Wait, you's need to leave the empties, thems three cent apiece."

We handed him the bottles, "Thanks again, Mr. George."

He quickly responded, "Now hold on there. I know you's well-mannered and your mamas won't approve, but sees we on equal footin'. You gives me fish, and I gives you cold drinks. See how that makes us equals? So my name is Amos, and that's what I 'spect yous to call me."

CHAPTER 20

It was four days before Rory and I were back on the marsh. Lawn mowing obligations, baseball games, and family commitments kept us otherwise engaged. But this Monday in late June there was nothing between us and another adventurous day on the water. However, from the outset, it was not a promising day. The skies were overlaid with slow moving, gray clouds foretelling a wet day. The air felt as if by cupping your hands and squeezing, a glass of water would be produced. A day with this little upside would encourage most fishermen to stay home, but then again, Rory and I weren't most fishermen. We were exceptional fishermen.

We caught the outgoing tide and traversed the shortest path through the marsh towards Fort George Inlet. As we glided into the inlet the skies opened. Pushing as quickly as possible we made for the cover of the bridge. Safely out of the elements, we decided to further scout the bridge's infrastructure. At the embankment, there was a solid concrete wall that ran the entire width of the bridge. Along the wall, exposed rusted rebar testified to the corrosiveness of the salty air. We attached the raft to one of these jutting rebar fragments and after considerable effort pulled ourselves onto the ledge.

The flat platform stretched about ten feet before connecting to the inclined portion of the bridge that rose to the apex where the bridge met the land. We walked up the steep grade and found it concluded with a cavity just big enough to lay in.

"Cool, this is like a cave," Rory said. "We could sleep up here, it would be awesome."

"Yeah, until you woke up, forgot where you were and sat up quickly. That might be the last thing you'd remember for a while," I said referring to the short ceiling.

My stomach growled. "What did your mom pack us for lunch?" I asked.

"Let's see," Rory said as he dug into the bag. "Two of our favorites, Beanee Weenees and chocolate Snack Pack pudding."

"Perfect," I said as I peeled back the metal top of the Beanee Weenees.

This combination of Van Camp's finest and a perfect size pop-top can of pudding was the foolproof companion for any adventurer. They had an unbelievable shelf life. My can was stamped, *good to infinity*. And the razor-sharp peel off metal lid could be attached to a stick to create a spear for fishing or fending off a grizzly bear.

Rory tore the lid off his pudding and callously ran his tongue across it. It gave me the willies as I imagined him slicing his tongue on the razor edge.

Our lunch finished, we resumed fishing, but we were just killing time. The weather was just too bad. When the next break in the rain came Rory and I pushed off the wall and headed back to Bent Tree Creek. As we guided the raft along the shallow creek, Rory commented, "I hope Amos is home, I could go for a soda."

"So, the man gives you a drink and now you're no longer concerned that he is going to chop us up and put us in his freezer?" I said. "That is all it takes to earn your trust, huh?"

"OK, you were right. He's just a nice old man. It's the cat I am afraid of… That's the biggest cat I have ever seen," Rory said.

"I heard that. It's huge, you know it's like some kind of mutation? Like those movies where the animals get exposed to radiation and they become gigantic," I said.

As we neared Amos' place the skies opened again. Seeing our approach, he walked to the railing and called to us, "Hurry and gets yourselves out of the weather."

We quickly clambered up the ramp and to the cover of the porch. "Whew!" I said wildly shaking my head like a wet dog.

"It's a frog choker ain't it?" Amos said before disappearing through the squeaky screen door. Rory looked at me with a smile of anticipation as he hoped Amos was heading to the fridge. While we waited, I surveyed the porch. It was open on three sides, and the left end provided a panoramic view of Bent Tree Creek and the marsh.

The floor felt solid enough, although the carpenters had been sloppy when they spaced the boards. Some boards had no space between them and others you could slip your hand into the crack. At various spots on the floor were puddles where rain had dripped through nail holes in the tin roof. There were two no-pest strips hanging from opposite beams. When bugs landed on the sticky strips their legs became stuck. Amos' strips were so laden with dead bugs you could no longer see the yellow sticky part. The screen door had numerous patches to repair tears and holes and next to the door a Royal Crown Cola thermometer hung on a nail.

Amos reappeared with two sodas and two towels.

"Here," he said. "Dries yourselves off 'fore you catch cold."

The towel was thin but very soft, and had a pleasant, reminiscent scent that I just couldn't place. I sat down with my back to one of the support beams and took a big gulp of soda. I again put the towel to my nose and on the second pass it hit me. This is how our towels smelled before Mom got a clothes dryer. I had forgotten how nice laundry smelled after hanging outside all day.

Amos broke the silence, "You catch anything?"

"No sir," Rory replied but then remembered, "Just some mullet that is, I'll get them for you when it stops raining. "

"No rush, they ain't going nowhere," Amos replied. "You know the fact that you boys even went out tells me you is optimists."

"What does that mean? "I said.

"You gots a dictionary at home?" he asked.

I nodded.

"Well you might wants to looks it up. Basically, it means you thinks positive 'bout things, even when things look bad. Like this day for instance, I knowed it was gonna rain, everythin' 'bout the morning said so. You two saw the same signs yets you went anyway. That's an optimist. Get it?"

"Yeah, that makes sense," Rory said then added. "We may not be optimists. We just really wanted to get out on the water, and this was our day to do it, so we went."

Amos thought for a moment, "Then perhaps you's desperate optimists. Now, I'll tells you my dictionary is important to me. Should be important to you too. Theys all kinda words in there that most people never know."

Being it was summer, the time of year that most kids avoided books like Rory avoided snakes, Amos' suggestion to embrace Mr. Webster's crowning achievement pretty much fell on deaf ears. Peering out to my right and seeing the expanse of the marsh I commented, "There's a nice view of the creek through here."

Amos' eyes brightened, "You knows that's right. In the fall the sun sets right across that bend in the creek," he said pointing. "God do paints some pretty pictures there, yes sir."

We sat quietly for a time, content to sip our sodas and listen to the rain beat its way across the tin covering. The drops would hang for a moment on the rusted edge of the roof, then cascade into the waiting creek. My quiet was interrupted upon seeing the feline behemoth emerge from under the porch, a mere two leaps from where I was sitting. Instinctively, I stood. The cat leaped effortlessly to the railing and walked towards me. His gait did not appear menacing so I held my ground. The closer he came, the bigger he was. He stopped right next to the post where I was leaning and sat down.

With this up-close view, I could see his left ear was split from the tip to where it connected to his head. It reminded me of butterfly wings.

In comparison, his left ear was in much better condition than his right ear which was gone altogether. His face bore several scars, including a particularly wide one that ran from between his eyes down to his nose. He also had extra toes on his front paws, like the Hemingway cats in Key West.

Looking to Amos I said, "Does he bite?"

Amos smiled, "Naw, lessen you a rat or snake."

Gingerly I slowly raised my hand towards the cat. I gently scratched the top of his head. The cat bowed his softball size noggin to allow me greater access to his neck and shoulders. He produced a rumbling sound like a timpani drum roll. "Is that his purr?"

"Somethin' ain't it? Likes rollin' thunder way off," the old man replied smiling broadly.

I continued to stroke the cat and Rory walked over to take a closer look. He slowly reached out his hand. Sensing Rory's presence the cat whirled around. When the cat focused on Rory I checked out his nub of a tail. What I saw so intrigued me I just had to stare. My trance was broken when Amos spoke up.

"He gots a pair, don't he?"

All I could do was nod my head in affirmation.

"That's why I calls him Mr. Rosco. I figures you gotta set like that, you deserves to be called Mister!" he laughed and his smile beamed like that of a proud parent.

As I stared at the two plums hanging underneath Mr. Rosco's stubby tail, I understood Amos' logic. If a cat ever deserved the respect of being referred to as Mister, it was this one.

"How long have you owned him?" Rory asked.

"Don'ts own him. Mr. Rosco's his own cat. We's got what you might call a gentlemen's agreement. See, Mr. Rosco keeps the rats and snakes down and I's share my food with him.

"Is he a good mouser?" I asked.

"Lawd yes!" Amos said. "You knows them big river rats round here?"

Rory and I nodded.

"Well some of them demons are the size of a opossum, and mean too. Sometimes I sits here and watch Mr. Rosco at work. It's like a scene out of one of them nature shows. Mr. Rosco lies in the grass still as the dead. When one of those rats comes scurryin' by, he strikes like a mongoose, *pow*!" Amos clapped his hands for effect. "Ole Mr. Rosco grabs the rat by the head and shakes it back and fro 'till he hears the neck snap."

"Wow," Rory said. "He's tough. But how did he lose his tail and what happened to his ear?

"I thinks he got in a scrap with a big coon. That's 'bout the only animal round here big enough to whoop him. As far as his tail go, that's probably some mean person's doing," Amos said.

"Like Wade Brown mean," I said to Rory.

Rory was scratching Mr. Rosco and his purring seemed to vibrate the porch. Rory moved his hand to Mr. Rosco's back, and the cat wailed what seemed to be a painful meow. Rory quickly pulled away his hand.

"It's all right boys. He just sayin' it feels good," Amos laughed, "You boys is good for the soul, yes sir." He then patted his leg and called Mr. Rosco. The cat leaped to the plank floors and began to curl in and around Amos George's legs. "You wants to know something really special 'bout this old cat?" he asked.

We both nodded.

"Now you needs to realize this here cat ain't never been no house cat. Most likely he's dumped when he was little and had to survive on his own. I don't know why he decided to lives with me, reckon the good Lawd knowed we needed each other. Anyways, on really cold nights he come scratchin' on the door. And I lets him in, all he want's to sleep on my feet. He stay there all night, and I don'ts know if he keepin' himself warm, or tryin to keep me warm."

"That's cool," Rory said.

"Seems that Mr. Rosco is a special cat," I said.

The old man bent down and cupped both his hands around the cat's giant head, "There ain't another one like 'im. They broke the mold when they made Mr. Rosco."

"Must have been a big mold," Rory said.

"Rain's stopped, we best head home," I announced.

Walking towards the raft I turned back to Amos, "Well, thanks again for the drink. And it was nice to meet Mr. Rosco," I said.

Amos smiled, rose to his feet, and stuck out his hand, "It was time well spent, Jake."

As I stepped on the raft Rory was handing the stringer of mullet to Amos. Seeing us struggle to maintain our balance he said, "Next raft you design plan to use some barrels for better flotation. See? Likes on my dock.

Rory and I pulled the raft next to the floating dock and more closely examined the barrels attached underneath. "Yeah, that would make a big difference," I said.

"Boys, buildin' rafts is a lot like life. You learns what works and what don'ts, then you trys to never make the same mistakes again. Now be careful goin' home and watch out for the Kraken."

We had begun to drift away with the tide and Rory shouted back, "What's a kraken?"

"Looks it up!" Amos George shouted.

CHAPTER 21

LATER THAT EVENING I SEARCHED in vain for a dictionary. Mom was cooking and by the tantalizing scent drifting through the house, Dad and I would soon be gorging on fried chicken and collard greens.

"Mom, where's the dictionary?" I asked.

"Where's the what?" she said from the kitchen.

"The dictionary."

"Jake honey, come here. I am elbow deep in fried chicken and can't hear what you're saying," she shouted back.

I entered the kitchen, "Mom, I need the dictionary."

She glanced away from the bubbling caldron and said, "Jake let me feel your head."

"Why Mom? I'm fine."

Smiling she said, "Well there must be something wrong with you if you're looking for a dictionary in the middle of summer."

"I just need to check out a word."

She suggested the right end table in the living room. There I found a sizable hard cover Webster's dictionary. I searched for the word with no luck.

"Mom, how do you spell Cracken?"

"You mean like crackling corn bread?"

"No like something you would find in the ocean."

"Oh, that's K-r-a-k-e-n," she answered. "Why do you want to know?"

"Because Amos George told Rory and me to watch out for the Kraken. I want to know what he meant," I answered.

"Found it" I said to myself. *Kraken - In 16th century Norwegian folklore a kraken was a huge sea monster shaped like a giant squid.*

Mom entered the living room just as I had finished reading the definition. Satisfied with my new knowledge of sea monsters I closed the book with a loud slap.

"Who is this Amos George person?" Mom asked.

This question was asked in the slow deliberate tone that conveyed her maternal sensors were fully engaged seeking to ascertain the danger level. Much like NORAD (North American Aerospace Defense Command) reacts when they detect an unfamiliar blip on the radar screens monitoring the Bearing Sea. Mom had immediately changed the status from Defcon 5, which means the world is a peaceful loving place to Defcon 3, which triggers the scrambling of fighter planes to investigate what the Ruskies are up to.

"Mom, he's just an old man that lives on the creek. Rory and I swapped him some mullet for Cokes," I answered.

Of course, this was not sufficient disclosure. Mama bear was on the scent of something and would not relent until all relevant facts were disclosed. She peppered me with questions about how we met him, how old he was, was there a woman living there with him, did he seem drunk? I was doing fine until she asked, "You two haven't been in his house have you"?

"No ma'am, not inside his house," I said.

Moms never miss the subtleties. She picked up on the *not inside* part and grilled me further. When she learned we had spent several hours on his porch she announced, "We are done with this until your father gets home." This meant Dad would be embroiled in the investigation that would eventually rival the McCarthy hearings in scope and magnitude.

After dinner mom ushered Dad into the living room and expressed her concerns. She was concentrating on the fact that young boys should not be taking sodas from some strange man on the creek. He could be a molester or an escaped convict.

Eavesdropping from the kitchen, I heard Dad respond, "Connie, take a breath. The boys are smart. I'm sure they've not put themselves in any danger. He's probably just a harmless old man. But just to be sure I'll speak with the sheriff."

"Well until you do, you tell your son to steer clear of that Amos character. I just can't stand the thought ..."

Dad stopped her in mid-sentence, "Connie honey, you can't go down this road every time Jake is out of your sight. You fear tragedy anytime the boy is five minutes late. Let's keep to the middle of the road and stay out of the ditches. How about you and me go help Jake finish the kitchen and then have a piece of that apple pie I saw on the counter?"

Later that evening Dad came into my room and said what I knew was coming. Until he had a chance to make sure there were no concerns with Amos George, Rory and I were to make no further contact. It was clear we would remain at Defcon 3 until Dad fully vetted the threat.

The next afternoon, Dad parked the Country Squire in front of the Nassau County Sheriff's office, fed the meter and approached the double glass entryway. The sheriff's office was situated in the heart of downtown Fernandina. It was directly adjacent to the County court house, which made it very convenient for hearings and trials. The jail, which consisted of six cells and an interview room, was housed in the rear of the building. The front of the office was welcoming and approachable. The rear was bordered with a twelve-foot fence capped in razor wire and floodlights.

In his work at the bank dad knew many people in town. As such he was acquainted with the deputy manning the desk, Ricardo "Ricky" Alvarez. Deputy Alvarez was in his early twenties and wore his hair slightly shaggy, which contrasted with the close cropped almost military cuts worn by the older men on the force. He also differed in that he was not the perfect picture of fitness, his paunchy gut and heavy jowls testifying to his over active sweet tooth. His uniform fit him as if he chose the size with the expectation he was going to lose weight, but never did. The most striking feature of Deputy Alvarez's appearance was his jet-black pencil thin mustache that blended perfectly with his dark eyes. He was also the newest man on the force, having recently completed his first year of service. This was a tremendous accomplishment for Deputy Alvarez. Considering eight months earlier he was ever so close to setting the record for the shortest time on the force.

Alvarez was affable, which made it all the more surprising that he pointed his service revolver at the wife of a County Commissioner. What began as a routine traffic stop quickly escalated after she refused to present her license and called him "Deputy Taco Head." This inference to his Mexican heritage was not only mean spirited, but also incorrect, as Ricky could trace his bloodline back to the original Spanish settlers of Florida.

Sheriff Buddie Jr. was aghast at Alvarez's lapse of judgment, and decided to fire him. However, phone calls from influential citizens and political power mongers began pouring in demanding that he not only dismiss Alvarez, but arrest him as well. If there was one thing the sheriff didn't cotton to, it was town busy bodies telling him how to manage his department. With spiteful indignation the sheriff not only retained Alvarez, but also gave him a pay raise.

Deputy Alvarez had made the most of his second chance and since the episode had been a model civil servant. The deputy knew my father as the banker who made him his first loan. It was for a red 1970 Ford Maverick. As my dad approached the desk, they greeted one another enthusiastically.

"How's the car Ricky?" Dad asked.

With an enhanced level of exuberance Alvarez said, "Oh she's a sweet ride now. I put 60s on the front and 70s on the back, and I've installed a glass pack muffler so now it has that throaty idle. The next thing on the list is a new engine, it really needs a V8."

"That sounds expensive Ricky."

"Yes I know, but it'll be worth it."

My father paused the way dads sometime do when they are about to rip a big hole in your poorly thought out plans. "Ricky with a V8 under the hood, I doubt the transmission and rear end will handle all that torque."

Deputy Alvarez was silent for a moment then his face wilted, "Gee you're right. Man, that's not going to work at all."

Quickly Dad redirected, "Ricky instead of trying to turn a Maverick into a Mustang, which it'll never be, why don't you start a muscle car savings account?"

The glow of residual optimism returned to Alvarez's face, "That sounds like a good plan. Thanks, Mr. Forrest."

"You're welcome Ricky. Now I wanted to see if Sheriff Buddie Jr. is available," Dad said.

"OK sure Mr. Forrest, I hope nothing is wrong?" Officer Alvarez asked, his police curiosity showing.

"Oh no, there's nothing wrong, I just need his input," Dad said.

Resigned that he was not to be involved in whatever Dad wanted to discuss, Alvarez escorted Dad to the sheriff's office.

Sheriff Buddie Jr. or Sheriff Junior Buddie, either worked, maintained an office that reinforced his importance to the county. His desk was a rich cherry wood monster that could have been a billiard table save for the missing six pockets and green felt. The top of the desk was largely unadorned except for a bronze nameplate with his name centered between two raised western style stars, and a desk lamp. The lamp was a typical office apparatus in every way except that the vertical support piece was made from a .44 magnum pistol.

As my Dad and Deputy Alvarez entered, the sheriff rose to his feet and extended his hand. "Hello mister banker, what brings you to my humble office?"

"Eric will do just fine," Dad answered. "And I just need to pick your brain on something."

The sheriff responded in a deliberate self-debasing manner, "Well I'm not sure what you'll find in my brain, I'm just a simple county constable."

Dad was always intuitive when it came to people's motives. He could ascertain which ones were genuine and which ones harbored ulterior intentions. He sensed Sheriff Buddie, Jr.'s self-deprecating comments were all part of his manipulation strategy.

As they sat down Dad glanced at the Buddie family's wall of fame. There were several pictures of Buddie Jr. and Sr. along with fellow officers and local dignitaries. However, one stood out, it was a huge, nearly poster size shot of the Buddies taken on the beach surrounded by bales of marijuana. A newspaper clipping included in the frame read: "Biggest Pot Seizure in Nassau History." Dad smiled as he recalled the truth about the incident. The term "seizure" was a bit of a misnomer. The sheriff's department did in fact seize the pot, but only after a local citizen alerted them that the "square groupers" were washing up along the beach. It was more of a cleanup effort than a sting operation. The only arrest resulting from the "seizure" was two guys caught loading the bales into their micro bus.

Dad began, "Sheriff what I wanted to ask.."

Sheriff Buddie Jr. quickly interrupted, "You know Mr. Forrest it has always confused me that there are lots of jokes about attorneys and police officers taking money from folks, but none about slippery bankers. Why is that you suppose?"

In relaying this encounter to me years later, Dad said he knew he was at a crossroads. His choices were to acquiesce to the Buddie Jr.'s need to be in charge or play hardball. Dad was never much of an acquiesce kind of guy, he knew it was the smart play, but he just couldn't roll over.

"You know Sheriff, I think that there are fewer jokes about bankers because we are more trustworthy than the other two categories."

"And why pray tell is that?" Buddie Jr. asked.

Without a pause, Dad said, "Because when people hand over their money to us, it's still there when they come back for it."

The sheriff said nothing for several seconds. He then tilted his head ever so slightly, much like a dog might do when straining to identify a noise. He slowly leaned back in his chair and resting his cleft chin atop his two index fingers focused his gray eyes on dad. "What can I do for you Mr. Forrest?"

"I wanted to ask about an old man that lives out on the marsh, his name is Amos George?"

"I know who you mean, an old colored man living in a piece of crap shack. Has he caused you a problem Mr. Forrest, do you want to swear out a complaint?"

"No nothing like that. See my boy and his friend have been fishing out there and it appears they have befriended the old man. They seem to have a good arrangement where they trade fish for sodas. Anyway, I just wanted to make sure he has no history I need to be worried about."

"Mr. Forrest, the man of which you speak has no criminal record with this department. As far as I am aware he has lived out there peacefully for decades. But there are other dangers besides those of a criminal nature," Buddie said.

Perplexed by the sheriff's answer Dad said, "I'm not sure I follow?"

"Mr. Forrest, the concern of which I speak is the agenda being forced upon us by those well intending folks in Washington, D.C. Why, they believe that the whites and coloreds should all work together, go to school together, attend church together, hell, I think they'd all be happy if we would just all live together. With a boy at such an impressionable age, I think I'd be more discriminating about the type of company he was keeping," the sheriff said.

"I see now. Thank you for clarifying it for me," Dad responded.

"Glad to help," Buddie Jr. said.

Rising to leave Dad said, "You know Sheriff, you do a terrific job of keeping this community safe. In fact, there are times I wonder why we even lock our doors." As Dad spoke Buddie Jr. was smiling at the compliment, "But when it comes to issues of moral or social significance, I prefer you keep your backwards views to yourself. Good day."

Leaving the police station Dad realized he would never again receive a mere warning for a moving violation.

CHAPTER 22

December 28TH 2003

After a long day sifting through my parent's possessions, followed by the dinner with Freddie Sadler, I should have been primed for sleep. But, there I sat in Dad's big lounger without any initiative to go to bed. A theory that held promise was that my gastrointestinal system was still trying to digest the three thousand calories of calzone I consumed at the DeLuca's restaurant. On the positive side, given the garlic saturation in my system, the town of Fernandina would be vampire free for at least a week.

In my bloated, miserable state, I gamely decided to clear out another room. Believing it was mostly purged at this point, I chose my old bedroom. The only remaining unexplored areas were under the bed and inside the closet. The dark recess under the bed held no treasure except an orphaned black sock. The effort of looking further agitated my too full stomach.

Crawling to the end of the bed, I leaned against the wall next to the closet door. I paused for a few minutes allowing Mount Vesuvius to settle. From my sitting position, I opened the door and was face to face with Joe Willie Namath. Once married, I no longer slept in my old room when I visited, and as such I had not seen the Hall of Fame quarterback in perhaps fifteen years.

Oh, the flood of memories this poster produced. They had absolutely nothing to do with Broadway Joe and everything to do with Farrah Fawcett. In 1976, Farrah Fawcett was without question the number one female celebrity in the United States and possibly the world. Her thespian skills were at best average, but it was her stunning looks that mesmerized a generation of young men. While at the peak of her popularity, her image was forever preserved in a pinup poster. The combination of her toothy smile, the big 70s hair, and that red bathing suit catapulted the poster's sales to unprecedented heights.

I was sixteen at the time, and like most teenage boys I thought it appropriate that Farrah adorn my bedroom. Once plastered on my wall, it took exactly 12 minutes and 17 seconds for my mom to spy it as she tossed a load of clean laundry onto my bed.

"Jake Forrest, get yourself in this room right now!" she said.

I walked in to find her standing in front of Farrah, hands on her hips. I was told in short order that Farrah and her much too thin bathing suit were to be removed post haste. Realizing by the tenor of her voice and the malice in her eyes this was not a negotiable situation, I gave her an obligatory, "Fine!"

Complaining loudly to myself about the oppressive, intolerant state in the Forrest house, I begrudgingly removed the poster. I steadied myself to crumple it and forever wrinkle sweet Farrah, but then I succumbed to a rebellious spirit which ushered me down a devious back alley to "Sneaky Town." I temporarily hid the poster under my bed while I weighed my options.

Ten minutes later a brilliant plan was hatched. I retrieved a stack of *Sports illustrated* magazines and tore away six of the covers. I walked through the kitchen holding a crumpled ball of magazine covers and proceeded outside before loudly clanging the garbage can lid.

The remainder of the night followed its normal pattern and by eleven the house was dark and quiet. I retrieved Farrah from under my bed and with the precision of a U.S. Mint engraver, I carefully attached the poster to the closet door behind Joe Namath. I examined my masterpiece the following morning and it was impossible for the unsuspicious eye to ascertain my dastardly deed.

It was exhilarating to know that I had put one over on Mom. Perhaps the ole girl was slipping. For the next month or so, whenever she angered me I simple retreated to my room and looked at Farrah, just for spite.

That haughty pride dissipated one afternoon several months later. I was rooting around my closet for a lost shoe and noticed Broadway Joe was ever so slightly skewed. Gently, I lifted the bottom of the poster, but there was no Farrah. In an emotion just shy of panic I lifted the Namath poster even higher. And that's when I saw it. A piece of Mom's personal stationary affixed to the door with the message.

Jake, I guess you're not as clever as you think!
Love, Mom

I was shocked. Part of me was enraged at her gall to snoop in my room, a room that happened to be in her house. And yet part of me marveled that she was in fact smarter than the average bear. I considered my next move carefully. If I confronted her, she had me on several counts of sneaky in the first degree. I therefore decided the best course of action would be no action. Just continue pretending that nothing had changed. Wait and see if her curiosity and conscience got the better of her. I was betting she would blink first, a seasoned bookie would call that a "sucker bet," with me being the sucker.

Once again, I had gravely underestimated Mom. She had no reason to bring it up—she had won. Poor Farrah was alone at the bottom of a landfill. Or worse, her crumpled beauty had been rescued by a sanitation employee and she now adorned the inside of a porta-potty at the city dump. Mom and I never spoke again about the Farrah incident. But for good measure, I left her note under Joe Namath. Just to leave a little doubt in her mind.

That night in late 2003, I sat there gazing at the decades old poster of Joe Namath. I carefully lifted the brittle corner and was relieved to find Mom's note still affixed to the door. It was one of those events that many experience along the grief highway, a moment with the duality of your heart smiling and your eyes weeping.

Deciding that Broadway Joe and Farrah had been apart far too long I tossed him in the trash pile. The note from Mom went in the keeper stack.

Resuming my examination of the closet I found two heirloom quilts on the top shelf and that was all.

Saying audibly, "Well that's one more closet done." I closed the door, but felt a strange yearning to take another look. Scanning it again I spied something in the back left corner, a sealed cardboard box. Once in the light I immediately knew Dad had packed this box. First of all, it was sealed with duct tape. My father was a zealous disciple of the omnipotent power of duct tape. The second clue was the inscription. It said "Will and Jake—more junk."

Now this box intrigued me. Like a kid on Christmas morning I quickly ripped away the tape. Opening the flaps, the first thing I saw was a stack of scratched 45's representing the best of the 1960s, the Beatles, Simon and Garfunkel, and the Beach Boys.

Laying the records aside and continuing the excavation of the box, I found several rubber band bound stacks of Topps baseball and football cards. There was a dozen or so Hot Wheels cars and a Hess Truck still in its original box. Like how the prize in a cereal box always seems to be at the bottom, such was my fortune when I reached the last item in this old box. As quick as my eyes registered the book's red cover a huge smile spread over my face. Pulling it from the box I examined the cover. The gold letters of the title gleamed *Webster's Collegiate Dictionary*. It was not in pristine condition, but then this book had not spent its life on a shelf as intellectual décor. Its cracked, taped binding and the red string fibers that hung from each corner gave evidence this was a beloved companion. Generally, the unearthing of a dictionary would not be as significant as say, the finding of the Dead Sea Scrolls. But this was not just any dictionary, this was Amos George's dictionary.

The first time I saw this oversized reference tool was a summer afternoon in 1972. It was still early in our friendship, and as usual, Rory and I had arrived thirsty after a morning of fishing.

"Hey Amos, you home?" I shouted as we approached his dock.

Amos emerged through the screen door, "Boys, good mornin's to you. How's the day's fishin'?"

Rory responded, "Great! We'll show you just how great in a minute."

We bounded up the ramp and Rory proudly hoisted a string of speckled trout and flounder. Amos carefully eyed the fish as the stringer spun slowly in a counter clockwise direction. "That's a fine mess of fish boys, fine indeed."

Rory removed a flounder and one of the trout and handed them to Amos. As always, he protested that we should be taking these home to our mamas, but he graciously relented.

"Where's Mr. Rosco?" I asked. "We've got a treat for him too."

Amos peered around the porch and said, "I don't know where he at this mornin'." Then he shouted, "Cat, cat!" Within ten seconds we heard the unmistakable thud of the Godzilla cat jumping from the railing onto the deck. I bent down to scratch his head, but he was wildly sniffing at my shirt and the small plastic bucket behind my back. I relented to his primal need and presented him with two pogies, each about four inches long. He somehow managed to grab both fish in his mouth and retreated to a dark corner. Amos had taken his fish inside to soak and returned with our reward, sodas and Snicker bars.

"Mr. Rosco sure likes fresh fish," I said.

"Yep, he do," Amos answered. "But you knows what's kinds he like best?" With a slight pause, he said, "sardines."

"Sardines?" Rory asked.

"You bet," Amos said. "If he hear me peeling back the top on a tin of sardines he come runnin' from a mile away. In fact, you sees all those tears in the screen door? That's cause of him. He climbs that screen like a black bear lookin' for honey."

Just as Mr. Rosco had done, Rory and I retreated to our favorite spot on the porch to enjoy our feast. Amos George sat in his rocker and drew a pipe from his shirt pocket. He pried open a can of Prince Albert tobacco, placed a scoop in the pipe and struck a match. He touched the flame to the tobacco leaves and gently puffed. Within minutes the fragrance pervaded the porch.

"That's great smelling tobacco," Rory said.

Amos smiled and picked up the tin of tobacco, "It's called Flyin' Dutchman. It do smell nice don't it? But lets me tell you somethin' boys, I has one pipe a day. I started with this pipe when I quit smokin' them cigarettes."

At this point he stared at us and pointing his finger for effect said, "Now listen to Amos, Don'ts you ever try them cigarettes. 'Cause once you pick 'em up, they's hell to put down."

We nodded in agreement and Rory said, "My mom used to smoke and she said the same thing—it was real hard to quit."

The conversation gradually veered to our favorite and most unifying topic, baseball. As our friendship deepened with Amos he shared more about his past, which included playing professional baseball. He had been a promising third baseman, and in his own words "quick as lightning on the bases." However, a knee injury when he was barely twenty-three robbed him of his speed. His career was washed up well before he ever reached his potential.

The lecture on cigarettes completed, Amos said, "Who the best pitcher all time?"

"That's easy," I said. "Sandy Koufax."

Rory chimed in, "Well I think it's Tom Seaver."

"Well those good choices for sure but, I's think the best pitcher all time was Satchel Paige."

"Who?" Rory and I said together.

"Satchel Paige!" Amos said again. He stood and briskly walked into the cabin. He returned with a framed picture and presented it to Rory and me.

"Here, this is Satchel Paige."

"Which one?" Rory asked as there were three ballplayers in the picture.

"The one in the middle," Amos said. "And that's me on the right."

There before us was a young Amos George. Even though he was fifty years younger, the broad smile unfurled across his face was unmistakable. In examining the picture, I saw there was no scar encircling Amos' right eye. Whatever injury befell him happened after his baseball career.

"Well if he's the greatest pitcher of all time, why haven't we heard of him?" I asked.

"'Cause he black, he played most his career in the Negro Leagues," Amos said.

"What was the Negro...." Rory hung on the word as if it was forbidden to say. He modified the question, "What were those leagues again?"

"The Negro Leagues. It's where black players played ball before Jackie Robinson brokes the color barrier in the majors. See boys, when I played, blacks and whites was segregated," he continued.

"What's segregated mean?" Rory asked.

"My Lawd have mercy," Amos said. He rose to his feet, headed back into the cabin, mumbling as he went, "What they teaching kids in school these days?"

He returned with a large red book. He passed it to Rory and me and said, "Now looks up segregation."

Rory and I opened it and thumbed toward the "S" section. Finding the correct page, Rory ran his thumb down the page. "Got it," he said.

"Read it," Amos said.

Rory cleared his throat as if he were about to give a school report. As he read it I saw that certain words were underlined, and in the margin Amos had made notes.

After Rory finished, Amos asked, "So does you know what that means?"

"Yeah, it kinda means that people of different colors lived in different places," Rory said.

"And it wasn't good," I added.

"Rights, so when I say I played in the Negro leagues it's cause I couldn't play in the majors. You boys see baseball on the TV and the teams has black, white, and even fellows from South America. You don'ts think nothing of it, but it weren't always that way. Yeah ole Satchel pitched in the Negro leagues and the majors for near forty year. He was 59 or 60 when he quit. It's a shame you boys ain't never heard of him."

He paused and settled back in his rocker. Inspired again he added, "A man can learn lots from a dictionary. I knows you got one at home, spend five minute a day readin' it and you'll grows up knowin' lots of good words."

CHAPTER 23

July 1972

Red sky at night….Rafters delight.

The last day of June that summer between 7th and 8th grade was spent as summer days should be spent. Rory and I knocked out several lawns in the morning, hit the 7-Eleven for a Slurpee, and caught the last currents of the afternoon tide.

It had been a rewarding day on the briny marsh. Our stringer was weighed down by three red fish and a handful of flounder. In mid-afternoon, a thunderstorm chased us to the safety of the bridge, but as with many summer squalls, it was upon us then gone in short order.

It would seem the air surrounding the marsh could not possibly become any more humid, but the brief rain managed to push the sticky needle even further into the red zone. Had the cloud cover from the storm remained it would have been a fair trade off, but the angry clouds had other people's beach days to ruin. All that remained were a few lines of clouds, appearing as though they had lost pace with the rest of the storm and were simply left behind.

We stopped at Amos' place late in the afternoon to engage in the commerce of bartering. A red fish and a flounder in exchange for Frosty root beers and Twinkies, seemed a fair trade for both parties.

After a short visit, we dutifully headed for home. Our Moms had relented to our adventures with some very simple, yet non-negotiable rules — never go past the bridge and be home before dark. Noncompliance with these statutes would not be met by the amazing grace of second chances, but instead by an immediate revocation of our captain's licenses. As Rory and I were regularly violating the rule of not going past the bridge, we felt the need for absolute adherence to the sundown policy.

Nearing the Twain lot, the sun was falling fast into the western sky. The heat of the day had reluctantly relented to a cool sea breeze that was too pleasurable to adequately define. At the perfect moment, a moment so precise that a sixty second window was the difference between experiencing it or missing it, the last rays of daylight filtered through the shallow straggling clouds and fashioned a fresco of pink and white on a blue ceiling. This display of God's handiwork was so profound that even a couple of boys were in awe. We both stopped poling the raft and simply stared towards the horizon. No words were exchanged, no analysis of the conditions was required. It was a stirring culmination of a nearly perfect day.

Flipping the calendar to July was met with great anticipation. Within the thirty-one days of July, two of our favorites events of the year occurred, the Fourth of July and the Major League All-Star game. In our little hamlet, the festivities of July 4th were part patriotic celebration and part county fair. In addition to speeches from local politicians, pie eating contests, sack races, and of course fireworks, there were also carnival rides. For many however, the primary attraction of the event was both the abundance and variety of food. The word "variety" does not imply there was all manner of food, including food with any redeeming nutritional value whatsoever. No, the reference to "variety" meant that the festival foods fell into one of three categories: greasy, fatty, or sweet.

The air was saturated with scents lofting from huge barbeque cookers, steaming vats of low country boils, as well as food trailers and tents erected by churches and civic organizations. It was impossible to separate the individual smells, but the concoction produced instant salivation.

The event was staged at the Northeast end of town at the main harbor. After traversing the brick laid crosswalks through historical Fernandina, your nose would drag the rest of your body towards the tantalizing scents that lay just across the tracks.

Rory and I followed a simple plan. Arrive early, find our friends, have the run of the place, and only locate our parents at the conclusion of the fireworks. Walking across the railroad tracks, I was given a small American flag by Chief Wolshisky. I turned to walk away but was halted by a sharp, "Swabbies!" Rory and I about faced and gave the Chief a crisp salute.

Yes, the Chief was a bit over the top and our respect was more feigned than genuine. But in high school I interviewed him for a history project and came away with a whole other level of admiration. In the summer of 1941, sixteen-year-old Francis Wolshisky lied his way into the U.S. Navy. He was deployed on a destroyer providing convoy duty to England. During our meeting the Chief shared the fear he experienced during the midnight watch.

"You didn't have to worry about going to sleep on watch, it was too damn cold. Good God, the North Atlantic was one miserable place during the winter, and it was always winter. Moonless nights were the worst though, every swell looked like a Kraut torpedo coming straight at you."

Later in the war the Chief had a front row seat to the greatest invasion in history, D-Day. His ship, the *USS Frankford* was part of a flotilla of destroyers which moved into the dangerously shallow waters just off Omaha Beach. Gunner's Mate Wolshisky and his shipmates blasted the German defenses with five inch guns enabling the pinned-down Allied troops to break out of the beachhead. As the Chief relayed this portion of his past, it was clear he felt tremendous pride to have participated in the invasion of Fortress Europe.

We soon collected the other members of our tribe. We located Clay Dawson at the DeLuca Pizza trailer. Big Freddy Sadler came along momentarily, and his purple mustache indicated he had already visited the snow cone shack. With great exuberance he explained, "They had righteous flavors and it was the best snow cone ever!" Sean Horrowitz, the guy who always makes things happen, was the last to show.

Everyone accounted for we set out for food and fun. While waiting in line for the Scrambler, Mary Grace, Lacy and Callie showed up and we agreed to meet later for the fireworks. After burning through our money, the fireworks were still two hours away. In other words, there was only one thing to do.... find trouble. And with Sean Horrowitz, trouble was never far away.

With an inspired grin Sean walked across the road to the corn dog trailer and discretely grabbed a handful of ketchup packets. The street where we stood was the main entryway to the festival and it was packed with folks strolling towards the bay front.

Sean retreated to our location, carefully threading his way through the crowd. Every few steps he dropped a ketchup packet to the ground. Soon, an unsuspecting sap would step on one of these ketchup landmines causing it to explode. Observing Sean litter the roadway with tomato claymores, Clay Dawson remarked, "One day that idiot is going to rile the wrong bull."

We concurred with Clay's assessment. It was a bad idea. I shudder to consider my parents' reaction if they knew I was a party to a prank this wretched. But alas, when you're thirteen sometimes your perspective of appropriate and inappropriate humor is skewed. Sean rejoined us sporting a dastardly grin. "Now fellas we wait for the pigeon."

A pigeon was not destined to trigger Sean's trap. A better ornithology characterization would be a full-grown male ostrich. We watched for several minutes as people paraded through the minefield somehow avoiding detonation. Approaching from our left an individual stood out and over the crowd. This man was well over six feet tall and husky like a lumberjack. A big bushy beard obscured most of his face and a bright orange ball cap donned his huge coconut. He was accompanied by, or he had kidnapped and brainwashed, a woman that was far prettier than he deserved. Tall and slender with long black curly hair, she wore a navy top and white pants. At that moment, I thought to myself, "*I sure hope that big redneck doesn't trigger one.*"

From my mouth to fate's ear.

His big hulking Yeti foot stepped on a packet. Red napalm sprayed upward. It hit his lady friend and resulted in a red stream from her calf all the way up her leg to her butt. Of course, he was clueless to his actions. Truth be known Sasquatch could have stepped on a small poodle and would have never felt it. But his date immediately felt the shockwave. She stopped short to examine the sticky wetness on her leg. The poor guy walking behind her was otherwise distracted and plowed into her nearly knocking her to the ground. She screamed and pulled her leg up as if she had stepped on a roofing tack. The big redneck reacted immediately by taking issue with the man who bumped her, all the while she hopped on one foot and screamed, "It's blood, ugh it's blood!"

We tried to remain as inconspicuous as possible, but of course Freddie started laughing and that settled it for the rest of us.

The redneck slowly figured out that the other man had no culpability and returned his focus to the woman with the ever expanding ketchup stain. He subsequently demonstrated he was not as dumb as he looked. Using a napkin to dab her leg he noticed another packet of ketchup on the roadway, an unexploded packet. His eyes continued further across the street, towards where we were standing and spied another packet. He was well on his way to developing a sound hypothesis, when our laughter reached him. His deranged topaz eyes shifted from the road to a group of hooligan boys. We were busted.

By now the woman had morphed from anger to tears, giving him more than sufficient motivation to exact a measure of retribution. He slowly rose, pointed his stubby finger at us and called us a name that implied our parents were never married. He then said in a growl, "I'm. Gonna. Kill. You! " From where he stood it was five, maybe six Bigfoot strides to where we cowered. Our laughter ceased.

He rumbled towards us while other festival attendees parted like the Red Sea. His fists and teeth were clinched, and thus, certain parts of my anatomy were feeling clinched as well. Rory was nearest to the raging skunk ape. He turned to the rest of us and quickly said, "Time to split." And in a flash, he was gone.

The man realized he had no chance to catch Rory and instead focused on the four remaining reprobates. I decided to pin my hopes of survival on the toad that got us into the mess. Sean was not fleet of foot, but he was sneaky. And given the circumstances I chose to place my trust in sneaky. We bolted to the right towards the harbor, passing mere inches from the giant's grasp. Sean and I booked it through the crowded roadway, never looking back.

Only two remained, Freddie and Clay. Given Freddie's girth, the redneck surmised he was easy prey. This was a flawed assumption as Freddie's sumo wrestler physique was complimented by a ballet dancer's feet. As the man approached in full gallop, Freddie rose slightly on the balls of his feet. At the last second, he sidestepped the man's grasp. He then ran towards the snow cone shack. Ignoring Clay, who stood calmly sipping a drink, the redneck reversed gears and tore out after Freddie. Freddie reached the snow cone stand and took a quick glance to see if he was still being chased. Sporting a demonic glower his pursuer yelled, "I got you now, fat boy!"

Quickly scampering to the side of the snow cone shack, Freddie deftly tip toed through an area of discarded ice. The charging man hit the ice patch at full stride. His feet slid and then left the earth altogether. He landed with a thud, flat on his back in a pool of icy slush. He let out a groan, pushed himself up on one arm, and screamed something about killing us in our beds. He was joined in his misery by the girl in the now red striped pants and together they hobbled away.

Freddy's exploits were unknown to Sean and me as they occurred while we ran for our lives. At this juncture of the events of July 4th, it is appropriate to discuss the concept of things coming full circle. In the Hindu philosophy it's karma, in the Bible it's *whatsoever a man sows, that shall he also reap*, and in homespun wisdom it's *if you are gonna dance you have to pay the fiddler.*

Sean Horrowitz acted as though he was immune to many of the rules that otherwise governed human society. And to a large degree there was a Teflon nature to him. Neither blame nor consequence seemed to stick to him, it was as if he were charmed. But on that muggy night the spell was broken. Karma was in hot pursuit of Sean, and she was closing fast.

We zigzagged through the human obstacle course way too fast for conditions that crowded. Approaching a group of slow moving revelers, we split up. As I cleared the group I saw open ground and sprinted for church row. At the same time, Sean cleared the group and saw the same opening. He also spied a large German shepherd, but he didn't see the thin black nylon leash attached to the dog. The dog's owner just happened to be down on one knee tying his shoe and the leash was therefore very close to the ground. Was it ill timing that prompted the man to lower the leash at the exact moment Sean Horrowitz was making a clean get away, or was it Sean's time to pay the fiddler?

At a full sprint, Sean hooked his foot on the leash and sprawled head long onto the hot asphalt. He gamely got up and attempted to walk off the hurt, but he was scraped something awful. Deputy Ricky Alvarez witnessed Sean's fall and escorted him to the EMTs.

I later caught up with the rest of the guys, and was regaled by Freddie's account of his amazing escape. Rory asked, "Where is public enemy number one?"

"I don't know. We were running together and then he disappeared."

Turning to Clay I asked, "And where did you run?"

Clay smiled, "I didn't run anywhere."

With great skepticism Freddie asked, "Yeah, right, you didn't flinch when that mad man ran towards you?"

"Nope!" Clay said. "See you city boys don't think things through."

"Really. Why don't you explain it to us?" Rory said.

Clay continued, "Here is how I saw it. He spooked you guys. Why? Cause you knew you were guilty that's why. I acted like I wasn't a part of it, and it worked. He barely looked at me before he took off after Freddie."

"Pretty smart there, country boy," I acknowledged.

"Guys, it's simple. The quail that get scared and fly are the ones that get shot, not the ones who stay cool," Clay explained.

That was Clay all right, calm and cool. I never knew if it was part of his upbringing or if it was a Dawson family trait, but Clay seemed unflappable. I recall a frigid November Friday night during our senior year when Clay and I went to a football game at Hampton High, a cross county rival. The only reason we drove to the boonies was to see Freddie Sadler in action. Freddie's size and quick feet collaborated to create the best high school left tackle in the state of Florida.

We both sported our Fernandina Beach Pirates letterman's jacket, although that's where the comparison ended. I had a lone baseball pin while Clay's jacket was so laden with pins and awards it was tough to see the blue F under all that gold. Our freshman year the wrestling coach caught site of Clay bench pressing one hundred and eighty pounds and asked him to try out for the team.

After only a few weeks of practice, Clay won his first match. By our junior year, Clay was first team all-state and the top wrestling colleges had him on their wish list. As we drove to Hampton that night, Clay shared with me that he decided to go to the University of Iowa.

The game was a blow out win for Fernandina, but it was worth the drive. That night Freddy was a freight train in cleats. Regardless of where he lined up, tackle, guard, center, even blocking fullback, you could easily spot him by the blond hair hanging out of the back of his helmet.

By the time we headed for Clay's truck the field was mostly deserted. Rounding the back of the gym we were suddenly face to face with five Hampton guys. They purposely stood in our path. We attempted to walk around them but they shifted to block us.

I muttered a less than assertive, "Excuse us fellas."

Laughing, one of them said, "You can walk around the other side of the gym. And don't act like you don't like it."

Clay's response was simple and direct, "Get the hell outta my way, peckerhead."

The biggest Hampton boy spoke next, "You stupid sack of crap, it's five against two." Laughing to the others he said, "Somebody's 'bout to get an ass whippin'."

Clay stepped towards the speaker, "Are you the lead dog, or just the loudest yapper?" Emboldened by Clay's moxie I too took a step forward.

The leader stared at Clay, "I'm gonna bust you up."

Calmly Clay took off his jacket and handed it to me. Facing the Hampton leader, he said, "Your town is no more than a pig sty with road signs. Let's see who goes to the hospital tonight."

I was thinking, *This poor shmuck has no idea who he's screwing with.*

Then I saw it. It was ever so slight. A momentary look of uncertainty crossed the leader's face. If I saw it, I knew Clay saw it. The Hampton boy painted himself into a corner and now had no choice but to see it through. He was far braver when the odds were five against two, but now Clay's steely glare was drilling a hole in his confidence. With as much mettle as he could muster he spoke to his friends.

"Back off boys, I got this." As he said "this" he pointed his finger at Clay. Quick as a cobra Clay snatched his arm and simultaneously twisted and raised it above his head in an awkward position. The boy screamed as Clay bore down on his shoulder. Above the ear piercing shrieking I heard Clay shout, "Shut up or I'll break it!"

The boy quieted somewhat but continued muttering, "Oh God, he's breaking my arm!" He was in full scale weep at this point.

Clay said to the others. "Now unless you heifers do exactly as I say, I'm gonna tear his arm off." He directed the other boys to back off and toss their keys across the fence. He then instructed me to go get his truck. Without thinking I said, "Yes sir."

Despite the coolness of the night, sweat was pouring down my face as I cranked the engine. Not entirely proficient with a stick shift I managed to get the truck rolling but couldn't get it out of second gear. As I approached Clay I shouted, "I'm not stopping—jump in!"

Clay kicked the ring leader in the stomach, dropping the guy to the dirt. He ran towards the truck, grabbed the railing, and heaved himself into the bed. Instantaneously he was up and banging on the back glass telling me to "punch it!"

Thankfully I found third gear and we disappeared in a cloud of Hampton dust.

Back at the 4th of July celebration, the four of us, minus Sean, decided to split up and hopefully avoid running into Magilla Gorilla. We agreed to meet at the harbor in time for the fireworks.

As Rory and I walked past several parked emergency vehicles we heard a familiar voice.

"Jake, Rory, over here."

It was Sean. He was sitting on the back bumper of the ambulance being attended to by several EMTs. We walked over and saw first-hand karma's handiwork. The front of his shirt was speckled with blood. Both knees of his Levi's corduroys were ripped and puffy white bandages protruded through the holes. His left arm had taken the brunt of the fall and he sported a serious raspberry from the elbow to his wrist.

"Holy cow Sean, are you OK?" Rory asked.

Sean nodded and half smiled bearing witness to the worst injury. There was a black space in the front of his mouth where a tooth once resided. "Yeah, I'm OK I guess. I just hurt everywhere," he said.

"Did the redneck catch you?" Rory inquired.

"No man, I fell. I tripped over a stupid dog leash," Sean answered.

"Is the dog all, right?" I knew it was cruel but too good to pass up.

Through the pain he managed a "hardee-har-har."

"Well, when they're done patching you up, meet us by the harbor," Rory said.

"No way guys, I'm hurting too bad. My dad's coming to get me. Why does stuff like this have to happen?"

I wanted so badly to remind Sean that his prank started the chain reaction that ended with his teeth flying like Chicklets across the asphalt. But I chose to be his friend instead.

There remained slight hints of twilight in the western sky when Rory and I caught up with the other guys at the harbor. Just prior to the first rocket exploding skyward, we located the girls and wedged ourselves into the space they saved for us. Mary Grace made sure she was next to Rory who fidgeted like a trapped animal. Freddie and Clay were relaying to Callie the encounter with the crazed redneck, and I engaged in mindless small talk with Lacy. She was sitting just to my right and slightly ahead of me. The rockets streaked into the dark sky, illuminating Lacy's profile as they exploded. I may have been the only person that night whose eyes were not directed towards heavenly explosions, my eyes were transfixed on an earthly angel.

The firework show was terrific but too short. We always wanted more. The final salvo was a crescendo of thundering concussions and giant red stars. The glowing tails of the stars extinguishing as they plummeted into the dark ocean. It had been an unforgettable day, especially for Sean. It ended as it should have, surrounded by friends with a red sky at night.

CHAPTER 24

An intense summer shower chased Rory and me from our livelihoods that steamy July afternoon. Despite racing hard to finish, the wall of slate gray clouds forced us to retreat to Mrs. Palmer's carport. Thunder and lightning soon followed and Rory attempted to time the *kabooms* as he hummed the *1812 Overture*. With no hint of blue in the sky, the day was done. Once the lightning ceased, Rory secured a plastic trash bag over the mower's engine and we walked home in the cooling rain. The streets resembled a volcanic landscape as steam rose from the sizzling asphalt. Its musky aroma combined with the smell of fresh cut grass authenticated it was summer.

As with most afternoons, Mom was in the kitchen preparing dinner. She inquired about my day and then gave me a meteorological explanation for thunderstorms and parlayed that into an obligatory maternal admonishment. "You two need to be extra careful out on the marsh. In fact, perhaps you should not even go out anymore in the afternoons," she said.

"Mom, you know we're careful, we understand lightning is dangerous," I said.

Desiring to truncate this session of "you boys should or shouldn't be doing something," I hurried to the den to watch TV while waiting for dinner. In those dark ages we only had three network channels and PBS. So, this time of the afternoon your choices were news, news, *The*

Electric Company, or news. By default, I chose news, and turned the channel to NBC because dad was a John Chancellor man.

Chancellor began the broadcast with a story about the public's reaction to an American woman meeting with North Vietnamese Communist troops. Hearing Dad close the back door, I hustled to set the table for dinner. It was a short window from the time he arrived until we sat for dinner. The window was measured by how long it took him to shed his tie, drop his briefcase on the couch, and pour three fingers of Coke in his John Wayne glass.

We must have been living right because it was meatloaf night. Mom's meatloaf was nothing short of amazing. She used just the right amount of sausage and bread crumbs and topped it with both cheddar and American cheese. The cheese mixed with the sauce to form a crispy shell that was sinfully good. The crowning touch to this meat fantasy was Heinz 57 steak sauce. We slathered it across the meatloaf like butter on bread. We were enjoying our meal and general small talk was flowing when I ask about the news report.

"Dad, who's Jane Fonda, and why did she meet with the North Vietnamese?"

There was a moment of absolute silence, all chewing and swallowing ceased. The quiet was shattered as Mom slammed her fork on her dinner plate. Dad calmly put down his fork, and shot me a distressed look before burying his head in his hands and slowly rubbing his forehead.

Mom quickly stood but her hands held fast to the edges of the table. Her grip was so tight that the color drained from her knuckles. As she leaned towards me an obscenity laden rant flowed from her mouth taking great exception to what she considered a traitorous act. The verbal onslaught so frightened me that I slid my chair backwards only to be cornered by the nook wall. She damned every person that ever protested the war, including celebrities, regular citizens, and even spiritual leaders.

It was the only time in my life I ever heard my Mom swear. I sat frozen. Promptly, Dad reached over and placed his hand on Mom's.

"Connie that's not—" But that was all he could say before she cut him off.

"Don't you 'Connie' me!" she snarled as she pulled away from Dad's hand. "This is my house and Will was my son!" At those words tears began rolling down her cheeks and her voice quivered. "And I'll say any blessed thing I feel. These people have no concept of what it means to kiss a son goodbye and ten months later pick him up at the airport in a flag draped box."

She walked briskly from the room, her sobs still discernable until they were curtailed behind their bedroom door. I looked at Dad for some measure of assurance, but his face had lapsed back into his hands. A muffled sniff escaped and I knew he was fighting back his own tears. I was dumbfounded, not only by my mom's reaction, but that my words had been the catalyst.

I sat quietly waiting for Dad. He sniffed again and wiped his eyes with his napkin. I softly said, "Dad I'm sorry I just...."

He raised his hand, which I knew was a sign to hush.

"Jake, son, you did nothing wrong. It's not your fault.... It's the damn war's fault. Just finish your meal and we'll talk later."

"I'm done," I said, my plate still half filled with meat loaf.

"Then clear the table for Mom."

Dad would now go to their bedroom and see if Mom would let him in, a familiar part of the routine. A good barometer for how intense this period of the "shadows" would be was Dad's success when he knocked on the door.

He soon returned to the kitchen, which was not a good sign. Silently we washed the dishes. As he folded the hand towel over the drying rack he said, "Bud, let's take a drive."

The rain had ceased and the skies were clearing. Driving through downtown we stopped at a gas station and Dad bought two bottles of Frosty root beer. Though he said nothing of our destination, I knew it was the harbor. Water was Dad's go-to elixir. When he needed to de-stress, pray, or think through a bad scenario, he headed for the closest body of water. We pulled into the harbor parking lot, which by this time of the evening was all but deserted. The torrential rain had vanquished the afternoon heat and the evening seemed more like spring than summer. There remained several hot spots in the parking lot and small clouds of steam drifted across the harbor like ghostly aberrations.

The city's harbor incorporated an upper retaining sea wall designed to provide extra protection against abnormal tidal surges. Periodically spaced along the sea wall were metal gang planks which provided a bridge to the floating moorings. Our rubber soled shoes squeaked and chirped on the wet metal, and this shoe symphony was accompanied by the shrill creaking of rusted joints and the end of the walkway grinding on concrete. The sound was like fingernails on a chalk board, and it caused the hair on the back of my neck to rise.

Stepping off the clatter gauntlet, Dad said, "Good thing we're not trying to sneak up on somebody. Hannibal's Elephants crossing the Alps made less noise."

The harbor hosted a variety of vessels from sailboats and luxury yachts to sport fishing boats and commercial trawlers. Warm light shining through portholes accented the darkened ship's silhouettes. At the end of the primary floating pier was an unfettered view of the Atlantic. To the west, the marsh witnessed the last colors of twilight.

"This is a fine spot," Dad said. He settled against a light post and fished his key chain from his pocket. Fumbling in the low light he oriented an odd piece of tarnished metal. "My lucky can opener," he said and popped the tops from our root beer.

"Why do you think it's lucky?" I asked.

"My drill sergeant issued it to me in basic training and told me not to lose it. Over the ensuing fifteen months it opened hundreds of bottles and more importantly my K-rations. It's lucky because like me, it came home in one piece." He then handed me my bottle of Frosty.

I took a big gulp and sighed as the carbonated burn tickled my throat. I gazed out over the expanse of the Atlantic and was struck by the evening metamorphosis. With the sun's departure, the water's once inviting blue transformed to a foreboding inky black.

"Son," he tentatively began, "you know your mom does not want to be like this."

He waited for my gaze to make sure I understood.

"Yes sir, it's just she's hurting over Will."

"Right," Dad said. "And you know we'll always hurt over Will. No matter the years or how old we are, there will always be that hole in our lives. And right now, it's a raw, searing, wound for your mother and me."

I nodded and we had a few more sips of root beer. "Dad, I sometimes think it would be better for Mom and for all of us if we talked more about Will. I mean, I walk by that table with his flag and Air Force picture and I get angry because I've forgotten so much about who he was and what he was like."

Dad looked at me a little sideways. I thought for a moment I had said something wrong. But he reached his hand behind my neck and stroked my summer length hair. "Jake, sometimes you are so much wiser than your years. In my heart, I know you're right. It would be better for us, especially your mom, if we could speak more about Will and all the good things we remember. And son, I'm confident that with time and the Lord's grace we'll get there. But until then, I need for you to tip toe a bit through anything to do with the war. Come to me, I promise I'll answer any question you have."

The conversation ebbed for a few minutes as we enjoyed the last colors of the evening. In the twilight, a lone star appeared. "Jake, you see that star?"

"Yes sir."

"Know what it is?"

"Venus?"

"Well most people think so, but actually that's Vega. Navigating by stars was something we learned in the Army, and amazingly twenty years later I remember enough to get my bearings," he said. "Jake is that star really all alone?"

"No, the rest of the stars are there, but we just can't see them yet."

"Correct, and right now your mom is like Vega. She feels like she is all alone. But she's not. She has us, she has good friends and her family back in Alabama. And there are thousands of other people simultaneously walking the same grief highway because of this miserable war."

"And she has God too," I said.

"Jake you're right about that, but truth be told your Mom is pretty upset with God. And when you're angry with someone it's hard to feel like they are there for you, understand?" Dad asked.

"I guess," I said.

"To help you, let me paint the whole picture. Your Mom and I got married when we did because I was being sent overseas to the War. As we know all too painfully, men do not always come home from war. After I left she found out she was going to have Will. The mail was so slow in finding me that I didn't even know about it until months later. By the time I came home Will was four months old, which meant your Mom had to go through the entire pregnancy and the first months of your brother's life not knowing if she would ever see me again. Every day she woke with the fear that a telegram could arrive telling her that I was killed, missing, or captured. That was a tough burden to bear." Dad paused long enough for a gulp of root beer.

"And you know of course that your mom lost a brother in World War II."

"Uncle Hank," I said.

"Right, so after losing her brother to war and then going through the hell of not knowing if she would be a widow and a new mom all at the same time, I think Mom felt like she had done her part and would never have to endure that kind of worry again. Well, she was wrong. Like a generational curse, it came around again eighteen years later. This time, however, it was not her brother or her husband, but her first born child."

Dad paused for a moment, and set down the bottle as if he wanted his hands free.

"Son, every military family's worst nightmare is two uniformed officers approaching your front steps. I stood there behind the door that night, wishing and praying they'd made a mistake." Dad paused as he wiped his eyes on his sleeve. "God, it feels like it was yesterday." Again, he needed a moment, "As I stood there behind our front door I thought that if I refused to open it, what was would never be."

Overcome by emotion Dad stood and walked to the end of the pier. I joined him and he grasped me tight in an embrace.

"It was just too much, Jake. Too much for Mom to get her arms around. I know in time she'll be the Mom and wife we remember. Between here and there..." Dad paused and peered skyward, "well, between here and there it is just going to be rough. And our job is to do what we can to help her through it, OK?"

"Dad, why did you and Mom wait so long to have me after you had Will?"

"Jake that was not a choice. When Will was born, there were some medical complications and the doctors told us Mom couldn't have any more babies. We were extremely disappointed but we dealt with it and life continued. Then boom, ten years later you came along. Son, you are what we call a blessing baby. You were truly a gift from God," Dad said with a broad smile.

"Maybe I was meant to be a replacement for Will?"

Dad turned sharply towards me, a determined glare piercing through his tear filled eyes. "Jake, don't you ever think that, not for a moment. You are your own person, and you have your own path in this life to follow. And just like Will, wherever it takes you, it takes you. And I will always be proud of you." With added emphasis, he asked, "Do you understand me, son?"

I nodded, "Yes, sir."

"OK, so back to your original question. As you know this war is not a popular war. By that I mean there are many Americans that think we never should have gotten involved in the first place and our soldiers, airmen, and sailors are dying for nothing. I know you have seen the news reports of students protesting and burning their draft cards, right?"

"Uh huh," I said.

"Now the reason behind the war was to try and stem the growth of Communism, and I encourage you when you're older to research it for yourself. Whether it was a noble cause and whether it accomplished its goal will only be clarified by time."

"But Dad, if the war was so unpopular, why did Will go?" I asked.

"Will chose to go, and that's an important point. He wasn't drafted, he had a college deferment. He chose to enlist despite our begging him not to."

"But why?" I asked again.

"Because he thought it was his duty. He loved America and he had a sense of obligation to serve his country."

"So, who is Jane Fonda?" I asked.

"She's an actress and is very much against the war. I guess she thought by going to North Vietnam she could help end the war or something. Now she wasn't the first American to visit North Vietnam during the war, but what makes her visit so notable is she was photographed wearing a NVA helmet and sitting on an anti-aircraft gun." Dad's eyes widened for emphasis as he continued, "The very type of gun that fires at our Air Force and Navy pilots, like the one listed on your MIA bracelet. Your Mom knows about the incident so your comment at dinner was like dropping a match into a can of gas.

"Jake, you should know that there have been incidents at airports where our returning service men have been spit on and called horrendous things. Granted, the troops returning from Korea didn't get a parade like the boys from WWII. But when I stepped off the *CG Morton* onto the San Francisco docks, I was met by the Salvation Army passing out hot coffee and donuts." Dad paused as he recalled the moment. "Best donuts I ever had in my life—Now compare that to our boys coming home from Vietnam being met by long hair hippie freaks screaming 'baby burner' in their face. They put their lives on the line in the name of freedom and this is the welcome they receive from some of their fellow Americans. It's a travesty. And yes, it's your right to disagree, but it is not your right to focus your anger on the soldier who's just following orders."

Dad turned away from and scanned the Atlantic. He was taking in deep breaths attempting to calm the rage that gripped him. "Jake, there is one other thing you must never question. Your mom loves you and me with her whole heart. And our love for her is what's going to get her through this."

My gaze returned to Vega. Alone no more, she was now bolstered by millions of her fellow interstellar companions. As we stood to leave, Dad gave me another long hug. Silently we retraced our steps to the car, all that needed to be said had been said.

The following morning, I awoke to find my parent's door closed, and Mom was nowhere to be found. The bed in the guest room was rumpled, further confirmation that it had been a rough night.

I really didn't feel much like fishing. The events of the previous evening resonated with me like the after effects of a stomach virus. But there was no reason to stay home either. Watching Monty Hall on *Let's Make a Deal* was certainly not going to improve my mental state.

The day seemed to mirror my mood. The clear star-filled evening had given way to a hazy morning. The sky was completely devoid of color. As Rory and I embarked on the marsh, the water seemed to match the sky's gray hue and produced no reflections. Even the green luster of the marsh grass appeared sluiced away by the haze.

The tide was beginning to come in, so it was impossible for us to make our way downstream to the inlet or Amos' place. Our only option was to flow upstream, and apparently, we were not the only anglers with this plan. Two dolphins came up from behind us following the tide. It was a mother and baby and like synchronized dancers, they surfaced and submerged in perfect unison. Approaching our raft, they crested within arms' reach. Their eyes were bright and they seemed to be smiling at us. Yes, I was aware that dolphins didn't smile, but it made me feel better nonetheless. Rory bent down and gently grasped the mom's dorsal fin. Immediately feeling his touch, she flipped her tail and the two disappeared beneath the gray water. Rory smiled, "feels weird, kinda rubbery."

We didn't give much significance to seeing a dolphin. Heck, the ocean was full of them. It was just another participant in the estuary food chain, and in fact, competition for the fish we pursued. Had we known that thirty years later people would pay gobs of money to experience a *dolphin encounter*, Rory and I would have conspired to catch a few and open our own marine tourist trap.

Perhaps it was the presence of the dolphins, but the fish weren't biting. My heart was not into it and mercifully, we ended the day early. Rory knew I wasn't right and probably figured it was related to Will, so he basically let me be. I guess that's how guys deal with deep, burdensome issues. We just let the other guy be.

With little conversation, we concluded our day. Hoping to provide an air of optimism, Rory reminded me that the next night was the Major League All-Star Game. He promised we would have a great day on the raft and then enjoy the game.

Pedaling towards home I wanted to believe that I would find Mom making dinner and recovered from last night's turmoil. But I knew in my heart the house would be quiet and she would remain secluded in her room.

CHAPTER 25

It is a common experience that a problem difficult at night is resolved in the morning after the committee of sleep has worked on it.

~ *John Steinbeck*

One of the benefits of youth is that adult type problems tend to have a limited shelf life. The following morning I was in a much better frame of mind as I rode to Twain's lot. A stiff sea breeze had peeled back the veil of haze leaving a carpet of blue and I couldn't wait to get out on the water.

Arriving ahead of Rory, I sat on the edge of the raft enjoying the simple beauty of the creek. The marsh grass was again a sprightly green and the sun glinted off the wet mud banks. A blue heron was patiently making her way along the opposite bank. The three-foot tall huntress would have made an excellent member of a marching band as she lifted each leg to a 45-degree angle before softly stepping forward.

My silent commune with nature was shattered by Rory's arrival. Startled by his boisterous greetings the heron took to the sky. We quickly packed the raft and shoved off for the day's adventure. It was fine fishing until midday. Then as if an underwater alarm sounded, all activity ceased. Deciding this was a sign to seek sunless sanctuary we hauled up the cinder block anchor and made way to Amos'.

Rounding the bend, we could see him slowly moving in his rocker. We shouted but he seemed unable to hear us. Once at his floating dock, we grabbed the stringer of fish and bounded up the gangplank.

"Hey there!" I said.

Amos responded somewhat curtly, "I knows you comin'. Heard you squawkin' like parrots a mile away. Good thing I didn't wants to catch any fish today, you done scared 'em off."

Rory and I were confused. This was a side of the kindly man not previously seen. We knew he sometimes fished from his porch, and I guess we were kind of noisy but…

"I don't means to be cantankerous, it's just my knee is givin' me all kinds of fits this mornin'. And if you don't know what cantankerous means, go gits my dictionary."

"Is that the knee you hurt playing baseball?" Rory asked.

"Yep, ain't never been right," Amos replied.

"Well, you won't have to worry about what you're having for supper," I said hoisting the string of trout. "I'll clean them for you after we've eaten our lunch."

"That's a pretty string of fish, yes indeed. Thank you, boys," Amos replied with more patience than before.

Rory cut a smallish one off, "This is for Mr. Rosco." He walked over to the west end of the porch and imitated Amos' unpretentious beckoning, "Cat, Cat!"

Soon the plodding paws of the super cat arrived on the porch. Rory held the fish aloft encouraging Mr. Rosco to rise up on his hind legs.

"Better be careful, or you'll end up with a nub for a hand," I said.

Mr. Rosco rose to his maximum height and reached his Hemmingway paws towards the fish. His paws reached Rory's stomach.

"What's for lunch?" Amos asked.

Rory chimed in first, "Bologna, an apple, and chips."

I followed with, "I've got PBJ, Fritos, and grapes."

Amos smiled, "Jake, you win. Can'ts go wrong with PBJ and Fritos. Go in the house and gits you and Rory a cold drink. Saves me a trip on this achin' knee."

Approaching the screen door, the significance struck me. I had never been inside Amos' house. In fact, I had never even peered through the door. Slowly, as if some dark predicament waited on the other side, I opened the patchwork screen door and entered. The wood flooring was rubbed bare in most places and throw rugs covered the walk paths. There was a shelf on the left containing books, photos, and several framed certificates with the letters CCC boldly printed. Proceeding further was a sparsely furnished living room containing a couch that despite its worn appearance looked extremely comfortable. A dated TV with an antenna made of a bent coat hanger adorned with tin foil sat in the corner. Perfectly positioned in a direct line of sight to the TV was a recliner. Its dark brown corduroy material was accented by gray duct tape. I smiled thinking my dad would like Amos immediately upon realizing he was also a loyal lodge brother of the Duct Tape Templars. Though not as secretive or politically motivated as the Free Masons, these gray tape apostles were zealots nonetheless.

Behind the couch two windows framed the wall and heavy, tan, roll up shades strained to keep out the strong sunlight. Despite the shades' efforts, lasers of light streaked through small holes. I continued through the sitting area to the kitchen where there was a fridge with the old-style latch handle. Clutching two RC Colas, I returned to the porch. I gave Rory his drink and sat down. Mr. Rosco emerged from the shadows, sat next to me, and began cleaning his face. He paused and seemed to be staring at Rory. It made me chuckle as I imagined Mr. Rosco was thinking, "*You know if I were really hungry, I could probably eat you.*"

"Well fellas, tonight's the big night," Amos said with a lighter tone. "Baseball at its finest."

"You bet," Rory answered. "We've looked forward to this all season long."

We spent the next hour talking about our favorite players and who was going to do what in the All-Star game. When a quiet moment replaced the baseball banter I asked Amos about the certificates and the CCC.

He smiled and regaled us with another chapter in the interesting saga of Amos George.

"You probably learns 'bout this in high school, but the CCC was the Civilian Conservation Corp. It was a plan by President Roosevelt, Franklin that is, not Teddy, to puts the men of America back to work. See, the country was comin' out of the Great Depression, and there wasn't no jobs. So, the government organized men to build roads and parks and fix up old buildings. And theys planted nearly three million trees. Three million." Clearly the number impressed Amos.

"In some ways it was almost like joinin' the Army, in fact some of the fellas were given old WWI uniforms. You wents away, they feds you and gave you a place to sleep. Buts the money you made, well most of that gots sent to your family. After I had to quit playin' ball I bounced around awhile tryin' to find decent work. Then a fella tells me 'bout the CCC and they's hirin' at a fort down Savannah way. So, I hitched me a ride down to Tybee Island."

He paused as if he were catching up to his thoughts, "You been to Fort Pulaski?"

"I have," I answered. "We went up there one time in the summer, and man was it hot."

Amos laughed, "You gots that right. Lawd that was one miserable place in the summer, whooo-we! Funny thing though, there's a preacher man on my crew, you know just tryin' to feed his family like the rest of us. Anyways, during the summer along about three o'clock in the afternoon we just 'bout couldn't stands it. We's hot, our tools's hot, and the walls of that fort was hot. Sooner or later, one of the new guys would say, 'It's hotter than hell out here!'"

"Then ole Preacher Buck he'd grab the moment. 'Naw son, this ain't hotter than Hell, but unlessen you gets right with the Lawd, you gonna know how hot Hell is!'

"Then the rest of us would pile on, 'Amen brother, preach on.' And then another fella might say, 'Hey there sinner, if-in you wants we can baptize you right here in the moat.'"

Amos laughed as he thought about Preacher Buck and then said, "Say, there's a picture I wants to show you. Jake, goes in the house and, oh never mind, I'll haves to find it."

Standing with a considerable groan Amos grabbed his walking stick and limped into the cabin. He returned moments later with a large book. "Take a look at where I gots it marked," he said as he passed me the book. I opened it and there was an old photograph of a baseball game. The caption read *One of the first pictures of a baseball game, 1862 Fort Pulaski, Georgia.*

"Wow, that's cool," I said. I then handed the book to Rory

"Amos, did you play baseball while you were at the fort?" Rory asked.

"Lawd yes, in fact it's probably the only time we gots along," he said. Sensing our lack of understanding he added, "Boys, remember I told you 'bout segregation. Well in the CCC, we was segregated, blacks lived in one barracks, whites in the other. In fact, some of the projects you's only have blacks working or whites, but nots both. So, there weren't the best relations because the white boys really didn't want us around. But the few times that them bad feelins' disappeared was when we was playin' ball."

We talked a while longer until the lengthening shadows hinted it was time to head home. Rory and I pushed the raft at a quick pace, as an important task remained before the big game.

CHAPTER 26

DRAGGING THE RAFT ASHORE WAS always daunting. Besides being heavier than a Mississippi River barge, we were usually sun baked and whipped. This afternoon however, we brimmed with energy in anticipation of the All-Star Game. We raced to the 7-Eleven hoping to acquire a baseball trading cup with one of the players suiting up for the big game.

As usual Doris was working the counter and joining her was her bone thin sister Frieder. Her given name was Frieda, but everyone added an "er" when pronouncing it. You would have never guessed they were sisters. Frieda was petite while Doris was robust and appeared fifteen years younger than Frieda. There was nothing about their facial structures or voices that indicated they were related. The only hint of their DNA connection was their deep and abiding love for tobacco. While Doris loved her Virginia Slims, Frieda went old school, preferring snuff.

Approaching the counter I said, "Hello Doris, you got two mighty thirsty cowboys here, set us up with your finest Slurpees if you please."

My chipper demeanor resonated poorly with Doris. She stared at us for a moment, then slowly trudged to the Slurpee machine and pulled two cups. The first one she set on the counter was Ron Santo, a Chicago Cub. Not a bad player, but neither us immediately jumped at the prospect. As she placed the second cup on the counter I heard angels singing the "Hallelujah Chorus." It was too impossible to believe. Perhaps we had been in the sun too long and this was merely a cruel mirage. Rory and I stared in silent disbelief. There sitting on the formica counter, in between incense sticks and pickled pig's feet was the most sought after cup in all of Slurpee land, Carl Yastrzemski. The "Yaz" was already a legend in 1972, and by the time he retired in 1983 he had played an incredible twenty-three years for the Boston Red Sox.

Instantly Rory and I said, "I'll take Yaz!" We looked at each other and it was on.

"It's mine," I said. "I saw it first!"

"That's bull, how could you have seen it first?" Rory fired back.

"Well, it's my turn to pick first, you got to last time," I said.

Rory responded, "Oh no pinhead. The last time we argued you got it."

"Really short stack, well which one was it? Huh, huh?"

"I'm short but not stupid, and I know it's my turn Mr. Concrete Feet!"

"You selfish piece of crap!" I said.

Somewhere between volleys of name calling we began pushing one another.

WHACKKKKK! A deafening shockwave echoed off the store's walls. The concussion was followed by a barrage of plastic shrapnel flying through the air. The cannonade sprayed Rory and me and we instinctively covered our faces. As the dust from the explosion cleared, we saw Doris. She was holding aloft the plunger stick that served as a bathroom key chain. She stared at us, her face void of kindness or feeling. She had shattered Carl Yastrzemski and the circular bottom of the cup was all that remained on the counter.

"Now, nobody's getting Carl Yaterminski," Doris said through clinched teeth.

The way she butchered his name was humorous, but neither of us dared crack a smile. Rory was however unable to restrain himself from correcting her. "Ahh, its Yastrzemski"

"Nip it Mr. Perkins!" Doris said.

Frieda spoke up, "Doris is a little cross today, she's tryin' to quit smokin'."

Doris glared at her sister, "Frieder, you just keep your nose out of my beeswax. These two little….." Here Doris paused. Despite her system being woefully devoid of nicotine, she kept herself under control and modified what she wanted to call us, "These two little ingrates need to be taught a lesson. I help them find good cups. I don't do that for anybody else and this is how they repay me. Well, let me tell you spoiled three-year olds something and you had better listen good. If you ever pull this crap again, it will be rookie cups from now on! Got it?"

"Yes ma'am," we both said.

"Now to show you I mean business," she turned to the Slurpee machine and began pulling cups out of the shoot. Ten pulls later she had the two cups she wanted. Passing the cups filled with cherry mix across the counter she said, "Here! Two loser rookies who are already back on the family farm, never to be seen in the big leagues again. Now beat it!"

Walking to our bikes we each exchanged a mumbled "sorry man" and the rift was no more. Later we would joke extensively about this day and the exploding Yaz cup. Though Rory and I collected cups for several more summers, we never had another shot at Carl Yastrzemski. I often wondered if Doris placed a curse on us that day.

CHAPTER 27

ALTHOUGH ONLY ONE DAY REMOVED from the month of July, the significance of August 1st could not be ignored. On the first day of August, a school age kid could be peering into the Grand Canyon or riding a roller coaster, yet in the back of their mind they were acutely aware the day possessed a dark side.

It's the beginning of the end of summer. It's a warning that the lazy days will soon be over and we'll be languishing again in a cramped sunless classroom. And it was a wakeup call, extolling youths everywhere to live these last days to the absolute fullest. The only day of the year that may have a more sinister soul than August 1st, is the first Sunday thereafter. For it is on that day that newspapers are jammed with multicolored advertisements proclaiming *Back to School* sales. Flyers filled with notebooks, protractors, pencils, and clear little bags that hold your pens. Then it's JCPenney and Sears ads for back to school clothes, new uncomfortable jeans, and scratchy shirts. And worst of all, the agony and shame of trying on pants with your mom. It's not enough that you are required to parade out of the dressing room for her visual inspection. She must then pull the belt loops and comment on the length of the crotch. This verbal indignation is soon overshadowed by her insatiable need to tug on the crotch in front of God, the cute young sales clerk, and curious onlookers.

With regards to the whole back to school fervor, Rory and I refused to go quietly into the night. This August 1st we would strike a blow for kids everywhere. A day to fish and barter from sun up to dusk.

We were quite proud of what we had accomplished this summer. We had planned and built our raft and had successfully navigated the marsh and inlet. In the process, we had filled our family's freezers with fish. We felt very grown up, very much in charge of things, and possibly a wee bit cocky.

That Friday morning brought a clear sky, with no signs of pending thunderstorms. The tide was heading out early and we planned to spend the day in the inlet pursuing big fish. Today the world, or at least this little corner of it, would be our oyster.

We made quick time down Bent Tree Creek and were drenched in sweat by the time we floated into the emerald waters of the inlet. As it had become somewhat of a tradition, we both cannon balled into the revitalizing water. Pulling back onto the raft, Rory shook his head like a wet dog and asked, "What do you think the other kids at school did this summer?"

I shrugged my shoulders, "Don't know, but no way it's as cool as this."

Rory beamed a big smile, "You are so right my man, gimmie five."

We steered the raft towards a particular spot on the opposite side of the inlet, near Big Talbot Lagoon where we had previously experienced great fishing. Shuttling from piling to piling we slowly traversed the inlet.

Our raft was very much like a kite. We were tethered to the bridge and our range was determined by the length of our rope and the degree of our brazenness. Throughout the summer our boldness had mushroomed. We started with twenty-five feet of rope and gradually added more until we were over two hundred feet or two-thirds the length of a football field. With this distance and a good cast, we were very much in range of the big fish which gathered at the mouth of the inlet. For a motorist traveling north across the bridge, our tethering rope would be invisible. All they would see were two boys on a makeshift raft floating dangerously close to the Intracoastal water way.

Truth be known, Rory and I did fear that a funky act of fate would spoil our summer freedom. All it would take is somebody's dad catching sight of us. Innocently he would share it with the matriarch of the house and within forty-five seconds a phone would ring at mine or Rory's house and life as we knew it would cease to exist.

We never considered we were being foolish. If the raft were to break free from the bridge, our plan was simple, abandon ship and swim to shore.

It was a great day on the water. It seemed our rods were bent more than they were straight. Our stringer was heavy with more than a dozen fish including flounder, sheepshead, and several big redfish. Eventually, the tide began its conversion and we slowly drifted back towards the bridge.

"Well, I guess we should leave some for tomorrow," Rory said.

"Yep. Besides I'm bushed," I answered.

Our lines reeled in, we began rolling up the slack in the rope. In less than ten minutes we were sheltered in the coolness of the bridge. We had just cleared the bridge and were back in the intense glare of the sun when the raft seemed to pause. The tide was moving but we weren't. We exchanged confused stares. Suddenly a sizable splash erupted behind the raft.

"Something's after our fish!" Rory snapped.

"It's probably a kingfish, I'll grab the stringer," I said placing my bamboo pole on the raft.

"Be careful, might be a barracuda."

"You're a funny guy. I'm sure there is something real scary on the end of our stringer," I answered as I began pulling the rope. Having to use substantially more effort than I expected I grunted, "whatever it is, there must be a school of them."

It was in fact a solo bandit. On my second tug, I put all my weight into it. As I strained, a dark grey object breached the surface. It was a shark! Grasping the entire stringer in its jaws, the six-foot beast thrashed its head side to side. The smart choice, the reasonable choice, the referendum that would be approved by nine out of ten intelligent people, would be for me to cut the stringer and go home. The tenth person in the survey would be Hollywood tough guy and World War II Marine, Lee Marvin. Lee would have exclaimed in his gravel voice, "Hell no you ain't taking my fish you thieving S.O.B.!"

Perhaps it can be blamed on youthful swagger bolstered by adolescent testosterone, but for some insane reason I chose to throw in with Lee Marvin. I was positioned between Rory and the shark, so for an instant he had no idea what we had on our stringer.

"Rory, it's a shark, bring the paddle!" Bring the paddle, yes, there was a prudent reaction. A small wooden paddle is the perfect weapon for a thrashing, blood crazed shark.

Despite my initial bravado, my brain wisely suggested to the rest of my body to move away from the shredding teeth. Stepping backwards my right foot became tangled in the anchor rope causing me to fall. In this trifecta of regrettable decisions, I was given one more opportunity to do the smart thing. In the process of falling, the logical play would have been to release the stringer rope. Clearly this boy vs. nature contest had become personal and thus the thought of letting go of the rope never occurred to me.... until I realized that by falling back, my weight had pulled the snapping shark further out of the water. Almost a third of his body was now arched over the back of the raft. My feet were on either side of his head, well within biting range.

Before I could perform another act that would undoubtedly worsen our predicament, Rory stepped over my shoulder to face the man eater, paddle raised. With the combined weight of Rory, the shark and me all on one end of the raft, it listed dangerously towards capsizing.

Rory swung the paddle downward like an ax striking the shark squarely on the head. The paddle shattered. All that remained was the handle and a jagged piece of the slats. Rory, who obviously had a little Lee Marvin in him as well, adjusted his grip on the handle and swung again. The downward arch of his swing caught the shark with an audible thud. This second strike resulted in a deep gash and cleaved a golf ball size chunk of flesh from the shark's head. Blood began to pour from the wound, but the shark remained firm in his intentions to keep his meal, as I remained firm in my convictions that I was not letting go of the rope.

Emitting a primal scream, Rory lifted the paddle once more and swung low and hard. Perhaps the shark's black eyes perceived another blow coming, or maybe he had just grown weary of the fight, but whatever the reason, as Rory was in mid-swing the shark slid off the end of the raft descending below the surface. Rory's mighty swing hit nothing but thin air. Losing his balance, he swung his arms wildly like a tight rope walker trying to regain his equilibrium. I released the stringer and reached for him. I caught a handful of his shirt but his momentum was too much. The shirt tore from my clinched fingers and I witnessed with horror as my best friend plunged into the churning bloody water. The water, where mere seconds prior an angry, injured shark had submerged. With the exodus of Rory and the shark, the front of the raft splashed back into the water.

I stood and scrambled towards the end of the raft with the sole intention of leaping into the water to save my friend. Moving quickly, I failed to realize my foot was entwined in the rope. As I jerked my foot to step forward, I tumbled on the raft landing hard on my stomach. Most of my frame landed on the raft, however, my head, shoulders, and arms folded over the end of the raft. Whereas my length most likely saved me from breaking my face, my outstretched arms slid across the jagged edges of the timbers. Instantly, a terrific burning racked my right arm. Ignoring the pain, I felt below the surface trying to grab Rory. Realizing this was futile, I got to my knees and was preparing to leap into the melee, when I heard Rory shout my name.

I turned as he was pulling himself out of the water at the opposite end of the raft. Though he was taking in big gulps of air, he sported a big grin.

"Rory, you're alive! God I was scared, I thought you were a goner."

"Not today!" Rory said half laughing. It then trailed off to a quieter voice, "not today."

Relieved to see Rory in one piece, I was suddenly aware of the excruciating pain in my arm. I was on my hands and knees still trying to get my breath when I noticed a red stream flowing from the underside of my arm. A puddle of blood encircled my hand. I was immediately nauseous. I rolled over and lay on my back, squinting against the afternoon sun.

"Jake, your arm," Rory said.

"Yeah, I hurt it when I fell. Is it bad? It feels real bad," I said.

"It's bad. Don't touch it," he answered and quickly grabbed a bamboo push pole. "We gotta get you to Amos, and fast."

With each second the pain became more intense. The wound was on the underside of my arm from above my elbow to just below my armpit. I could feel the blood continuing to spill down my arm.

"Rory I'm bleeding bad! Hurry!" I said in a half sob.

Rory stopped pushing the raft and reached into the gear bucket. He pulled out an old piece of a t-shirt, folded it lengthwise, and placed it over the wound. "Here, now hold this on tight."

My well intending friend had just placed the filthiest rag in North America, outside of the rotating drying towel in the 7-Eleven bathroom, on my open wound. We used that rag anytime we had fish blood or guts on our hands. Being this was the original rag from our first day on the marsh, it held the DNA of countless fish. It's entirely possible that the fluids contained on that cloth were mixing with my DNA, and in essence, I was now a blood brother to a flounder.

Rory resumed pushing the raft and I tried to sit up. "Be still!" he said. "And hold that rag in place."

"I was going to cut the stringer line. We don't want that shark coming back," I said.

"It's already cut. That's why he fell back into the water, he bit the line. Hope he chokes on it."

"Rory, listen," I started, but he cut me off.

"Shut up Jake and be still!" he said.

"No, man you've gotta listen," I pleaded. "You can't say anything about the shark, or that this happened on the inlet. If my Mom gets wind of it, we'll never get on the water again. I tripped and fell, that's all."

Rory agreed with a breathless, "OK."

The sun was unmerciful as I lay there on the raft trying to ward off being sick, but it was no use. I vomited and Rory kept poling. Rounding the final bend to Amos' cabin I heard Rory shout, "Amos, Amos, help! Jake has been hurt. Help!"

Feeling groggy and confused I began to lose track of the events. I was aware that Amos and Rory half carried me up the ramp to the cabin. I remember hearing the screen door squeak and then slam. I recall Amos looking down at me and saying, "All rights boy, just be still. It's gonna be fine."

I later understood I was lapsing into shock which accounted for my inability to remain fully conscious. I do remember the cool wetness of a rag rubbing my face and something being poured on my arm that stung. There was also something about someone named Lilly. The next thing I recalled was Dad's voice. He was lifting me up to a sitting position, "Son, its Dad. Can you hear me?"

I mumbled a feeble "Yes."

"OK, we need to get you to the doctor. Can you stand up and walk with me?"

With his and Amos' assistance they walked me to the car and laid me in the back seat. I heard my dad profusely thank Amos and he responded, "Now tells the doctor that I poured hydrogen peroxide in it before I bandaged it up. But they's a big splinter wedged real deep that gots to come out. And Mr. Forrest would you please lets me know when the boy's OK?"

My dad later told me that the compassion in Amos' voice was so compelling, it was as if I were as important as his own child.

When I fell on the raft my right arm slid over the end of a log with an uneven cut. It sliced my arm open and a two-inch splinter imbedded deeply into my muscle. Twenty-seven stitches were required to close the wound.

Mom, Rory, and Miss Perkins were waiting at the emergency room when we arrived. It was nearly midnight when we finally left the hospital. Although the shock of the injury had eased, I was disoriented from the effects of the pain killers racing through my veins. I recall lying down in the back of my Mom's Impala and her placing my head in her lap. The air-conditioned car, the pain killers, and the velour seat covers were wonderful in comparison to the blistering sun and searing pain I experienced on the creek. But those comforts paled in comparison to the peace I felt as my mom gently stroked the hair from my eyes.

The next morning as I fumbled to eat my breakfast with my left hand, I realized my summer was over. The stitches alone would require two weeks to heal, and the trench created in the muscle tissue from the wood splinter would take even longer. Of course, this scare to my Mom would be a fresh decree authorizing her to hover over me for months. I just hoped her maternal need to ensure my safety would not lead to crazy ideas like home schooling.

Rory came over around noon to check on me. I was on the sofa watching an episode of *Dragnet*, when I heard him banging on the door like an angry Viking.

"Hey buddy, how you feeling?" he asked.

"Good man, good!" I said with dishonest gusto. "The bandage makes it look worse than it is."

"Then you won't mind pitching me some balls this afternoon?" Rory asked.

"I don't think I'll be tossing any strikes for a while."

"What's new? You could never throw strikes anyway. That's why you play left field!" he said with a laugh.

Ahh, the difference between girls and boys is never more clearly illustrated than when a comrade is injured. We talked in hushed tones about the incident and again I swore him to secrecy. We agreed that by the time school started we could share the story because it was just too cool to keep to ourselves.

CHAPTER 28

Several days later, Mom and I went to Amos George's house. They had not met and she wanted to express her appreciation for helping me. She thanked him in the manner preferred by Southern women—food. In addition to her award winning meatloaf, there was fried chicken, squash, butter beans, white acre peas, cornbread, and a fresh baked apple pie.

"This shore a lot of food Miss Forrest," Amos said as Mom and I placed the bowls on his table.

"Well Mr. George, I wasn't sure what you liked and hopefully this will provide a few meals for you," Mom said.

Amos expressed his deep appreciation. They continued to talk for a few minutes exchanging pleasantries.

Amos turned to me, "That's a big bandage Jake. How many stitches?"

"Twenty-seven!" I said as if the number was a point of honor.

"Twenty-seven you say? My, my," Amos responded shaking his head. Looking back to Mom he said, "Miss Forrest I knows I don't need to tells you but your son, and Rory too, are fine boys. Yes ma'am, they's good boys and I do enjoys their company." Amos dropped his head slightly, cut a big grin and said softer, "And the fish they brings ain't bad either." He then laughed heartily.

"A mother never tires of hearing words like those, Mr. George." She looked at me and I knew it was time to go. "Well, I've got a couple errands to run. Mr. George, would you mind if Jake stayed with you for a while?" This request signaled she had no lingering concerns about my friend.

"No indeed," Amos said with a smile.

Mom picked up her purse to leave, "Now Jake, you mind your manners and don't eat all of Mr. George's fried chicken."

I settled on the couch and Amos handed me a drum stick. He sat down in the old recliner with a chicken wing and a wedge of corn bread. We talked about my arm and what really happened that day. I was breaking my agreement with Rory, but I knew he wouldn't mind. I just felt like, well, Amos should know the truth. He was enthralled as I described in vivid detail the battle with the boy-eating shark.

"Nows you know they out there, how you gonna make sure this don't happen no more?" he asked.

"I don't know, hadn't really thought about it," I answered.

"Here's what you do, no more stringers. That's just like chum in the water. Next time gits a small cage to puts the fish in," he said.

"Yeah, that makes sense."

We continued to talk about fishing and baseball. There was a slight pause in our conversation as Amos went back to the stove for another piece of corn bread. I decided this was the time to ask, "Amos, who's Lilly?"

Amos stood straight, his face betraying that my question caught him off guard. "Why you ask boy?"

"Well, I don't remember much about the other day, but I do remember something about Lilly," I said.

Amos walked over to the bookcase on the far wall and picked up a framed picture. "This was sittin' right there when you and Rory showed up," he said. "In your deliriousness, you was asking all kinda questions 'bout who was these people."

I took the picture to examine it closely. Inside the frame was a grainy 8x10 black and white photo of a young couple standing next to an old Ford truck. The woman was smiling in a summer dress, holding a baby.

The man sported a shirt, tie, and a stylish fedora. One of his feet was resting on the truck's side step and his arm was around the woman. In the bottom, right corner of the frame was a school photo of a little girl.

"Is this you?"

"Yep, that's me. I's a good lookin' fella weren't I?" he said with wistful smile.

I too smiled, "Yes, you were a handsome devil."

"Well, you closer there than you know. Anyways, that's my wife, Thelma. And the baby she's holding is, well.... that's Lilly."

"Wow, Amos, that's neat. Is this picture in the bottom Lilly too?" I asked.

"Yep, she's 'bout seven there," he answered.

"So where did you meet your wife?" I asked

"In Savannah. See the big treat for a hard week's work was goin' to town. We put on our bestest clothes and rode the bus to Savannah proper. Now remember in them days everythin' was separate, there was a white town and a black town. In black town was a main road with shops, a couple restaurants, and a church on either end. Anyway, I'd just come out of the general goods store, and there she was. Land sakes, I saw me the prettiest little gal ever. She's wearing a yellow dress and a white hat. My, my she was somethin'.

"Now I weren't never much with the ladies. I was always sort of shy. But somethin' inside me demanded I meets her. So, real casual, like *Mannix* on TV I followed her from the other side of the street. Well I's so focused on her that I walked full on into a wrought iron bench. *Wham!*" Amos slapped the palms of his hands together for effect. "My bad knee hit the arm rest, and the backrest caught me square in......my man area," Amos whispered as if there was a lady present. I, of course, laughed.

"Now you thinks that's a hoot, don't you?"

I said through giggles, "Yes, especially since you did it to yourself."

"Funny or not I dropped to the sidewalk like a sack of potatoes. Thankfully, there's a car parked near the bench that hid me. By the time I's able to stand that little gal's long gone. But I figured I found her once, I'd find her again.

"The next Saturday I grabbed me a spot outside the barber shop where I could just hangs around and see if she walked by. Around lunch time she come out of the shop, and headed down the sidewalk and into a diner.

"So, I straightened my shirt, slid my hat to the left side, and sauntered across the street. It was false courage though, I'd had sooner gotten beaned by Satchel Paige than to grabs the door handle, but I did it. Sure 'nuff I did.

"She's sittin' at the counter, empty stools on boff sides. Ever so smooth I sats down at the counter leaving an empty stool betwixed us. I ordered coffee and was lookin' at the menu. She was reading a book and sippin' hot tea. With no warnin' she said, 'How's your knee?'

"'Pardon, ma'am?' I said.

"She eyeballed me and repeated, 'How's your knee?'

"Without thinking I said, 'Oh it ain't nothin' just an old baseball injury.' And as I said it I wondered how in the world she knowed I had a bum knee.

"'Baseball injury huh? As I saw it, you fell over a park bench.'"

Amos' smile betrayed a hint of adolescent embarrassment. "She had me. I knowed right then she's somethin' special. And that's how our romance begun. Late the next spring, we's married. And Jake that first year was the best year of my life."

"Even better than when you played baseball?" I asked.

"Yep, even better than playin' ball. Yes sir, mighty fine times. Well, weren't long 'till Lilly's born, and things gots even better," Amos said. He then sat back in his chair and gnawed the last bits of chicken from the wing.

I had gone this far so I decided to ask one more question, "Where are they now?"

He shifted in his chair, then crossed and uncrossed his legs. He cleared his throat, leaned towards me, clasped his hands together and said, "Jake we's friends that's for sure. And I knows you don't mean no harm in askin'. But you needs to understand that some things just ain't good conversation."

I stumbled with a couple of "OKs," but he saw the confusion on my face.

There was a long awkward silence as Amos was lost in his thoughts. He then stared at the ceiling and exhaled out his nose.

He started slowly, "Jake, you camps a lot right?"

I nodded.

"OK," Amos said, "So the next mornin' where the fire was there's a pile of ashes. Now if you takes a stick and churn up them ashes, what happens?"

"Smoke and dust float in the air," I said.

"Rights, that's exactly what they do. And once them ashes gits agitated it takes 'em a long time to settle back down, understand?"

Again, I nodded.

Amos continued, "Well that's how some things in life are too. Once you gits talkin' about 'em, the feelings gits all churned up and it takes a long time to settle down."

He paused and I considered how Mom struggled when her feelings about Will's death became too much. I then said, "I understand, I'm sorry."

Amos smiled, "It's alright. No ways you could know."

CHAPTER 29

DECEMBER 29TH, 2003

I AWOKE MONDAY MORNING WITH what could only be described as a food hangover. My tongue was swollen and my mouth tasted of old leather and garlic. I surmised I had consumed a year's worth of sodium in one evening and vowed to never eat another calzone.

While sipping very weak coffee I reviewed the yellow legal pad for what remained on my list. Today's first task was a trip to Jacksonville to empty one of Dad's safety deposit boxes. The Great Depression had imprinted on him to never place all his eggs in one basket. Therefore, even though he worked thirty-five years for the local bank, his personal accounts were spread out over several institutions.

I hoped this last safety deposit box would be loaded with uncirculated silver coins. But it might just as likely contain the original house mortgage or artwork created by Will and me in elementary school.

The road to Jacksonville took me over the beloved Fort George Inlet. On this morning, the sun's rays filtered through puffy clumps of clouds creating random patches of emerald across the water. This is as the inlet should be, inviting yet harboring a modicum of mystery and danger. The inlet gave up its treasure during that next summer of 1973, but it required we conquer the most debilitating of all emotions—fear.

CHAPTER 30

May 1973

Out eighth grade school year was much like every school year, a treadmill of boring classes with daily homework. By October my arm was fully healed from the shark incident, but a pink, jagged scar was a permanent reminder. Thankfully our moms never learned the truth about what really happened on the inlet.

High noon, Friday June 3rd, was the official start of summer. We were finished with eighth grade and ready for high school. Outside of Christmas, there is no sweeter day on a kid's calendar than the last day of school. Three months of unfettered freedom and adventure awaited us. Alice Cooper's new single expressed it perfectly — *no more pencils, no more books, no more teachers' dirty looks—School's out for Summer!* However, my excitement was shattered by Lacy McAlister's announcement that she was leaving Fernandina.

Her father accepted a transfer to a YMCA in North Carolina. She had no other family in Florida to come and visit, and on a map the distance from Fernandina to Black Mountain sure seemed like a long way. Therefore, it was very likely I would never see her again. On the edge of fourteen, I had little understanding of romantic love. But I knew how I felt about Lacy, and I sensed or maybe hoped, that she regarded me differently than the other guys. It may have been too simplistic on my part, but it seemed perfectly logical that one day our friendship would grow to love and that would be that. Sadly, I was terribly mistaken.

By Friday evening I was feeling some better. Heart abrasions at my young age healed quickly and it helped that Rory was spending the night. But what really pulled me from the doldrums was the anticipation for Saturday morning. We were building a new raft, and this time Dad was helping from the start.

After dinner Rory and I were in the living room playing *Stratego* while Dad watched TV. The Friday night movie was the world television broadcast premier of *The Planet of the Apes*. Immediately *Stratego* was pushed aside and our eyes were glued to the tube. When the movie was released in 1968, my friends and I were too young to see it, but we all knew about it. Two sequels had subsequently been released and the apes were plastered on everything from action figures to lunch boxes.

Midway through the movie, Charlton's Heston's character, Taylor, escapes his cage and begins running through the village market. Of course, he is unlike the grunting animalistic humans inhabiting this bizarre upside down world. Rather he is an astronaut from earth that strayed off course and landed on a future Earth where apes are in charge and humans are the animals. Heston's character had been captured, and in the process, was wounded in the throat rendering him temporarily unable to speak.

In perfect Hollywood timing, his vocal chords heal just about the time he escapes. After running amok through the ape church and into the outdoor market, he is caught in a large net. The apes celebrate like, well, apes grunting and jumping around. The camera pulls in tight on Heston's face as he snarls, "*Take your stinking paws off me you damned dirty ape!*"

The line was a complete shock, not only to the apes surrounding Charlton Heston, but to Dad, Rory, and me. Dad howled with laughter.

Mom was in the kitchen tenderizing cube steak. But Dad's caterwauling somehow overcame the concussions of the Coke bottle slamming the counter. She wandered into the living room to investigate.

"Eric, what in heaven's name is so funny?"

Now he was in a pickle. If he told her what was so funny, then he was trouble for endorsing swearing in front of impressionable young boys. There was no swearing in the Forrest home. The rule was equally agreed to by my parents and strictly enforced by Mom. It was her educator's sentiment that swearing was just a weak expression of emotion when there was a better word available, but people were just too lazy to think of the better word.

Dad's answer to Mom regarding the Charlton Heston line was truthful yet slightly incomplete.

"Honey, Charlton Heston just said something funny. It's weird to see Moses and Ben Hur arguing with these monkeys."

Satisfied, Mom left to resume bludgeoning the steak. Dad leaned over to Rory and me and whispered, "If you two repeat that line, we're all dead."

We agreed, but it was just too good of a line to leave by the side of the road. That night in my room, Rory and I were too excited about the next day to quickly fall asleep. We took turns saying the line and laughed with each utterance.

Rory said, "You know the next time Wade Brown grabs me I'm gonna use that line, 'Get your paws off me you damned dirty ape!'"

By seven thirty Saturday morning Rory and I were ready to go. Dad shuffled into the kitchen, peering at us with droopy eyes.

"We're ready," I said.

Reaching in the fridge for orange juice he said, "I can see that. Where's all this gusto on school mornings?"

Momentarily, Mom entered the kitchen.

"You boys take a seat and I'll whip up some eggs," she said.

"Connie, don't bother. We're going out for breakfast," Dad answered.

"Where, June's Diner?"

"Nope, McDonalds."

"You're going to feed these boys burgers for breakfast?" Mom asked.

"No babe, they serve breakfast now."

"At McDonalds?"

"Yes.... McDonalds. They've got this new sandwich called a Macmuff or something like that."

"You're telling me you would rather have a mac-thing than a plate of my eggs and toast?"

Dad turned on the smooth, "No sweetie, your cooking beats any restaurant in the world. Think of this as an experiment. We'll see if McDonalds has made a blunder with this breakfast thing."

Enjoying the banter Mom replied, "Fine, go to the golden arches for breakfast. And while you're there see if they are willing to iron your shirts too."

By midmorning we had acquired the materials and were laying out the project at Twain's lot. Dad recruited a carpenter friend to assist with the framing, which made things go much quicker. Our second raft design used six twenty-five-gallon metal drums for flotation. The deck was no longer rough logs but smooth plywood giving us an 8'x 8' platform. Using dad's car and a much sturdier tree this time, we slid the raft towards Bent Tree Creek. It plowed into the water with a swoosh, and settled high and dry. Rory and I jumped aboard with no worries of capsizing. The drums perfectly supported the raft. We joked with Dad about erecting a mast for a sail. He responded by wiping the sweat from his forehead and proclaiming, "I'm done!"

It was late afternoon when we piled in the Country Squire. We were hot, filthy, a little sunburned, but anxious for our first day's outing on the new raft. Even with the car moving I thought I was going to melt.

"Dad, you need to get an air conditioner in this car," I said.

"Jake, it's got a 450 air conditioner," Dad said smiling.

"A 450 air conditioner?"
"Yep, four windows rolled down going fifty miles an hour."
"Corny Dad, real corny."

CHAPTER 31

THE FOLLOWING MONDAY MORNING, RORY and I peddled toward Twain's lot with high expectations for the first summer voyage. We planned to float down to Amos' to show off the new raft, then proceed to the inlet. In addition to the regular provisions hanging from my bike's handlebars, today's cargo included a brush and a small can of red paint. Rory and I had significant deliberation the night before about what to name the raft. We finally agreed on a winner. Rory's hand writing was much better than mine so he had the honors. Once he finished we stood back for a moment.

"*Nessie*," Rory said.

"Yep, it fits," I agreed.

Our gear stowed we pushed *Nessie* into the outbound tide. She floated magnificently.

"This is going to be a great summer," I said to Rory.

"Are you kidding, it'll be the best!"

Using my foot, I pointed to the small pet cage sitting near the back of the raft. We found the cage in the dumpster behind the local veterinarian's office and with several modifications converted it into a fish keeper. "And no sharks this year either," I said.

As we approached his place, Amos spied us and was waiting on his floating dock as we landed.

"My, my, my," he said. "Let's take a look at this new raft."

He took his time, looking at it from stem to stern. He then read the name, "*Nessie*, nows I like that, yes sir. Is she sturdy 'nuff for a ole man?"

"Yes sir, climb aboard," Rory said.

Amos took our hands and very carefully stepped onto the raft. True to Rory's word the raft barely tilted with the extra weight. He stepped fore and aft then said, "You boys outdone yourselves, indeed this is a fine raft. And I sees the edges is all smooth." He looked at me while making this observation. "Real good boys, real good."

We helped Amos disembark and promised we would be back later in the day, our cage loaded with fish and our parched throats ready for a soda.

Entering the inlet, we enjoyed our first cannon ball of the season. However, in the back of my mind was the recollection that the last time I was on this body of water we had the epic battle with the shark. Unsettled, I returned to the raft rather quickly. The fishing was slow that day, but it was of little concern. We were on *Nessie*, and we had our freedom.

Growling stomachs drove us to the bridge where we clambered up to the flat concrete buttress. With two *pops* lunch was served. Rory had Vienna sausages and I had the old standby, pork and beans. Grape Kool-Aid and chips completed the entrée. Rory was tearing the rapper off a Little Debbie raisin pie when he said, "It's like the beer commercial, it just doesn't get any better than this."

During the first few weeks of June we settled into our summer routine. We mowed yards, played baseball, fished, and hung out with Amos. Our parents were also benefitting from Rory and me being back on the marsh. When I arrived home with a string of fish, Mom would say with genuine excitement, "Clean 'em, bag 'em, and throw 'em in the big freezer. "

We never tired of talking baseball with Amos. We constantly begged him to share stories with us from his playing days. Not just about the magnificent feats on the baseball diamond but also the hi-jinx's that happened off the field. We mostly wanted to hear stories of the road trips. For Rory and me the thought of traveling with our friends, playing baseball, and getting paid sounded like heaven on earth. Amos assured us that was not the case, "I tells you the truth, that road'll wear a man down, and quick."

Rory was on the cusp of learning something about traveling to play ball. He was selected as an All-Star for our age group, and for the remainder of the summer, he spent his weekends playing tournaments throughout North Florida.

The situation at my house was improving as well. Mom was having fewer and fewer bad days and the "shadows" had all but disappeared. I guess Dad was right about time taking care of Mom's healing. She did seem to be closer to her old self. However, there was still almost no discussion or reminiscing about Will.

We hated to see that afternoon end. We had feasted on Amos' secret recipe of smoked mullet, which I confess I was beginning to really enjoy. But the tide was flowing towards home and the sun was tracking to the west, both signaling it was time to go.

Arriving at the Twain lot with plenty of daylight to work with, we decided to stop by the 7-Eleven. We remained on the hunt for another Carl "Yaterminski," cup. Like Captain Ahab, it had become our "great white whale." As usual we parked our bikes next to the ice freezer and strolled in under the clang of the cowbell. There was Doris standing behind the counter, a Virginia Slims between her fingers. She exhaled heavily and smiled, "Hello boys, two Slurpees?

"Yes ma'am!" Rory said as we proceeded to the candy bar section.

The tragic occurrence that was the shattering of the Carl Yastrzemski cup was in the past and highly unlikely to be repeated. Partially because Rory and I would never again argue over a cup, but mostly because the soothing effects of nicotine again coursed through Doris's veins. Her effort at quitting had been a dismal failure. It was rumored that in the throes of withdrawal she snapped at the local IGA when the clerk refused to apply an expired twenty-five cent coupon to a package of toilet paper. After shredding the clerk's ears with a stream of curse words no lady should employ, she threatened to torch the store and all its employees. Later after careful consideration of her actions, Doris decided the consequences of living without nicotine were perhaps more dire than the risk of lung cancer.

When we arrived at the counter Doris asked, "Will these do?"

We discovered that Doris had in fact pulled two winners, Catfish Hunter, and Gaylord Perry. It was Rory's turn to choose and he took Catfish Hunter—no surprise, what a cool name. Exiting the store both of us were engrossed in reading the stats on the back of the cup.

Without warning, something slammed my hand and my cup flew into the parking lot. Another cup sailed across my field of vision also landing in the parking lot. Upon impact the cups cracked and blueberry puddles formed on the hot asphalt. There was no need to wonder what happened. The inbred laugh identified our assailant, Wade Brown.

"How does that feel piss ants?" Wade said. "In two short months, you'll be with me in high school. And I'm gonna make your lives a living hell."

Rory was as mad as I had ever seen him. It sounds bizarre but when he lost control his eyes seemed to change shape. They would narrow, darken, and recede further into his skull. It was weird.

"Wade, you pizza faced freak. God, I hate you!" Rory said.

"Don't blame me, you and wiener lips here seem to have butter fingers."

I lost my Slurpee and now I was being insulted by a nimrod that can't even pass ninth grade. I saw Rory leaning towards the much bigger Wade, his fists clinched, he was ready to erupt.

"Well Tiny Tim, what cha' gonna do? Hey, I got an idea, what if I stay here and you go get your dad to help you beat me up? Wait, no that won't work cause your daddy left. He high tailed to Oregon to live with a bunch of hippies, right?"

A half smile crossed Rory's lips. "Yeah Wade, my Dad's in Oregon. But you know what, he calls me all the time and I'm going out to see him this summer. What I want to know is how rotten does a family have to be to make their mom just disappear in the middle of the night? Your mom decided you were all losers and just blew town. By the way, how did ninth grade go this year? Are we all going to be in the same class come September?"

Like a fighter that just caught a vicious uppercut, Wade appeared stunned. Was Rory's verbal assault so harsh that Wade would simply slink away? Unfortunately, no. Wade reached down and grabbed a discarded Nehi bottle. Holding the tapered end, he slammed the bottom part against the concrete. Glass shattered in all directions and I jumped as a piece flew past my shin. Wade smiled as he brandished the lethal bottle.

"That mouth of yours just got you more hurt than you can handle," Wade said and it was clearly not a bluff.

Rory and I were completely defenseless, but with fairy tale timing a cowbell announced the arrival of our protector. Our heroine was wearing Kelly green polyester slacks and a Virginia Slims 100 hung from her lips. She brandished a plunger handle, the same weapon that killed Carl "Yaterminisky."

"Hey Boy! Yeah, you with the bottle. You better scram 'cause I just called the police and Deputy Bowers is on his way."

Wade paused.

"I believe you and Deputy Bowers are old friends, right Wade?" I said.

"Yeah," Rory followed, "I think you two have been on a first name basis for some time."

Rory then pinched his fingers together and brought them to his mouth like he was smoking a joint. Wade's angered glare turned inquisitive. He was trying to figure out how Rory and I would have known about the episode the year before, when he and his friends were caught smoking pot. Choosing to flee the scene he turned to leave. He stopped and looked directly at Rory, "You're dead runt."

We rode home in silence. I knew Wade's words about his dad had stirred up painful feelings for Rory. He missed his dad terribly and he couldn't comprehend why he had left his mom or why he chose to move so far away. As for Wade, it seemed we were on a course for a showdown. Rory, blinded by his anger towards his dad and his general proclivity to stand his ground, seemed to welcome this Armageddon. I, on the other hand, worried that Wade's size advantage and his capacity for cruelness would take things further than just a fist fight.

I hated Wade, but then I had a healthy sense of when it was time to flee rather than fight. Rory seemed to default increasingly to a fight first mentality, and because of that I feared greatly for my friend.

CHAPTER 32

It was barely light as Rory and I rolled out of my driveway. Peering through the oak limbs there was crystal blue to the east but pink clouds with gray undertones stretched to the west's horizon. The sky appeared unsettled, as if it could not decide what kind of day to offer us. Our bike handle bars were saddled with a day's worth of provisions as we planned to be out until nearly dusk. We had recently confessed to our parents that we did in fact fish in the inlet and that the bridge provided an excellent harbor for us in case of trouble. Mom was of course concerned, but dad as usual talked her off the ledge. She would have skinned us alive however if she knew we were floating on the east side of the bridge. Especially when the only thing between us and the enormous cargo ships traversing the Intracoastal waterway was a spliced marine rope.

Amos was on his porch reading the paper as we approached.

"Mornin' boys, you ats it early," he said.

"Yep, and we plan to hit it all day too," I said.

"Alrights, be mindful out there, it's gonna be a scorcher," he said. Rising from his rocker he walked to the railing and peered at the morning sky. "Weather's takin' a turn."

Rory and I stared skyward, "I don't see anything," Rory said.

"Yeah, it's just a regular summer sky," I said.

"My bum knee says otherwise," Amos replied. "You be smart, hear?"

Assuring him we were always careful I pushed away from the dock and felt the current take hold of the raft, "We'll be back late this afternoon," I said. "You better make some room in your freezer."

The tide carried us straight to the bridge where we tied off before floating towards the Intracoastal. Rory and I were rigging our gear and anticipating the first strike of the day when a group of brown pelicans glided in from the ocean. They were in perfect formation, just like a squadron of Japanese dive bombers from the movie *Toro, Toro, Toro.* Committed to protecting Fernandina Beach, Rory and I manned our Browning .50 caliber bamboo machine guns. With realistic sounds and imaginary bullets, we quickly dispatched the winged marauders.

We enjoyed good success for the next several hours and reeled in our lines only when hunger drove us to the sanctuary of the bridge. Our bellies full, we laid back and took a little siesta. Dad stopped by while we were lounging on the buttress.

"So, is this what you two do all day? Now I can understand why you come home too tired for chores," he said with a smile. He sat down and opened his brown bag.

"What did Mom make you?" I asked.

Sniffing the sandwich through the wax paper he said, "Umm boy! Peanut butter and banana. If it's good enough for the King, its good enough for me," referring to Elvis who had a known penchant for the delicacy.

Midafternoon, as if giant gears in a machine were reversed, the water began its slow turn from draining the estuary to replenishing it with a fresh offering. The tension on the tethering line eased and we gradually floated back towards the bridge.

Once clear of the bridge our lines were back in the water. Like a Norman Rockwell image, Rory and I dangled our feet into the water as we fished side by side. We had been there perhaps a half hour when Rory commented on the serenity of the western sky. It was blue with white puffy polka dot clouds.

"I guess Amos' knee isn't always right, look at that sky."

I was foraging in my tackle box for a new hook when I perceived the change. Initially it was faint, almost imperceptible. There was a slight coolness intermingled with the overpowering heat. Much like it feels in the car when the air conditioner is on but the windows are down. Minutes later a cool wind blew across our backs displacing the heat altogether.

"Oh, man that feels good, it's like someone opened a big refrigerator," I said.

I turned to face the cool breeze and my heart stopped. Beyond the bridge, a veil of inky blackness concealed the sky. I had never seen nor could have fathomed a more menacing cloud. Its color was completely uniform, a deep blackish gray that covered the eastern horizon. Its ever widening grasp was rapidly encircling either end of the bridge. Westerly it was a pleasant sunny day, easterly however, a demonic darkness was pressing in and would soon engulf us.

"Rory, we gotta move!" I said with what I thought was adequate urgency.

"Bingo! Got another one," Rory exclaimed as his rod bent. He sprung to his feet and began reeling in his catch.

"RORY WE GOTTA MOVE!" I shouted as loudly as possible. "NOW!"

"Man, what is the prob….." That's as much as he got out before turning and seeing the apocalyptic blackness descending.

"Holy Crap!" he said.

As if the storm desired to reiterate Rory's proclamation a jagged lance of lightning split the darkness and a deafening thunder crack caused us to drop to our knees.

"That was close!" Rory said.

Shouting to be heard over the rushing wind I said, "We gotta get to the bridge!"

Rory pulled his knife, cut his line, and threw his rod to the deck. I was already at the front of the raft pulling against our mooring line.

Rory joined me, and we pulled hand over hand as fast as possible. The raft was moving towards the bridge, but far too slow for our situation. Not only the incoming tide hindered us, but also the effects of the storm. The wind blew fiercely and churned the inlet into waves of white caps. Several swells crested the front of the raft, and the surge of water rose above our ankles. More lightning strikes lit up the sky and reverberated like cannon fire under the bridge.

"Owww, my eye!" Rory screamed and released the rope. He pulled his hand away from his face and his palm was covered in blood. A red stream ran down his face soaking into the collar of his shirt.

"Something cut me, felt like a rock," he said.

There was a nasty gash just outside his eye. Before I could deduce what happened I was pelted on my arm by a dice size piece of hail.

"It's hail! We've gotta get to cover!"

Rory joined me on the rope and we frantically pulled as hail pelted us and bounced off the deck of the raft. Finally, the raft edged beneath the protection of the bridge. Safe for the moment, we paused to watch the barrage of hail and lightning assault the inlet.

In between heavy breaths Rory said, "Wow, that was close. How's my eye?"

Using the hem of his shirt he dabbed the wound and I took a closer look, "It's OK, just a nasty cut. You'll have a cool scar to remember this."

"I won't need anything to remember today," Rory said.

"I'm just glad we're out of the worst of it," I added.

We hastily tied *Nessie* to the rebar hooks jutting from the bridge buttress and placed our gear on the concrete ledge. The raft was being tossed violently prodding us to move higher. Once on the ledge we ventured to the eastern side of the bridge and witnessed the teeth of the storm. The hail had yielded to torrential rain. The small beach was no more than twenty yards from where we stood, but it was completely obscured by the storm. Overhead water channeled through fissures in the roadway before cascading down in oversized droplets. A bright flash of lightning chased us back to the middle of the bridge. The temperature dropped drastically, and as odd as it may seem on what was a ninety-five-degree day, Rory and I were shivering.

"I have never, ever seen anything like this!" I said, shouting to be heard above the storm.

Rory peering at the thrashing water below the ledge said, "It's like a hurricane."

The easterly wind intensified, blowing the rain further under the bridge. We were standing in the dead center of a thirty-foot-wide bridge span, and it was raining on us as if we were still in the middle of the inlet. To escape the downpour, we moved higher up the embankment. Suddenly, a stout gust of wind blew under the bridge lifting *Nessie* and upending it before slamming her back into the water. The raft continued to float but the drums were bobbing up and down within the frame.

"Are you kidding me?" Rory said. "You know how heavy that raft is and the wind just flipped it like a feather!"

"Thank God we were so close to the bridge when this thing hit," I added.

Sitting in silence on the inclined section, I began feeling an odd sensation. It started at a low octave, more vibration than sound.

"What is that, a ship?" Rory asked.

"No, doesn't sound right." I stood in an effort to hear the sound more clearly. The volume and intensity both amplified. It reminded me of standing next to railroad tracks as a train approached. The mysterious sound seemed to be getting closer, which further unnerved both of us.

"Rory, this isn't good, come on," I said.

"Where?"

"Up to the ledge," and I pointed to the narrow place between the end of the bridge and the roadway.

"Not without my gear," Rory replied. He scooped up the rods and poles and used his foot to slide the tackle boxes further away from the water.

The thunderous roar grew louder with each passing second. Rory started ascending the inclined concrete but slipped and fell to his knees. I went to him, grabbed the rods, and helped him to his feet. Together we moved to the crevice. Throwing down the gear we pressed ourselves against the back wall and lay on our stomachs, head to head.

With a panicked tone, Rory asked, "Jake what's happening?"

Straining to be heard above the cacophony of the storm, "I think it's a tornado!"

Powerful gusts of wind swept across the bridge pilings producing shrill whistles. Had we remained on the buttress we would no doubt been blown into the churning water. The sand which littered the bridge's ledges became tiny airborne missiles that peppered our faces, while the deafening roar rang in our ears. I squeezed my eyes tightly and prayed God would protect us. Torrents of water swirled beneath the bridge, continually blasting us with spray. I briefly opened my eyes and saw giant water plumes, like high pressure fountains dancing across the inlet. I wondered how much more the old wooden bridge could sustain. Again, I closed my eyes and prayed.

After another minute the roar began to soften. Rain continued pelting us from various directions but the ferocity of the spray diminished. The water in the inlet seemed to calm slightly. "I think the worst is passed," I said.

"I don't care, I'm not moving!" Rory responded.

We remained hunkered down in the crevice for another five minutes as the storm gradually subsided. Cautiously rising, we surveyed the infrastructure of the bridge. The underside was darkened giving evidence of the spray that soaked the entire span of the bridge. The inlet remained a menacing gray and three foot swells slapped loudly as they struck the pilings. Carefully, we inched our way down the slippery incline to the flat buttress.

"Gosh, I hope Amos is all right," Rory said.

"Man, you're right. His old house would never stand through that."

"Well as soon as this rain lets up, we've gotta go check on him," Rory said. It was gratifying to see Rory's affection for Amos. He had come a long way from his initial reluctance to befriending him simply because of his color.

It appeared the rain might never let up. We sat there for what seemed like another half hour as waves of strong wind and rain continued to roll through. When a light drizzle was all that remained of the tempest, we stowed our gear as best we could on the underside frame of the raft, straddled the drums and pushed off from the safety of the buttress.

Though the sky remained cloudy, the shades were lighter and far less ominous. Despite flowing with a strong incoming tide, our progress was slow with the upturned raft. Positioning the raft to enter Bent Tree Creek, I was anxious to get to Amos. Having survived the onslaught of the storm, Rory and I should have been chattering like a couple of monkeys, but the concern for our friend dampened any celebratory emotions.

Before we cleared the last bend, we were calling to Amos. Sweet relief washed over us as his place came into view. Miraculously it was standing. He was on his dock looking at the underside of the porch when he finally heard our shouts. As he turned, his face reflected relief.

"Sweet Lawd is you two a sight!" he shouted. "You had ole Amos scared somethin' awful."

"We're fine," Rory said.

"Yeah, we thought you were the one in trouble," I said.

The tin roof of the porch had been peeled back from the easterly corner to midway of the porch. The sight reminded me of an open sardine can, which made me think of Mr. Rosco.

"Is Mr. Rosco OK?" I asked.

"He's fine. He gots better sense than most people. He stayed hid under the cabin. Unlikes two boys who didn't listen to their elders when he tolds them the weather weren't right," he said. "So where did you holds up, the bridge?"

"Yes sir," Rory said. "And it was a good thing we were so close. I've never seen anything like it."

"It was a tornado for sure," Amos said. "I's seen a couple in my life and that sound is somethin' you don't forget. We all OK, but you better gits home and fast."

Looking at the patches of blue emerging in the sky I asked, "What's the hurry, the storm's past."

Amos George shook his head side to side. "Boys you gots to trust ole Amos when I tells you this storm ain't over, now gits home!"

Doing as we were told we resumed poling up the creek. Several more bends in the river and we began to see additional signs of the tornado's path. There were numerous trees uprooted and at one bend it as though a bull dozer had driven through the marsh grass. A road wide path, stretching at least fifty yards had been cleared as precisely as if it had been done by a CCC crew.

"Look at that rainbow," Rory said. "I swear I don't know what Amos meant by 'the storm ain't over.'"

A double rainbow stretched in a perfect arch from horizon to horizon. It was a beautiful display of color set against the remaining dark clouds as the storm raced west.

I too wondered why Amos was so adamant that we scurry home. However, all too soon, we would grasp the wisdom of his words.

CHAPTER 33

THE JOURNEY FROM AMOS' TO Twain's lot was painstakingly slow. The inverted raft was difficult to steer resulting in continual collisions with the mud banks. It was also nearly impossible to use the bamboo poles effectively while attempting to balance on the bobbing drums. All too quickly the sun disappeared, and by the time we made Twain's lot, only faint blue highlights remained on the horizon. After the long day and the troubles that accompanied it, we were exhausted and our conversation had been minimal since leaving Amos's. Rory however broke the silence, "Jake isn't that your mom?"

Peering into the twilight I could make out the silhouette of a woman by the edge of the water. Despite the darkness, I knew it was Mom by the way she was standing.

"That's her, wonder why she's here? Hey, wait, your mom's here too."

Rory's mom was leaning against the hood of her car. She was smoking a cigarette and the embers glowed bright red with each deep draw.

"Rory, this can't be good."

To measure the degree of our predicament I called out, "Hey Mom! What are you doing here?"

She offered no response, she only repositioned her arms, pulling them away from her hips and folding them across her chest. I interpreted nothing positive in her gesture.

Rory said in a hushed whisper, "I think this is what Amos meant."

The raft slid into the sandy bank with a crunch. As we stepped off I said, "Wow, some day huh? Sorry we're late, got caught in a storm."

Neither woman acknowledged I had made a sound. Mom's emotionless stare made me uncomfortable. She mustered four words through clinched teeth, "Get in the car!"

Rory's mom gave him similar abbreviated directions, "Car, now!"

I glanced towards Rory, "I'll see you tomorrow man." He nodded.

In a terse non-negotiable tone Mom replied, "Not likely."

"What is the problem?" I said.

"We'll talk when we get home."

Given her tone, my best course of action was to shut up. Besides, maybe the ride home would give her time to consider how much she loved me and it might mellow her mood. These ignorant musings confirmed that I still had much to learn about women.

Arriving home after our silent commute, all I wanted to do was take a bath and go to bed. Whatever we needed to discuss or whatever punishment I had coming, I hoped we could defer until tomorrow. Walking into the house I was grateful for the greatest invention of all time—air conditioning. I started for my room and Mom said, "Where do you think you're going?"

"To get a bath and to go to bed."

"I don't think so mister. You'll go sit at the kitchen table and wait until your father gets home," she said.

I was tired. I didn't know what the big deal was and just wanted to crash. That was my only excuse for snapping back, "Mom what is with you?"

She spun around and her eyes were like fire, dampened slightly by a thin sheen of tears. "What is with me? Are you serious son? How about this, my only child was out on the water today during a tornado. He was on a frail raft with not even a basic life preserver. How's that for starters?"

"But Mom, I'm fine."

"So you are, and don't think for a second I am not grateful with every part of my being for that fact. But for the last four hours your father, Sylvia, and I have been scouring the inlet and the marsh for you two. Earlier today I was in the kitchen when the National Weather Service issued an extreme weather warning, with possible tornados. I called your dad and Sylvia in a panic and we all headed out in different directions to try and find you two. Your dad drove to the bridge but couldn't get out of his car because of the golf ball size hail. After seeing the damage to his car, I imagined you and Rory out there in the marsh being pelted to death."

Tears were streaming down her face and her voice had risen to hysterical octaves. "Jake, don't you understand, you could have been killed! It's only by the grace of God that your father and I aren't at the hospital identifying your body. Can't you see how tragic this day could have been? And it's all because of stupid boyhood adventures. That's what got Will killed you know, macho adventure seeking!"

The introduction of Will triggered an emotional avalanche inside me. My hurt and resentment regarding Mom's handling of Will's death boiled over in a venomous tirade.

"And what if I had died today, Mom? Would you stick a picture of me on a table in the foyer and never speak about me again, just like you've done with your other son? What was his name again? I forget sometimes because it's never mentioned around here!"

Mom raised her open hand and I steeled myself for a slap to the face. Feeling no impact after several seconds I opened my eyes. She stood there with her arm raised, motionless, as if she were frozen in place. Tears ran down her face before dropping to the carpet. Slowly, she withdrew her arm, snatched up her purse and walked briskly out the front door. The door slammed with sufficient force to crack one of its three window panes.

I didn't know what to do. I wished Dad were home. I wished we hadn't gone out today. I finally went to my room and cried myself to sleep.

Dad awakened me sometime later in the night. He asked where Mom was and I mumbled a few words about her leaving mad. Dad turned off my bed side light and then I felt him kiss me on the forehead. That is only time in my life I recall my father kissing me. I was a boy on the edge of manhood. I smelled to high heavens of fish, sweat, and marsh mud and my Dad chose that moment to tenderly kiss my forehead.

I didn't wake until midday. Fearful of what I might find outside my door, but propelled by hunger, I cautiously headed for the kitchen. It was empty but there was a plate of eggs and bacon left on the stove. I inhaled the plate's contents and wolfed down two bowls of cereal before I was satisfied. There was a note from Dad instructing me to call him. As we spoke, I chose not to ask about Mom, but he volunteered that he had seen her earlier and she was alright. I dialed Rory's house and hoped he rather than his mom would answer the phone.

"Hello," came his familiar voice.

"Hey bud it's me."

"Oh, hey Jake. How are things?"

"Quiet for the moment, no one's home except me. How 'bout at your house?"

"Much quieter this morning. Mom tore me up one side and down the other last night, but she is at work. She told me I couldn't leave the house and I wasn't supposed to talk to you."

"Yeah, I think lying low is the best course of action today. We need to let the rest of the storm pass before we even mention the word 'raft' again."

Unsure what to do, I decided to improve my circumstances if possible. I cleaned my room and made sure all the dishes were washed. I watched some TV and occasionally went to the window when I heard a car drive by. I was hoping it was Dad coming home, but I needed to prepare in case it was Mom. The extent of my preparedness was considering whether under my bed or in the attic would be a better hiding place.

Dad arrived home at his normal time and carried a bucket of Colonel Sanders' finest. After dinner, curiosity or concern got the better of me. "Dad, when's Mom coming home?"

"Later."

That was the extent of his answer. The lack of an explanation as to where she had been for the last twenty-four hours meant we were not finished with yesterday's events. Around dusk I heard a car door slam. My first instinct was to disappear, but I knew I needed to be a man and face the music. The front door opened and closed, this time without shattering any panes. I heard Mom's heels *clip clop* through the foyer. She bypassed us in the living room and went straight to the kitchen. Dad joined her, while I chose to stay right where I was.

Historically speaking, important family discussions occurred around the kitchen table. These summits were always handled with both parents present and dealt with issues like restrictions, punishments, and areas of my life that needed improvement. These kitchen conferences never announced good surprises, like, say, all of us going to Disney World.

Dad returned from the kitchen and Mom called me to join her. It was clear I would be facing the guillotine alone. I tentatively approached the table, then pulled out a chair. Mom was seated directly across from me, her hands wrapped around a steaming cup of coffee. She was wearing the same dress from yesterday. Her face was red and her eyes were puffy. Knowing full well that anything I might say at this point would most certainly be the wrong thing, I said nothing.

"Jake, I think we need to clear the air from last night," Mom said. Her voice calm and measured.

"OK."

"It was a rough day for all us, don't you think?"

"Yes ma'am." I doggedly stuck to my plan of saying as little as possible.

"Jake, do you understand why I was so distraught last night?"

"Yes ma'am, I think so."

"Then tell me what you think."

"Well, I think you were scared. You thought maybe Rory and I had gotten hurt in the storm."

"Or worse," she said.

"Yes ma'am, maybe even worse."

"So, I was well within my rights as a mom to be upset?"

My mind was desperately trying to stay one step ahead of her but, she was painting me into a tight corner. True, she had the right to be upset I guess, but not to go all psycho on me.

"Yes ma'am, you were entitled to be upset, but, but.."

She cut me off before I could say more. "Then you agree I had the right to be upset when I thought your life was in danger?"

"Yes ma'am, but you were *too* upset."

"So there are degrees of upset and what happened yesterday does not merit the top tier of upset. Is that what you mean?"

"Yes ma'am."

"Then let's put the shoe on your foot. Exactly how upset were you when Rory fell in the water with the shark?"

What the heck, how did she know that? I thought. Rory and I never said anything about the shark to our parents. These are the instances that cause kids to wonder if all moms are secretly part of the CIA. I was trying not to let my face reflect the extreme surprise my mind was attempting to process. She had me. I had no avenue but to fall on the mercy of the court.

"I see your point," I said sheepishly.

"Good, now we have some common ground," she responded. "Now Jake before we go any further, I want you to understand one absolute truth. Regardless if I had one child or ten, I would have reacted yesterday with the same fear. I didn't react the way I did just because you are now our only living child. Do you understand?"

"Yes ma'am," and continuing in the most respectful tone I added, "Mom there is also something you need to understand. I'm not stupid or reckless. That was a freak storm, and we'll probably never see another like that. Rory and I were just fishing. You can't prevent accidents—they just happen. Sure, you can never let us on the marsh again and that'll keep me safe. But no, it won't, because I ride my bike, and kids get killed on bikes all the time. So, you get rid of my bike, fine. I still play baseball and I bet some kid somewhere has died from a freak baseball injury. And what about Boy Scouts, do I have to quit Scouts—heck, they do all kinds of dangerous outdoor stuff. Where does it stop? Mom, we're careful. We did the right thing yesterday. We got out of the storm. What more do you want?"

There was a long pause during which Mom took several sips of coffee. She then slid her hand around the back of her head and rubbed her neck. "Son, those are very valid points. And under normal conditions perhaps I would have handled it better."

"Mom, these *are* normal conditions for our family. Will's death will always be a part of our lives. Like Dad told me, our definition of normal changed forever the day those two Air Force officers knocked on the door."

She looked down and absent mindedly folded and unfolded the napkin in front of her. Through watery eyes she reached out her hands and closed them around mine. "Jake, you are so wise for your age. And I want you to know that I am very thankful to God for your special insight."

Tears pouring from my eyes I said, "Mom, if Will's death will always be part of who we are, shouldn't we try to make his memory a bigger part of our daily lives? It's not like it can hurt worse than it already does."

She completely broke down and for a moment laid her head on the table. Several minutes later she rose and walked from the room, pausing as she passed me. Bending down she placed her arms around me and laid her head on mine. She whispered, "I love you Jake, please forgive me."

Breaking the embrace, she went to the living room and fell into Dad's welcoming arms. Feeling like this was no longer where I should be, I stepped outside. Perched on our front stoop, I watched the random blinks of countless fire flies as they proceeded on their nightly journey. I glanced behind me and stared for a moment at Will's star. The small flag with a gold star set against a white background and bordered in red, hung in our front window. No family desired this honor. The star signified to all that passed by that this family lost a son in military conflict. The peacefulness of that moonless evening was a welcomed culmination to the previous day's trials. Above me was Vega. She and her innumerable friends strewn like pixie dust across the heavens.

I knew our family's and my Mom's challenges would not suddenly be transformed overnight. The scale of healing required for us would be evolutionary in its nature. Occurring slowly, but hopefully always moving forward.

In the life of a forest a seemingly destructive wildfire is actually beneficial. The flames clear the debris which encourages a generation of healthy new growth. Sitting under the stars that summer night, I was confident that the tornado of '73 had initiated a measure of healing for our family that far overshadowed its destructive results.

CHAPTER 34

Due to lengthy discussions regarding new rules for our marine outings, it was nearly a week before Rory and I were allowed back on the marsh. One of the proposed rules was the wearing of life preservers, the bulky orange version seldom seen on kids over the age of seven. We attempted to negotiate around this requirement, pointing out that these devices were more likely to kill us from heat stroke than save us from drowning.

Thankfully, Dad came through as the voice of reason. He told the moms that despite our promises, we would remove the contraptions as soon as we were out of their site. He proposed ski belts as a reasonable alternative. Dad's recommendation was sound – so long as we were conscious. Whereas a ski belt is comfortable, it is not engineered to keep a swimmer's face out of the water. Therefore, if we hit our heads before falling in, the ski belt would merely make it easier to locate our bodies for a proper burial.

Rory suggested that if the parents were serious about our safety they should purchase a 10-horsepower Johnson outboard. That perfectly sound recommendation was quickly vetoed.

Mercifully, we were finally permitted back on the raft on a sultry morning during the last week of June. We stopped as usual at Amos' and the conversation turned to the big storm.

"Amos, why didn't you tell us my mom was here looking for us?" I asked.

"Wouldn't served no purpose. I knews they'd be waiting for you and it weren't gonna be a happy homecoming. No sense getting you all worried." As we untied from the dock he stretched over the rail and handed Rory and me a cold cola.

"This is early payment for the fish you gonna catch today. My freezer's a little slight so don't come home with no sad stories 'bout they weren't bitin'."

We fished for several hours on the east side of the bridge before the tide turned. With the incoming tide we drifted back to the respite of the bridge. I was standing at *Nessie's* bow and just before we broke back into the sun something on the inlet floor caught my eye. Unable to identify it, I yelled for Rory to toss the anchor.

"What is it?" Rory asked.

"I don't know. The light glinted off something near the base of the piling. It was blue or purple. I want to check it out."

I shucked my shirt and fitted the official Lloyd Bridges *Sea Hunt* swim mask over my face.

"How deep do you think it is?" Rory asked.

"Well considering the tide just turned, eight feet maybe. I can reach the bottom easy."

Jumping feet first I descended to the sandy bottom. The water was clear and I had no trouble swimming to the base of the piling. Jutting from the sand was a shard of purple glass. I carefully placed my hand on the exposed end and gently pulled. It moved only slightly.

I resurfaced, pulled myself back on the raft, and was immediately besieged by Rory.

"What was it, why didn't you bring it up?"

"It's a piece of purple glass. It's broken on the end but most of it is under the sand. Hand me one of the gloves."

"Well how 'bout you give me a try?" Rory asked as he rummaged in the gear bucket.

"No way man, I saw it first."

"Hey, remember, whatever we catch we share," Rory said.

"Fine, I'll be happy to share a sharp piece of purple glass with you, now give me the glove."

Rory complied by slapping the glove into my hand as hard as possible. He wasn't mad, he just hated to lose.

Returning to the bottom I moved the piece of glass back and forth further loosening it. Freeing it, the water clouded with sand and silt. The murkiness briefly obscured it but a wave or two of my hand dispersed the sediment revealing an unusual piece of glass. It was a purple bottle but unfortunately the neck was broken and much of the exterior was coated with hard sediment. My lungs screaming for air, I kicked against the inlet floor and shot to the surface.

Back on the raft we examined the bottle. It was about the size of a half-gallon of milk, but below the neck it spread out to more of a rectangle shape rather than a cube. It was deep purple and there appeared to be intricate details fashioned on each side.

"What do you think this is?" Rory asked.

"No clue. But I do know someone we can ask."

"Amos," we said simultaneously.

We gently stowed the bottled in one of our buckets, hoisted the anchor and began pushing towards Bent Tree Creek. Amos saw us navigating around the bend.

"Yous back early. Did you catch your limit that fast?"

"We caught something all right, just wait'll you see," I said.

We scampered up the ramp to his porch, "This is what we caught, any idea what it is?"

Amos examined the bottle. He rubbed the side with the bottom of his shirt and held it up to the light to have another look.

"Well?" Rory asked.

"Boys I do believes I know what this is. It's a rum bottle, and an old one at that."

"A rum bottle? Are you sure, that seems awful fancy for a rum bottle," I remarked.

"Agreed Jake, it is a might fancy for a rum bottle. But that's why I remember it. The company what made the rum wanted the bottle to be exquisite—now if you don't know what exquisite means we can grab my dictionary."

"No, we know what that means," Rory said groaning with impatience. "What was the name of the rum?"

"Can't recalls the real name, we's called it the 'King's Rum' on account of how nice the bottle was."

"Well why did the company want the bottle to be so nice?" I asked.

"Two reasons actually. First, the rum weren't no good and second, they purposely wanted the bottle not to looks like a rum bottle," Amos responded. "In the late teens, that be 1919, a laws passed called Prohibition, what made the distillin' and sellin' alcohol illegal. All of a sudden, the folks who likes their spirits gots no place to buy it. So, gangsters and such bought whiskey from Canada and rum from the islands. Then they'd smuggle it into the States."

"If it was illegal how did the smugglers get it into the country?" Rory asked.

"Son, where there's a will, there's a way. There's big money to be made by bringin' liquor here, so lots of folks were more than eager to help. Here's how they'd do it. The rum runners would fill a cargo ship with booze. Then they'd stop at designated spots along the coast, makin' sure they stayed at least three miles off shore. See that'd be international waters and the Coast Guard couldn't touch 'em. Then under the cover of night smaller boats would comes along side, load up, and head for the shore. At some secluded beach, they'd meets men with trucks and the boozes disappeared into the night."

"Weren't they afraid of getting caught as they came to shore?" I asked.

"That's one of the dangers, but if a smuggler was being chased, they'd just throws the stuff overboard. They'd lose the load but not gets arrested. There'd always be another load. You know that little beach on the northeast side of the bridge? That'd be a good drop site."

Excitedly Rory asked, "So you think where we found this bottle there may be a whole crate full that was dumped?"

"Not's likely. See the inlet is real shallow and if there's crates of liquor sittin' on the bottom they'd have been spotted. No, the loads that weren't recovered would be in the Intracoastal. You knows it gets pretty deep right there. This here bottle probably wound up where you found it 'cause of the Army Corps of Engineers and that big storm we had."

Rory and I were thoroughly confused at this point.

"The Army Corps dredged the Intracoastal last winter. This bottle was probably buried in the mud that was scooped up by their cranes. Now theys supposed to takes all that mud with 'em, in a big barge, but you know, sometimes folks get sloppy and some of the mud gets dumped on the sides. So, then that big storm comes along and your bottle gets swept into the inlet. That's what probably happened."

"Amos, you said the rum wasn't any good but people bought it anyway, why?"

"Folks really missed their drinks, so any hooch would do. The other unique thing about this rum was this fancy bottle. Folks would buy it and use it for other things, cause of how pretty it was."

"You sure seem to know a lot about liquor," Rory said.

"That's a fact, and a sad one too. I do knows way too much about liquor, and I tells you it ruint my life. So, don't you boys even start with it, you hear?"

We nodded our heads.

While we were entranced by Amos' story, Mr. Rosco joined us on the porch.

"Sorry Mr. Rosco, no snacks for you today," I said.

"And to thinks I's planning to have fish for dinner," Amos said.

"Oh, no we've got four nice sheepsheads in the cage. We just didn't snag any Rosco size fish today," I said.

"Well that's OK then, you had me scared. I thought you's treasure huntin' when you should be getting old Amos' dinner," he said with a smile.

"If there were more of these bottles, and they weren't broken, could you get the sea mud off them?" I asked.

"Sure. First soak 'em in some mineral spirits, then hit 'em hard with stiff brushes," Amos answered.

"And if we had some that were clean, do you think they would be worth something?" I asked.

"Probably so. The company what mades this rum weren't in business long. As soon as Prohibition ended the distillers that had been makin' rum for hundreds of years took the market back. So, it's for sure likely that there ain't too many bottles like that anywhere. They'd be valuable to the rights person. Why you so curious boy?"

"I was thinking if there were other bottles out there, maybe Rory and I could figure out a way to find them. We might become treasure hunters instead of lawn mowers."

"Well, you knows where you need to start?"

"Where?" Rory said.

"The library. Do some research on Prohibition and try to finds out more about this bottle."

"That sounds like the right next step, do some research," I said.

"Now, I wants your promise that no matter what you boys learn 'bout this bottle you ain't gonna take that raft anywhere near the end of the inlet. That big storm gave your mammas and me all the scare we can stand for a long while. Promise?"

Rory and I nodded and said, "uh huh."

"I wants to hear it," Amos said.

"We promise," Rory and I said.

Amos smiled and reached into his shirt pocket for his pipe. He tapped it three times on the arm of his rocker, brushed away the previous day's ashes and opened the tin of tobacco. Moments later, thin aromatic trails of the Flying Dutchman rose from his pipe shrouding the porch in the sweet extract.

Rory and I planned to be at the library as soon as it opened. Prior to leaving, mom quizzed us about spending a summer day in the library. The educator in her was pleased, but she was also somewhat suspicious. As I walked to the front door she inquired if we were going to look at naked people in *National Geographic*. My face contortion begged the question "*are you serious*?" Rory and I had research to do. There was no time for naked natives.

By midafternoon we had exhausted the library's resources. We knew more about rum runners and their tactics, and it seemed very likely that liquor would have been smuggled into the North Florida area. If that was true, then the inlet would be a prime location for the offloading. We struck out however on anything resembling the recovered bottle. Further exploration would require a trip to the big library in Jacksonville.

"You disappointed?" Rory asked as we peddled away from the library.

"I wish we would have found more information, but then again, if there were tons of books about it…well, it probably wouldn't be valuable. I'm thinking this bottle is so rare few people have ever seen one."

"Rare—you mean like a Carl "Yaterminski" Slurpee trading cup?" Rory said in a laugh.

"Exactly."

"Hey, I was thinking. What if we bought another swim mask and while we're out on the inlet we could scan the bottom just to see if there are any other bottles. Who knows, the storm may have washed in others." Rory suggested.

"Great idea, let's hit Tyson's before we head home."

The next morning we couldn't wait to get to the inlet. We did not even slow as we passed Amos'. He called out to us from his porch, "Boys what's the hurry? Fish ain't going anywhere."

With his hand cupped to his mouth Rory said, "There's treasure out there, and we're going to find it!"

"Yous be careful out there," Amos said and gave us a wave.

Cruising down Bent Tree Creek, Rory and I strategized that we could survey the inlet floor by dividing it into grids using the bridge pilings to define the sections. Once we had tied the raft to a piling, we released the line and took up positions on either side of the raft. Placing our faces in the water we scanned the bottom as we floated.

Amos was most likely correct that the inlet did not conceal any secrets. The shallow, clear water would have long ago given up any treasure. But, since the storm had disturbed the bottom, why not take a look. The previous summer's encounter with the razor toothed demon was in the forefront of our minds as we dipped our heads beneath the surface. We not only looked for purple bottles, but also for sharks and barracudas.

The charts in the library showed that the depths of the Intracoastal at the point where it received the inlet, was anywhere from twenty-five to fifty feet deep. If there were more purple bottles in the transitional area, finding and salvaging them was going to require significant ingenuity.

CHAPTER 35

THE FIRST DAY OF OUR underwater survey was panning out as Amos had forecasted. We found plenty of bottles on the inlet floor, but they were brown and the raised letters read "Budweiser." If old sinkers and lures were in high demand, Rory and I could have been millionaires. The inlet floor was littered with rusting hooks, sinkers, and the occasional anchor. Of the three anchors I saw, all were in good shape and there was a rope or chain attached to the eyelet. This meant that some chowder head tossed his anchor overboard, only to realize the line was not connected to his boat. Each time I saw one it made me chuckle.

We were, however, enjoying a good day with our rod and reels. At least I was. It appeared I was casting from the "right" side of the raft. I had pulled in three nice flounder, a Spanish mackerel, and a giant red fish. It was at least fifteen pounds, and I couldn't wait to show him to Dad. Pulling the mooring line hand over hand, much like the mariners of sailing ships have done for centuries, we slowly drew to the bridge for lunch and a much-needed escape from the sun. This had been an especially hot week, with the afternoon temperatures flirting with triple digits.

By late afternoon the sun had taken its westerly course. The resulting glints of light danced upon every ripple of the water. While enchanting, this glare was tough on the eyes. Some evenings the muscles around my eyes and cheeks would be sore from an afternoon of constant squinting. The tide was close to turning and soon we would be drifting back towards home.

"Well buddy, you ready to call it a day?" I asked.

"Yep, in fact I should have called it a day much earlier," Rory said referencing his poor luck.

As I stowed my gear I caught a whiff of something intriguing. Somewhere in the middle of the scents that surrounded us, the saltwater, the pressure treated boards, and the bait my nose perceived an enticing fragrance.

"Rory, do you smell that?" I asked.

"Sure do."

Turning like bloodhounds towards the source, I said, "That's charcoal, somebody's grilling on the beach."

Peering towards the small beach on the Northeast side of the inlet I saw a group of picnickers. They were milling around placing folding chairs and colorful umbrellas on the sand.

"Man, that smells good," I said. "Wish we knew them. I wouldn't think twice about bumming a burger."

"Do you know them?" Rory asked.

"I can't tell, sun's too bright and we're too far."

Just then a racing green MG crossed the berm and drove onto the hard beach.

"Hey, isn't that?" Rory started but I quickly cut him off.

"That's Lacy's dad's car!"

"But I thought they moved already?" Rory questioned.

"They were supposed to. Maybe he sold it before they left?" I said.

"No way, he loved that car," Rory said.

What I saw next had to be a mirage. The passenger door opened and a blonde lass emerged, my breath caught for a moment but I managed to mumble, "Lacy McAllister."

Rory reiterated what my heart had already perceived. "Hey, that's Lacy. I guess they haven't moved yet. And there's Callie."

After noticing Callie, Rory paused then groaned. His eyes registered the pursuer of his heart, Mary Grace DeLuca. "Oh man, why did she have to be there? Otherwise we would have gone over."

I looked at Rory incredulously, "Sorry pal, I know Mary Grace annoys you, but this RAFT is going to THAT beach. If you don't want to come, I suggest you put on your ski belt and start swimming for home."

Rory turned to me, then back to the beach and back to me again. "We'll stay just long enough to eat. That's all. Right?"

I didn't agree to Rory's demands. In fact, I could not have cared less what he was babbling about. I just wanted to get to the beach as fast as possible. Quickly we maneuvered from piling to piling towards the northern end of the span.

"Do you think they know it's us?" Rory asked.

"I doubt it, we're pretty far off. We wouldn't have known it was them if it wasn't for Mr. McAlister's car." This of course was a lie. I would have known that was Lacy walking across that beach a mile away. Pausing to catch our breaths at the channel lattice, I yelled to the girls.

"Hey Callie, Mary Grace, Lacy!"

All three girls turned in our direction. They shielded their eyes from the glare of the sun trying to determine who we were. Mary Grace figured it out first and shouted back,

"Hey guys. Come over here!"

We had been officially invited, exactly what I was hoping for. As we neared the beach I recalled that earlier in the day Rory said I smelled like Krystal onion hamburgers were stuck to my armpits. It had been a smoking hot day and I guess I was a little rank. Discarding my shirt and legionnaire's cap I dove into the cool water. Coming back to the surface, I was confident my saltwater bath had negated much of the stink.

Wading ashore I said, "Hey girls, what cha' doing here?" Immediately thinking it was a stupid question.

"We're having a beach cook out, what does it look like?" Lacy said.

"Well good, cause that's exactly what it looks like." Hearing the crunch of timber sliding on the sand I turned to see Rory hop from the raft into the shallows. "Hey, guys," Rory said.

Quick as a whip Mary Grace said, "Rory, did you row all the way over here to see me?"

Boys hovering at the edge of fourteen are not skilled in handling questions of this nature. Mary Grace's query was the equivalent of what men will face many times when asked, "Does this make me look fat?" Rory addressed it honestly, "Well, actually it was the smell of charcoal that brought us."

I was struggling to remain cool, but I feared my eyes betrayed me. They were uncontrollably drawn towards Lacy. She was wearing a pink one-piece bathing suit with a pair of light blue terry cloth shorts. I have no idea what the other girls were wearing, what I was wearing, or at that moment what year it was. I was blissfully lost in Lacyland.

Callie spoke up, "So is this your.... boat?"

"Raft!" Rory said. "Yes, this is our raft."

The girls waded into the water and surveyed the raft. Mary Grace stepped onto the deck, "Guys, this is really cool. Did you build it yourselves?"

"Designed, paid for, and built by us!" Rory said, conveniently omitting the help from Dad and his carpenter friend.

Lacy walked around the other side of the raft, "*Nessie*," she said. "I like that."

I had stepped back onto the deck to retrieve my shirt when Lacy approached the front and said, "Captain Jake, permission to board?"

"Permission granted," I held out my hand for her as she stepped up. I wished that moment would have lasted longer, but all too soon she was steady on the deck and released my fingers. The girls asked several questions and seemed genuinely interested, which only reinforced what Rory and I already knew—we were having the best summer ever!

Mr. McAlister approached along with a man I did not know. He greeted us and introduced the man as the new director of our YMCA.

Immediately, the two men began examining the raft. They quizzed us about the size of the drums, how many 2'x 4's it took, and were most curious about how we managed to navigate so far from home. Finally, Mr. McAlister said,

"Boys I am envious. This is a fine craft."

This compliment was within Lacy's earshot. I felt ten feet tall.

"Dad, can the boys stay and eat with us?" Lacy asked.

Stammering he said, "Honey, I don't mind them staying." Then looking at us, "Boys you're more than welcome. It's just that we are a little light on food. We had planned to catch some fish to add to the burgers we brought, but so far we can't even get a nibble."

Rory, seeing a window to escape the wanting stare of Mary Grace chimed in, "We understand Mr. McAlister, everybody has a bad day fishing occasionally."

No, we do not understand, I thought to myself. Leaving now is not how this is going down. I walked to the back of the raft and pulled the rope attached to the submerged fish keeper. Straining I hoisted the big redfish.

"Mr. McAlister would this help?"

"Land's sake boy, let me see that monster!" He waded out into the water and I passed him the fish. Lacy's dad questioned me about the tackle I used and where in the inlet I hooked it. He then attempted to pass the fish back to me. "Here son, you need to take this home."

"No sir, it's fine. Our freezer is already full of fish this size." OK, that last part was a tiny fib. This was by far the biggest fish I had ever landed. But like a poker player on a roll, I was all in.

"Are you sure?" he asked.

"Yes sir. Please take it."

"Well that would certainly solve our food shortage." He then turned to Lacy and held up the fish smiling. "Your friend is quite the fisherman."

You could have knocked me over with a feather when Lacy walked over and examined the redfish. "Wow, Jake you catch monster fish and build cool rafts. You're just full of surprises."

"Honey," Mr. McAlister shouted. "Look at this fish Jake brought us." Lacy's mom smiled and gave me a thumbs up.

"Mr. McAlister, I'll clean it if you like."

"No, no, son you've done enough. Lacy, why don't you get this champion angler a drink? Yes sir, that's a beaut," he said as he walked away.

Lacy approached me and softly took my elbow. "Come on, the cooler is over here."

I followed her lead. Heck, I would have followed her into a mine field at that point. Poor Rory was left standing by the raft, but all too soon Mary Grace's smothering attention was upon him. Lacy flipped open the lid on a green metal Coleman cooler, "OK, we have Shasta cola, root beer and black cherry."

"That's easy, black cherry."

I pulled the tab and felt the spray of black cherry mist. I downed the entire can in two large gulps.

"Thirsty there, Jake?" Lacy said smiling.

"It was a furnace out there today."

Our conversation was interrupted by Lacy's mom calling to her. Lacy handed me another soda then went to her mom. She returned carrying two paper grocery bags filled with ears of corn.

"Jake, would you mind helping me shuck these?" she asked.

"No," I said. As I looked at her a slight breeze was moving her golden hair and the western sun was perfectly illuminating her face. At that moment, she could have asked me to chop off my big toe and eat it and I would have put up only token resistance. I relieved her of one of the bags and we walked towards the shaded side wall of the bridge.

As we shucked the corn I asked, "I thought you'd moved?"

"No, the new house wasn't ready."

"Oh. Are you excited?"

"No, I'm dreading it .....and I do worry," she started, "I worry about going to a school where I don't know anyone."

I chuckled slightly, "Lacy, you of all people shouldn't worry about that."

"Why?"

"Because."

"Jake, 'because' is not an answer."

"Because people are drawn to you like a magnet."

"Really?"

"Lacy I'm not shining you on. You're nice, and you really care about people and you're not a phony. Don't worry you'll always have friends."

She smiled, "So where were you when the shark attacked?"

"About fifty feet on the other side of the bridge, there," and I pointed.

"Were you scared?"

"Terrified, not so much of the shark, but mostly when Rory fell in the water with the shark."

"Does the scar hurt?"

I twisted my arm to expose the still pink scar. "No, it doesn't hurt, but it feels sort of weird."

"I'm sure it was scary, but it made both of you legends. I mean that's a hard story to top."

The way she said it made me want to crow like a rooster, but I shyly smiled and turned away.

"Oh, hello there," she said excitedly.

Peeling back one of the ears of corn she found a caterpillar. It was about an inch long with brown and tan alternating bands.

"He's so cute," she said, as she placed it in my hand. The worm continued to arc its middle to move forward.

"I can put him to good use on the end of a hook."

"No, you will not, Jake Forrest." With that she scooped the worm from my hand and gently placed him on a strand of sea oats. "Be free little guy and stay away from Jake's hooks," she said.

This was all very strange. Lacy and I had been friends for years, but this somehow seemed different. Callie and Mary Grace made no effort to join us, and Lacy seemed in no hurry to rejoin them. However, once we were finished with the corn, Callie approached us to announce we were going to play Frisbee "monkey in the middle" and of course Rory and I were the monkeys.

Prior to dinner, Mr. McAlister drove Rory and me to the 7-Eleven so we could call our parents. Upon returning to the beach, we were presented with plates piled high with bacon burgers, corn on the cob, and baked beans. I was more than happy to let the adults enjoy my redfish.

The setting sun and the incoming sea breeze conspired for a perfect evening with our friends. There was to be a full moon that night and given our location it would be a magnificent spectacle as it rose from the Atlantic. Mr. McAlister brought over a shovel full of hot coals and I used my Boy Scout skills to get a fire going. As dusk rolled over Florida's northeast corner, the five of us were settled around a crackling fire.

We were conversing about nothing when Callie reacted as though she just remembered something. She reached into her tote bag and produced a box of sparklers. "Let's do a sparkler wish."

"What's a sparkler wish?" Rory inquired.

Mary Grace answered, "You light a sparkler and wait until it is almost burned out. Then you throw it in the water. If it is still sparkling when it hits the water, you get your wish."

"Seems simple enough, I'm in," I said.

Callie handed each of us a sparkler. Rory quickly moved his towards the fire, but was rebuffed by Mary Grace, "No we have to light them together or it won't work."

"Holy cow, there's a lot of rules with this sparkler wish thing," Rory said.

Upon Callie's command, we placed the tips of our sparklers in the fire. Rory's fired first and with quick succession the remaining rods began to sparkle. We walked around making sparkler circles and shapes. Rory left the group and headed to the water. "Not yet Rory, you have to wait until it's real close," Callie cautioned.

Rory's body language gave witness to his impatience but he reluctantly rejoined the group. At the appropriate time, we made our way to the water's edge. Mary Grace, Rory, and Callie threw theirs first. Watching Mary Grace's sparkler soar into the air, the rest of us could have never imagined that one day she would rocket to the stars on the Space Shuttle Endeavor, STS 77.

Lacy and I were standing next to each other, slightly separated from the group. "Well, here goes," she said and launched her sparkler towards the dark water. As her sparkler arched skyward, mine left my hand. In full burn the two sparklers broke the plane of the inlet and were immediately extinguished.

"So..." Lacy said.

"So what?"

"What did you wish?"

"No way, if I tell you it won't come true," I said.

After a slight pause, she leaned towards me until her shoulder was against mine. "I bet I know," she said.

Never taking my eyes away from the inlet I said, "Yeah... yeah I bet you do."

Our special moment was all too soon interrupted by her Dad, "Lacy, you guys need to put out that fire and gather your stuff, time to go."

The fire doused we moved towards the cars. As we walked, the activities of the long day caught up with me, and perpetual yawns were hindering my ability to complete sentences. I received several more glowing remarks about my angling abilities and how I rescued the cookout. Rory and I placed our rods and tackle boxes in the trunk of Mrs. McAlister's Oldsmobile. Earlier we had moved *Nessie* to the protection of the bridge, confident she would be safe until we returned at first light. I sat down in the back seat and Lacy slid from the opposite side until she was right next to me. Realizing the premier shotgun seat was available, Rory jumped at the chance to remove himself from Mary Grace's clutches. His scheme backfired as there were six of us in the car: Callie was in the back with Lacy and me, and so Mary Grace took the middle spot in the front. Had she slid any closer to Rory, she would have been in his lap.

My house was the closest so I was the first to be dropped off. As I exited the car I leaned in the front window and thanked Mrs. McAlister. I glanced back to Lacy one last time and mouthed "bye," then walked towards my front door.

"Jake, wait." Lacy said as she pushed open the car door.

I turned as she approached. "Are you going to the July 4th celebration?" she asked.

"Of course," I said.

"Well…. would you like to meet and hang out?"

"You'll still be here?" I asked.

"Yes, we leave the next morning."

"Well sure. I'd expect the gang would meet for the fireworks, just like always," I said with slight confusion.

"No, before the fireworks, just you and me."

Giving my brain a chance to wake me from this dream, I paused for the briefest second before I said, "Sure."

"Here," she handed me a slip of paper. "Call me and we can plan where to meet."

"OK, 'night."

"Goodnight Jake," she said with a smile and returned to the car.

I walked up the steps to my door but it really wasn't necessary, I could have floated. Mom heard the door shut and called me into the kitchen.

"Jake honey, is that you?"

"Yes ma'am!"

"Well, come tell me about it," she said.

I wandered into the kitchen. Mom was at the table placing S&H Green Stamps into a collection book.

"There" she said. "I have enough for my new lamp."

"I thought Dad was saving stamps for a bike?" I said.

"No, he only thinks he is. So, did you have a good time?"

I nodded.

"Well, good." By this time, the musky scent of my long day enveloped the kitchen. "Whew, you smell like a long shore man. Go straight to the bath, and use soap this time."

Later I lay in bed, enjoying the comfort of cool sheets, and replaying the events of the evening. I was puzzled by how things worked out. *Lacy was stuck to me like glue, and then she asked me out on a date, what the heck?*

At that moment, solving such a riddle was impossible. I didn't have near the required maturity and Mr. Sandman was about to ambush me. It was much later in life, after I had learned a bit more about women and their intricate confusing nature, that I formed a plausible theory. Our entire lives Lacy had seen me as a humorous friend. But when I presented that giant redfish to her dad, something in her brain clicked. She no longer saw me as just a kid. Suddenly I was a young man capable of being a provider. I had morphed from a goofy middle schooler to a guy who fought a shark, built his own raft, and braved the savage deeps to produce a mighty fish for their family feast.

Girls are so confusing.

CHAPTER 36

If we were to solve the mystery of the purple rum bottle, Rory and I needed the resources of a more substantial library. We pitched the idea to Dad and tossed in the notion that since we were going to Jacksonville, we could also take in a minor-league baseball game. Ever the trooper Dad quickly agreed.

We left the house around noon, but at the edge of our neighborhood Dad turned the wrong way.

"Where're we going?" I asked.

"I talked your mom into switching cars, we can ride to Jacksonville in air conditioned luxury."

"Good job Dad!"

"Well, it wasn't easy champ. You know your mom hates a hot car. And considering how the Country Squire is looking these days I'm surprised she went for it."

Dad was not exaggerating about the car's appearance. Because of the hail storm, the hood and roof were peppered with marble size dents, and the windshield was a spider web of cracks.

"Boys, there is one catch."

"What's that Mr. Forrest?" Rory answered.

"When we switch cars with Jake's mom we need to switch keys as well. Somehow, perhaps purposely, she lost her key to this car."

"So, what's the flaw?" I asked.

"She's at the beauty parlor."

"Hah! No way am I going in there," I stated.

"OK, have it your way," Dad said.

"Come on Jake, it can't be all that bad," Rory said. "I'm already sweating to death."

"Rory, you have no idea what you're agreeing too. It's a deathtrap. Dad, why can't you go in?"

"Jake, that's one of the reasons I wanted kids, so I would never have to walk in that place again. Those women and the smell, it gives me the willies," he said as he shook his head and shoulders.

I said to Rory, "This is a bad plan."

Dad pulled into the parking lot of Mindy's Beauty Shop and spotted Mom's Impala. With a theatrical voice, he said, "There she is lads, our magic carpet. And all that is required to prove your worthiness is to step through that portal and lay hold to the enchanted keys."

"You're really enjoying this aren't you, Dad?" I asked. "Come on Rory, since you were so keen on this you get to go in first."

Rory confidently grasped Mindy's front door and swung it open. He stopped and attempted to step back, but I was directly behind.

"Too late, go on," I said and pushed him forward.

The shop was small, but Mindy incorporated Henry Ford's assembly line concept to its fullest: wash, cut, dry, and pay on the way out. There were wet headed women parked everywhere. Beyond the disturbing visual images, the breathable air had been removed and replaced by noxious chemicals. We covered our noses with the hem of our t-shirts. Rory and I had no difficulty with fish guts languishing in the broiling sun, but this mixture of hair toxins was more than we could bear.

I managed to locate Mom, but she looked like she just walked off the set of *Star Trek*. There appeared to be tin foil interwoven through her hair. Rory and I quickly approached her, trying desperately to keep our eyes diverted to the floor.

"Hi boys, ready for your big day?" she asked.

"Yes ma'am, but dad said we needed to swap keys," I replied.

"I suppose your father is waiting outside? The big fraidy cat. Here you go," she said and leaned over to give me a kiss.

"Mommmm, not here. Besides you look like you're from another planet," I said.

She smiled and gave us a wave.

We retreated from Mindy's quicker than the British fled Andrew Jackson's troops at the Battle of New Orleans. Once outside we took long joyous gulps of clean air. Dad was standing by the Impala as we approached.

"Well done men!" he proclaimed. "I am in the presence of true courage."

"That was horrible, Mr. Forrest. I think my lungs are ruined," Rory said.

Dad cranked the Impala and immediately pushed the AC lever to high cool. Soon we were cruising south on A1A in wonderful chilled comfort. This route to Jacksonville required us to cross the Intracoastal on the Mayport ferry.

Pulling onto the boat, I noticed an odd white car in front of us. It was very small yet it had four doors. I had never seen anything like it.

"Dad, who makes a Corina?" I asked.

Dad looked at the car and smiled. "Son that is a Toyota. It's Japanese."

"Japan!" I said with surprise. "They sell Japanese cars in America?"

"Yep."

"Would you ever buy one, Mr. Forrest?" Rory asked.

"Me? Heavens no. I remember Pearl Harbor. No, I can't imagine why any American would buy one. It's a fad, won't last."

Rory and I exited the car and walked to the railing. "You know," I mused, "Amos is probably right, there wouldn't be any treasure in the waterway, it would be on the edges. The problem is how we get to it."

Rory and I had been mulling over this problem ever since we found the rum bottle. We had thoroughly surveyed the inlet locating nothing of value. No, if there were more of the purple bottles or other loot it would most likely be at the mouth of the Intracoastal where the depth increases dramatically. It was too dangerous to take *Nessie* that far, so we had to devise another way to safely reach the deeper areas.

"Guys come on, we're about to dock," Dad said.

Prior to leaving the rail, I noticed a crab fisherman hauling up his pot. "Rory check that out."

The crabber pulled a small cage to the surface. It was not much different than our fish keeper. Instead of lifting the pot all the way onto the deck, he had rigged an old surfboard, alongside his boat. He placed the pot on the board, emptied the contents, rebaited it, and slid it back into the water. The man's ingenuity intrigued me.

Once downtown we located the architectural tragedy that was the main library. It contained far too many angles and was highlighted in lime green tiles. Lime green is great on a Plymouth Road Runner, but bad for a repository of books. However, with three stories, it represented our best chance to solve the mystery of the bottle. We commandeered a six-chaired table and quickly covered its surface with books. Dad had been reading the *New York Times* and came by to check on us. Upon seeing the mountain of books, he said,

"Did you guys leave any books on the shelves?"

"This is serious research Dad," I said.

He smiled, "So, it looks like you guys are going to be at this for a while. I'm going to take a walk down by the St. Johns River. I'll be back in an hour or so."

Locating detailed information about not only rum runners, but also their activities in North Florida, it seemed increasingly plausible that our beloved inlet may have served as an offloading point for illegal liquor. Rory was flipping through a book entitled, *Rums of the Caribbean* when he said, "Eureka, I found it!" I sprung from my chair and it slid back with a loud squeaky scrape. For these egregious infractions the librarian directed a stern look in our direction.

I quietly came to Rory's side. There before us in all its glory was a color photo of our bottle. The caption said, *Blood Bay Rum.*

"This is fantastic!" I said way too loudly and received a second stern look accompanied by a curt "shish."

There were two short paragraphs about the rum. It listed the manufacturer, that it was only produced for four years and in addition to the unique bottle, the rum was flavored with a hint of apple.

"Rory, this is perfect. It means that one of these bottles could be worth big bucks," I whispered.

"Hundreds? Thousands?" Rory asked excitedly.

"Maybe?"

Shushed again, we quickly stepped outside.

Rory said excitedly, "OK, we found one bottle which means there is a good chance there's more. We know they're rare and we have a logical guess of where they would be. Now we have to figure out a way to get them."

"Exactly. I've been thinking about that crabber with the surfboard we saw this morning," I said.

"Yeah, that was pretty smart."

"Right, so what if we figured out how to float some kind of retrieval device to the edge of the Intracoastal?"

"Something that would sink." Rory said. "I think you're definitely onto something."

As we spoke Dad approached and announced we needed to pack up and head over to the ball park if we wanted to catch batting practice.

We enjoyed the minor Leagues' version of America's favorite pastime to the fullest that Saturday evening. After a wholesome meal of roasted peanuts, ball park hot dogs, and several sodas, we settled back into our seats, to scrutinize every pitch.

Rory and I were mostly quiet on the drive home. I'm sure like me he was pondering how to salvage the purple treasure that we were convinced littered the darker recesses of the inlet floor. The Blood Bay bottles were jettisoned by desperate rum runners nearly fifty years' prior. Perhaps the very night that Lindbergh crossed the Atlantic or the evening that a bookstore owner in Nuremburg placed the first copies of Hitler's *Mein Kampf* on his shelves. For decades, the bottles silently waited for the right treasure hunters to locate, salvage, and share them with the world. The wait would soon be over.

CHAPTER 37

By July 3rd, our deep-water salvage system was finally ready to test in the inlet. If it performed well, we would employ it at the edge of the Intracoastal Waterway, the most likely resting place for the Blood Bay bottles. We modified the fish keeper pet cage by securing a piece of plywood to the open door. This would scoop anything on the bottom as we drug it across the floor of the inlet. To ensure it sank upright and stayed firmly on the bottom, we placed a bar bell weight in the back of the cage. The final hurdle was to devise a way to place the cage in deep water before sinking it. This brought us back to the crabber's surfboard. We solved that problem with a kid's Styrofoam surfboard from Tyson's.

Placing the salvage cage on the surfboard, we could let the tide take it out. With a yank of the guy ropes, the cage would slide off the surfboard and sink. We ran another rope through a hole in the surfboard which we reinforced with duct tape.

The natural curve of the inlet into the Intracoastal waterway meant that we could adjust the place where the cage would end up based on how far into the middle of the inlet we released it. In our sea trials, the cage pulled smoothly along the bottom and once scooped up a beer bottle. The prototype was ready for a deep-water dive.

We were both excited as we pulled *Nessie* onto the little beach on the Northeast side of the bridge. With the cage positioned on top of the surfboard and all ropes in place, Rory looked at me and said, "Well, here she goes." He pushed the surfboard into the current and it floated as planned towards deeper water.

I held the rope attached to the basket while Rory held the rope on the surfboard. Patiently, we watched as it slowly drifted to the area we targeted. "Now!" I said. Rory snatched the line and the surfboard leaped forward causing the cage to slide off and immediately sink.

"Just like we planned it," Rory said.

I took in the slack of the two ends of the rope that looped through the cage. Once the reins were tight, I slowly pulled the cage along the inlet floor. In these early efforts, we became prematurely excited each time the cage snagged on the bottom. But immediate success was not to be. Seven times we launched and seven times an empty cage was hauled to shore. The eighth effort proved successful…sort of. Two softball size rocks lay nestled in the back of the cage. We were elated. If it could scoop rocks, it could certainly scoop rare rum bottles. Several launches later we felt tension on the lines and knew we had something. Anxiously, we pulled the cage to the shallows and Rory bolted into the water to retrieve it.

"There's something in here, and it's not a rock," Rory said.

"Is it a bottle?" I asked.

"Nope, not a bottle either. It's a… a…." Rory was rubbing the object attempting to remove some of the sediment.

"Well, what is it?" I demanded.

He looked at me and smiled, "It's an alarm clock."

"What?"

Rory tossed the clump of barnacles towards me. As it landed, one of the bells made a faint "ding" sound.

"Well, it's a step up from a rock," I said.

While stopping for lunch Rory suggested we move *Nessie* just off shore. That way, we could launch the surfboard further into the current allowing us to reach even deeper water.

Anchoring forty feet off the beach, we again released the treasure finder. Just as the board neared the target drop zone, I picked up the faint sound of an outboard motor. This was worrisome as a thick piece of rope was stretched across the inlet. If a boat were to run over the tow lines it would destroy the prop and we would lose our cage.

"Rory, pull it now!" I said. Rory snatched the rope and the cage descended. Quickly he tried to reel in the surfboard. As the boat entered the inlet we both groaned. It was Wade Brown. Upon seeing us he revved the motor bringing the boat up to plane and steered towards the surfboard.

As Wade neared the float, he cut the engine. There was another person in the boat and when he turned towards us, I immediately recognized him. It was Skyler, the older boy that Deputy Bowers roughed up the previous year when he caught them smoking pot on the Twain lot.

Shouting to insure he could be heard, Wade said: "Well, well, look what we got here, Turd #1 and Turd #2. You num-nuts got a surfboard huh?" Wade brought the boat alongside, pulled a knife from his pocket and cut the rope. He examined the board, then used the knife to enlarge the rope hole to the size of a dinner plate and placed his face in the opening.

"Hey, look Sky, little Rory and Jake made a picture frame." They both laughed. Wade looked at us, smiled an evil grin and proceeded to stab the board into numerous pieces. The remnants, big and small drifted off with the tide towards the ocean.

I considered arming myself with a couple of sinkers. But, we were somewhat trapped and with two of them we were definitely outgunned. Wade re-fired the motor and approached us.

"What are you twerps doing with a kid's surfboard tied to a rope?"

"We're fishing Wade. So, buzz off!" I yelled back.

"That's bull crap and you know it. Y'all are up to something, and I'll figure it out. And if it's something that I want.... I'll just take it from you."

Rory sneered back at Wade, "Oh yeah Wade, you'll figure it out, just like you figured out how to fail ninth grade, again!" Wade's eyes contracted to mere slits and his face reddened with anger.

"Perkins, you've been asking for it for way too long." He looked to Skyler and pointed to the bottom of the boat. "Sky, I think Gilligan over there has given us permission to board."

Though bigger and older than Wade, Skyler was obviously his subordinate and content to do his bidding. He stood up in the boat, awkwardly trying to keep his balance. He hoisted a rope from the bottom of the boat, dangling from the end was a Danforth anchor. As it slowly spun, the silver coated prongs glistening in the sun. Wade's boat was less than ten feet from us when Skyler engaged his arm in a circular motion. Releasing the rope on the upswing, the anchor soared high into the air, then like a Dauntless Dive Bomber arched over and began its descent. Calculating its trajectory, I stepped back. The anchor crashed into *Nessie's* deck. The claw impacted with sufficient force to penetrate the plywood.

Rory, who was also transfixed by the nautical missile, suddenly screamed out in pain.

"Ahhhggh!"

I turned and he was holding the side of his head and ear. His face contorted and eyes tightly shut. He fell to his knees and in a mix of anger and tears shouted,

"Damn it! Damn it!"

Next to Rory lay a partial bag of ice. Much of the contents, ping pong sized cubes, were spilled across *Nessie's deck.* I looked to our tormentors who by this time were laughing riotously.

While Rory and I were distracted by the thrown anchor, Wade hurled the bag of ice catching Rory squarely in the ear.

I wanted to kill Wade. I wanted to comfort Rory. But Skyler was pulling hard on the anchor rope and in a matter of seconds he would be able to board. I leaped to the embedded anchor and desperately moved it back and forth trying to free it from the deck. It broke loose and I lifted it fully intending to return it with extreme prejudice. Skyler anticipated my intentions and violently yanked the rope. Feeling the friction burn my hand, I released the anchor but not before losing my balance. I stumbled two steps before falling into the water, my head landing dangerously close to the side of their boat.

I surfaced to their laughter. As I attempted to clamber back onto the raft, Wade cranked the motor and whipped the boat around. He pulled the motor forward, lifting the prop from the water. The blades spinning at full throttle passed within inches of my feet as I rolled onto *Nessie*.

"Later losers," Wade said and steered up the inlet.

I lay on the raft breathing hard. My heart raced and I could feel the vibrations through the plywood decking. Rolling over I looked at Rory. He was sitting on the deck, his knees pulled to his chest gently rocking back and forth. No longer balling, he had somewhat collected himself. The remaining tears in Rory's eyes were attributed not to pain but to raw fury. His right ear was fire truck red and swollen.

"You gonna be all right?"

With fire burning in his dark eyes, he said "Jake, I hate him so bad." He sniffed again, and then rubbed his forearm across his eyes. "I'll be all right. But I'm gonna kill him. Just let me have a chance and I swear to God I'll kill him."

Rory's words were measured, not spoken with boisterous bravado, but rather very matter of fact. The certainty of his tone unnerved me.

"This could be a problem," I said. "If that weasel learns what we're searching for, the jig is up."

With a determined gaze, Rory responded, "Well, we're just going to have to be extra careful, aren't we?"

CHAPTER 38

I WOULDN'T TURN FOURTEEN FOR another month, yet here I was on the cusp of my first date. Lacy McAlister and I would be celebrating our nation's 197th birthday, as a couple. The first part of the day was painfully long, worse than waiting for Christmas. Late in the afternoon, I was in my room trying to make my hair look cool when Mom tapped on my door.

"Jake honey, you about ready?"

"Yes ma'am."

"Good," she said as she walked into my room. "Before you leave I wanted to talk with you."

My Spidey sense activated. A "chat" with your mom usually signals trouble.

"Jake come sit with me for a minute," she said as her hand patted the bed.

Sitting down I asked, "What's up?"

"Well, I must confess I overhead your phone conversation the other night and I understand you will be in the company of a young lady this evening?"

Confirmation again that Mom was secretly with the CIA. "Yes ma'am, Lacy and I are meeting up."

Brandishing a sweet smile, she said, "I think that is just wonderful. You two have been good friends for so long and I know they're moving so this will be a nice night for you two."

"Yes ma'am," my mind still wondering where this was going.

"Honey is that the shirt you're going to wear?"

This seemed to me a terribly obvious question. My shoes were on, my hair combed, and I was about to walk out the door. Of course, this was the shirt I was going to wear. Later as I became more enlightened about such inquiries, I understood they weren't really questions at all. They were opportunities for me to reconsider what was clearly a bad decision.

"Well, sure Mom, I love my Joe Namath jersey."

"Yes, I know you do. In fact, you're wearing it in just about every picture I have of you over the last two years. But since you're going to be with Lacy tonight, might you consider wearing something, well, a bit more handsome?"

A bit more handsome, what does that even mean? I thought.

She walked to my closet. "Since its July 4th, what if you wore this nice blue shirt?" She retrieved a collared shirt with three buttons.

"No way mom, that's a dorky shirt."

Reaching again into the closet she came out with a solid red Hang Ten t-shirt. By this time, Dad had wandered down the hall and was leaning on the door frame, "Go with your Mom on this Jake, ladies like a man that knows how to dress."

I agreed to wear the red shirt, but she continued loitering in my room. There was clearly more on her mind.

"Now there's one other thing. Here," and she tried to hand me a five-dollar bill.

"Mom thanks, but I have money."

"Jake, I know you do. And I want you to know your father and I are so proud of how you work for your money. You are quickly becoming a grown up young man. "

She paused for a moment, glanced at the floor, and then turned back to me. Reaching out she took my hand, "Son, you should also know that Will would be very proud of you. He loved you so much and if he were still with us, I guarantee you he would be out on that raft with you and Rory."

I paused to consider Mom's comments about Will. This was the first time I heard her speak of him in casual conversation. Immediately tears flooded my eyes.

"I know he would Mom," I quietly said. We embraced, both crying on the other's shoulder.

Momentarily Mom cleared her throat, pushed back her hair, and dabbed her eyes before returning her focus to the five dollars.

"I want you to take this money. Use it to buy both you and Lacy something to eat and then take her on the Ferris wheel."

"The Ferris wheel is kind of lame Mom. I want to ride something fun."

"Jake, this is one of those times you need to trust your Mom. There are few things in life more romantic than a ride on a Ferris wheel."

"Are you sure Mom?"

"100% sure, Jakey."

Thump, thump, thump, came loud knocks on the front door.

"That's Rory, thanks for the money. Bye!" I said as I raced to the door.

Rory and I rode our bikes to the harbor arriving nearly an hour before I was to meet Lacy. This allowed me some quality time with the guys. Had I known what I was walking into I would have avoided my sensitive, caring friends all together. No sooner had I dismounted my bike, then they set upon me like a pack of wolves. I was called a traitor for abandoning my buds in favor of a girl. The neatness of my hair and my red shirt also seemed to be fodder for their enjoyment. I took it all in stride because I knew every one of them would cut off their hand to trade places with me.

After they finished roasting me, we recalled the previous year's celebration with the redneck escapade.

Sean proudly defended his actions, "You can't deny that I make things exciting. And none of you knot heads will ever forget that 4th of July!"

We reluctantly agreed, none of us would ever forget it. Of course, near death experiences tend to stick with you.

I arrived at the DeLuca Pizza trailer a few minutes before Lacy. Standing there I desperately trying to be cool. However, I was fearful my exterior revealed a nervous little boy. Then, through the crowd, my princess approached and my heart stopped. She wore a blue shirt, white shorts, and sandals. Her summer blonde hair was down but was held in place by a hair band covered in American flags.

"Hey Jake," she said and seemed so calm, so normal, so unlike I felt.

"Hey Lacy," I responded. *Yes, that's good Jake just repeat everything she says, that'll impress her.*

"Well, you look nice in your patriotic red shirt."

Holy cow, my mom was right! Now I am in a pickle, she complimented me, what do I say?

I went with the first thing that popped in my mind. "I like your hair thingy, very American."

"Oh, thanks, that's sweet of you to notice."

My mind eased, *Yes,* I thought. *It is very sweet of me to notice, because that's the kind of sweet guy I am.*

Desiring to be a good date I inquired, "What would you like to do first?"

"How about we get something to drink and take in the sights?" she answered.

Approaching the DeLuca trailer, I was pleased to see Mary Grace's older brothers were working. This meant half price sodas and pizza. Lacy reached in her pocket for money, and I said, "No way, tonight is on me. Consider it a going away gift."

"Thank you, Jake, you're a thoughtful gentleman," she said with a smile.

As we sipped our drinks, I considered that *now I was sweet and a thoughtful gentleman.* I was hitting on all cylinders. But sometimes, when things are going well, fate has a way of sticking out its big foot to trip you. From behind I heard the inbred voice of Wade Brown.

"Well if it isn't my old friend Turd #1. Hey where's your Siamese twin, little Rory? Is he at home icing his ear? Get it…ice in his ear?"

I spun around, ready to spit venom. But I found myself face to face with not only Wade, but also his Neanderthal partner Skyler and four other skuzz buckets. I was greatly outnumbered and had no real options. But then again, it's not like they were going to attack me in front of the whole town. Besides there were cops everywhere.

"Wade, why don't you do the world a big favor and kill yourself?"

"You're lucky I don't feel like messing with you tonight, you little prick."

Lacy touched my arm, "Come on Jake, let's go."

"Lacy baby, you are looking foxy tonight," Wade said with a repulsive leer.

"Bug off Wade," Lacy said.

"Don't be that way Lace. Besides," and he held up a can of Sprite. "We got some good stuff."

"I've already have a drink, no thanks," she said.

"You ain't never had anything like this. It's not Sprite, its homemade cherry wine. And it's got a real kick. Come on…try some."

I took a half step forward partially shielding Lacy, "Oh yeah, we want some of that. You probably squished the cherries with your stank fungus toes. I'd sooner drink my own pee!"

Lacy shot me a glare that implied she could handle this. "So, that's why you're saying such ugly things, you've been drinking."

Lacy was like a kindergarten teacher, gently admonishing a little boy. Of course, I was thinking, *No, no you don't gently admonish Wade Brown. You hit him across the bridge of the nose with a pool cue. That's what he understands.*

Wade responded to Lacy, "Are you sure you don't want to ditch the twerp and have some fun with us?" With a sleazy grin, he added, "You're old enough to have a good time."

My mind ginned up a perfect response, *Yes Lacy, don't you want to forgo everything that is sweet and gentlemanly and join Beelzebub here and his hoard of minions.*

"No thanks Wade," she said. And with that she lightly grasped my arm, and we walked away. I was amazed how effectively she handled

Wade. Granted, she was a pretty girl, and that was certainly an advantage. But it was still impressive.

We made our way through the craft tents browsing the local artisan's wares. Then, as Mom had been spot on about the Joe Namath shirt, I chose to go with her suggestion regarding the Ferris wheel. However, the line was terribly long and I decided to circle back later in the evening. I was about to suggest we find something to eat when I saw Wade and his fellow delinquents in line for the Tilt-A-Whirl.

"Lacy, come here," I said as I walked to the railing encircling the ride.

"What is it?" she asked.

I pointed towards the riders waiting in line, "It's Wade and his posse."

"So?"

"Don't you see what he's doing?" Wade was wolfing down a foot-long corn dog and taking huge gulps from the Sprite can. "Wade is about to get on the Tilt-A-Whirl full of cherry wine and a corn dog. This could be great."

"Jake, I wish you had a kinder attitude about Wade. You know he has a terrible home life. He's probably not a bad guy, he just needs some guidance."

Lacy's attitude regarding Wade explains why she would spend her adult life ministering to children in Panama. While attending nursing school, she fell in love and eventually married a medical student. Forgoing a pampered country club life, they instead established a free clinic serving rural areas in Central America.

"You know, Lacy," I began. "That's one of the things I really like about you. You see the good in everybody. And that's groovy, but I've got to ask you. Has anyone ever bent your arm so far behind your back that you thought it was going to tear out of the socket? At the same time, this person is calling you names that I couldn't even spell in front of a girl. Then your face is shoved into a mud puddle. I mean completely under water, to the point that you when you took a shower that night dirt ran from your ears? And if a mud puddle wasn't available, a pile of dog crap was even better."

Lacy slowly shook her head sideways.

"Well the boys in this town who have crossed paths with Wade know exactly what that feels like. And for most of us it has happened more than once. Yesterday, he and Prince Valiant attacked us in the inlet. They destroyed some of our stuff and lobbed an anchor at us that punched a hole in *Nessie.* And, oh yeah, Wade hit Rory in the head with a bag of ice that almost knocked him out. I think he needs more than just some guidance."

Lacy was quiet as I vented. "I know you like to see the good in everybody, but with Wade there just isn't any good."

Realizing I just "went off" off on my date, I halfway expected her to leave. But she didn't. She said nothing as she processed what I said.

"Jake that's a good point. I guess since he's never hurt me I didn't think about it from your side. I can't imagine being bullied like that."

She paused and we stood silent for several moments. Then looking towards Wade she said, "OK, so what are you hoping to see here?"

"Something for the ages, something memorable."

"All right, let's hope for that," she said. A short moment later she asked, "So what's the other thing?"

"What's the other thing what?" I answered with genuine confusion.

"You said that finding the good in everybody was one of the things you really liked about me. What else?"

Was she messing with me? What's the other thing? The other thing I really liked about Lacy was a very long list. You name it and I liked it. Her smile that was a little crooked on one side. The light sprinkling of freckles across her nose, and the way she pulled her hair back over her left ear. I liked the little scar under her chin, a souvenir from a bad fall at the skating rink. I liked how her laugh raised several octaves when something was really funny. How was I to answer?

I decided to go with her smile. However, meeting her gaze, her face bathed in the softening afternoon light, I was drawn to the deep spherical pathways to her soul.

"It's your eyes."

"What about my eyes?"

I knew what I wanted to say but was afraid it would sound dumb. She stared at me, patiently waiting for my response.

"Well, it's…it's just that the color of your eyes reminds me of the ocean. You know that deep blue when the afternoon sun hits it just right."

She offered no reaction. For a moment, I thought she was going to break into her high-pitched laugh at my stupid compliment. But then a blushing smile passed over her face. She softly patted my hand, "Jake Forrest you're one in a million."

The Tilt-A-Whirl screeched to a halt and the next group of riders, including Wade Brown, climbed aboard.

"Here we go," she said. "Let's see something memorable."

CHAPTER 39

THE RIDE'S WORN GEARS CREAKED and the undulating platform groaned to life. Slowly, the Tilt-A-Whirl rotated counter clockwise, causing the cars to roll back and forth on their rails. This simple amusement ride relies on the physical laws of centrifugal force to thrill its passengers. As the platform moves over a series of dips, wicked gravitational pulls cause the cars to spin at extreme speeds. This was the ride Wade Brown willingly boarded after consuming a corndog and unknown quantities of homemade cherry wine.

Lacy and I were standing at the back side of the ride, directly across from where the passengers entered. Wade, Skyler, and another guy clambered into a car, with Wade sitting in the middle. As the ride began turning, Wade and his friends were the loudest passengers by far. As his car came past us, he was shouting, "Faster, faster!" Wade and his friends appeared to be having the time of their lives.

Lacy said, "Well what is so memorable about this? They're just acting like idiots."

"They haven't hit the perfect spin yet. Just wait."

The next time Wade's car passed us it had entered a perfect spin. Whirling faster and faster, the car was a red blur and I mentally counted—five, six, seven revolutions. Just as quick as it began, the spinning ceased and the car rolled back and forth like a pendulum.

Wade's jubilant reveling had also ceased. He was sitting perfectly still with his head back and eyes closed. The next time he came by he was leaning forward and rubbing his forehead. The guy sitting to Wade's right said something to him. Wade glanced in his direction and that's when it happened. With no warning and apparently, no regard for his friend's life, Wade Brown exploded. It was not just a little vomit. The term, throw up was woefully inadequate to describe what occurred. A red stream of cherry wine, corndog, and bile blasted from Wade's mouth with the pressure of a volcanic geyser. The torrent swathed his friend's chest in sticky red hurl that resembled half chilled Jell-O. The kid looked like he'd been shot.

"Oh gosh, that is so gross!" Lacy cried as she turned away.

Lacy wasn't the only one turning away. Wade's friend Skyler had no intentions of being the next victim. He stood up in the moving car intent on jumping, but his escape was foiled as the car began another spin cycle. I, however, wasn't turning away. I was going to enjoy every second of Wade's cherry wine reversal.

Given the sheer amount of the initial discharge, it seemed logical Wade had nothing left inside him. That would be an incorrect conclusion. The next group of riders stood single file on the metal gang plank that ran parallel to the rotating platform. The majority of them were clueless of Wade's intestinal carnage. Like ignorant old world peasants, the helpless rabble stood unaware that a fire breathing dragon was poised to rain hell upon them. Wade's stomach convulsed again and every muscle in his body seized causing him to recoil from his slumped position. He faced forward this time, which was good for his car mates but bad for the peasants on the gangplank. The turning of the platform, the revolution of his car, and the proximity of the waiting riders came together in perfect synchrony. He wretched violently. The cherry red fountain landed on the metal space next to the platform, splattering the feet and legs of those in line.

Reminiscent of a 1950's grade "B" horror flick, the girls in line screamed and stamped their feet while the boys vaulted the rails attempting to escape. Finally, aware that red vomit was raining down on his Tilt-A-Whirl, the operator pushed the kill switch and the ride grinded to a halt.

The operator stormed towards Wade shouting a stream of obscenities. The gist of the message was "Get off my Tilt-A-Whirl!" Two of his friends shouldered Wade to the exit.

"Is it over? Can I turn around?" Lacy asked.

Through joyous laughter I stuttered, "Yes, it's over. At least I think it is."

Wade was jelly legged as he was led away from the ride. Lacy asked, "Was that memorable enough Jake?"

"From now until doomsday nothing will be more memorable!"

"Then let's go before that smell makes me do 'something memorable'."

Walking away I realized I should be a better person. I know my mom expected so much more of me, but I just couldn't resist. "Hey Wade, very nice," I said and clapped my hands in applause.

Wade glared at me and appeared to want to say something but was overcome by the dry heaves and dropped to all fours. With great determination, he gamely lifted his hand from the ground and gave me a trembling one fingered wave. I must confess, at that moment I halfway respected his moxie.

"Come on," Lacy said as she grabbed me by the arm. "Let Wade limp off with some dignity."

We walked away and I could not get the smile off my face. On one hand, it was a shame that the other guys, who had all been his victims, were not there to see Wade explode. Conversely, as I was the sole witness, I would get to tell the tale. In the ensuing years, the guys would gather around me and beg, "Jake tell us the Wade Brown cherry wine Tilt-A-Whirl story again."

Realizing we still had an hour before the fireworks I said, "Come on Lacy, there is something we have to do."

"Where are we going?"

"You'll see."

We wandered through the growing crowds slowly making our way towards the Ferris wheel. I stopped in front of it and pointed up. "Whatta ya say?"

"I say No Way!"

"Are you kidding, it's a Ferris wheel. A nice slow ride, with no spinning," I said spinning my finger in little circles for effect.

"I don't think so Jake. It hasn't been that long since we had pizza."

"Did you also have cherry wine and a corndog?"

My question needed no answer, she just smirked at me.

"Have you ever ridden a Ferris wheel?" I asked.

"No."

"Me neither. Come on."

"OK, but you better not laugh if I get scared."

I raised my right hand in the Boy Scout sign, "Scout's Honor."

Dusk was quickly overtaking our little corner of the world allowing the big wheel's bright lights to take center stage against the darkening sky. As our turn neared I turned to Lacy just to make sure she was still game.

"Don't look at me, I'm not chickening out."

We moved up the metal ramp preparing to enter our car. As Lacy sat down, the car rocked backwards startling her. She asked the operator, "Is it supposed to swing this much?"

"Absolutely little lady, that's what makes it fun."

I carefully sat down trying not to cause more rocking. The man closed the waist latch and inserted a cotter pin.

As we moved backwards Lacy exclaimed, "That's it? That little bar is all we have to keep us in this thing?"

"Lacy, this is a Ferris wheel. It doesn't go upside down."

"Jake, I could easily stand up and jump to my death."

"But, why would you? And what would I tell your mom?"

Appreciating my humor, she smiled. Every minute or so our car would move upward, but then stop as new passengers boarded. This process continued until Lacy and I were at the top of the circle.

"Wow," she said. "What a sunset."

Over the marsh shades of pinks and blues stretched clear to the horizon. "This is amazing Jake, good choice."

"I'm glad you like it."

Just as I said that, the car moved forward at full speed. As we plummeted towards earth, our stomachs hesitated slightly before catching up half way down. Lacy let out a short scream, and then grabbed my hand. She held it tight in her left hand and grabbed my wrist with her right hand. I was holding hands with a girl. If I had only known this was the effect of a Ferris wheel, I would have brought my entire summer's lawn mowing earnings and we could have ridden all night. Unbelievably, my mom was right again.

As we rounded the top for the second time, Lacy again squealed but this time it was in fun. The wind rushed past us and our stomachs dropped each time we crested. All too soon though, the ride slowed and we were the third car to exit. Our legs were just a little wobbly as we ran down the ramp.

"Jake, that was so cool!" she exclaimed.

The darkening sky suggested we head to the harbor and find the gang. Zig-zagging through the crowd I began to consider if the hand holding was not because she liked me, but because she was scared. Whatever the reason, it counted in my book.

This close to the start of the fireworks the harbor was a tightly packed sea of people, and it took some time to find the gang. They had secured a primo spot right on the sea wall where we could dangle our feet over the edge. As Lacy and I stepped around strollers and leashed dogs, I said to Freddie and Clay, "Make some room."

To my great relief none of the guys hounded me further about spending the evening with Lacy. Not being able to refrain any longer I relayed, in graphic detail, Wade's infamous ride on the Tilt-A-Whirl. I told it in a grand, but truthful fashion. An episode that amazing required no embellishment. I overheard Lacy tell Mary Grace and Callie, "If I live to be a hundred, that scene will be forever etched in my brain."

Perhaps it is perspective that can only be appreciated as an adult, but at that period of our lives Rory and I were obsessed with finding sunken treasure. However, on that magical night *real* treasure surrounded us. We were the best of friends, but no assemblage lasts forever. Just as water and time erode the shoreline, life, and the changes it brings erode even the tightest of groups. Our little troop was all there that July 4th of 1973. And we would remain intact until the town exhausted its allotment of fireworks, and then one of us would leave forever.

The first rocket pierced the night sky and exploded with a canopy of green sparks that trailed toward the dark water. Lacy and I were sitting next to each other on the sea wall. I placed my hand at my side and it brushed hers. Our fingers interlocked and remained that way so long as concussions shook the night. As it was with the Ferris wheel, the firework show was too brief. The finale was six huge fireballs, bursting in brilliant red, white, and blue. And then all was quiet.

We stood there not knowing what to say. Mary Grace and Callie were crying. Sean, in one of his less than stellar moments, made a smart aleck comment and was harshly rebuked by the girls. Final hugs were traded and like the smoke from the fireworks, our friends gradually drifted away, leaving Lacy and me alone at the harbor.

"So where do you need to meet your parents?" I asked.

"On that side road, just across the tracks."

As we stood there, the last of the crowd slowly made their way past. The wharf light above us began to blink and then went out altogether. A harbinger perhaps that our time together was ending.

"Jake, I really had a great time tonight. Thanks for making me ride the Ferris wheel. I'll never forget it."

That meant she would never forget me. And that thought brought a big goofy smile to my face.

"What's that smile about?" she asked.

"It's about you, I'll miss you Lacy. But I'm glad we could hang out tonight."

"Well I guess there is nothing left but goodbye," she said solemnly.

With a scale of boldness never previously known, I said, "No, there's one more thing." And I leaned forward to kiss her. Our lips met and held fast for a heavenly moment.

We parted and looked at each other, before a simultaneous blush overtook us.

"Goodbye, Jake." And with that she let go of my hand.

"Bye, Lacy."

CHAPTER 40

UNDER A LESS THAN PROMISING sky, I arrived at the Twain lot well ahead of Rory. Gun metal gray clouds blanketed the sky and the air was heavy with moisture. Rain, so long as it was not accompanied by lightning or deadly hail, was no reason to ruin a good day's fishing. And the quest for fish would have to be sufficient for today, as the tides were not agreeable for treasure hunting.

Despite the gloomy conditions, I whistled happily as I stowed my gear on *Nessie*. With each recollection of the previous night's events, I sported an uncontainable smile. Sitting on the raft I slid my feet into the flow of the creek. The cool briny water instantly saturated my shoes. These Keds were my raft shoes and the daily exposure to sun, saltwater, and mud had taken its toll. Once navy blue, they were now the color of old denim jeans. I moved my feet up and down hoping the sloshing action would suppress their dank musty stench. They smelled so bad that Mom forbid me to bring them in the house, nor was I to leave them on the back porch. She jokingly suggested I tie them in the oak tree to keep bears away.

Rory arrived and jumped from his bike. "Hey man, did you bring your rain slickers?"

"Rain coats are for sissies!" I responded.

Rory clambered aboard and placed his gear in the second five-gallon bucket.

"So, I saw you holding hands with Lacy last night."

"So, what?"

"Well?

"Well, what?"

"Don't play dumb with me pal, you know what I want to hear."

"No, I don't know what you are talking about," I said through a grunt as I pushed the raft to loosen it from the muddy bank.

"Did you kiss her?"

I gave Rory my best, *what are you talking about?* expression, and accented it by holding my hands palms upward.

"You did! You sure did, you sorry dog. I can't believe you kissed Lacy McAlister. My buddy kissed the prettiest girl in school. Man, oh man, wait'll the guys find out. My boy Jake got him a little smooch. Wow!"

"Are you finished?"

"I just can't believe you pulled it off. I would have bet my half of this raft that you'd chicken out at the last second."

"Can we just go fishing now?"

Inside, I was feeling mighty proud that Rory was making such a fuss. However, I refused to give him the satisfaction of a "kiss and tell."

Poling down the creek, I silently considered the risk and the resulting feat I had managed to pull off. It had been a truly magical evening. Lacy and I hanging out together, Wade losing everything he ate since Christmas on the Tilt-A-Whirl, and the best Ferris wheel ride of all time. The kiss was absolutely, without question, the perfect ending.

But what if she had turned away when I leaned in to kiss her? Although I had worked up a sweat pushing the raft, the thought of Lacy rejecting me sent a cold shiver up my spine. The awkwardness of that moment would have been unbearable. But such are the risks of life. It's like a favorite quip of Dad's, "You don't ask…you don't get." Last night had I not leaned in and asked for her kiss, this morning I wouldn't be reflecting on the best two seconds of my young life.

Large rain drops began pitting the surface of the creek. Within several minutes, it had become a steady, soaking rain.

"Looks like we'll be spending the day with Amos," I said.

"Yep, but we can't go empty handed," Rory answered as he laid his pole on the raft's deck. "And if I'm not mistaken that's a school of mullet over there."

Rory skillfully flung the cast net and hauled aboard five mullet.

"Now we can go to Amos'," Rory said.

The sounds of countless drops landing in the creek would have been an enjoyable symphony had Rory and I been sitting on Amos' porch, but we were still a few bends in the creek away. Finally, *Nessie* nudged his floating dock. Amos shouted to us,

"What in heaven's name has washed up on my dock? Lawd, Lawd you two is some kind of wet. You best be careful, ole Rosco might mistakes you for water rats and gets you. Especially Rory, you just eatin' size!"

Amos, who was always pleased with his own humor, laughed as we walked up the wooden ramp.

"Hey Amos, fine day for fishing," I said.

"Fine indeed," he responded.

Once under the covering of the tin roof, Rory and I shook like a couple of Labradors.

"Whew, it is really coming down. I am soaked to the bone," Rory said.

Amos groaned and slowly rose from his rocker. "Let's me go gits you two a towel. If-in you catch colds, I'd never hears the end of it from your mammas."

"What a sucky day!" Rory exclaimed.

"Hey now Rory, don't talk like that. Besides this ain't a bad day at all. In fact, I sort of likes listening to the rain bounce off the roof and splatter in the creek. So long as there ain't no tornados tearing up the marsh that is."

Amos returned with towels, sodas and Snickers candy bars and Rory and I settled in our customary spots along the porch railing.

"Where's Mr. Rosco?" I asked.

"Oh, he's holed up under the house somewhere, he be along 'rectly. So how goes the treasure huntin' boys?" Amos inquired.

Rory popped the cap off his drink and tossed the bottle opener to me. He then shared with Amos the details of our initial efforts with the salvage system. I added the part about Wade and Skyler hassling us.

Tapping his lips like he was thinking Amos asked, "Is this the boy what gots a white wooden boat and needs a haircut?"

"Yep, that's him," Rory answered.

"That boy seem like trouble, I bet it sticks to him like mud on a pig," Amos said. Commenting on our treasure hunting success he said, "Well, two rocks and an alarm clock. That ain't a bad start. Oh, I's been meanin' to shows you somethin'." He disappeared into the cabin and returned with the original bottle.

"Whoa! It's like a purple diamond," I said.

"Yep, it did clean up nice," Amos said.

"And there's no sharp point," Rory said.

"Nope. I snipped off the bad end and sand papered it." Amos passed the bottle to my anxious hands. I turned towards the sky. Even in the dull light of a rainy day the color was unbelievable. Together, the deep purple and the detail of the etching made for an astonishing piece of glass.

"Amos this is amazing. It's like something you would find in a fancy museum. No wonder people kept these bottles after the rum was gone."

"So, the rum was really bad, huh?" Rory asked.

"Better believes it. Today it'd be called rot gut. But folks gots to have their booze, so as long as it had a kick and it didn't make 'em go blind, they'd pay big for it." He took a big gulp of his Coke and smacked his lips, "Ahhhhhh, that's the good stuff."

After a short pause, he said, "Boys, they's somethin' needs sayin'. Now mind you I ain't proud of it, but I think you needs to hear it. I just pray you don'ts think no less of me once I'm done."

I was using the pointed end of the bottle opener to peel the rubber seal from the inside of the bottle cap, but stopped as Amos spoke.

"The stuff from this bottle, from any liquor bottle, is poison. Likes I said before, it ruint my life. Its ruint a many life and before you two is ever faced with a choice to take a drink, I wants you to know the truth."

He leaned forward and rested his elbows on his faded dungarees.

"Boys my mama raised me right. She's a God fearin', saintly woman, didn't tolerate no drinkin' or gamblin'. And if you valued your life, you best not take the Lawd's name in vain either. Buts when I started playin' ball, well I's on my own. So, it weren't too long before I started taggin' along with the older men to the beer joints. And if in you in the beer joint you gots to have a beer. This went on four, five nights a week.

"Well, once I gots to likin' beer, I started takin' a little nip of the hard stuff. Seemed like on those late-night bus rides there's always a bottle passed around and I's enjoyin' my new freedom. But then, well, then I hurts my knee. Whatever I tore up, weren't ever gonna be right again, and the team cut me. I'll never forget it, a Monday evenin', mid-August, just outside of Wheeling, West Virginia. The boys passed the hat to get me a ticket home, and that was that. I stoods on the side of the road and watched my dreams roll away." Amos paused for another sip of Coke.

"Yes sir, that was a hurtful night, uh-huh. The next bus weren't till mornin'. So, guess where I headed? That's right a beer joint. It'd been a pretty bad day, and I deserved a drink. Well, one led to two, then two led to four, and next thing I knowed I's awakened by a man saying, 'Get up boy, this ain't no hotel!' I opened my eyes and there stood the bus depot manager. I'd passed out against the front door of the depot.

"I finally gots home, but there weren't no work there but I heard that the CCC was needin' men at Fort Pulaski," Amos said. He then looked at Rory. "Now Jake done heard part of this story but lets me catch you up."

He proceeded to give Rory an abbreviated version of how he met Thelma. He highlighted the part about running over the park bench which Rory thought was hilarious.

Amos continued, "I worshipped the ground Thelma walked on. But they's a problem. She was a regular church goer and I weren't. One afternoon we's sittin' down by the river and she said to me, 'Amos, I know you loves me, but I ain't marryin' no man what ain't right with the Lawd.'

"I said, 'Thelma, I knows the Lawd.'

'Yes, but you ain't right with him, I knows you a drinker.'

"How'd she know I's a drinker? Did I smell? Did the Lawd tell her? I don't know but she's worth any sacrifice, so I decided right there to gits myself into church and stop drinkin'. And I did, for the most part. But I convinced myself that havin' a beer or two weren't really drinkin'.

"Well, when Lilly came along I didn't wants to be away from 'em all week, so's I left the CCC and tried to find a job in town. That didn't pan out so well and we's strugglin'. During those times when I should've been the strength of my family, I was the weakness as my drinkin' gots worser and worser. Thelma was patient longer than she should have been. But one Friday night I just went and shattered whatever hope she had in me. Lilly was 'bout two year old and I came home drunk as a skunk and had lost my paycheck in a card game. Thelma was up, madder than a wet hen. She started cryin' and the baby was cryin' and I just wanted to be left alone. I shouted, 'Woman, shut that baby up!'

"Through her tears, she said, 'You know why she's crying, cause she's hungry. Amos there ain't no food in the house and you done lost your paycheck. So, it's your fault Lilly is suffering. You sorry rascal!'"

Amos stopped. He reached into the pocket of his shirt and pulled out a faded red bandana. "And a sorry rascal I was boys." He sniffed and then wiped his eyes.

"She hurt me deep, 'cause it was true. But in my drunkenness, it just made me fightin' mad. I walked towards her, real mean like and snatched Lilly from her. Then's I lifted her up in the air and shouted,

'You love this baby more than me, you don't even care 'bout me no more!'

"Thelma pleaded, 'Amos, please don't hurt her, taint her fault. Please, please just put her down!'

"I couldn't believe what she's sayin'. I weren't gonna hurt Lilly, I loved that little girl with all my heart. I handed Lilly back to her, said a few more terrible things then went to bed. When I woke the next afternoon, Thelma, Lilly, and everythin' she could pack in the old truck was gone."

Amos shifted his eyes towards Rory and me. "Now boys, I didn't go after my wife and child, cause the booze was more important. You lets that sink in.

"You mights think I couldn't gits no lower, but you'd be wrong. I still had one more fall before I hit rock bottom. Now it weren't long before I's throwed out of our place and wound up in an old motel that'd been converted to rentals."

Like a pastor eyeballing a sinner on the front pew Amos stared hard at Rory and me.

"Guess where that motel was?" he asked.

I shook my head and Rory offered an "I dunno know."

"On the road to Damascus," Amos said.

He was quiet for several moments then tilted his head and nodded slightly as if he were waiting for us to respond.

"Paul," Rory said.

Immediately I followed with, "Saul."

Amos' smiled in approval. "You both right. Saul ran slap into the Lawd on the road to Damascus. And on account he was persecuting Christians, God blinded him and gots his attention. Three days later he gots his sight back and a new name, Paul, and become the Apostle Paul."

Hem-hawing somewhat Rory asked, "So... you were blinded by God?"

"Near 'bout," Amos said. "But lets me tell you the rest of the story.

"So, havin' lost everythin' I settled into a mighty pitiful life. I'd find work where I could and when I gots my pay I headed to the bar. Come Monday I's broke. Then I do the same thing the next week. That was my life for nearly two year.

"But things came to a breakin' point on a raw night in January. When I says it was a raw night, I ain't exaggeratin' like you two do 'bout the fish I's never see."

Rory and I smiled at Amos' levity.

"A wicked cold front blowed in and when I left the bar it was way below freezin'. Course I weren't feelin' it none, I's full of bad whiskey. Turnin' up the collar on my coat, and jammin' my hands in the pockets I braced myself for a long walk home. I's 'bout half way and was focusin' best I could on stayin' in the middle of the road. I knows if I gots on the shoulder I's liable to fall in the ditch and they's full of water. Rectly lights were comin' up from behind me and a horn was blowin'. Didn't know where I was on the road, just knowed I had to get to the grass. I run to the left side of the road. And you know that woulda been a good plan 'cept for one small thing."

He paused allowing us to be drawn further into the story.

"But what?" I said.

"I's on a bridge!" he said. "At the edge of the road instead of grass, I found a metal railin'. The rail hit me cross my thighs and pin wheeled me over. My face slammed into the side of the bridge…..and it all went dark.

"Thankfully the bridge was only ten feet or so off the crick. Shoot, didn't make no matter to me how high it was I never knowed it when I hit the water. Comin' to I's on the bottom of that crick. Somehow I gots to the surface and floundered to the bank. That water was some cold. But I reckon that's what saved me, it woke me up. Otherwise I'd drowned.

"I crawled up the bank and stumbled to the road. Soaked to the bone it's a plain miracle I didn't freeze to death before I gots home. In addition to the bitter cold, it felt like the whole side of my face was gone. Every shiver and chatter of my teeth sent pain waves to the right side of my face. Staggerin' into my little place weren't no better. It was as cold on the inside as it was outside. With no kerosene for the heater and no firewood, I broke up the old table and chairs and set 'em ablaze. I grabbed my bed covers, throwed 'em down next to the fireplace and collapsed. Boys, this is the God's honest truth, I didn't 'spect to wake in the morin'. But I did. Comin' aware of light in the room I knowed I's alive." Amos leaned towards us and scrunched his eyebrows, "Know how I knew I weren't dead?"

We both shook our heads.

"Cause bein' dead couldn't hurt that bad." Amos said and nodded his head up and down for emphasis.

"Liftin' my head to get up caused the blanket to lifts from the floor. I's confused then figured out, the blood comin' from around my eye glued the blanket to my face. Dreadin' the pain it's gonna cause, I gripped the blanket and peeled it away. It made a sickenin' tearin' noise as it separated, and fresh blood starting pourin' out."

By this point in the gospel of Amos, I must confess my stomach was a bit queasy.

"I needed a doctor, but weren't no colored doctors. Closest thing was a man what lived down the road. He'd been a corpsman in France during the Great War. Walkin' towards the door I caught sight of myself in the mirror.

Amos closed his eyes and shook his head from side to side. "Boys, what I saw was like somethin' from a freak show. Never wantin' to forget what rock bottom looked like, I let that image burn. My head was swelled, the right side of my face was covered in dried blood and pieces of blanket, and clumps of mud clung to my hair. I saids to myself, 'Amos, wouldn't your mama shore be proud of whats you done with your life.'

"The old corpsman sewed me up but said all the bones around my eye was busted. He said if I could keep my face away from bridge rails for 'bout two month, they might mend and I'd keep the eye. Back home I spent the day chewin' aspirin and thinking 'bout my life. Later that evenin' I walked back to the bridge and poured my last bottle of hooch in the creek. Never took another drink. The Big Man was sendin' ole Amos a message, and I knowed I better heed it. It weren't easy, but gradually I gots myself back together."

"What happened to Lilly?" I asked. "Did you try to find her?"

Amos being touched by my concern peered at me in the kindliest manner.

"Why yes, Jake, I did learn where they was. Two year later after I knowed my bein' sober was gonna stick, I began searchin'. It took 'bout six month but I found 'em."

"Where were they?" I asked.

"In Fargo."

"They were in North Dakota?" Rory asked.

Amos smiled, "No boy, Fargo, Georgia. A little town on the Suwannee River, up near the Okefenokee swamp.

"And then what did you do?" I impatiently demanded.

"Easy Jake, I'm gettin' there. I put on my best Sunday go to meetin' clothes, borrowed a truck and headed over there one Saturday mornin'. It wasn't hard findin' her place but nobody seemed home, so I parked down the road a ways.

"Couple hours later my ole pickup came down the road and pulled into the drive. I's so surprised to see that hunk of junk still rollin'. Thelma got out of the truck carryin' bags of groceries. Suddenly the house door burst open and a little girl came out screamin'. Then a big fella, I mean a mountain of a man, runt out of the house and start chasin' her. And he's hollerin' like a maniac. I reached behind the seat and found an ax handle."

Amos briefly paused from the story to share a morsel of wisdom, "You know a man can do some serious damage with a good piece of hickory." He winked at us after he said it as if it were something we should tuck away in case of an emergency.

By this point Rory and I had moved closer to Amos and were hanging on every word.

"As I open the door, the man caught the little girl by the back of her dress, and in one move he yanked her off the ground and held her above his head. Just as I was roundin' the front of the truck the big man fell to the ground and the girl started bouncin' on his stomach. Then a little boy run from the house and he too started jumpin' on the man. Realizin' there weren't no danger I stepped back to the truck. Then the big man got up on all fours and them kids rode him around the yard like a pony. Thelma walked over and the man pulled her down into the melee and I watched her give him a big kiss. So I cranked the truck and drove home."

"That's it?" I snapped. "You never even said hello to Lilly, you didn't tell your wife how you had changed?"

"Nope," he said in a painful whisper. "Jake, much as I wanted to it weren't right. I saw how Thelma and Lilly's lives was better. They were in a nice house and that fella appeared to be a good man, and Lilly had a little brother. If I marched over there and said, 'Hey it's me Amos, I'm all cleaned up and ready to be your husband again.' What would that've accomplished? Nothin' but hurt and confusion. Nope, as hard as it was it were the right thing to do—for them. I's payin' for my sins, weren't right to make them pay too."

We were quiet for several minutes. It was clear that relaying the story had taken the wind out of Amos. Curiosity got the better of Rory, "Have you ever tried to find Lilly since that day?"

"No, Rory. I figured if she ever got curious she'd find me, just like I found 'em. I ain't hidin', gots the same name I always had.

"Now boys, I didn't tell you this to make you feel sad for me. But it's important you understand that choices got consequences, good and bad. Some consequences are temporary, like the effects of that big storm on the marsh. And some consequences carry with 'em long reminders of bad things, like that scar on your arm Jake."

The rain never let up that afternoon, and it seemed fitting given our moods. What Amos shared gave Rory and me a much deeper understanding of our friend, and it also imprinted on me his lesson in the effects of choices. In a pond, the ripples from a thrown rock cease at the bank, but a rock thrown in the soul creates waves that can affect a man for a lifetime.

CHAPTER 41

Many days were spent dragging the modified pet cage along the deeper portions of the inlet. For lesser fortune seekers, this seemingly fruitless effort would have been quickly abandoned. Rory and I held no such notions, we were immersed in the place we felt most alive. When the tides were cooperative we dredged, when they weren't, we fished.

Over the weeks our dredging efforts produce a substantial pile of rocks, sticks, bottles, and other assorted garbage. Thus, far, our most valuable find was a pair of lady's eye glasses, while the creepiest thing was an artificial hand. When that disembodied hand tumbled from the cage we jumped back three feet. It looked so real that for several minutes neither one of us dared touch it. There had to be an interesting back story surrounding the artificial hand, but the truth remained locked away in Davy Jones' locker. Inventorying our collection Rory joked that we should send the Army Corp of Engineers a bill for dredging services.

Though immersed in our quest for treasure, we maintained a wary eye for Wade Brown. To disguise our prospecting, we always kept our lines in the water. Anytime we heard a small launch approaching, we abandoned the drag rope and picked up our rods. We were so focused on the hunt that when a fish did hit one of our lines, it was a bit of an annoyance. These deception efforts were "feel good" at best. Wade could be lurking in the shadows of the bridge and we would never see him.

Late on a Thursday afternoon I was manning the dragline and felt resistance. My first thought was *Oh boy, more rocks*. However, based on the effort required to drag the cage to shore I changed my prediction and was certain it was a rusted anchor. As the cage broke the surface, I could see the contents were definitely not rocks nor an anchor.

"Rory, I think I got something!"

With less than genuine enthusiasm he responded, "Terrific, another piece of a lawn mower."

Hauling the cage from the water he shot me a big grin, "Jake, I think I see purple!"

He lifted one of the muck encased clumps from the cage and held it up to the sun. "Yes! I see purple too!" I exclaimed.

We had not one, but two of the Holy Grails we had so diligently sought, and they were both intact. We cut our celebration short. If we scooped two at once, odds were there were more. We tried to calculate the exact path the cage had taken, which was next to impossible as the water had no landmarks. Our only means of reckoning was to line up a tree across the inlet in Big Talbot Lagoon. In the years to come, famed undersea explorers Mel Fisher and Bob Ballard would make finding wrecks seem routine with their million dollar vessels and mini subs. Let them try it with a Styrofoam surfboard and a discarded pet cage.

We toiled for another hour without recovering any additional bottles. Regardless, the day had been triumphant. As the tide turned inward we poled as quickly as possible to Amos' to share our success.

Amos examined the two bottles. "Boys, theses' gonna be somethin' once I gets 'em cleaned."

I spent the night with Rory and we stayed up well after eleven. We couldn't have been more excited if it had been Christmas Eve, but there was a problem—we were short on time.

"Based on the tide chart we have two maybe three more days this week to search. By the time the cycle comes back around, I'll most likely be in Oregon with my Dad," Rory said.

"Well, we better make the most of the next three days," I said. After a brief pause I asked, "So how do you feel about seeing your dad?"

"A little weird, I mean I'm excited about flying for the first time. But I don't know what to expect. It's been over a year since I've seen him. What if he has a girlfriend, what if he has joined some hippie commune and lives in a teepee?"

With best friend conviction, I answered, "Whatever you find, remember he's still your dad. It'll be all right."

CHAPTER 42

December 31st, 2003

Continuing to chip away at the items remaining to settle my parent's affairs, it occurred to me that the verse in the Old Testament book of Job that states "naked I came from my mother's womb and naked I shall return" described only part of the arrangement. There should be an additional phrase, "and all that stuff I'll leave behind is somebody else's problem." For five days, I had emptied, sorted, shredded, and given away several tons of stuff that filled my parent's home. Thankfully, I was nearing the end and would be able head home in a couple of days. Earlier in the week I had surrendered any notion of celebrating New Year's with Karen the girls. After only a week I was terribly missing my wife. It caused me to consider how lonely Dad must have been without Mom.

Being absent from work for a few more days was not an issue, as few tourists venture to snowy Gettysburg the first week of January. For whatever reason, folks seem less interested in the exact location of "Pickett's Charge" with the thermometer hovering at nineteen degrees.

The day's tasks included a trip to nearby Yulee for a beveled pane of glass. I needed to correct a permanent reminder of a dark night in my family's life. Ironically, the upheaval of that night was the turning point in our family's and in particular my Mom's coming to grips with Will's death. It was the day of the infamous tornado that nearly killed us.

When I harshly but honestly screamed at Mom that our actions were dishonoring Will, she stormed from the house, slammed the door, and in the process cracked the top right pane. It was odd to consider that for thirty years, despite the other improvements my parents made to the house, they never replaced the original front door or fixed the cracked pane. I felt a sense of obligation to replace it before I turned the house over to the realtor. It was as if that broken pane was a testimony to a private tragedy endured by the Forrest family. It was our business and it should not be there when I closed the door for the last time.

Deciding that eggs over easy and bacon trumped a cold bowl of cereal, I began my day at June's Diner. There is much to admire about a perpetually full cup of coffee enjoyed amongst a symphony of small town conversations. Though it anchored Fernandina's historic district, it could have been in any small town in America.

I was reading the newspaper while gorging on my second grape jelly biscuit, when my attention was drawn to a section entitled "The Year in Pictures." In the middle of the collage was a photo of hundreds, maybe thousands of people, in a snake like line at a convenience store. They were waiting to buy tickets for a Powerball lottery. The photo's caption noted the odds of winning the big jackpot were one in two hundred million. I would venture that most people reading that statistical expectation would dismiss those odds as impossible. Unfortunately, our family knew all too well that regardless of long odds, anything is possible.

I was just shy of my eighth birthday when Will announced he was joining the U.S. Air Force. Despite my age, I vividly recall sitting at the dinner table as the situation boiled over. Will was attempting to explain that although he was joining the military my parents worry was unfounded. He argued that in the Air Force the chances being killed were extremely low.

Dad threw up his hands, "Will we are in the middle of a war for God's sake! How can you sit there and tell us we shouldn't worry?"

Will calmly responded, as the recruiter had no doubt coached him, "that Vietnam was ground war and that's where the casualties were happening."

"The sky didn't protect your Uncle Hank," Mom said. "He's in a cemetery in France."

"Mom, that was World War II. There were people dying all over the globe. That, well, that," Will seemed to lose track of his argument and then stammered, "that was different." Regaining his focus, he launched back into his argument, "I won't be trudging through the jungle with a rifle, or flying into hot landing zones in a Huey gunship. I'm joining the Air Force as an enlisted man. It's not like I can be a pilot. The recruiter said my test scores showed an aptitude with electronics. I'll probably end up at a radar station in South Dakota."

Mom rolled her eyes as Dad offered, "Son, a recruiter's job is to get boys to sign up. They are always going to paint a rosy picture."

"I've thought a lot about this, and I want to be in the Air Force. I want to do my part for my country. It's not like I'm joining the Marines."

Having experienced military conflict first hand in Korea, Dad was not having any of it. "Son, I want to ask you a question and if you are man enough to go fight for your country, I expect you to be man enough to answer me honestly."

"OK," Will said.

"Let's just say that after completing boot camp, the Air Force gave you the choice of a radar operator in South Dakota, or radar operators on a B-52…Which do you choose?"

"You know the answer Dad, I'd take the B-52."

Dad continued, "Son, I know full well that given the opportunity you would volunteer to serve in combat. And when I was your age I felt the same way. War was all wrapped up in the stars and stripes and being a patriot. It was the ultimate proving ground for boys who wanted the honor and privileges of being a man in uniform, but had no idea the potential cost. But now that I'm older and a bit wiser, I understand there is one undeniably fact of war… young men die!"

"Dad you went," Will said.

"I was drafted! I had no choice," Dad said sternly. He paused and took a deep breath before continuing. "Son, you have the benefit of a college deferment, take it. If you really want to serve your country, join ROTC and in four years you can go in as an officer."

"The war will be over in four years, and I'll have missed it," Will said callously.

With that, Mom could no longer contain her tears and left the table. Will, feeling like he was being piled on, tossed his napkin with disgust and left the table. Dad muttered something about "dumb idealistic kids" and choosing to flee the scene altogether, exited the back door. As so many times previously the kitchen table's ability to bear the weight of tough discussion was proven. This one began because of five words. In between bites of stroganoff, Will simply said, "I'm joining the Air Force."

That evening and over the next several days my parents did all they could to dissuade Will, but it was to no avail. Once all avenues to change his mind were exhausted, they had no choice but to be supportive and take solace in the odds. Dad even accompanied Will to the recruitment office to sign the papers.

Will was also correct that his aptitude with electronics would be of value to the Air Force. After boot camp, he was shipped off to Texas for unspecified training. One evening in early June he called home and excitedly told us that he had finally flown in a BUFF.

Dad said, "Neat!"

Mom asked, "What in the world is a BUFF?"

Will explained that BUFF (Big Ugly Flying Fellow) was the nickname for the B-52 bomber. Dutifully my parents expressed excitement about Will's flight. However, some years later Dad shared with me that he viewed the B-52 as a dangerous woman seducing his son.

My parents' worst case scenario was realized as Will's orders directed him to Southeast Asia where he would in fact be flying in the war zone. He assured us he was not assigned to a bomber, but for security reasons could not divulge anything else. He stressed that his missions would be important and lifesaving. It was strange to hear my big brother, who I fought with over everything from the bathroom to a last piece of cake, sounding so much like a man. After Will finished talking about his orders there was nothing but silence on our side of the receiver. Will tried to displace the awkwardness by talking about the guys he was working with and how much he missed Mom's cooking, but still got no response. Finally, he said, "I know you're worried, but I thought you'd be proud."

I heard mom sniffle on the second phone and Dad gently pulled the receiver away so I could no longer hear. "Son," he weakly said then cleared his throat. "We are deeply proud of you. Truth is there's no way we could be more proud of you." Then through a fake half-hearted laugh, "I must confess we were really looking forward to seeing Mount Rushmore when we visited you in South Dakota this summer."

"I know being stationed stateside would make you feel better. But I'll be making a real difference where I am going."

The remainder of the evening was overcome by an uncomfortable quiet. The mystery of Will's assignment was worse on my parents than if he had told us he'd be flying over North Vietnam in a B-52. It was the beginning of when our lives would never be the same. Life went on of course, there were joys and good times, but always at the peripheral edge, close enough to feel......was fear. A fear that can only be understood by those required to balance their daily lives with the knowledge that their loved ones abide in harm's way.

Will was assigned to the 553rd Reconnaissance Wing stationed at Korat Royal Thai Air Force Base. His plane, a Lockheed Super Constellation, was known as a Batcat. These prop powered, unarmed planes relied on the cover of darkness and electronic counter measures for protection. However, the Batcats' missions were so secret that it would be decades before families of those who perished would learn the circumstances.

The Batcats' advanced electronics monitored movement along the Ho Chi Minh Trail, the main supply line for the North Vietnamese. As the plane orbited, electronic sensors which had been previously deployed by parachute or planted in the ground would detect vibrations of trucks and other vehicles. The capabilities of the systems were so advanced it could distinguish the vibrations of a single man walking the trail.

Unfortunately, my brother was never able to astound me firsthand with his personal exploits. On the evening of April 25, 1969, Will's plane Batcat 21 took off on a routine mission. Shortly after takeoff, the pilot requested permission for a hard right turn, due to storm related turbulence. That was Batcat 21's final transmission. The plane crashed within four miles of the airport, killing all eighteen aboard.

From August 1964 to March 1973 nearly three and half million U. S. active duty personnel served in Southeast Asia. Of the 52,280 names etched on the Vietnam Memorial Wall, Air Force personnel accounted for 2,586 of those casualties, or less than 5% of all deaths in the Vietnam War. Statistically speaking this was an extremely small percentage resulting in very long odds.

Because of Will's death, I mentally wince when I hear an assertion decrying the odds of something unfortunate occurring. Peace of mind derived from long odds is a mirage. The absurdity of chance matters not, if you happen to be the "one."

CHAPTER 43

Filled to the brim with coffee, I left the diner and drove towards the town of Yulee. It had been a frigid start to the day, but a spotless blue sky and climbing sun foretold I could soon shed Dad's Levi's jacket. I located it earlier in the week and knew it most likely pre-dated me. Having been washed dozens of times it was as soft as the cotton used in its making. As the jacket aged, Dad cautioned Mom that it was to be washed on the gentle cycle. He'd say, "Connie be careful with ole Blue, it'll be worth something one day." He was right, it was priceless to me.

Yulee is a little town just southwest of Fernandina and the closest place I could locate the specialty glass I required to replace the door pane. Cruising along State Road 200, otherwise known as Buccaneer Trail, various landmarks hinted that I was close to the turn off for Clay Dawson's house. As I sped past, I craned my head to peer down the dirt road. I briefly considered driving by to see if the place was still there, but I was on a mission and reasoned myself out of the idea. It had been twenty-three years since Clay's death. If I were to stop by unannounced, his parents would think I was a nut. Who knew if they still lived there, or were even alive for that matter?

I purchased the window pane and several other necessary items and began the drive back to Fernandina. The closer I got to Clay's turnoff, the more it weighed on me that I should stop. *There could be no harm just driving by to see if the place was still there*, I reasoned.

Proceeding down the dirt lane, the surroundings seemed strangely different than I recalled. There was a mature pine forest where I would swear there was once grazing pastures and corn fields. Rounding the final corner, the house came into view. Even from a distance I could see it was a rough shell of its former charming self. The country blue exterior was faded as if it hadn't been painted since we were kids. The roof was a tapestry of new versus old shingles, and shutters were hanging precariously from several upstairs windows. The manicured landscaping that had once perfectly framed the front of the house now grew wild and obscured much of the downstairs.

For reasons I could not explain nor dismiss, I felt compelled to stop. With great reluctance, I turned into the driveway. Exiting the truck, I was greeted by the symphony of wind strafing through the pine trees. It was punctuated by the haunting cry of a red-tailed hawk. Standing there, I secretly hoped no one was home. If that were the case, I could applaud myself for doing the right thing by stopping and that would be the end of my involvement. I walked up the grass choked sidewalk which led to the screened front porch. The screen appeared similar to the roof with patches on top of patches. I prepared to knock on the screen door but hesitated fearing my tapping might cause the rusted hinges to disintegrate. Giving it three stiff raps triggered a cascade of paint chips that drifted away on the light breeze.

"What you want!" A gruff voice emitted from a man sitting on the porch. Having not previously noticed him, I was startled by his response.

"Oh, uh excuse me sir, I was looking for Mr. Dawson."

"That's me and I don't need whatever you're selling, even if it's Jesus."

His answer, though not intended to be humorous, caused an awkward chuckle. "Oh, no sir, I am not here to sell you anything. My name is Jake Forrest. I was a friend of Clay's."

"Forrest, Forrest.... you the banker's boy, right?"

"Yes, sir."

In an even tone void of any emotion he replied, "Son, I don't think I can help you. Clay's dead."

Strongly regretting my decision to stop, I was however obliged to see this through. "Yes, Mr. Dawson, I know Clay's dead. But I happened to be in town this week and I was driving by and—"

He cut me off mid-sentence, "Your daddy died last summer, wasn't it?"

"Yes sir, that's why I am in town, taking care of some final things."

"I didn't know him well, but never heard anyone speak ill of him."

"No, sir." At this point, there was a long pause and I squinted to see Mr. Dawson through the screen. "Sir, would you mind if I came on the porch?"

"No, come on in, appears you ain't planning to leave anyway."

For the second time in this short encounter I was questioning the forces that compelled me to stop by and see friendly old Mr. Dawson. Reluctantly, I swung the screen door open, fully expecting it would break off in my hand. He was slowly rocking in an oak colored chair. He briefly glanced at me as I entered the porch, then turned away and resumed staring straight ahead. I gently lowered myself into a straight back wooden chair, its deer hide seat practically devoid of fur from years of service. It creaked and groaned under my weight, repercussions of my double biscuit breakfast perhaps. He wore white rubber work boots, a pair of torn khaki colored Dickies and a double layered flannel shirt. The shaded porch had not warmed from the night's chill and I regretted leaving Dad's jacket in the truck.

"I apologize, Mr. Dawson, if I've troubled you."

"No trouble son, how'd your daddy die?"

"He had a bad stroke."

"That's what took Clay's mom too, been nine years now."

Another period of silence convinced me I would have to channel our conversation. "Mr. Dawson, as I said Clay was one of my best friends, and I'm not sure if you recall it but our gang spent more than a few nights camping in your barn. "

"I do remember, son. Clay was blessed to have good friends. You was all city boys, but good boys."

I continued, "You know as I drove up here there seemed to be more trees than I remembered."

"Yep, all that in front of us used to be corn, and the other side was pasture. But when I couldn't work the fields no more I leased it to a company for growing pine trees. Makes for good deer and quail space but ain't near as pretty as a field of corn when a breeze catches it."

After managing to string together a few more minutes of trivial conversation, I sensed it was time to go.

"Well, Mr. Dawson, I got quite a list waiting for me at the house. I appreciate you taking a few minutes with me. Seeing your place brought back a bunch of good memories."

"Yep."

As I stood to leave his face never yielded from the distant stare. It was as if he were intently watching for something, but there was nothing to see but uniform rows of pine trees. With no glance from him I surmised a hand shake would be inappropriate. As I reached the door it registered with me how completely drained of life he appeared. He had lost his son, his wife, and his ability to till his land. There seemed to be nothing left. Gazing at him it struck me that this was a man very near the end of life's road.

"Mr. Dawson," I waited for him to look at me, "I want you to know I think about Clay often, and I still miss him." He nodded his head ever so slightly then slowly redirected his eyes to the pine forest.

I walked slowly to the truck, surveying the old place. My eyes were again drawn to the uniform rows of pine trees. Like an advancing army, the trees seemed poised to eradicate what remained of the Dawson homestead.

Reaching for the door handle on Dad's truck, I felt a hand on my shoulder. I turned to discover Mr. Dawson had quietly followed me. He held out his hand and I extended mine. We shook, but he refused to release his grip. He cleared his throat then said, "Son, thank you for what you said, and thank you for not forgetting my boy." Before I could respond, his released my hand and turned back towards the house.

Backing out of drive I paused and took another long look at the old barn. On those Friday nights, we'd sit around a fire conversing on important subjects, like sports and girls. Once in the loft and after we assured Rory there were there were no corn snakes about, we rolled out our sleeping bags on a mattress of hay. Now peering at the barn through the windshield it seemed neglected and exhibited a distinctive lean to the left. Like the old man sitting on the porch, it was empty and forgotten.

Both the suddenness and the circumstances of Clay's death hit all of us hard. In January of our senior year in high school Clay accepted a wrestling scholarship from the University of Iowa. Just as it had been in high school, his combination of strength and leverage was formidable. As a college freshman he was competitive, by his sophomore year he was All Big Ten Conference, and after his junior season he was named All American. This honor came with an invitation to compete for a spot on the 1980 Olympic team.

Many expected the trials to be a formality. Barring an injury, Clay was projected to be the U.S.' best chance for gold. It was exciting to think my friend Clay Dawson, a country boy from Yulee, Florida, was going to represent his country against the premier Eastern Bloc wrestlers in the Kremlin's back yard.

Little did Clay know, or any of us for that matter, that an event the previous December would change his and all the American Olympian's lives forever. December 27, 1979 was just another day of Christmas break for us, but a half a world away the brunt of the Soviet military invaded a country few of us had heard of, Afghanistan. The United States along with democratic countries around the globe immediately condemned the action as blatant Communist aggression. The Cold War was alive and well in 1979 and this represented a fresh barb in the ongoing struggle. The Soviets refused to withdraw their troops and on March 21, 1980, President Jimmy Carter announced the United States would boycott the Moscow games of the twenty-second Olympiad.

Clay was bitterly disappointed. He had trained so hard and was at the top of his sport. The thought of waiting another four years was devastating. But his country hard perspective kept him grounded and he set his sights on Los Angeles in 1984. Concluding the spring term, he returned home to Yulee and did what he always did in the summer, worked on his parents' farm. As with previous summers he also worked part-time as a farrier. He had been shoeing horses since he was a kid, and his reputation as a farrier kept him busy. It is not a job for the weak or lazy. Sometimes he worked under the shade of a barn but most times it was in an open corral in the blistering summer heat. The plus side, as Clay liked to remind those of us who were working for minimum wage, was that it paid well.

On a Tuesday morning in late July, Clay went to the Raulerson farm in Callahan. There were three horses that needed shoeing, two mares and a big stallion. The police investigation was unable to determined what actually occurred, but they speculated that a snake or perhaps a bobcat spooked the stallion while Clay was shoeing its back hooves. He was found lying on his back in the middle of the corral as if he had simply fallen backwards. There were no outward signs of injury but the medical report indicated a kick to his chest had shattered his sternum and crushed his heart. Whether the facts were accurate or it was an attempt to assure his parents that he did not languish, the medical examiner noted death was instantaneous.

It was late afternoon before the farm's owner discovered his body. Mr. and Mrs. Dawson had no insight that anything was amiss until early evening when Sheriff Buddie, Jr. and the family's pastor knocked on their door. For nearly ten hours that miserably hot July day, the world continued to spin and people in Fernandina went about their normal lives while Clay lay dead in that corral.

Clay Dawson should have spent that summer in Moscow having the adventure of his life. He should have been flirting with

Australian swimmers, sampling Russian caviar, and bringing home a gold medal. But instead my friend died alone in a filthy corral in Callahan, Florida.

CHAPTER 44

"You Can't Run from Trouble, There's no place that far."

UNCLE REMUS

JULY 1973

WE PROPELLED *NESSIE* TOWARDS THE inlet with unbridled vigor that Friday morning. Bolstered by the discovery of two bottles the previous day, we were anxious to sink the cage and drag for more treasure.

Nessie's bottom scraped the sand of the inlet beach and we moved quickly towards an unassuming pile of driftwood. The wood and a leaning palm tree in Big Talbot Lagoon served as a reckoning marker to the previous day's success.

So overcome by treasure fever we neglected to retrieve our rods to continue the charade that we were fishing. Rory positioned the salvage cage on the surfboard barge, and released it into the flow. Once in the target zone, he yanked the rope dispatching the cage to the murky depths.

Six or seven launches later, I felt encouraging resistance. Carefully Rory and I pulled the cage aboard *Nessie*. To our great delight, the cage contained another intact rum bottle. Upon further examination, this one appeared to have the remnants of the original cork still wedged in the mouth.

"We are definitely on it," Rory said. "I just wish we could snorkel out there and see what else there is."

"We'd need skin diving gear out there," I said, "I bet it's thirty feet at least."

The cage reloaded we launched again. An hour later and a dozen more attempts the cage was again heavily laden with treasure. This time there were two bottles.

"We've found the mother lode!" Rory said.

Like pirates celebrating a successful raid, Rory and I danced around hoisting our bottles skyward. It was because of our reveling we failed to hear the growling sounds of an outboard motor approaching from under the bridge. By the time we were of aware of it, Wade Brown and Skyler were cruising directly in front of us, less than twenty-five yards away. We ceased our celebration, but it was too late. Wade had witnessed our "miner finds a big nugget dance" and was justifiably curious. However, they seemed content to keep their distance, for now.

As they cleared the bend and entered the Intracoastal Rory asked, "You think they know we have something?"

"Yep! And you can bet they'll be back."

We launched the cage another handful of times but scooped only rocks. Our total for the day was three intact bottles. These, plus the two at Amos George's house, could be the makings of a small fortune. We should have been elated, but our uneasiness regarding Wade and Skyler dampened our enthusiasm.

The tide would flow out for another hour, so we had no choice but to stay put. However, at the first sign of the inward flow Rory and I shoved off and feverishly pushed *Nessie.* I felt an overbearing sense that evil was lurking, waiting just out of sight.

Rounding Darlington bend, we paused to catch our breath. Bent over, grasping my knees I felt pocket blisters forming on my palms. We had poled the raft as if it were a race. All too soon we would understand it was in fact a race, a race for our lives.

"Wait, what's that?" Rory said in a breathless whisper. I tried to listen, but all I could hear was my heavy breathing and pounding heart. Then I caught it. "Crap, it's a boat motor, it's gotta be them. Hurry! Push!"

We dug our bamboo poles deep into the Bent Tree creek's muddy bottom leveraging all our strength. Amos' place was close, but the sound of the motor quickly grew louder. Rounding a tight turn, I ventured a quick glance behind us. Just before we disappeared around the bend I could see the bow of Wade's boat coming out of Darlington bend. Skyler was sitting at the bow and beating the bow as if it were a horse in the home stretch. There was less than a football field between us. "They're gaining Rory! Go, Go!"

Amos' place was almost in sight, but our motorized pursuers were rapidly closing the gap. If we could clear one more small bend, we could call for help. We rounded the last bend and began screaming for Amos. Why today? Why of all afternoons was he not sitting on the porch? Rory and I called him repeatedly. But it was no use, the hounds were upon us.

Wade throttled back and brought the boat parallel to us. I raised my pole to prevent them from grabbing the raft. Wade countered my move by speeding around us, the bow of his boat arching as he gunned the engine. Rory too had his pole out of the water, holding it like a javelin.

Wade began to circle the raft, all the while sporting a satisfied smirk. "Where're you girls going in such a hurry?" he said.

Wade positioned his bow against *Nessie* and opened the throttle pushing us towards the shore. Skyler had moved to the rear of the boat so both were out of our reach. Rory and I put the poles against their boat trying to force it away from the raft. It was useless, the strength of two boys was no match for an Evinrude. We grounded to a halt on the bank just down river from Amos' place. Less than twenty yards from safety.

The raft settled on a small delta that was normally covered by the tide. The bank was flat and level for ten feet or so then it rose with the beginnings of marsh grass. Directly in front of the raft between us and Amos' place was a natural mud jetty. We were trapped. Wade stepped to the front of the boat and jumped to the sodden bank, Skyler followed. Both wore rubber boots and seemed immune to the quicksand characteristic of marsh mud. Rory and I stood defiantly, poles in hand. I glanced one last time towards the cabin but there was no sign of Amos. We were on our own.

CHAPTER 45

"So, WHAT'D YOU FIND IN the inlet?" Wade asked. "Y'all been looking for something, and we know it ain't fish."

"It's none of your business you stupid prick, and if you come any closer I'll jam this pole up your ass," Rory said.

"Whoa, I am so scared. Hey Sky, listen to little Rory trying to cuss like a real man," Wade said. "You're all alone, you got no options Perkins. Let's see what's in the bucket."

"Hey, big boys, you's back off! Leave Jake and Rory be, you hear?" Amos shouted from his back porch.

Yes! Amos had come to our rescue. Wade gave a disdainful glance at Amos and shouted back, "Hey blackie. You best mind your own business. Otherwise you might have a fire one night."

Sternly, Amos responded, "You best move on, boy!"

Wade responded with his usual one finger wave. To my horror, Amos paused at the railing then walked back into the house. *That's it? Amos tosses out a warning and he goes back into the house?* Again, Rory and I were on our own.

"Last chance to do this the easy way, get off the damn raft," Wade said.

Rory and I stood our ground. I was scared, but given the effort to recover the bottles the thought of Wade Brown taking them induced a rage greater than the fear. Skyler and Wade stepped toward the raft. Rory and I thrust the poles at their heads. They ducked and grabbed the ends. With his superior size and strength Wade easily pulled it from my hand. Skyler was unable to separate Rory from his pole so he jerked it sideways causing Rory to tumble into the shallow water. He landed on his feet but the slippery mud caused him to fall face first into the muck.

Wade and Skyler laughed mercilessly as Rory emerged covered in gray mud. Unable to see or even stand in the slippery quagmire Rory fell again into the knee-deep water. They turned their attention to me. I grabbed the five-gallon bucket containing our treasure.

"Hand it over!" Wade said.

I shook my head.

Shouting Wade said, "You got no place to go, butt-face. Give it up or I am going to beat the hell out of you!"

In a feeble voice, I said, "No, we worked hard for this. It's ours."

"Sniff, sniff. Hey Sky, I think he's gonna cry," Wade whined.

Laughing at their moronic gibberish, the two sons of Lucifer stepped on the end of the raft and moved towards me. I hastily snatched a bottle from the bucket and tossed it in the creek. Being filled with mud the bottle sank instantly. I quickly grabbed another and tossed it as well. Before I could clutch the last one, they were on me. My only defense was to wrap my arms around the bucket in a bear hug. Wade pulled at my arms while Skyler repeatedly slapped me in the face.

"Let go Forrest, you're only gonna get hurt," Wade said.

At this point he began punching me in my arms. With each blow his knuckles bore deep into my upper arm. Skyler was now slapping my face with both hands. As I moved my head to avoid his onslaught he caught me hard in the left eye with the heel of his hand. It hurt so badly that I felt tears welling up. I was mere seconds from giving up.

"Take your stinking paws off him you damned dirty apes!" Rory exclaimed.

Though my head was ringing from the blows I could appreciate the significance of Rory quoting the immortal line from *Planet of the Apes.* No doubt, Charlton Heston would have been proud.

Wade and Skyler turned towards Rory who was standing on the bank covered head to toe in creek sediment. He had procured a piece of driftwood and was swinging it like a baseball bat.

Wade calmly jumped from the raft and waded ashore. He retrieved a knife from his pocket and walking towards Rory flicked open the four-inch blade.

"I'm gonna cut your nuts off."

BOOM! A thunderous explosion echoed throughout the marsh and a plume of water exploded in front of the cabin. The four combatants turned in unison towards the source of the concussion. There on the porch, leaning against the rail stood Amos brandishing a double barrel shotgun. Amos' head turned slowly towards us and through a devilish grin said, "That shore was a big water rat. Did you boys see him? I do loves shooting rats!"

Our attackers stood like statues, momentarily frozen by the audacity or perhaps fearing that Amos may turn the gun on them. Seizing the moment Rory swung the drift wood, slamming Wade's arm. He dropped the knife, and backed up several steps. Wade swore a blue streak and cradled his arm in obvious pain. Rory tossed the stick aside, and boldly approached his distracted nemesis. Wade finally took notice of Rory just about the time Rory's foot slammed into his crotch. Wade groaned, clutching his genitals. Rory then grabbed Wade's hair and pulled his head forward while simultaneously bringing his knee upward. The audible impact sent Wade tumbling backwards, landing spread eagle on the muddy bank. Wade was defenseless at this point, dazed and gagging on blood that poured from his nose and mouth. Unfortunately for Wade, Rory wasn't finished.

Rory picked up the knife and leapt towards Wade landing in a sitting position on his chest, the impact causing him to emit a wet gurgling moan. Rory pinned Wade's arms with his knees.

"This is for me and Jake and every other kid you've hurt during your miserable worthless life," Rory said through clinched teeth.

In stunned horror, I watched Rory raise the knife above his head.

KABOOM!

Another shotgun explosion reverberated across the marsh. Snapping my head to look at Amos I saw the shotgun pointing skyward.

"Rory!" Amos sternly shouted. "Puts that knife down boy!"

Rory paused, the knife still raised. He glared at Amos, a silent declaration that his was an unwelcome intrusion.

"Now Rory," Amos said, his voice dramatically softer than before, "Boy you needs to listen to ole Amos. Decisions got consequences. Sometimes what's done can't be undone. Now you knows I'm tellin' the truth, caused I've lived it. He ain't worth it Rory, no sir. That sorry, worthless, piece of white trash ain't worth it."

Returning his attention to Wade, the knife still raised Rory stared down at him for a harrowing moment. I gasped as Rory swiftly yanked his arms downward. A hair's instant before the knife plunged into Wade's chest Rory altered the trajectory and drove the blade into the mud less than an inch from Wade's neck. Wade squealed shamelessly.

Rory grabbed Wade's hair, lifting his head from the mud.

"You better listen good Wade Brown 'cause this is your last warning. If you ever mess with me, Jake, any of our friends, or any kid, I'll gather up some boys and we'll catch you and take you down. Then Freddie Sadler will jump on your chest cracking all your ribs. After that we'll all take turns punching you till the splintered bones rip through your lungs. And that's how we'll leave you, gasping and dying like a fish on a dock. You got that?"

Wade didn't answer, and frankly I wondered if he even could at this point.

Rory balled his fist and punched Wade in the ear. Wade groaned. "I asked you a question Wade."

"I, I understand," Wade said in a painful whisper.

Skyler had been distracted by Rory and Wade's showdown and stupidly turned his back to me. Setting the bucket down I grabbed Rory's fishing rod. It was rigged with a multi hooked lure and a six-ounce pyramid sinker. I swung the rod with all my might at Skyler's head. The narrow tip of the rod whistled as it cut through the air before striking him. It whipped across his right ear and wrapped around his face, the sinker opening a finger long gash above his left eye. He screamed and grabbed his face. He turned slightly towards me and I swung the rod again with short quick strikes, *whack, whack*!

With each wallop, I yelled, "Get off my raft!"

Skyler retreated towards the water side of the raft before falling into the creek. He quickly surfaced and attempting to orient himself placed his hands on the edge of the raft. As he tried to stand I brought the rod down like a sledge hammer striking the crown of his head and splintering the rod. He lurched towards deeper water, only resurfacing once he was in the cover of Wade's boat. There he stayed, cowering behind the motor.

At this point in the melee, Rory had just obtained Wade's agreement that his bullying days were over. Rory raised his fist to give Wade one more for good measure.

"Rory, that's enough now!" Amos shouted from the porch. "You! Boy in the water," Amos said to Skyler. "Go picks up your friend and git!"

Skyler slowly crawled out of the creek. He was bleeding profusely and continually wiping the blood from his eye. Rory stepped in his path.

"Screw with us and you'll get the same."

Skyler placed Wade's arm over his shoulder and half carried him to the boat. The guy who had tormented me for years was bloody, helpless, and begging Skyler in pathetic moans to go easy. Skyler helped Wade onto the wooden bench then released him to push the bow back into the creek. Emitting an anguished groan, Wade tumbled to the bottom of the boat. Skyler left him there and slowly motored away.

Rory glared at me. "Jake you're so stupid! I can't believe you threw our treasure back in the creek!" He waded out and dove under the brackish water. I stood there not knowing what to do. My heart was racing. I was drenched with sweat and my mouth was like cotton. I felt my hands trembling.

"Jake, come on over here," Amos said.

I gestured towards Rory.

"Let him be, now gits on up here."

I made my way to his floating dock then up the gangway. It felt good to be in the shade of his porch. Amos met me with a bottle of Coke, a wet towel and told me to go sit down in the corner. He then turned to leave.

"Where are you going?" I asked.

"To get some ice for that eye."

I touched it and it felt puffy. Across the porch, I noticed Amos' shotgun leaning against his chair. It occurred to me that I never knew Amos had a gun nor had he ever bragged about shooting rats. I reflected on how lucky Rory and I were that Amos came out when he did. It was perfect timing. So, perfect in fact that even in my scared, trembling condition it didn't seem coincidental. Before I could consider it further Amos handed me a rag filled with ice.

"Let me see boy?" he said as he lifted my face to the light. "Yep, you gonna have a nice shiner. Good luck 'splaining it to your mama," he said with a chuckle.

At that moment, Rory shouted from the creek, "Jake, you baboon! What an idiot thing to do!"

I stood up and walked over to the rail. "What about Rory?"

Amos joined me leaning on the rail "He be all right. Swimmin' round trying to find them bottles will do him good. You know cool him off a little. Rory gots lots of knots in his tail, mostly 'cause his pappy's gone. What you saw him do with that big boy was pure rage, all that anger he's bottled up over the last few years just let loose."

Amos paused to light his pipe and through puffs he said, "Had to happen sooner or later, Jake."

"What?"

"Facin' down somethin' bigger than you." Reading the old man's eyes I saw profound approval. His rough hand gently clasped the back of my neck "You done good boy, done good."

With that Amos walked back into the cabin. I stood watching Rory repeatedly dive under the water searching for the bottles. I felt vibrations through the railing and knew Mr. Rosco was trotting down to see me. He rubbed against my arm and I scratched his scarred head.

It took Rory twenty minutes to locate the bottles. When he came to the dock, I met him and gave him a soda. He responded with a grunt. I gave the rum bottles to Amos and he placed them in a large galvanized foot tub filled with water and solvents.

Rory never did come up to the porch. After he finished his drink he retrieved the raft from the delta and brought it to Amos' dock. I climbed aboard *Nessie* and waved at Amos. He smiled and exhaled a cloud of smoke.

"Boys gets a good bath and a big dinner. You earns'd it."

Rory never said a word or even looked at Amos. He focused on the creek and was very deliberate in poling for home. I tried to talk with him several times but he only grunted or ignored me altogether. After pulling the raft ashore, we mounted our bikes and headed for home. At the road split between our houses Rory said, "See you tomorrow."

"Wait, man," I said. "Mom told me three times this morning to make sure you came home with me for dinner and to sleep over."

"I know, my Mom told me the same thing, but I just don't feel like a sleep over. I just wanna go home."

The importance of Rory spending the night was unknown to me. The truth was his mom was having male company for the evening and did not want Rory around.

I finally convinced him to come home with me and at least get some dinner. During dinner Rory remained silent and ate very little. My parents were concerned, but chose not to push the issue. Mom inquired about my eye and I wiggled through an explanation that I banged it on the raft. This was mostly true. I was on the raft when Skyler banged me in the head.

After dinner, Rory announced he was going home. My dad took him aside and in quiet tones told him that his mom said he needed to stay with us. He offered to let him sleep in Will's room if he wanted to be alone. That seemed a reasonable compromise and Rory went directly to bed. My parents cornered me and asked what was troubling Rory. I told them he had just had a bad day and that he was really missing his dad. I doubt they bought it, especially with my gradually darkening eye, but surprisingly they pursued it no further.

The following morning, I bumped into Rory outside the bathroom. I said "Hey" and waited for his response.

"Sorry bout yesterday man. I, I …."

"No problems man," I said. "It was a tough day all around."

And with that we were good again. Later in the kitchen while eating our second bowl of Frosted Flakes the phone rang. The phone was next to the coffee pot which at that time of the morning was right next to dad.

"Hello?" *Pause.*

"Oh, good morning Mr. George, how are you?" *Pause.*

"You're where?" Dad said with a very concerned tone. Rory and I moved towards Dad.

"What is it?" I said in a loud whisper. Dad immediate pinned the phone receiver against his ear with his shoulder and gave me the time-out sign.

"This is not good, not good at all," Dad said, then listened. "No, I'm not aware that anything like that happened yesterday. However, the boys did seem a bit off last night."

We could hear Amos talking but it was too muffled to understand.

"Well Mr. George, just sit tight. I'll talk to the boys and get to the bottom of this. Try not to worry…. We'll figure this mess out."

Dad and Amos exchanged goodbyes and before the avocado green receiver was returned to its cradle, I asked, "Dad what's wrong with Amos George?"

For several seconds Dad rubbed his cheeks as if he was checking to see if he needed a shave. He then looked at Rory and me. “Amos is in jail.”

CHAPTER 46

DAD PREPARED AS BEST HE could for the encounter with Sheriff Buddie Jr. After consulting with his attorney friend, Jeremiah Kent, he had an extra strong cup of coffee and a quick prayer. Shortly before noon, Dad dropped a quarter into a parking meter in front of the police station. There had been no direct communication between him and the sheriff since the previous summer when Dad told him to mind his own business regarding our friendship with Amos. He knew Buddie, Jr. was unaccustomed to folks disregarding his authority, and he also understood Amos was a pawn in this situation.

Approaching the steps, a sharp whistle garnered Dad's attention. He turned and crossing the street was Jeremiah Kent.

"Eric, wait up," Jeremiah said. It was full on summer and Jeremiah was sporting his seasonal best—a blue stripped seersucker suit, bright red bow tie, white belt and bucks, and a stylish straw hat.

"What are you doing here?" Dad asked.

In his soft Carolina way Jeremiah said, "Well, I started thinking about what we talked about this morning, and I thought you might... well, want some back up when you talk to the sheriff."

Placing his hand on Jeremiah's shoulder Dad said, "While I greatly appreciate the gesture, this really isn't your problem. I hate to drag you into it."

"Eric, bullies are everybody's problem. And there's no bigger bully between Orlando and Tallahassee than Earl Buddie, Jr. I relish the opportunity to take him down a notch."

Dad smiled, "You sure?"

Jeremiah put his arm around Dad and ushered him towards the door, "Let's do some good."

Deputy Ricky Alvarez caught site of Dad and Jeremiah entering the station and greeted them.

"Good Morning, Mr. Forrest," Ricky said with a smile and extended his hand.

"Hello Deputy Alvarez, good to see you." Turning towards Jeremiah Dad said, "Jeremiah have you met Deputy Ricky Alvarez?"

"No, I do not think I've had the pleasure. Good to meet you Deputy."

Dad continued, "I expect this fine young policeman will be sheriff one day."

Alvarez smiled broadly and quickly moved to change the subject. "Mr. Forrest, I'll let the sheriff know you're here. He's expecting you."

"I'll bet he is," Dad said.

"If you'd like a cup of coffee, you know where it is, help yourselves," Alvarez said.

Dad made his way to the coffee pot. He didn't want more coffee but holding the cup would give his hand something to do. As Dad and Jeremiah entered his office, Sheriff Buddie Jr. remained firmly seated behind his desk. He made no attempt to greet them or extend his hand.

"Well, if it isn't my old friend, the banker. And it seems you're represented by council today. What could the Nassau County Sheriff's Department possibly do for you?"

Intent on remaining neutral Dad responded, "Thank you for seeing me."

At which point Jeremiah interrupted, "I'm not here as Eric's council, I'm here as his friend."

Buddie Jr.'s lips parted, transitioning to a sly smile, "Well now, that's...that's precious."

Quickly Dad reengaged, "I'll try to be brief as I know your time is very valuable. I understand that you have Mr. George in custody."

Tapping his desk with his index finger, the sheriff gazed towards the ceiling as if he was trying to recall something. "Mister banker, we arrest many people. Lots of miscreants in this county you know." He opened a folder on his desk and ran his finger down a list, "Yes, yes you are indeed correct. We do have a Mr. George in custody."

Dad later shared with me that when Buddie, Jr. played dumb it made his blood boil. But it was the snake like smile Buddie wore when he acknowledged Amos was in custody that nearly sent Dad leaping across the desk. "May I ask what he is charged with? And my name is Eric or Mr. Forrest, either is appropriate."

"Well mister banker, are you family? Of course, I mean no insult by that question. I just don't know what with all the time your son spends with Mr. George if perhaps your family has adopted him, or vice versa. So, if you're not family perhaps I shouldn't divulge the details of his situation."

"You know full well we're not kin," Dad answered.

Jeremiah added, "But a citizen charged with a crime is public information."

"Ah, now those of us with inferior intelligence are showered by the wisdom of Jeremiah Kent, Esquire. Very well....Mr. George is charged with discharging a firearm within the city limits, threatening a minor and attempted assault with a deadly weapon. In other words, his ass is grass."

"Those are serious charges," Dad remarked.

"Yes sir they are. You know a wise man would've heeded my warning last summer 'bout your boy hanging out with this...this person of color shall we say. I expect your boy will need to find himself a new father figure.... cause this one's going up the river."

"Sheriff I must confess I find it interesting that neither you nor anyone from this office contacted me about speaking with my boy or Rory Perkins concerning the incident. They were of course eyewitnesses. Would you like me to get them so they could provide a statement?" Dad asked.

"As much as I appreciate you telling me how to do my job mister banker, I interviewed several witnesses and quite frankly didn't feel it beneficial to speak with two impressionable boys who regularly obtain free drinks and God knows what else from the accused."

Dad bit his lip and somehow retained his composure.

"The two witnesses, would that be Wade Brown and a boy named Skyler?" Jeremiah asked.

"I am not required to share that," Buddie, Jr. said.

"Sheriff my boy told me who was there, so let's cut the BS," Dad said.

"Well you just seem to know everything about everything, don't you? Have you ever considered running for my job? You appear imminently qualified," Buddie, Jr. said.

Ignoring Buddie, Jr.'s barb Dad opened his portfolio, revealing a yellow legal pad. "I questioned both boys, separately I might add, and their stories lined up. My boy and Rory were attacked by those other two, one of which I believe is over the age of eighteen. And secondly, whereas Mr. George did in fact fire his gun, he was merely shooting a water rat. Something we've all done while out on the marsh. My boys swear that Amos never pointed the gun in their direction and never made any threats to Wade Brown. In fact, it was Wade that threatened to burn down Amos' place."

Extending the yellow pad towards the sheriff Dad said, "Would you like to see these notes?"

"Banker man I find your boy's version of the events riveting, yet not very plausible. You say for example, that your boy was attacked? Then how come the other boys were the ones requiring medical attention? The Brown boy has a broken nose, a stitched-up lip, a fractured arm, and two severely bruised testicles. While the Skyler boy needed eight stitches to close a cut that nearly took out his eye. A cut I believe caused by your boy cowardly hitting him from behind."

Dad responded his voice growing in frustration, "So you're saying Jake and Rory attacked two older and much bigger boys?" In a decidedly sarcastic tone he added, "That's a real plausible story. And for the last time my name is Eric."

Gesturing to calm Dad, Jeremiah lightly touched his arm. He then posed a question to the sheriff. "It sounds like you just confirmed Wade Brown is your key witness, is that correct?"

Sheriff Buddie, Jr. rested his chin on his thumbs and placed his two index fingers over his mouth. He smiled. "And now we have been edified by the legal insight of Mr. Atticus Finch." Buddie locked his slate gray eyes on Dad, "Banker man this meeting's done."

Again, Jeremiah intervened, "You know these charges won't stand. The grand jury will compare Jake and his friend with the Brown boy and it's over."

The sheriff stood up quickly, the momentum causing his chair to roll and crash with a thud into a file cabinet. "Let me be inordinately clear as it seems you Black Panther wannabes are having trouble with reality. This is my jurisdiction. And the District Attorney's office will prosecute any case I tell 'em too. And I promise you I'll have a jury that convicts his black ass. I don't care how they do it in Chicago or New York, down here coloreds don't point guns at white folks. Now, this meeting's over, unless you want to spend a night in jail. What'll it be banker man?" Buddie walked briskly from behind his desk to where Dad and Jeremiah stood. He opened the door and told the dispatcher to locate Deputy Bowers and have him remove Dad and Jerimiah from the building.

Jeremiah whispered to Dad, "Eric, we're playing at his field, we can't win this way. I'll talk with the DA, no chance he'll bring charges. At worst Mr. George will be in jail a couple more days."

Dad looked incredulously at Jeremiah, "And what if some accident befalls Amos while he's here? Given what you just saw, would you put that past Buddie Jr.?"

Jeremiah didn't answer but his countenance revealed he concurred.

"I didn't slog through the mud in Korea to protect these kinds of injustices. I didn't lose a son in Southeast Asia so this jack-ass of a sheriff could trample the Constitution." Dad's voice crackled briefly, but then the fire returned to his eyes, "Hell no I didn't!"

Buddie stepped back in the office followed by Deputy Bowers, "Deputy Bowers will show you out, or to a holding cell...your choice."

"Not just yet he won't. Sheriff, you may be done with this but I'm not. We both know what happened out there. And you're railroading that old man for the simple reason that he's colored and you can do it. No doubt Wade Brown went home all busted up and his daddy, in perhaps his only sober night of the month, came down here and demanded justice for his boy. And from there it was easy to just blame the poor old black man. This isn't about the truth. No, this is simply an abuse of power, and so help me God I'll do whatever is required to make sure you don't get away with it."

"Are you threatening me, banker man? Do you realize Deputy Bowers could arrest you right now? And can you imagine the consequences of your picture being on the front page of the *Fernandina Observer*, 'Local Banker Arrested.' You'd be fired immediately."

Dad's eyes met Buddie's. The sheriff now had shiny handcuffs dangling from his hand. At the mention of him losing his job because of the arrest being in the newspaper, Dad had an epiphany. He stared at Buddie Jr. and glanced back at Jeremiah. In those few seconds the thought became a plan.

"Sheriff, let *me* be inordinately clear as it appears you're having trouble with reality. If Mr. George is not released by this evening, I'll take these notes and the reputable boys that were involved and I'll drive down to Jacksonville."

Smiling, Buddie Jr. shook his head as if Dad was an idiot. "You go right ahead, I don't cotton to nobody in Jacksonville."

"Well I'm not going to see the authorities...I'm going to the *Florida Times Union*. It's a big city paper and I imagine there's a young beat reporter on the staff, a woman most likely that graduated from some left leaning northeastern college. You know one of those do-gooder types that wants to fix what's wrong in the world, especially here in the Deep South. I'd bet a year's pay that a story about a black man, a particularly likable man like Amos George, being railroaded by an arrogant white sheriff would be too good to pass up. And you know those reporters are just like a blue tick hound. Once they get on the scent of a racoon, they chase it till they tree it…or, in this case, till they tree you."

"The hell you say. I ain't afraid of no little girl reporter with a notepad…..this is my county! I control things around here! You hear me?" Sheriff Buddie, Jr. turned and returned to his chair.

"Ball's in your court Sheriff, this thing doesn't have to go any farther. But if Amos is not released by four o'clock or if he is harmed in anyway, I'll be sharing this story with a reporter by five o'clock."

Just after four o'clock our phone rang. Rory and I raced to it scooping up the receiver before it completed the second ring. "Hello, Dad is that you?"

"Yes, it's me son. I have a dear friend of yours with me. How about you and Rory hop on your bikes and meet us at June's Diner."

Amos George was a free man.

Jubilantly we grabbed our bikes and made it to June's in record time. Dad and Amos George were waiting outside. I walked up to Dad and gave him a big hug, "Thanks Dad."

He smiled, "Son, I want you to always remember, doing the right thing isn't always easy, but it's always worth it."

Rory and I greeted Amos as if it had been years since we had seen him. I know he was pleased, but he seemed a bit overwhelmed with all the hugging.

It had been an incredible couple of days. The experiences and lessons from that short window were more profound than any I would ever experience in my life. In facing Wade and Skyler, I took tremendous strides towards manhood. But, in my father's example, I learned that a man must stand not only for himself, but at times he must also stand in the gap for others.

CHAPTER 47

THE ENSUING WEEK FOLLOWING OUR showdown with Wade Brown, Rory and I returned to our first love, fishing. The quest for the purple bottles had been thrilling and we hoped financially rewarding, but we longed to return to the simple pleasure of wetting a line.

Each time we stopped by Amos' we pestered him to show us the bottles' progress. He had concocted a recipe of Spic-n-Span, mineral spirits, and Turtle Wax. It smelled something awful, but Amos was convinced it would restore the bottles to their original luster.

One week. That's all that remained of our summer together. The start of school was still four weeks away, but Rory would be spending three of those weeks with his dad. I made the mistake of lamenting to my parents how boring it was going to be without Rory and how I would have nothing to do. The next morning a list was taped to my bathroom mirror, "Jobs for Jake while Rory is gone." These last seven days were all that stood between me and forced servitude.

Rory was dreading the trip for reasons I did not clearly understand. I knew he really missed his dad, but he was now accustomed to it being just him and his mom. This certainly was not how Rory wanted it, but it became his new normal. Soon he would travel three thousand miles to foreign surroundings and to a dad he had not seen in more than a year. Three weeks could seem like an eternity if things went poorly.

Two days before Rory's departure we had the best fishing day of all time. On the way home we of course stopped at Amos'. Rory and

I retreated to our usual spots on the porch to enjoy our respite. Mr. Rosco was gnawing the head off a sea trout and Amos was gently puffing on his pipe.

"Well boys, I thinks the sun looks right. Is you ready?"

"Ready for what?" I asked.

"To see the fruits of your labors, that's what." He stood from his rocker, clapped his hands and excitedly and said, "Come see."

"Are the bottles ready?" Rory asked.

Amos did not respond but beckoned us to follow him into the house. Near the front door was a horizontal window that opened to the western side of his house. It provided light to the front part of the house, and it also had a wide sill that made a handy shelf. Rory and I walked into the narrow, darkened hallway, and were fully entranced by what we saw. His sense of timing was perfect as the sun had dropped just low enough so that a direct beam of light shone through the window. The summer sun filtering through the six bottles created purple streams of light which enshrouded the hallway. Dust particles floated into the light, and seemed to dance like tiny fairies.

"Ain't that something?" Amos asked.

"Amazing," Rory muttered.

"How did you know to do this?" I asked.

"It was accidental. Once they's clean I needed a safe place to keep 'em. This seemed as good a spot as any. Yesterday I just happen to walk past 'bout this time of day. I tells you boys at first it scart me a little. It was so bright and seemed to be moving, I didn't know what if it was a poltergeist." Amos paused and we knew it was coming, "You boys know what a poltergeist is don't you? If not we'll grab the dictionary."

We assured Amos we knew poltergeists were ghosts and we were soon drawn back to the fantastic light show. Rory and I carefully lifted two bottles and walked back into the living room for closer inspection. They appeared brand new. There was nothing to indicate they had been at the bottom of the channel for fifty years.

"It still amazes me that these were filled with cheap rum," I said.

Rory added, "Cheap rum or not, I bet these things are worth some money now."

"I think you're right Rory. The trick's gonna be findin' the right buyer," Amos added. "Yes sir, you boys find the right buyer and you might be surprised what they fetch."

Rory and I both wanted a bottle to keep and Amos insisted on taking the first bottle we recovered, the one with the broken neck. He said, "This here bottles' gots character." That left three bottles for us to sell.

The following Saturday Dad and I visited a local antique dealer who offered me fifteen dollars for one bottle. Dad politely declined but prior to leaving the shop purchased several trade magazines. We combed the magazines for other dealers and mailed nearly twenty-five letters with photographs. Now came the hard part…waiting for a response.

In the meantime, Rory returned from Oregon with tall tales about the size of the trees and the trout. He said it was a little awkward the first few days, but I could tell he really enjoyed the time with his dad. So much so, that he was already talking about going back for Christmas. Mr. Perkins was a sales rep for a timber company, and according to Rory the only thing his dad disliked about the job was he had to cut his pony tail.

The Tuesday after Labor Day my friends and I officially entered high school. This was the big-time–Friday night football games, lockers with real locks, and vending machines filled with soda. It also meant we were going to be in the same building with everyone's favorite Mensa candidate, Wade Brown.

As fate directed, Rory and I crossed paths with Wade the first day of school. His nose had healed but his arm remained in a cast. As we approached I stared straight at him, and before we passed he shifted his eyes to the floor. Clearly, he had not forgotten the beating administered by Rory, and throughout the remainder of high school Wade never bothered any of our group. Part of it was no doubt the lesson we taught him, but another factor was he stopped growing. By our sophomore year all of us were sufficiently big enough to handle him. Regarding his partner in terror, Skyler, well we never saw him again. But wherever he is, he'll remember Jake Forrest every time he sees that scar in a mirror.

The first week of October I received a letter from an antique store in Skaneateles, New York offering one hundred dollars for one of the bottles. In 1973 one hundred bucks was a small fortune to a couple ninth graders. Several weeks later we received another request from a man in Providence, Rhode Island offering one hundred sixty-five dollars. With this trend, Rory and I fully expected the next offer would be much higher. But that was not the case, the third and final letter we received was a not an offer at all, it was a request for us to donate the bottle. After reading it several times Rory and I asked Mom to confirm that "donate" meant what we thought it meant.

She laughed, "Yes, Jake, donate means you give it away for free."

After reading the letter Dad said, "Oh, this is great. I never even considered something like this."

"Great would be more money, Dad," I said.

Completely ignoring my comment, he continued, "OK boys, it says here that The Museum of Industry and Transportation in Chicago has an exhibit on Prohibition. And they want to add your bottle as an artifact. It goes on to say that they had no idea any of these bottles existed and it would be a wonderful addition. How about that?"

"We'd rather have another one hundred sixty-five bucks," Rory said.

"All right, that's honest," Dad said as he pulled off his reading glasses. "A bit greedy, but honest. Boys, I'm not going to tell you what to do, you worked hard to find these bottles and you should decide. But I want you to consider that the two previous bottles you sold are most likely in somebody's home being seen by only a few people. It you agreed to let the museum have the last one, it would be seen by hundreds of people every day." He paused to let that sink in. "Also, the museum would give you two credit for donating them the bottle."

"Is credit like money?" Rory asked.

Chuckling Dad said, "My goodness, you two certainly have a firm grasp on capitalism. No Rory, credit means the museum would note that this bottle was donated by Rory Perkins and Jake Forrest, probably on a little plaque under the bottle."

"So, every day in the city of Chicago people would see this bottle and know that Rory and I are the ones that found it?" I asked.

"Yep," Dad answered.

"Well, that *is* pretty cool," Rory said.

"OK Dad, that is kinda neat. We'll think about it."

While the thought of being recognized for finding the bottles was cool, our subsequent decision to donate it was made easier by the lack of any further offers. In mid-November Dad helped us package the bottle to send to Chicago. We included a letter outlining how Rory and I located and recovered the bottles.

The following March Rory and I received a response from the museum thanking us for our donation. A picture was included showing the bottle displayed. It was encased in clear plastic and had several lights behind it to reveal the intricate etchings. Next to the bottle was a bronze plaque. With the aid of a magnifying glass we could read the inscription, "Black Bay Rum Bottle, circa 1929. Discovered off the coast of North Florida by Treasure Hunters, Jake Forrest and Rory Perkins."

Rory and I were as proud as peacocks.

We made two hundred sixty-five dollars selling the bottles and were struggling on how to spend it. What we really wanted was an outboard motor for *Nessie*. But Dad said any motor we could buy for that little would be more trouble than it was worth. Mom was opposed to the idea thinking that we might dare go into the Intracoastal Waterway or worse, the open Atlantic. I never understood where she got such crazy notions.

We decided to keep some of the money for ourselves and do something nice for Amos George. After several suggestions were rejected we settled on buying ceiling fans for his house. We approached Amos with our plan who at first seemed angry. Dad helped soothe the situation by making sure Amos understood this was a gift, not charity. He said, "You helped them with cleaning the bottles. You're their friend and it's OK for friends to give each other gifts."

For whatever reason Dad failed to mention that Amos saved us from a terrible beating when Wade and Skyler attacked us. Either way, Amos gradually softened and finally agreed. He would not be the only one who benefited from the ceiling fans. One was installed on his back porch which greatly improved our comfort too.

As our freshman year continued, Wade kept his distance. There were no taunts or threats, he ignored us and we did likewise. There was unfortunately one more incident that we suspect was Wade's handiwork. The first morning of Spring break was warm with an outbound tide, a perfect day to be out on the marsh. *Nessie's* winter moorings of course were also her summer moorings, and comprised nothing more than a cinder block anchor on the shore of the Twain lot. Reaching the water's edge, we were met by a tragic site. *Nessie* was destroyed. She had been set ablaze, the fire completely consuming the decking and leaving only charred sticks of the support timbers. The flotation drums had been punctured on both ends by something sharp, perhaps an ax. She was a total loss.

Yes, it was just a wooden raft, but it was *our* raft and she had taken us on many adventures. Rory and I vowed come summer we would rebuild her, but that never happened. Rory was more involved in baseball than ever before. He was playing on two teams, and other than at school, I barely saw him. Even during summer, we were unable to spend time together like we once did. His time was spent with a travel baseball team and I was very involved with the Boy Scouts. When we could plan a day together we usually rode our bikes over to Amos' or to the inlet bridge to do a little fishing. We still had some great times, and Rory was still my best friend, but it just wasn't the same as when we had *Nessie.*

Once baseball was finished, he immediately flew out to be with his dad. They were reconnecting very well which was imperative as his mom continued her struggles with life. I never knew all the details, but Dad later said it was mostly alcohol and the wrong men. Unfortunately, this was to be our last summer together. During Christmas break of our sophomore year, Rory moved to Oregon for good.

The baseball prowess he had shown in his younger years grew as he did. He earned a full scholarship to Oregon State and was a four year starter. He possessed terrific instincts for the shortstop position, had a rocket arm and could run like a gazelle.

In his senior year of college, he was drafted in the mid-rounds by the Minnesota Twins. He performed well in their pioneer league and moved quickly to Single-A. The following year he moved up to Double-A ball, but by season's end his batting average was thirty-seven points short. That was all that separated him from progressing to Triple-A and a shot at the majors. Rory's speed, glove and arm that had always elevated him as an elite player, were no longer special at the Double-A level. Every player on the roster possessed those same skills. The difference between players who eventually get to the "show" and those that languished in the minors was their batting average. Rory played Double-A for two more years trying everything he could to boost his average, but it was not to be.

I lost track of him after he left baseball. We had long since stopped writing, we lived on opposite ends of the continent and other than old adventures we no longer had anything in common. Then sometime in the early 1990s I happened to flip the channel to the College World Series. Oregon State was one of the teams playing that night and I paused to watch a few minutes. The camera did a close-up of a Beaver player who had just hit a single and was talking with the first base coach. The coach tilted his hat and when I saw his eyes I had no doubt, "That's Rory!" I said. My wife came running to see what the commotion was about, "That's him honey, my best friend of all time, Rory Perkins!"

The destruction of *Nessie*, Rory's departure from Fernandina Beach, and my becoming more involved in other activities did lessen my time on the marsh and thus my visits to Amos were less frequent, but overall our friendship continued to deepen. As I matured, the time we shared became about more than fish and baseball. He was another mentor to me. And it was his reflections of his time with the Civilian Conservation Corps that played a part in my choosing a career with the National Park Service. For my sixteenth birthday Mom and Dad gave me a secondhand boat with a Johnson outboard. With the boat, I could visit Amos anytime, regardless of the tides. On many occasions he would join me and we'd cast for mullet. However, try as we may, we could never coax Mr. Rosco into the boat.

CHAPTER 48

January 3rd, 2004

Ever so carefully I loosened the screws from the fragile wood framing. These screws were installed some forty years earlier by a capable American workman in Cleveland, Ohio. Centering the new pane, I replaced the screws and brandished a smile of achievement.

"That's it!" I said to myself.

My re-immersion into my childhood home was soon to be over. I would be heading north tomorrow and longed to be reunited with my wife and daughters. However, visiting with old friends and unearthing long forgotten treasures had largely balanced the sadness associated with my visit.

There was one more thing I wanted to do before departing, and with the completion of the window pane, there was nothing holding me back. One of Dad's neighbors had a small fishing boat and had encouraged me earlier in the week to take it out if I had the time. I now had the time.

Driving towards the Fort George Inlet I detoured through town for a sandwich. Making a rolling right on a red light I heard the sharp *woop-woop* of a police car's siren. Pulling into the adjacent gas station I waited as the sheriff approached the truck. To clarify, that would be Sheriff Ricky Alvarez.

"Hey Jake, surprised you're not back above the snowline by now," he said thrusting his husky hand towards mine.

"Hey Ricky. No, I didn't plan on being here so long....it was just harder than I anticipated. I'm leaving tomorrow."

"Well, it's been good seeing your dad's truck cruising around downtown again. I miss the ole coot...he was good people."

"Yep, I miss him too."

"Well, be safe going home, and come back sometime. Bring the 'quail killer,' we'll fill the freezer."

Driving away I smiled at Ricky's reference to Dad's shotgun. It seemed it was as popular in town as Dad was. I also smiled at the irony of Ricky becoming sheriff. He was almost fired several months into his career for pointing his service revolver at a County Commissioner's wife, and yet he went on to be sheriff. And the most interesting part of Ricky's rise to chief law enforcer was who he replaced, the infamous Sheriff Buddie, Jr.

Though both Buddie's left office in distinctly unusual manners, Jr.'s departure was far more salacious. In the late 1980s, Buddie, Jr. purchased a lot on the St. Mary's River with the intention of building a retirement cabin. During the initial stages of clearing, he latched onto the notion that he could reduce the overall cost by using prisoners from the county jail. Many weekdays men wearing orange jump suits could be seen removing debris, felling trees and building a rock bulkhead. It is a given that most citizens in Nassau County would not have objected to this utilization of free labor, rather it would have been viewed as rehabilitative.

However, once the site work was complete Sheriff Buddie Jr. needed skilled labor to commence vertical construction. To accomplish this, his free labor concept had to broaden. He announced to his deputies that the county had a drunken driving problem, and construction workers hitting the bars on Friday nights were the main culprits. The sting operation called for deputies to stake out county bars and stop anyone leaving in a work truck. If the individual was indeed intoxicated, he would be arrested. Buddie, Jr. even established an under the table bounty system to reward the deputies' efforts.

Once arrested the accused would be offered a deal. If they helped build the cabin the DUI would disappear. According to the investigation, these DUI amnesty arrangements had secured free labor and materials for the foundation, framing, electrical, and plumbing.

However, Fernandina is too small for an operation involving dozens of extorted people to remain secret. At some point, Buddie, Jr. leaned too hard on one of the "volunteer" laborers and they reported it to the state authorities. Due to the good old boy system and influential friends, Buddie, Jr. avoided criminal prosecution and was allowed to resign. However, for a man like Sheriff Buddie Jr. leaving in disgrace was possibly worse than incarceration. The Buddies had controlled law enforcement in Nassau county for more than sixty years. Overnight Buddie Jr. transitioned from being the most powerful person in the county, a valued crony to politicians and a man who never paid for a meal, to being the community leper. It was rumored he was spotted some years later working as a security guard in a Panama City Beach amusement park.

I exited A1A onto the little beach on the northeast side of the bridge. It was a terrific afternoon to get out on the marsh, just warm enough to roll up my sleeves and bask in Florida's splendid winter sun. This little beach was the site of many wonderful memories. Will, my dad and I fished from this beach on many Friday afternoons. It's also where Rory and I joined Lacy's family for the fish grill, and it's where Rory and I finally tasted success in our quest for the rum bottles.

I shoved the boat's bow away from shore and set the engine at a slow idle. As I approached the edge of the inlet where it flows into the Intracoastal, the water turned from an inviting aqua to a mysterious dark blue. Looking back to the shore I guessed this was where Rory and I located the cache' of purple bottles. I wondered how many bottles still clung to the murky bottom, perhaps there were dozens lying alongside the rusted remnants of a Tommy gun.

I motored under the remains of the old bridge, immersed in a flood of recollections. It's where we retreated from the sun and enjoyed pork and beans, and snack pack puddings. And it was the only thing between us and certain death during the big storm of '73. As a dad, I shudder to consider how narrowly we escaped being swallowed by the tempest. It's a wonder Mom ever let me leave the front yard again.

A little way past the old bridge, I could see the small break in the shore line, the gateway to Bent Tree Creek. Turning into the tributary I felt confident that even after thirty years, if blindfolded I could flawlessly negotiate every bend and turn.

The creek began a long bend and I quietly said, "Darlington." Only one more turn and I would arrive at Amos George's place. Approaching the spot, I cut the engine. The boat gently glided between the remaining splintered pilings. I looped the bowline around one of the barnacle encrusted posts and exhaled a heavy sigh. It was quiet, nothing stirring except the outbound tide softly lapping against the boat.

In my mind I could see it all, the floating dock and rickety ramp that led to the porch, a tin roof with patches of rust, and a tattered screen door that closed with a loud slam. Prowling the rail was a giant cat with one ear and no tail. And I could see my friend Amos sitting in his rocker, tapping his pipe on the armrest, and brushing away the ashes

A hurricane had been the final death knell for the old place. The resulting storm surge displaced the main support posts and the house simply collapsed into the marsh. Due to environmental concerns, the city hauled off the pile of debris leaving only a few pilings as proof that an amazing man once lived here in a humble shack. At the time of its watery demise, the old place had long been deserted.

Early February of my senior year of high school I was summoned to the principal's office. When I arrived, Dad was waiting for me.

"Hey Dad, what's up?" Without answering his face conveyed it was bad news.

"Son, it's well.... Let's talk outside." Once outside Dad faced me, placed a hand on my shoulder and said, "Its Amos son, he's had some kind of spell. It's not good."

"What kind of spell, where is he?" I asked.

"Jake, you need to calm down and take a breath. He's at the big hospital in Jacksonville. I think we should go.... now."

Driving to Jacksonville I peppered Dad with questions. All he could say was Amos's pastor called and said he had some type of episode, maybe an aneurysm or a stroke and that he was in bad shape.

Arriving at the nurse's station for the ICU ward, Dad inquired about Amos. The nurse considered us before asking, "Are you relatives of Mr. George?"

Dad responded, "Ma'am we're as close as you can get and not be related. I would very much appreciate it if you could share his condition with us."

The nurse paused briefly before reading off a long list of medical terms that went right past me. When she finished, Dad asked, "May I see him?"

Again, she thoughtfully considered whether a rule violation was warranted, but relented. We walked towards the locked door separating ICU from the waiting room but Dad stopped me. "Jake, let me go first."

"No Dad, he's my friend," I stammered fighting back tears.

"Son, I'm not trying to keep you from your friend, but this is going to be tough. Let me go first then I'll come back and get you."

It was maybe five minutes before Dad returned to the waiting room. His face was stoic but sad. He motioned for me to join him on the couch.

"Son, based on what the nurse told us and what I just saw I doubt Amos is going to make it." Hearing this I sniffed and wiped more tears.

"Jake, Son, this is a time for you to be strong." He handed me his handkerchief and told me to go to the bathroom and wash my face with cold water. The water helped some and when I came out I was ready to see Amos. As we approached the door Dad said, "Do you want me to go with you?"

I shook my head no and pushed open the door. The ICU ward was unsettling, not at all like normal hospital rooms. An older nurse spoke kindly to me and walked me to Amos' bed. Had I not known it was Amos, I would not have recognized him. Numerous tubes ran from his arms and a big contraption was attached to his mouth. A machine sitting next to the bed would engage every few seconds, and when it did Amos's chest would rise. A monitor above his head beeped with each heartbeat. He seemed bigger than usual, like he was all puffed up. I slowly approached the bed, placing my hand on his. It was warm and I guess I was expecting him to squeeze it or open his eyes but there was no response. I said his name several times, again hopeful he would react. I was desperately seeking a sign that Dad was wrong, but there was none.

When those closest to us pass, some are curious on whether there was time for an appropriate goodbye. I've never understood that thinking. If someone means enough to you that an appropriate goodbye is important, they should mean enough to you that an appropriate goodbye is not required. Whereas, that afternoon I told my friend goodbye and that I loved him he most likely didn't hear it and honestly didn't need to. He already knew it. A couple of days later when that sweet man passed away, he entered heaven with the knowledge that I thought the world of him. Not because of what I said that day, but because of our deep friendship.

After spending as much time as allowed I was ushered back to the waiting room. Dad and I entered the elevator which was packed with hospital staff and other visitors. Despite the presence of these strangers, I broke down and sobbed. Dad encircled me with his arms as if I were again but six years old.

The ride home was mostly silent. I was lost in my thoughts and grief. However, as we neared the turnoff to Amos' I suddenly remembered, "Mr. Rosco."

"What about him?"

"How long has Amos been in the hospital?

"Couple days?"

"Mr. Rosco is probably starving."

"I'm sure someone is taking care of him."

"Who Dad, who besides us even knows Amos has a cat? We've got to check on him."

"OK, we'll run by and take a look."

Dad pulled the car into the 7-Eleven.

"Why are we stopping?" I asked.

Smiling he said, "Son, I don't keep cans of cat food in the glove box."

Arriving at Amos' I exited the car and began calling for Mr. Rosco. He was nowhere in sight.

"I'll probably need to go around back," I said.

"Jake, can you do that without getting wet?" Dad asked.

"Yes sir, there's a beam wide enough to walk along."

"I'll pass on the beam walking," Dad said as he walked to the front door. Then in a harsh whisper he said "Jake!"

He put his finger up to his mouth to shoosh me and motioned for me to come over. Joining him at the door I saw what concerned him. Amos' front door was halfway open.

"Go to the car and get my stick," Dad said quietly.

In Dad's trunk under the mat was a three-foot-long shovel handle that he referred to as his "just in case stick." Pushing the door open with the stick we crept inside, something Mom would have never endorsed. The place was ransacked.

Dumbfounded I asked, "What happened?"

"Somebody heard Amos was sick and decided it was a good time to burglarize him."

"It's like they just trashed the place," I said and began picking things off the floor. "We have to clean this up before Amos gets home."

Dad stood quietly and then it hit me. Amos wasn't coming home.

"Well let's see if we can find the mountain lion," Dad said in a rather sarcastic manner. He had always been skeptical of my stories about Mr. Rosco's dimensions.

Venturing out the back door, there was no sign of Mr. Rosco. Opening one of the tins of sardines, I rubbed the metal lid back and forth creating a loud scraping noise.

"If that noise doesn't bring him maybe the smell will. Wow, those are pungent," Dad said as he walked to the porch railing.

I heard a thump on the other side of the wall, I called him again and he trotted down the rail to where I was standing. I tried to pet him but he put his paws on my shoulder like he was going to climb on my head to get to the sardines.

"Whoa Jake, you weren't exaggerating. No way is that a domestic cat," Dad quipped. He cautiously edged over for a closer inspection, "Good granny that cat has some big cods."

"Yep, that's why Amos calls him 'Mister'."

I dumped two tins on the rail and they disappeared in a flash. Dad and I reentered the house and were again stunned by the devastation. Nothing remained in its place and anything made of glass had been shattered. I found several shards of purple glass and knew Amos's rum bottle had been smashed. Moving my foot in a sweeping motion across the floor a smiling face caught my eye. It was the picture of Amos and Satchel Paige. I picked it up and recalled the friendly debate Rory, Amos and I had about who was the greatest pitcher. I swept my foot across the floor again and caught the corner of a frame. It was Amos' CCC certificate. Tapping the frame against the edge of the table the remaining pieces of glass dislodged.

"Jake, there's nothing more we can do here. I've got a hammer in the car. We can nail the door shut for the time being."

Walking down the hall I said, "Dad wait."

I approached the bookshelf and searched the floor for one of Amos' greatest treasures. Amongst the strewn contents, I spied a red book.

"Ah ha! There it is." Near the window partially hidden by a pile of papers was his Webster's dictionary. Walking out I tucked the photo and certificate in the dictionary.

Amos never regained consciousness and died two days later. Dad and I attended the funeral and initially received confused expressions by the other mourners, almost as if we were in the wrong place. This was most likely because we were the only white people in the church. During the service, several people spoke about their relationship with Amos. With each story or anecdote, I found I knew the ending. It seemed as if I knew him as well as anybody knew him.

After the service, the pastor approached us. With a smile, he said, "You must be Jake." He extended his hand. "My boy I have heard all about you. Amos talked about you and Rory like you were family."

Heading home Dad suggested we stop for a root beer. As he paid I noticed the can goods aisle and immediately thought of Mr. Rosco. Back in the car I made my pitch.

"Dad, you know what we need to do for Amos George."

"What?"

"We have to adopt Mr. Rosco."

"No, we don't have to adopt Mr. Rosco."

"Dad, we can't just leave him there to fend for himself. He's an old cat, and he is used to someone taking care of him. You saw how hungry he was the other day."

"Jake, Jake.... not a cat. What if we take him to the humane society?"

"And what are the chances that somebody wants to adopt a one eared cat with no tail that's big enough to eat a small child? It would be more humane if we just shot him ourselves." And yes, that last part was terribly manipulative but I was desperate.

Dad sighed loudly. "Do you have any idea what your mom is going to say when we bring that cougar into the house?"

"She'll say we did the right thing."

Dad smiled, "Jake you really don't know your mother very well, do you?"

Exiting the car at Amos' we found Mr. Rosco waiting for us at the front door. "See Dad, he's ready to go."

"Jake has Mr. Rosco ever ridden in a car before?"

"I don't know, why?"

"Well, I just envision us merrily going down the road and all of sudden the cat gets scared and goes bonkers. And by bonkers, I mean he tears the car and us to pieces. I can see the newspaper headline, '*Man and Naïve Boy Plunge into Fort George Inlet, Suspicious Giant Cat Found in Car*'."

"I'll feed him while we are heading home, he'll be fine," I said almost confidently.

"All right, since you have your whole life in front of you and will have limited options to marry a nice girl if your face is shredded, I'll pick him up and take him to the car." Dad approached Mr. Rosco and stroked his head. "OK big fella, here we go." Dad scooped him up and his face reflected the strain. "Good grief this is like carrying an anvil. I'll need a truss tomorrow."

"What's a truss?"

"You don't want to know," Dad groaned. "Hurry open the door."

To our great relief once Dad placed him in the car he was completely calm. All the way home he lay on the seat between us munching on sardines. Pulling into the drive Dad looked at me, "Alright, this is your deal. You wanted to rescue him so you get to introduce him to your Mom."

Dad had the front door open and waited for me brandishing a wicked smile. "Better you than me bud."

Once inside I called for Mom and she met us in the living room. I had set Mr. Rosco on the floor and he was stretched out reclining. She entered the room, saw us, and then laid eyes on our new pet.

"Oh, my God, what in Noah's Ark is that?

"Mom, meet Mr. Rosco. He was Amos George's cat, and now he's ours."

Mom's bewildered eyes turned to Dad who said, "Yes honey, it appears this is what Amos left Jake in his will."

I'll give Mom credit, she handled it pretty well.

"Is it tame?" she asked.

"Sure Mom, it's just a regular cat."

"Jake, honey that creature may be many things, but a regular cat is not one of them. I tell you right now he's not staying inside. I couldn't close my eyes knowing he was roaming around in this house."

"Why?" I asked.

"Because Jake, I'd be afraid he'd eat me in the middle of the night."

"You two are so funny. Mr. Rosco is a just an overgrown ball of fur," at which point I lay next to him and stroked his head.

In time Mom developed a real affection for Mr. Rosco. While she demanded he be an outside cat, we know she brought him in every morning when Dad and I left the house. Whenever she had ladies over she would present him and say to her friends, "I want you to meet the biggest, and bless his heart, the ugliest cat in all of Nassau County."

Our new giant cat secured a permanent place in Mom's heart several weeks after we brought him home. It was a particularly frigid night and Mr. Rosco who always slept outside began meowing and clawing the back door. Thinking he was cold she let him inside. She watched with amazement as Mr. Rosco walked through the house searching for me. He jumped to the bed and curled up on top of my feet, just like he did with Amos George. Mom thought this was the sweetest thing ever.

Restarting the boat's motor, I headed further up Bent Tree Creek. Savoring the sight of every bend and tributary I instinctively steered around the shallows where oyster beds stealthily hid just below the surface.

Approaching what I knew to be the area of Twain's lot, I slowed. The continual string of houses obscured the landmarks on the north side of creek but the old curved stump on the south side was unmistakable. The tree that Dad bent when we used it as a pulley to drag our first raft into the creek managed to continue growing almost parallel to the creek. However, its own weight and the same hurricane that brought down Amos' place finished it off.

I was keenly seeing Twain's lot as it was before, just trees and a stack of logs. The place where our adventure began and where Rory encountered the killer corn snake. I caught myself laughing aloud as I remembered his face when the snake latched onto his shoe.

"What's so funny?" The voice rattled me from Rory's nightmare. It had come from the dock attached to the home on Twain's lot. An older man was fishing with a young boy. I was so enthralled in my memories I had not even noticed them when I tossed the anchor.

"Oh, hello there. I was just recalling something from 1972."

"1972? Wow that's been a while."

"Yes it has. When I was kid my best friend and I built a raft here, it was a vacant lot then. We spent the entire summer fishing on the marsh."

"I'm trying to teach my grandson here how to fish. You know catch it, clean it, and then put it in a frying pan. Kids today have no idea that fish aren't 'fish stick' shaped. Trouble is we can't get a bite."

"Well, if you have a cast net, you can probably snag some mullet," I suggested.

"Mullet. Yuck, I want something that we can actually eat."

I laughed, "I once felt the same way, but a dear friend showed me they can be very tasty, you just have to know how to cook them."

"So how do you cook mullet?"

Thirty years earlier I posed the very same question to Amos. With deep respect, I answered this man as he had me, "You smokes 'em!"

CHAPTER 49

January 4th, 2004

By ten thirty the next morning the house was empty, Dad's truck was full and it was time to leave. Since there was no way to cram all the stuff I was keeping in the truck's cab, earlier in the week I had invested in a second-hand bed topper. Though it wasn't specifically made for Dad's truck, it fit.... almost. Admittedly there were some gaps along the side but these were sealed with man's best helper—duct tape. Dad would have approved.

The beautiful weather I enjoyed the previous afternoon on the marsh was eclipsed by thick overcast skies and a cold drizzle. I walked back into the old place for one last look. On the kitchen counter sat a large coffee I began sipping first thing this morning. Picking it up I judged there was at least a third remaining. I thought of Dad's coffee philosophy, "I can drink it old, I just can't drink it cold," I smiled and put it in the microwave returning it to scalding hot.

Stepping out to the small back porch I eased down onto the top step before settling against the railing's support post. The coffee warmed my bones against the morning's chill that recast my breath into vapor. Surveying the backyard my mind could only conjure a fraction of the memories created in this fenced plot of sparse grass. In the southwest corner, buried under Mom's dogwood tree, were the remains of a giant cat.

That was some big cat, I thought and smiled at the memory of Dad trying to hoist him into the car.

I glanced towards the garbage can rack Dad was working on when he collapsed. For whatever reason, I had left it as he had left it. It was the last thing he touched and I just couldn't bring myself to dismantle it. There was something white tucked on the small window ledge above the rack. Curiosity beckoned me and I discovered it was Dad's coffee cup. He had most likely been drinking from it while he was working that morning. The cup bore an advertisement for a diner in Maggie Valley, North Carolina. Dad did love him a good diner.

"Ah Dad," I said, tears filling my eyes.

Clutching the cup as if it were a treasured chalice I walked back through the house, locked the front door and left home for the last time.

I stopped by the cemetery to pay my respects to Mom, Dad, and Will. Not knowing if I would ever return to Fernandina, it felt as if I were losing them all over again.

Cloaked in Dad's denim jacket I sat on a stone bench near their graves for the better part of an hour. The cemetery was deserted except for me and several wild turkeys foraging near the edge of the woods. The falling mist gathered on the leaves of the massive oak tree that sheltered me. Once the volume of water reached the leaf's tipping point, a collective drop would fall to the sand with a gentle *plop*.

The mist suited my mood that morning. While I missed my wife and girls terribly and was anxious to be home, my time in Fernandina had been such a wellspring of treasured memories there was a part of me that regretted leaving. All to soon the gentle mist became a torrent.

Scampering back to the truck, I quickly closed the door. In the front floor board was a cardboard box crammed with newspapers and old towels. Padded and sheltered beneath the packing was a purple rum bottle that represented some of the best of times in my life.

Adjusting the rear-view mirror, I caught the glint from a pair of brown glass eyes on a 12-point buck that seemed to be staring back at me. "Well, Cousin Zeke, any objections about going to Pennsylvania? ......Alrighty then, let's go home."

Cruising south on A1A towards the interstate was slow going, but this route would afford me one more opportunity to cross the inlet. Rounding the point at the end of Little Talbot Island the bridge was just before me. Driving over I alternated glances to the Intracoastal on my left and Bent Tree Creek on my right. The water was not the inviting jade of a clear summer day, but a menacing gray highlighted by the white pitch of cresting waves. I interpreted this as another sign it was time to go home. Feeling it was long overdue I picked up my phone and dialed 411.

"City and State please," the operator said.

"Corvallis, Oregon please. Do you have a listing for Rory Perkins?"

IN MEMORIAM TO THOSE
WHO GAVE THEIR ALL
THE UNITED STATES AIR FORCE
553RD RECONNAISSANCE WING

Lockheed EC 121R Batcat Super Constellation

Batcat 21, Crashed April 25, 1969

TSgt.	James H. Belflower
Major	Thomas M. Brandom
TSgt.	Albert N. Booker
A1C	Michael J. Cotterill
SSgt.	Jerald C. Davis
A1C	Ronald C. Deforrest
TSgt.	Warren C. DeLaney
SSgt.	Paul Faulk
TSgt.	Kenneth W. Fowler
Lt Col.	Emerson E. Heller
Capt.	George R. Kidd
Major	Paul R. Lunsford
1Lt.	John A. Marsh
LT Col.	William C. McCormick Jr.
Sgt.	Mitchel Messing,
SSgt.	James D. Moore
Sgt.	Mark M. Steeley
Sgt.	William D. Stepp

Batcat 19, Crashed September 6, 1969

Sgt. Julius C. Houlditch Jr.
Jr. Major Joyfull J. Jenkins
Sgt. Arnold Noel Jaco
SSgt. Gunther H. Rehling

For more information about the Batcats or the 553rd Reconnaissance Wing
http://www.westin553.net/Batcat00.htm

JAKE'S BLACK MIA BRACELET HAD TRUE LIFE MEANING TO THE AUTHOR

COMMANDER MICHAEL G. HOFF
UNITED STATES NAVY, USS CORAL SEA
MISSING IN ACTION

On January 7, 1970, Lieutenant Commander Michael Hoff was launched from the *USS Coral Sea* in a Sidewinder A7A Corsair aircraft. His mission was to perform armed reconnaissance over Laos, west of Vietnam.

Lt. Com. Hoff's aircraft was completing a strafing run near the city of Sepone when he radioed that he had a fire warning light and was going to have to bail out. Immediately afterwards, the aircraft impacted and exploded. No parachute was seen, nor were emergency transmissions received. Heavy ground fire prevented rescue efforts which resulted in his "Missing in Action" designation. He was promoted to Commander during the period he was missing.

Though his remains were never found, Commander Hoff was subsequently declared dead on November 28, 1978.

Mary Hoff, the Commander's wife, was passionate about finding a way to honor those who had not returned from serving their country. She contacted Annin & Company, a flag maker who had obtained a degree of notoriety for refusing to produce flags for communist China when they joined the United Nations. When the design was complete, Mrs. Hoff was asked if she wanted to own the rights to the flag—she refused. According to her son, Joe, "Mom told them it wasn't about owning something that everyone should own." What Mrs. Hoff was responsible for creating is one of the most recognizable images of American solidarity – the POW-MIA flag.

While in college I had the distinct privilege to room with one of Commander Hoff's sons. Like most twenty-year-old students, I was very naïve about the real world and things bigger than college football games and my GPA. However, because of his father's sacrifice, the circumstances of this young man's life stayed with me.

The lingering effects of the Vietnam War weave throughout *Coastal Treasure* like the many tributaries entwining the saltmarsh. It is my sincere hope that I've treated its history with the reverence it so duly deserves. – *Mark Alan Griffis*

64550427R00192

Made in the USA
Lexington, KY
12 June 2017